Francesco Merighi, a successful journalist, in an attempt to impose order on the doubts and confusions that beset his middle-age, begins to record in diary form the truth about himself and his wife Cora and his twenty-year-old step-daughter Baba.

His wife Cora bores Merighi to distraction – and knows that she does. Baba excites emotions in him that are far from step-fatherly– and knows that she does.

And so the diary begins.

The pursuit of truth, however, is a tortuous business. No sooner has he pinned down Cora or Baba in one of their many moments than they immediately undergo a protean change. Finally the diary is completed, but now Merighi is alone: Cora is dead - of cancer - and Baba has departed to a loveless marriage. But the truth remains . . . except – there is a lingering doubt in Merighi's, and the reader's, mind: the diary, as a way of defining its author's relationship with reality has raised one profound question that it is beyond Merighi's power to answer. . . . It is to do with the nature of our waking dreams.

This deeply disturbing picture of the human situation, as expressed in Merighi's account of his life with Cora and Baba, puts Alberto Moravia in the very front rank of contemporary novelists.

*Also by Alberto Moravia in the
Panther 'Modern Society' series*

The Red Book and the Great Wall
(An impression of Mao's China)

Alberto Moravia

The Lie

translated from the Italian by
Angus Davidson

A Panther Book

Contents

First of all I must explain why I kept a diary. There are many reasons for keeping a diary: to make a note of facts that one considers important; to open one's heart, to give vent to one's feelings, to make confessions; from the instinct of economy which sometimes encourages a writer to make good use even of the smallest crumbs of his life, so that he may have one more book to publish; or again from vanity and self-satisfaction. This diary, on the other hand, has been kept in order that it may afterwards be made into a novel: that is, as a collection of material that can be used for creating a novel. But, since someone will wonder why I did not write the novel directly, instead of preceding it by a diary, it will perhaps be not altogether pointless to give an account of the happenings and the considerations that suggested my keeping the diary before writing the novel.

In the first place, then, there was the shame which the past aroused in me. This shame would have been understandable if there had been, in my past, something objectively shameful; but this was not so: there was nothing in my past for me to be ashamed of; that is, there was no act which I would have wished not to have perpetrated and which, at the same time, aroused in me a sense of guilt. In short, I was ashamed, but of what I did not know. I would like now to say something about the character of this shame. Let me make a comparison. Thinking about the past was, for me, like recalling, on the following morning, an evening during which I had drunk a great deal and had performed acts of extravagance under the influence of alcohol. Thus everything which, during that evening, while I had been in a state of drunkenness, had appeared to me to be justified, to be real, significant, necessary and coherent, all at once seemed senseless, false, unreal, gratuitous. Underlying this shame that the past aroused in me there was, therefore, the mortifying idea that I had allowed myself to be led by the nose, that I had succumbed to an illusion, that I had been deceived by a mirage. And the question that I could not help putting to myself was not so much. 'Why did I do these things?' as: 'Was I really the person who did these things? Was it I or somebody else?'

The shame aroused in me by the past can be partly explained by my career as a journalist. Superficially my career has had a fairly ordinary character; I was a student of letters as well as a writer of short stories and articles for a left-wing paper. Unexpectedly I was given the opportunity of becoming a contributor to a conservative daily, and I did not hesitate to accept the offer. Although I was not a member of any party, my political ideas were well known, and thus there were quite a number of people who judged my conduct severely and who said that, after all, I had behaved like so many ambitious men who, having established a position on the Left, sold themselves to the Right. But it was not like that.

In actual fact my transferring from a left-wing to a conservative newspaper could not be explained either by financial profit (even if unconsciously) or by a change of opinions which, as often happens, coincides with financial profit. I had no self-interest, in the first place because I was not ambitious, in the second place because I was not interested in money, being neither poor nor greedy. As for my political ideas, I had not changed them; all I had done was to shelve them, like something which, no doubt temporarily, had ceased to have any importance in my life. No; the reason for which I had transferred from the left-wing to the conservative newspaper had nothing to do with financial profit or ambition or politics. By way of comparison let us imagine somebody who sets fire to his own house in order to light a cigarette. Obviously he has some sort of an interest in starting a fire; but the damage so far outweighs the advantage and the means is so disproportionate to the end that it might well be remarked that our smoker, in burning down his own house, is aiming not so much at lighting a cigarette as at giving vent to a pathological inclination, in other words, pyromania. If this comparison does not suffice, here is a moral fable that seems to throw light on the matter. In transferring from the left-wing to the conservative paper, I was behaving rather like the madman in the well-known story who, after a long sojourn in an asylum, was at last declared to be cured.

Before sending him home, however, the director of the asylum wished to submit the rehabilitated madman to a test. He summoned him and said: 'Well, let us see; you're a normal man now; just imagine that you've inherited a fortune of several millions. What would you do with it?'

The madman replied firmly: 'I should buy a catapult.' Disconcerted but not yet resigned, the director persisted: 'Come on, think before you answer. I said several millions. A catapult costs only a few lire. Come on, just consider for a moment; what would you do with these millions?"

This time the madman replied: 'I should take a wife.'

'Ah, splendid. Now you're talking like a sensible man. You'd take a wife: and how would you do that?'

'I should be married in church and then go away with her on a honeymoon.'

'Where to?'

'To Paris.'

'A very good choice. And then what would you do, once you'd arrived in Paris?'

'I'd go with my wife to an hotel.'

'Excellent. And then?'

'I'd shut myself up with her in a bedroom.'

'And what would you do in the bedroom?'

'I'd undress my wife. First I'd take off her dress, then her petticoat, then her brassière, then her drawers, then her shoes, then her stockings, and finally her garters.'

'And then?'

'Then I'd make a catapult out of her garters.'

The story does not tell what finally became of the poor lunatic who loved catapults, but it can easily be imagined. Now I myself had acted rather like that lunatic. I had transferred from the left-wing to the conservative paper neither in order to advance my career, nor to earn more money, nor because I had changed my political opinions, nor for any other suitable reason; but merely in order to travel. The left-wing paper was poor and could not afford the luxury of sending special correspondents abroad. That was why I became a contributor to the conservative paper.

Someone may wonder why, seeing that I was not poor, I did not pay for these journeys with my own money. My answer to that is that, although I was not poor, I did not have sufficient means at my disposal to travel continuously. Besides, in order to travel, I required a show of professional justification. Otherwise, since it was not so much travelling in itself that interested me as the effects of travelling, I might perhaps have had recourse to other, less innocuous, means in order to achieve these effects.

I will now explain why it was important to me to travel so much. It was important to me to travel because I did not wish to remain in Rome where I had lived during that past time of which, as I have mentioned, I was ashamed. And this was not because the past, reawakened by the suggestiveness of places, came back more often to my memory than I should have wished. No; my past in Rome had a name, a physical appearance, an age, a sex, and lived under my roof; what I mean is that it was my wife. I travelled, therefore, so as not to remain with my wife, or to remain with her as little as possible – that is, merely in the intervals between one journey and another.

I have already said that, even though I was ashamed of my past, I still could not manage to find anything in it that was shameful. This contradiction was certainly strange and would have deserved serious and painstaking attention; but it was precisely this kind of effort that I did not wish to make or rather – more probably – that I did not feel capable of making. I came to the conclusion, therefore, that, for the present at any rate, the most suitable course for me to take, in relation to the past – that is, to my wife – was to preserve an attitude which was the exact opposite of attentiveness, in other words, an attitude of detachment. What does a detached person do? He looks on from afar and – perhaps even with the aid of a powerful telescope – sees perfectly clearly the ruins of a town which has been destroyed by an earthquake during the night, But at the same time he fails to notice that the ground is caving in right under his nose, and that his own house is on the point of collapsing. So it was with me: in my contributions from abroad I was concerned with the civilization of the Mayas, or with industrialism in Japan; but, at first by an act of will and afterwards automatically, I had come to ignore everything to do with my wife, even, in fact, to ignore her personally, although she was living together with me under the same roof.

At this point I feel I ought to provide a little information about my wife. Cora – for that was her name – was a woman of the working class, a dressmaker by trade, daughter of a washerwoman and a market gardener. Why I, a young man of the middle class, son of middle-class parents, well-educated and comfortably off, should have married Cora is quickly told: finding that I had been born into a society that was divided into spheres superimposed upon one another and progressing upwards from the hellish pains of poverty to the paradisial bliss of wealth – those spheres which are commonly called classes; and living, myself, in paradise, I had been struck by the artificiality that prevailed there. This artificiality was of a special and very precise kind; that is, it was the falseness which is an essential quality of any parody that is not a parody for those playing a part in it because it is involuntary and unconscious. Now, by way of contrast to this falseness – with the slowness, but also the naturalness, of the process which brings to birth the nucleus of a pearl inside an oyster – a myth had taken shape in my mind, the myth of the working class as sole depository of all that was genuine in the world. This was in 1947; this myth had received confirmation from Fascism and from the War, two catastrophes which, on examination, are seen to have been due to false attitudes. This is the explanation of how, at my first encounter with Cora, I fell in love. The myth, in fact, worked as all myths do, automatically and mysteriously. There is no need to explain here how I met Cora. To prove that it was real love all I need say is that, on the day of our first encounter, after I had left her, I started walking alone through the streets, repeating aloud, in exaltation: 'She's the one, she's really the one; I've been looking for her for such a long time and now at last I've found her.'

After this flash of illumination, the story of my relationship with Cora is that of a fundamentally normal love affair. I continued to see her, at first at rare intervals and only for an hour or two in a rented room, then more and more often and outside the room as well. As I have already said, Cora was a dressmaker, that is, she worked in a dressmaker's shop in order to maintain herself and a little girl whom she had had during the war by a German soldier. It was not long before she asked me to help her set up a small workroom on her own. There followed an intermediate period during which I gave Cora an allowance and saw her every day but lived with my family; Cora lived with the little girl in a small flat adjoining the workroom. Then, since my love for her continued – increased, in fact – I suggested to her that we should live together. To my surprise, Cora showed no enthusiasm. She said she wished to remain free, that she did not want to be controlled in any way, that she had her own life and I mine.

What necessity was there for us to live together? Everything was going so well as things were at present, I in my home and she in hers, with love-making every day, for an hour or two, in the room adjoining the workshop. I then thought that Cora might be expecting me to give her a more binding proof of my love than merely living together – in other words, marriage. And, carried away by a sense of loyalty, I asked her to marry me. This time she accepted, though without any excess of delight; but she circumscribed her acceptance with the same conditions as before: Whether as mistress or wife, she wished to remain free, independent, to have a life of her own separate and different from mine. These precautions on her part ought to have caused me to reflect; however I attributed them to the spirit of independence of someone who, like Cora, had hitherto managed on her own and had always worked and earned her own living. So in the end we were married and became husband and wife.

That same year my father, who was a widower, died, and his estate was divided between myself and my only brother. In the portion of it which fell to me there was included an old, but large and airy, apartment on the top floor of a *palazzo* in the neighbourhood of Piazza Mazzini. I went to live there with Cora and the little girl. For some reason – perhaps out of an unconscious loyalty to the tastes of the class from which I came – I did up the flat in the style, then in fashion, of the first half of the nineteenth century, from Empire to Louis Philippe. My intention on going to live in this flat, furnished as it was like the house of a provincial lawyer, was to devote myself to the writing of a novel, an old ambition of my life. In this novel I should tell the story of my relationship with Cora, from our first meeting until our marriage. It did in fact seem to me that my life, after many storms, had reached a quiet haven: I had a small income which permitted of my not having to work in order to live; I had a wife whom I loved, a little girl whom I considered as my daughter; I was at peace with myself, that is, I felt no need to change either my ideas or my mode of existence; what more could one want? My circumstances in short, had the stability which seemed to me indispensable if I was to start on the composition of my novel. But at that very moment an unforeseeable thing happened: I ceased to love Cora.

To say I ceased to love her is putting it mildly. Not merely did I no longer desire Cora, not merely did I no longer find anything attractive or significant in those working-class characteristics which had made me fall in love with her; but I also felt an unreasoning aversion which expressed itself mainly in an uncontrollable, acutely painful, spasmodic uncommunicativeness. This started with the physical relationship: the simplicity, or rather the clumsiness, of Cora's manners and of her person, which formerly had pleased me because I perceived in them the genuineness which I so desperately needed, no longer meant anything to me now and indeed actually repelled me. Lying motionless beside her, I could not now manage to give her a single kiss with my lips, a single caress with my hands, a single embrace with my body. But, strange to relate, there was nothing in my mind of the indifference which, after all, still allows one to be polite, affable, even affectionate, in fact to display the sympathy to which all human beings have a right by the mere fact of existing. No, there was, instead, an obscure and unshakeable hostility that surprised and frightened me. It was then that the past began to affect me like a night of drunkenness and extravagance upon which one looks back sober-mindedly next morning. And Cora, who had been at my side during that same past, aroused in me precisely the feeling of dislike that one may have, on the following day, for the person who has been one's accomplice in the excesses of such a night. Cora had been my unwitting accomplice in the illusion to which I now felt I had succumbed in loving her and marrying her; I realized that it was no fault of hers; nevertheless I could not help hating her in exactly the way in which one hates the innocent cause of some error of one's own.

Apart from my uncommunicativeness, my aversion also expressed itself in a haunting, compulsive feeling of alienation. While we were sitting at table, or in bed while she was asleep, the thought would come to me: 'Who is this woman sitting opposite to me and talking to me and smiling at me? This woman who is lying beside me in bed, turning her back on me and snoring? What have I to do with this woman? How on earth does she come to be here?'

Every now and then I would repeat to myself: 'Cora Mancini'; and it seemed to me that I was uttering, not the name of my wife, but a name read by chance in the telephone directory or on a shop sign; and I would say to myself: 'What can

13

there be in common between myself and the person called Cora Mancini?'

My uncommunicativeness finally reached a point when I avoided turning my eyes towards her, so as to allow her not even the thing that one refuses to nobody – a glance. I made some excuse for changing my seat at table, placing myself so that I should not have her opposite me. Another mean trick was that, if she came into a room, I would contrive to slip out as quickly as possible; not merely did I not want to see her but I did not even want to be seen by her. In short, a kind of positive creeping paralysis stiffened me more and more into an attitude of complete taciturnity, of detachment, alienation and disgust.

Naturally this paralysis implicated all those who were in any way connected with Cora. It was easy for me to break off relations with my father- and mother-in-law who lived in a distant quarter of the city; but it was more difficult for me to do so with Gabriella, nicknamed Baba, Cora's little girl, whom I had hitherto looked upon, and treated, as a daughter. I should have preferred not to see her any more; but since this was impossible, I could only manage partly to conceal my embarrassment. Then one day, in an impulse of stupid exasperation, which I at once regretted, when Baba called me 'Papa' I answered her: 'Don't call me "Papa", because I'm not your father, d'you see? That's understood. Never again.' I noticed her looking at me with a quiet, even rather inquisitive, expression that disconcerted me. But thenceforth, from that day onwards, this term of affection disappeared from her conversation; and I remarked, with a relief that was mingled with a certain remorse, that the child avoided me, or at any rate no longer sought me out as she had done in the past.

To give an idea of the angry feeling of alienation aroused in me by living with Cora and her daughter, let me say further that, to myself, I no longer called them by their names but by nicknames. Cora was 'the dressmaker'. I would say to myself: 'What does the dressmaker want? What is the dressmaker doing?' And Baba, I am sorry to say, was 'the bastard'. I would ask myself: 'What is the bastard screaming about? When will the bastard stop running up and down the passage?' Far-off indeed were the times when my day had been divided into two equal parts, the first in which I longed for my meeting with Cora, the second in which I regretted that it was over; or when I used to take Baba to the public gardens and, clasping her hand in mine and listening to her chatter, I seemed to have a truly paternal feeling towards her, as though she were really my daughter.

There remained my work, that is, the writing of my novel, in which I had placed all my hopes for a future which had once seemed so secure and was now extremely uncertain. I had written a first draft of it in a single outburst, three hundred pages in little more than six months, and now I was preparing to re-write it, or rather to copy it out and correct it. I had written it with undoubted felicity of expression, with the sensation that I was becoming more and more of a writer and novelist at every page; and thus, as regards that side of my life, I felt protected and sure of myself. My marriage had failed, but at least it had served to make me write my novel. I must here note one important fact: the novel had been begun and finished before the crumbling of domestic affections, at a time when I still considered myself to be a happily married man. In the novel, in fact, my relationship with Cora was described as some thing positive and successful. But it is also true that the narrative came to an end on the eve of our marriage.

One day I sat down at my desk, opened the copy-book containing the novel and started typing. But I went no further than the first lines. Suddenly, assailed by a misgiving, I put the typewriter aside and began re-reading the book. I went on reading the whole of that afternoon and in the end closed the copy-book with the alarming sensation that my life was now entirely open and exposed, with no protection left, even from the literary point of view. An unmistakeable air of falseness, of unreality, of artificiality, in fact, emanated from every word of the manuscript.

Nevertheless I do not wish to be misunderstood. The novel might be said to be successful and certainly would not have made a bad impression amongst the output of fiction during those years. Situation, characters, style, construction and form all contributed quite naturally to create a complex organism that had all the appearance of vitality. However, this story of a search for genuineness through love for a woman of the working class was, itself, absolutely lacking in genuineness. Yet this lack of genuineness was not in the written word but rather, one might say, in the actual facts that were related. It was, so to speak, a constitutional artificiality, as though the events I had sought to relate had been irremedi- ably false even in their origin, even before they were related. But these events had not been invented by me; I had drawn them from my most recent past. I myself was the protagonist; the working-class girl whom the protagonist loved and mar- ried was Cora; the girl's father and mother were Cora's father and mother; the protagonist's brother was my brother; his parents were *my* parents; the girl from a rich family, whom the protagonist finally rejects in favour of Cora, had been en- gaged to me for a year; the city in which these characters lived and moved was that same Rome in which I myself lived and moved. Once again, then, it was not so much the book which lacked genuineness as the reality from which it had been drawn.

I am not sure that I am capable of expressing the feeling of horror that this discovery aroused in me. By way of com- parison, it was as if I had all at once discovered that God, when He created the world, had patched it up, so to speak, with substitutes, that is, with materials that looked like, but were not, those which they should have been. Or again that Adam and Eve, the first people to function in this world, had believed they loved one another whereas the reason for their union had in reality been something different; and so their descendants and consequently the whole of humanity, cen- tury after century, had acted from motives that were devoid of genuineness, thus multiplying, by geometrical progression, the initial unreality. Seen in this perspective, history appeared as a cemetery of false ideas which were made use of by degrees and then abandoned; as a storehouse of deceits whose appearance of reality had never even once been stripped away. It was natural that a novel in which the writer had sought to relate events that had occurred in a world like this should turn out to be corrupted by an intrinsic and ineradicable false- ness.

To return to my novel: I felt that the protagonist loved his working-class girl for reasons which were not genuine, so that it might in fact be asserted that he did not love her at all. But, at the very moment when this discouraging thought was taking shape in my mind, I knew that Cora was close by, in the next room; and I knew that the public official who had married us was still living; and I recalled the many times I had made love with her and how I had done it; yes indeed, I had loved Cora and had married her; but these actions, upon examination, revealed their own complete and irreparable falseness. So complete and so irreparable as to make me doubt whether the things that had happened had really happened at all. How, in fact, could something which was not there, something which did not exist – something, that is, which was devoid of genuineness – give rise to something which *was* there, something which *did* exist – that is, the thing which had really happened? And yet so it was; existence had sprung from nothingness, reality from unreality. To return to the comparison already made, it was as though God, in creating the world, had created it by mistake. Nevertheless the world was there to bear witness that it had actually been created, even if falsely; just as Cora was there, in the adjoining room, to bear witness that, even though our relations were entirely lacking in genuineness, we had actually loved one another and got married.

I do not wish to dwell long upon the catastrophe to my story. All at once, almost without thinking, and with the automatism which belongs to despair, I took up the manuscript and went over to a window of the flat that opened at the side of the house and looked down on a building site enclosed by a palisade. This site had become a kind of rubbish-heap; piles of rubble rose here and there; cats, street urchins and tramps wandered amongst the hollows and hillocks. I started tearing up the manuscript on the window-sill, throwing down the pieces by handfuls, which fluttered and turned slowly in the air before settling on the ground. I remember that, while I was performing this operation, I was looking at the avenue in which stands the building I live in, and at the far end of it I could see the double row of plane-trees along the road above the Tiber, and the bank on the other side with its line of houses, and above the houses a rocky hill, and on top of the hill a grove of pine-trees, and above the pines the blue sky of the lovely summer day; and I thought that, after God had created the world, perhaps He too had felt that it was completely lacking in genuineness and had for a moment been tempted to destroy it. But then He had refrained, and had thus been more courageous than I and more obstinately persistent in error. And so the world had gone on, from one falsity to another, becoming less and less genuine. I threw the last pages of the manuscript into the air without tearing them, and then watched them as they circled round, making their way – one might almost have thought intentionally, deliberately, with relief – towards the piles of rubbish down below on the building site. And I realized all of a sudden that in this rudely symbolical manner I had liquidated not merely my literary ambitions, but the whole of my past life.

Immediately after this I fell into a state of profound depression. As sometimes happens in dreams, I seemed to find myself clinging to a smooth, vertical wall, hanging over an abyss and incapable of climbing either upwards or downwards or of staying where I was. I was married to a woman older than myself and who was now a perfect stranger to me, with a child who was not my daughter; I no longer had any belief at all in the things in which I had hitherto believed, nor did it seem to me that I could replace these things with others more valid; and finally I had surrendered to the idea that the work for which I had been preparing myself, it could be said, all my life, had been a failure. The only element that was, in a certain way, positive, was that I was only thirty years old; but this consciousness of my youth made me resent, with even greater bitterness, the state of absolute importance into which I had plunged. I felt, in fact, that although I had limitless possibilities I had no available means of making use of them.

It was characteristic of this period of despair that I never for a moment thought of leaving Cora, as perhaps anyone else in my place would have done. Separation, in point of fact, would have been an active step, and I now felt entirely incapable of taking action one way or another, since I had recognised that taking action would mean telling lies, that is, creating new and worse artificiality as one action arose and developed out of another. Instead, it was Cora – who, so it appeared, did not share my ideas on the artificiality of taking action – who provoked the rupture which I did not feel able to face.

One afternoon, after long and inconclusive reflection upon my situation, I fell asleep on the sofa in the sitting-room; and all of a sudden, in my sleep, I had the impression that somebody was sitting at the end of the sofa, looking at me. I opened my eyes, sat up hastily, and there indeed was Cora, leaning on the arm of the sofa beside my feet and gazing at me in silence.

Cora's face was slightly reminiscent of that of an archaic,

painted statue of some Greek god or hero; this was perhaps owing to the simplicity of her features and the crudeness of her colouring – a very white complexion, raven-black hair, enormous blue eyes, a large, straight nose of the German type, a very red, full mouth, capriciously and cruelly sinuous, with the corners curling upwards as if in a perpetual smile. And now, just as though she were in truth a statue, she was sitting motionless with her eyes fixed on me, her face narrow between two long, snaky locks of black, glossy hair, her body stiff and upright, her hands clasped together in her lap, her bosom thrust out. This attitude, together with her continued silence even though I was now awake and looking at her, almost frightened me. Disconcerted, I exclaimed: 'Why, what's wrong? What's the matter with you? Why do you look at me like that?'

Almost without moving her lips, mumbling between her teeth, she answered: 'I'm going to the workroom in a moment. But before I go there's something I must say to you.'

'What is that?'

'You don't love me any more.'

I made an effort to speak but could not manage it. She went on: 'You said we mustn't go on making love because you had to devote yourself to your novel. But you're not writing your novel. What d'you suppose? That I haven't noticed that you spend your days in here listening to records and smoking? You're not writing your novel, and we're not making love either.'

Again I said nothing. It was true, I had made my literary work an excuse for breaking off our physical relations; but now, after I had torn up the manuscript, it gave me a feeling of shame to think of repeating the same excuse over again. Cora looked at me and then asked suddenly: Why, what's the matter, Francesco, can't you tell me what's the matter with you?'

I replied, with a feeling that I was telling the truth: 'Nothing's the matter.'

'Before, we used to make love every day, even twice a day, and it was I who had to tell you not to overdo it, for your health's sake, too. Now, on the other hand, you never look at me.'

'It's just a temporary thing: it'll pass.'

'You don't feel anything for me now.'

'That's not true, but . . .'

'Oh yes, it's true. . . .'

I was on the point of denying it again: not that I was afraid of admitting that particular truth to which she was alluding; but, as usual, I felt that to admit it would be adding another falsity to the one that already existed. Then she made one of her own characteristic gestures, at once both plebian and immodest: without moving the upper part of her body or her face, she stretched out her powerful arm and with her large white hand grasped my sexual organ, still staring me straight in the eyes, with an enquiring look in which there seemed to be a certain hopefulness of, so to speak, a technical kind. She retained her hold for a moment, and then, disdainfully, took away her hand and said: 'You see. Once upon a time I had only to look at you and you responded immediately, but now it's just as if you had nothing at all down there. You're only thirty, don't tell me you've become impotent.'

'Goodness knows,' I said, 'perhaps I really have.'

'Yes, with me.'

'That's not the only thing between a man and a woman.'

'What else is there.'

'Affection.'

'If there isn't that thing between a man and a woman, there's nothing.'

I did not dare to contradict her. 'I know,' she went on, 'I know what's the matter with you.'

'What is that?' I asked, my curiosity genuinely aroused.

'The matter is that you can't bear me any longer.'

'Who told you that?'

'There are some things that one feels.'

Again I hadn't the courage to contradict her. Cora continued, this time in a slightly sarcastic tone: 'Your passion for me has soon come to an end, hasn't it, Francesco? You said you would love me all your life. D'you know it's barely a year since we got married?'

Once more there was silence on my side. Cora was now looking at me with an indefinable look of appraisal, much as one looks at a piece of furniture or other cumbersome object and wonders where to put it. Finally she enquired: 'D'you want us to separate?'

I shook my head. Then Cora said hurriedly, as though she

were afraid of being interrupted: 'You want us to stay together?'

'Yes.'

'In this house?'

'Yes.'

She was silent for a moment, then she resumed: 'As you wish; in that case I propose that we should manage in this way. From now onwards you can live your own life, without being under any obligation to me: either to sleep or to eat with me, or to bother about me and the child. I earn enough money – which means that you need only give me enough for the household expenses. I'll make up a bed for you in the room near the front door; you'll have your study to work in, the sitting-room for entertaining; all you need leave for us is the bedroom and the kitchen. You can come and go just as if I wasn't there. But I'll take charge of everything as regards the flat, and all I ask in return is that I should be able to stay here. Is that all right?'

I nodded in agreement. I was struck by the precision with which she had set forth this programme: evidently she had been thinking about it for some time. By way of conclusion, she said: 'Everything, in short, will remain as it was, only we shan't be keeping up any pretences with one another. And now I must leave you, because I have a customer waiting for me.' She looked at me for a moment, put out her hand and lightly caressed my cheek, then as she rose to her feet, asked me: 'D'you want to go to sleep again?'

I mumbled an affirmative. I watched her as she went to the window and drew the curtains; and then, in the half-darkness, herself a shadow, she left the room.

Some days later, in the morning, the telephone rang in my room. I took up the receiver and heard a woman's voice saying: Good morning, this is Gianna.'

'Gianna who?'

'Gianna, Clara's friend.'

'And who's Clara?'

'Clara is a friend of Rina.'

'But who's Rina?'

'Rina, don't you know Rina?'

'No.'

'But it was you who gave your telephone number to Clara, who gave it to me. Well, anything doing? Would you like us to meet? D'you want me to come along?'

For a moment I was in doubt. I had understood perfectly well what it was all about; and all of a sudden, to my surprise, I felt a profound and gloomy kind of excitement that seemed to derive both its justification and its force from the idea that the sexual act was a thing of nullity and that all that was left to me now, in my present state of despair, was to plunge head-long into this nullity. So I answered Gianna telling her to come, and that I would expect her that same day, at five in the afternoon.

She arrived punctually, and I will not stop to describe her; perhaps I could not do so even if I wished, for in my memory she has a body but not a face. Gianna, the friend of Clara, the friend of Rina, was only the first of a long series. After her there was Luisa the friend of Gianna, and then Pina the friend of Luisa, and then Silvia the friend of Pina, and then again Mirella the friend of Silvia, and so on from day to day, from telephone-call to telephone-call, from visit to visit. Without intending it, I had found the end of a skein; I pulled it and the skein unwound itself smoothly. At first I limited myself to one visit a week; then I got the girls to come twice a week, then three times and finally almost every day. For almost a year I gave myself up in this way to love affairs of this type, thus putting into practice an act which I have already described as a nullity. In a different situation I might even have been able to consider these visits from girls as the carefree outlet of a superabundant energy. But, in my state of complete and resigned inertia, the mercenary sexual relationship appeared to me to be the only alternative to the artificiality of all other modes of action; and therefore I was unable to conceal from myself that I was going to bed with these call-girls with the conscious intention of systematically squandering something precious of which, however, I was neither able nor willing to make use. Moreover I recognised that this was the case, from the deathlike sensation which I had every time I poured out my seed lovelessly upon these complaisant and un-known bodies. I would sink back exhausted on top of the girl, saying to myself: 'I'm dying, yes, I'm dying. I shall go on living, but I shall no longer be alive, ever again; I'm dying, I shall die and I shall not realize it and I shall continue to go about alive, but in truth I shall be dead.'

One afternoon I was, as usual, expecting one of these many

girls, a certain Gina who had already been to my house on other occasions. But when I went to open the door I found myself face to face with a woman whom I did not know. She asked me if I was Francesco, I answered that I was, and then, with the self-assured air of one who knows she can take the liberty of doing what she is doing, and without another word, she walked in in a leisurely, conceited, proprietory manner, strutting and swaying her hips. I looked at her as she walked in front of me: she was very young, perhaps not more than twenty, her round head topped by a helmet of smooth black hair, with a fringe down to her eyes which were of a light, greyish colour. Her face was round and full and fresh like the face of a child; a very small nose and a very large mouth confirmed the childish impression. I noticed that she was wearing a tartan skirt that came down below her knees and was very wide and full of pleats. At each step, as she moved round the entrance-hall pretending to look at the prints hanging on the walls, these pleats in her skirt undulated seductively, from the points of her hips right down to her robust calves. I reflected that she must have a full, soft, rather plump figure – the figure, in fact, of a little girl who has grown in too much of a hurry; and, taking her lightly round the waist, I asked her: 'What is your name?'

She freed herself with a pirouette and said in a playful tone: 'Mr. Francesco, I don't know *your* name. Gina was unwell and asked me to come and see you, that's all.' She uttered these words in a decisive tone, and immediately afterwards asked impatiently: 'Where's the bedroom?'

I pointed it out to her and she walked in front of me and opened the door with the same proprietory air. We started undressing beside the bed, she on one side and I on the other. I kept my head bent while I was undressing; then I looked up and saw that the girl had lain down naked on the bed; and for a moment I stayed where I was, motionless and astonished, staring at her.

I saw in front of my eyes, not the soft plump, childish female body I had pictured; but rather a skeleton covered with skin. The roundness of the hips which, shortly before, I had thought I divined beneath the undulations of her skirt was in reality nothing but an optical illusion produced by the pleats in the material and the width of her pelvis. In her, the only fleshy parts were her face, her neck and her calves; all the rest was nothing but bones. Her thighs, like two sticks attached to her pelvis at right angles, lay parallel on the bed-cover, with a large space between them in which her groin, with its tuft of long, soft black hair, looked like the head of a new-born baby; her thorax, projecting sharply above her hollow, wrinkled belly, revealed every rib beneath the stretched skin; her breasts were nothing but flattened creases; the two bones of her arms branched off from the bones of her shoulders with the stiffness of an anatomical diagram. I looked at her in silence, and she looked back at me without shyness, in fact almost with a kind of self-satisfied challenge. Finally she asked: 'Well, what's the matter with you, why don't you come to bed?'

I said nothing. Between her thighs, below the tuft of pubic hair, I caught a glimpse of the cleft of her sex, with its tender, bulging edges, like the cleft of a fruit which has split from ripeness but which, by some miracle, has not yet fallen from the branch. At last, with an effort, I managed to say: 'The trouble is, I didn't know you were so thin. How d'you come to be so thin?'

She answered with indifference: 'For no particular reason. I've always been like that. That's how I'm made.'

'Yes, I see,' I said; 'but how d'you manage? What I mean is, don't you find it's a disadvantage to be so thin, in the job you're doing?'

She laughed, lifted her arm and drew her small, plump hand along between her thighs, stroking herself; then she replied: 'Why, don't you know? – it's just this thinness that men like. At first they're surprised, like you, but then they like it. There are plenty of them that want to see me again. Foreigners, especially, always want to do it again.'

She was silent for a moment and then, talkative and conceited, she went on: 'The other day there was a German who simply couldn't stop. He said he liked me better than any other girl he'd met here in Italy. He said something in German – wait a moment – ah, yes – *totentanz*. What does that mean?'

I translated mechanically: 'It means "dance of death".'
'And why "dance of death"?'
'It was a painting they used to have in the churches. You could see Death dancing first with one person then with another, with a king, with a beggar, with a young man, with

an old man, with a poor man, with a rich man, and so on.'

'So what?'

'It was intended to mean that death does not respect anybody, but carries them off, one and all. It wasn't very complimentary to you.'

'Why?'

'Because that German was treating you as a skeleton, he was calling you Death.'

She stroked herself again between her thighs in a self-satisfied immodest way, then shrugged her shoulders and said: 'As far as I'm concerned, they can call me what they like provided they pay me. That German with his *totentanz* gave me a nice little amount. Very well then, I'm Death; what about it? Come along, let's get on with it.'

I must admit that in the meantime, having got over my surprise, I had begun to feel a certain desire of, so to speak, an intellectual kind. Yes indeed, I thought, she was Death, the Death of the *danse macabre* in the church frescoes; but she was also that nullity round which I had been hovering for so long and which was at last presented to me in its true likeness. So I climbed on to the bed and threw myself with adequate fervour upon that pile of bones. Besides, after all, I reflected as she clung to me, clasping my sides with her two thighs and pressing the bones of her pelvis against my belly, after all it was a novel sensation, and a strange one, to possess a skeleton, penetrating into the soft, living sex that seemed to have stayed caught up inside it, rather as a warm bird's nest remains caught up in the dry, cold boughs of a winter tree.

Afterwards, we stayed together for a little, lying side by side, then she dozed off and I looked at her while she slept. She was in truth a skeleton; and, like a skeleton, she lay untidily, all right angles and acute angles, giving the impression that, if shaken, all the large and small bones of which she was made up would come apart from each other and fall in confusion on the bedclothes. Finally she roused herself, got off the bed, went into the bathroom, sat down on the lavatory seat with her legs spread out and urinated for a long time. I watched her through the doorway, as she had not troubled to shut the door: it seemed to me almost incredible that so great a quantity of liquid could come from so dried-up a skeleton. After she had washed, she came back into the bedroom to dress: as she walked naked round the bed she moved her bones in a somewhat disjointed manner which was, nevertheless, fairly logical and coherent. When she was dressed, I gave her the money and then showed her to the front door. In the doorway she said to me: 'Did you enjoy the *totentanz*? If you want to do it again, telephone Gina and make an arrangement with her.' I watched her as she walked out on to the landing: her pleated skirt undulated provokingly this way and that, counterfeiting a roundness of the hips; but I knew it was undulating, not over a pair of muscular buttocks, but over fleshless, hollow bones. The lift came to a halt; Death waved back at me and disappeared.

The visit of the skeleton-girl marked the end of that period of my life. Negotiations had already been going on for some days between me and the editor of a Milan newspaper. They had liked some articles of mine on Sardinia which had been published in my usual left-wing daily, and they thought I might start contributing, in the first place, as a foreign correspondent. As soon as the girl had gone, I sat down almost automatically at my desk and wrote a letter accepting their offer. Then I put the letter in an envelope and went out to post it.

Thus began a life which was entirely different from the life I had hitherto led. I travelled for six or even eight months out of the twelve, with an average of two or even three journeys a year; and my sojourns in Rome never lasted more than two months, during which I spent the greater part of my time writing the articles about my last journey so that I should be ready to start off again as soon as possible. 1953, 1954, 1955, 1956, 1957, 1958, 1959, 1960, 1961, 1962: during these years I visited almost all the countries inscribed, in alphabetical order, on the pages of my passport. At this point someone may perhaps wonder how it was that I managed, in so short a time, to become such an active and sought-after special correspondent. On thinking it over, I can suggest two reasons: in the first place I did not travel in order to make money or because I was ambitious in my career but, as I have explained, in order not to remain with Cora in Rome; and this disinterestedness was in my favour; the less eagerness we show for things, the more easily do we obtain them. The second reason was that, although a passion for literature had not sufficed to make me into the novelist I should have liked to be, it had at least given me a mastery of the means of expression such as is indispensable even in the profession of a journalist.

But perhaps the chief reason of my success must be sought in the character of the articles I wrote. This character sprang directly from the reasons which urged me to travel, that is from the necessity not to think about my past. In such conditions, travelling could not be so much an experience – for any personal experience would have brought me back to myself, that is, to my past – as a kind of drug. What is it that drug addicts generally seek? They seek to pass over from their accustomed reality into another one which, according to them, is better, and is in any case different. And that was precisely what I sought in my travels.

There is a French word which is highly expressive of the sensation my travels gave me: *dépaysement*. What was this sensation? I will try to describe it. It was the sensation of a traveller who, after flying for some hours across an ocean or a continent, disembarks at the airport of an unknown city and then, as he sits in the bus which takes him to his hotel, observes the streets through which he is passing. The traveller is tired and bewildered, he knows nothing of the country, he is entirely unprepared, he has no curiosity, he has no intention of stopping for long, he is perhaps merely in transit. Finally, he does not know the language in which the shop-signs are written and which is being spoken by the other travellers round him. In such circumstances a house is truly nothing but a house, a tree nothing but a tree, a woman, a child, a square, a cloud merely a woman, a child, a square and a cloud. This *dépaysement* skimmed off, so to speak, all significance from the countries I visited, leaving nothing but their superficial appearance. I was, therefore, a superficial traveller; but this adjective must be interpreted not in the sense of 'thoughtless' that it usually has, but in its literal meaning. I was superficial in that I did not go beyond the surface in my observations; not in that I was myself superficial in my intimate consciousness.

If, on the one hand, this superficiality kept me in the slightly drugged state of *dépaysement*, on the other, it allowed me to speak of countries in the abstract, reducing them to diagrams, to formulas, to concepts, without giving me the trouble, that is, of going and verifying whether these diagrams, these formulas, these concepts corresponded in any way with reality. I travelled a great deal, as I have already said, and I travelled carefully, that is, I traversed the countries about which I had to speak in my articles from top to bottom, making use of all the means of transport and not neglecting even the most remote and insignificant corners. But it was only in appearance that I travelled for the purpose of my newspaper contributions; in reality I travelled in order to drug myself. The articles, in any case, I wrote in Rome, at my own desk with the aid of books by other journalists, of encyclopedias, of guide books and manuals; and these articles, beneath their apparent precision, were unreal and far removed from any direct experience. Two important results followed from this; in the first place, extreme readability: my articles, thanks to the absence of a reality in which my mind might have stumbled and become entangled, were manufactured like little machines for reading – smooth, easy, transparent, fluent, in the second place, owing to the lack of any sort of sentimental participation, a detached, lackadaisical way of presenting the material which succeeded in giving the illusion of impartiality and impersonality which the more serious newspapers consider to be so important. Readable and objective as spelling-books, my contributions from abroad had a notable success. So much so that many of my colleagues, I noticed, tried to imitate me – without succeeding however. They, in fact, travelled really in order to write their contributions, not to drug themselves, as I did; and they did not have a past to forget; nor, once the journey was completed, was the past waiting for them at home in the person of a wife to whom they did not speak and whose existence they wished to ignore.

Of those ten years, between 1953 and 1962, I have a confused memory, as of things seen and done in a state of continual aloofness. I can see trains carrying me through landscapes that are endlessly different, aeroplanes taking off, flying, landing at airports, ships leaving or entering harbours, cars moving through city streets and country roads. Hotel rooms in which I slept seem to me to be all the same and seem all to share the same appearance of anonymity; sea-coasts, mountains, forests, countrysides, cities and all other kinds of landscape appear superimposed one upon another like pictures in a photograph that has been exposed several times by mistake. And the faces of the crowds of the whole world leap out of my memory and are scattered in the air like grains of corn sprayed furiously from the funnel of a threshing-machine.

Moreover this aloofness, this non-involvement, did not cost me any effort; I felt myself borne along by it by natural inclination. My head, in truth, was like a glass or china shop in which a bomb had exploded, so that all the objects in the shop have been reduced to fragments. A bomb had exploded inside my head – when, I did not know, perhaps when I realized I no longer loved Cora; a bomb which had given me the aloofness of a sleep-walker. In other words I was perhaps, as it were, asleep on my feet, or anyhow my mind was asleep. I was asleep and dreaming that I was awake, that I was a special correspondent, travelling from one country to another and coming back to Rome and writing my articles and then leaving again on another journey. Nevertheless this condition of sleep seemed to me preferable to that of wakefulness; and I therefore did nothing to rouse myself.

At this point I wish to say that those ten years of travelling had, as a consequence, not merely the aloofness of which I have already spoken, but also the unforeseen consequence of chastity. I did not deliberately decide to abstain from the sexual act; this too was a natural and anyhow a gradual thing. After some few encounters with prostitutes or casual women in the countries in which I happened to be travelling, gradually and almost without my realizing it these fleeting relationships, from which I no longer expected anything, not even the proof, already obtained in Rome after the collapse of my love for Cora, that they were purely negative – these relationships, I say, gradually ceased altogether. One day, for some reason or other, I happened to think about this subject and discovered, almost with astonishment, that it was now nearly a year since I had touched a woman. I asked myself whether I wanted to do so and realized that I did not. Then I started to reflect upon this coldness of mine; and this was the outcome of my reflections.

I had loved Cora, or at any rate had been convinced that I loved her. Then this love had fallen in ruins, from top to bottom, sweeping away, in its fall, all the things which at that time constituted my reasons for living. This collapse had been followed by a period – not very long, not even as much as a year – of mercenary love affairs. But mercenary love had revealed itself to me as something that could be experienced only at the cost of life itself, in other words as that nothingness which is death. I did not now feel like returning to that nothingness; nor was there any woman at hand whom I could love. There was, indeed, implicit in my chastity the idea that only love, the kind of love that I had once thought I felt for Cora, could make me abandon this chastity, and that, if I did not have this kind of love, then it was preferable to remain chaste. It may seem strange to some people that a man in the flower of virility could so easily renounce a natural relief, considered by many to be indispensable. But it is not so. The sexual act is one of those things that, if done frequently, is done more and more; and if done seldom, is done less and less; in the end one can even cease to do it at all. I had been on the point of doing it more and more, at the moment when I had ceased to love Cora; now, by dint of doing it less and less, I realized that I could give it up altogether.

Of course I did not give up the idea of love; but it became very difficult for me to imagine that a time could come when I should love once again. The illusion of genuineness, the illusion which had filled that past of which I was now so ashamed, had been the cause of my love for Cora, that I had no illusions left; and without illusions it seemed to me impossible to love. It was true that, having been taught by experience, I suspected that the conviction of having no illusions left might in fact be itself an illusion, even if of a new and different kind; but I was unable to imagine what sort of woman it might be whom one could love because one had no illusions, because one no longer believed in anything and because, as in my case, one felt attracted by negativeness. A woman, in short, whom I might love simply because I was no longer capable of loving.

In the meantime I went on travelling for my newspaper, methodically and diligently, adding with every year that passed a fresh stone to the edifice of my non-involvement. I have already spoken of the manner in which I travelled; it remains for me to describe the relationship that had become established between myself and what I still looked upon as my family, during my sojourns in Rome between one journey and another. I was, then, in every respect like a kind of lodger. And what is a lodger but somebody who preserves his detachment in relation to the people in whose house he lives? The lodger goes in and out, he sleeps, eats, works and lives under the same roof as other people whom he yet manages somehow or other, to ignore. Or rather, he ignores them and at the same time is conscious of their existence in a dim, painless, irregular way. To make another comparison, my detachment with regard to my family was rather like the insensibility produced by an anaesthetic. One no longer feels anything; yet at the same time one feels that one no longer feels anything, which, after all, is a manner of feeling. So it was with me, in my home. I did not ignore Cora as one ignores someone who for us really does not exist; I ignored her as one ignores someone whom one knows all the time to exist and is therefore conscious of ignoring. My non-involvement was, therefore, a feeling of a suspension of involvement, not purely and simply a lack of involvement. I *felt* I was not involved; and the more I felt this, the more I succeeded in being so.

Certainly, if somebody in the past had told me that I should end up by living in my own home like a stranger who rents a room from a needy family, I should have immediately protested that this was not possible. Now, to my surprise, I realized that not merely was it possible but that it was also much easier and more convenient, for myself at least, than its opposite.

Cora, moreover, helped me in my non-involvement which, it must be believed, now suited her far more than it displeased her, She had developed, with the years, a practical sense which, coupled with an extraordinary discretion, or reticence, not to say mysteriousness, had become one of her chief characteristics. The taciturn, sensual young working-class woman of former times had been transformed into a sort of business woman who, in the spare time allowed her by her dressmaking, had found means to be an excellent housewife as well. But, with a sure instinct, she had known how to mark out a precise limit between the attentions due to me from her as a lodging-house keeper and those which, on the other hand, would have been proper in a wife, such as she had been and had decided to be no longer. Since I myself had the same ideas about our relationship, everything went wonderfully well between the two of us, with an almost excessive perfection that might have seemed disquieting to anyone who did not have reasons for behaving as I did.

I travelled, then I went back to Rome for a month or two, and then I went off again. In my home I had finished by occupying the room beside the front door, in which I both slept and worked; and I left all the rest of the flat to Cora and her daughter. I knew that they slept in separate rooms; that Baba, now a student at the University in the faculty of Letters, worked in her own room; that they had their midday meal in the sitting-room, where they were waited on by the daily servant, their evening meal, prepared by themselves, in the kitchen; that my study, in which were my books and papers, was kept locked, and that no one entered it except, occasionally, Cora, to dust it and keep it tidy. I knew all these things, but all I did was to know them; in ten years I may have happened to go into the other rooms of the flat perhaps ten times. It is true that I sometimes had a strange and not easily definable impression: that, when I wished it, I could become the perfect husband and father which I knew I had never been. All I had to do was open a door and sit down at table with Cora and Baba in order to find myself back in the bosom of my family. This was the dream of involvement, right in the midst of the most complete non-involvement. And I was fully aware that it could be no more than a dream. Furthermore, while I now knew perfectly well what non-involvement was, I could not yet manage to understand what involvement might imply.

But one thing remained unaltered amongst so many changes – my passion for literature and, in particular, my ambition to write, some day, a novel. Gradually, with the years, the novel had become for me far more than a literary *genre;* it was actually a way of understanding life. I knew in fact that it was not possible for me to establish a genuine relationship in real life with myself and with others; and I was convinced that the novel was the only place in which genuineness was not merely possible but also, so to speak, inevitable, if the novel was truly a novel. And it often occurred to me now to wonder how in the world my novel, once I had written it, had revealed itself to me as also lacking in genuineness. And in precisely the same manner in which my actions had been proved artificial; that is, not in its wording but in the very nature of the events that were portrayed in it.

I realized that the answer to this question lay in the novel itself; or rather, in the things I had tried to relate; and so, again and again, I went back in memory to my work and analysed its aspects one by one, searching doggedly for the secret flaw which had caused the ruin of the whole edifice. Certainly I could have solved the problem in the quickest and simplest way by admitting that, when all was said and done, perhaps the only reason for my disaster lay in the fact that I was not a novelist. But this answer, just because I continued to cultivate my ambition to succeed some day in writing a novel, that is, to reach the only genuineness of which I felt capable – this answer was the only one that I had not the courage to make myself. Partly because I did not at all aspire to write a masterpiece, but merely to express myself in a genuine manner, with the means and talent at my disposal. The modesty and legitimacy of this aspiration convinced me that the cause of the failure of my attempt to write a novel must be sought rather in the things I had aimed at relating than inside myself.

In the end it seemed to me that I had an inkling of this cause. I had tried to tell the story of my relationship with Cora, from our first meeting until our marriage. This story was in fact a story, that is, a series of events which did not belong to the sphere of everyday life and were not included in the category of things that may happen to anybody at any moment, in other words it was a drama, by which I mean a combination of different actions by different characters. Now here lay the truth of the matter: the artificiality of the novel derived from the action that took place within it. I had in fact verified that in the reality of life it was not possible, for me at any rate, to act in a genuine manner. In consequence – like a subtle poison which has become blended with the soil and which passes through the roots of a tree into its most intimate fibres – artificiality had penetrated, from the things I had tried to depict, into the very words I had used to depict them.

All this was not, at the time, as precise and lucid as it now appears in my explanation. It was, on the other hand, the fruit of a long, obscure and, so to speak, instinctive reflection carried on by me for years during my professional peregrinations. I travelled, I returned to Rome, I started off again; and every now and then I thought about my novel, picking up the thread of my reflections at the exact point where I had let it drop perhaps a month or two before. In the end this literary meditation took shape in a fairly simple project, which I may summarize in this way: 'The novel as a story, as a series of events, with a beginning, a development and an end, as a drama, in short, has in your case been a failure. Try and see, then, if you can manage a novel without a story, without a series of events, without drama, a novel in which nothing happens. What is the opposite of dramatic action? The opposite of dramatic action is the ordinary run of things, the routine, as they say, of everyday life. In your first novel you wished to recount a drama and you left out the everyday; now you should try to describe the everyday, carefully avoiding drama. As for the genuineness that action could not but deny to you, you will see that you achieve it in a representation that excludes every kind of action.'

The thought occurred to me at this point that, after all, very few dramas happen in the life of a man; for the most part it is the daily round, the everyday routine that prevail. For every story, every drama or series of events with a beginning and an end and obviously fated to last only a short time, how many years there are of everyday routine during which one takes no action but is, so to speak, acted upon, while life flows on shapelessly, with neither head nor tail, and nothing happens that could not happen to anybody and at any moment: I thought of my life and recollected, especially, the periods of everyday routine during the brief visits I made to Rome, between one journey and another. During these visits, as I have already said, nothing happened that was not strictly limited to ordinary day-to-day life. My purpose, in fact, in these visits was solely to write my articles, so that I could start off again as soon as possible. Thus I decided to make a kind of experiment: I would keep a diary during one of these brief Roman visits between two journeys. A diary of two months of my life. Then, from this diary, somehow or other, I would extract the novel, that is, an objective narrative, in the third person and the past definite tense. After the novel of artificiality based on action, it would be the novel of the genuine, based on everyday life.

I then asked myself whether, in my diary, I would recount the facts with absolute faithfulness, or whether, as I recounted them, I would add all the things that seemed to me useful for the novel I was intending to extract from it; and I decided for the second alternative. Absolute faithfulness, indeed, even in a diary kept day by day, was not possible; obviously a diary could only recount the things which the person who was keeping it had noticed; no less obviously the writer would make a choice amongst the things he had noticed, reporting some of them and failing to mention others

– and this according to a criterion of his own dictated by the purpose he had set himself. Now my purpose, as I have said, was to extract a novel from the diary. It was therefore natural that I should not only make a choice amongst the material offered day by day for my observation, but also that I should complete and develop it whenever this became necessary; just as a palaeontologist, starting from a fragment of bone, reconstructs the entire skeleton of a prehistoric animal. In any case I should have to effect this reconstruction of reality at every point where it was lacking, when I came to face the actual writing of the novel. So all I would be doing was partially to anticipate it, at the moment when my impressions were still vivid. Nevertheless, in order not to create confusion between things that had really happened and those I had reconstructed, I promised myself that I would indicate in some way, in the diary, all those places where imagination had replaced direct observation.

I was in Iran when I made my decision to keep the diary. It had been a short journey, concerned merely with an enquiry into the question of Persian oil production. I was counting on not having to write more than five articles; after that all my time would be available for the diary. On my way back from Abadan I stopped to visit the ruins of Persepolis. Then, at Teheran, I took an aeroplane which brought me back to Italy in a few hours. The diary which now follows begins immediately after my return to Rome.

DIARY

Tuesday, October 13th

My return to Rome happens always in the same way. I do not notify anyone of my arrival; I creep stealthily into the house, like a thief; and immediately, without troubling to find out whether Cora and her daughter are in the flat, I set about doing the same things as when I arrive in an hotel in a foreign town during my journeys: I open my suitcase, I undress, I take a shower, I dress again, I make a few telephone calls. The only difference is that in Rome I am in my own home. That is to say, I am continually conscious, though in a dim and painless way, of that particular state of mind which I have called non-involvement, which in itself allows me to live at home as in an hotel.

After I have dressed, I usually sit down at my desk and examine the post which has arrived during my absence. Cora diligent in this respect too, and methodical, like a good lodging-house keeper, places the post on my table in different piles: one for registered letters, express letters and telegrams; one for normally stamped letters; one for open envelopes containing invitations, advertisements, announcements and suchlike.

This I have done today. I opened my suitcase, I undressed, I took a shower, I dried myself, I went back into my room, I dressed again, I sat down at the desk and began the scrutiny of my correspondence.

It was an express letter. It was the third I opened. The envelope was of the commonest type, of the kind called 'commercial', such as can be bought in tobacconists' shops. It contained a sheet of typewriting paper folded in four. The letter was typewritten on both sides of the paper and was not signed. I read it and then sat quite still for a moment with the sheet of paper in my hand, looking straight in front of me. Then I read the letter over again: it was written with correctness and even with a certain affected, almost courtly, elegance; one might imagine that whoever wrote it was a bureaucrat or a teacher or even perhaps a journalist like me. But the letter was also horribly vulgar, with a sour, hypocritical vulgarity. It suggested someone who, beneath the cloak of a moralist, was giving vent to some corrupt, too long repressed inclination.

I noticed also the rather special technique of the letter. On the first page the anonymous writer, who introduced himself as one of my readers, heaped one eulogistic phrase upon another. These eulogies were excessive and too insistent not to be intended as a mockery. But then, when the page was turned, the accusation exploded, with blasphemous violence, in four or five lines of coarse, pitiless words. It was clear what effect the anonymous writer had wished to obtain: first, a climax of confidence and of indulgence in self-satisfied vanity, then, by way of surprise, a sudden anticlimax of savage, sarcastic revelation.

I read the letter a third time, and then, all at once, I felt the blood ebbing from my face. It seemed to me that the false calmness of the eulogies on the first page, followed, on the second page, by the contrast of the unrestrained vulgarity of denunciation, was a positive proof – I myself did not know why – that the letter was telling the truth. If one could reconstruct a personality from a few lines, this anonymous writer, I thought, must be a serious, meticulous, even a pedantic, character. A man of that type did not invent anything; and he did not make any move until he felt he had his feet on firm ground. I seemed actually to see him, this anonymous writer, sitting down at his desk in a book-filled study, typing his letter and then reading it over, placing it in an envelope and stamping it. For some reason I pictured him as thin and very tall, middle-aged, with a long, sad, bilious face, a sharp nose, tight lips, and wearing spectacles. A man of culture, a studious man, a well-read man.

Finally I roused myself from these imaginings, put the letter in my pocket and left the room. Strange to say, it never occurred to me to dismiss the whole affair with a shrug of the shoulders and a phrase such as: 'It's their affair, it has nothing to do with me'; or with a quick decision, not very different in tone: 'I shall leave the house at once, I shall go to an hotel and stay there for this month or two while I write my articles, then I shall go away again and that's that.' No, in a curious and unexpected way, the task I had set myself, to keep a diary and extract a novel from it later, had given rise to the idea that I could not now, as in the past, behave as a mere lodger. I decided that I must move from non-involvement to involvement; I could not go back to non-involvement, for the sole reason that I had received the anonymous letter.

As I came into the passage I noticed again, as if seeing it for the first time, the tedious, symmetrical style of the most conventional kind of nineteenth-century decoration which I had thought it right to adopt when I was setting up house: the two curtains with broad vertical stripes masking the windows that looked out on the courtyard; the three Empire console-tables surmounted by mirrors, between one door and another; the four prints framed in dark wood in the spaces between the curtains. I realized that I was looking at these things, well known as they were, with news eyes. Why had I done up the flat in so conventional a way? It seemed to me that I now understood: it was due to an unconscious aspiration for some kind of order, even a mean, out-of-date middle class order, which should conceal from me the profound disorder of my life, still at that time unknown to me. The passage turned at a right angle as it followed round the courtyard. Beyond this corner the last door, right at the end of the passage, was the door of our bedroom, of Cora's and my bedroom at the time when we were still sleeping together. To it I now went.

I remembered this room as being the remotest, most silent and least-well-lit in the whole flat, facing as it did, not on to the street, but on to the courtyard, with one small window just below the attic cornice. And – after the anonymous letter – the room was suddenly revealed to me in a character which had hitherto escaped me: withdrawn, secret, shadowy, it must be, for Cora, not so much a bedroom as a refuge, or even positively a kind of lair. When I reached the door I knocked but no one answered; I turned the handle and looked in.

The room was in half-darkness, and empty. A sour, cold smell came to my nostrils, a smell of cosmetics, of stagnant air, of dirty linen, of drawers filled with bits of old rubbish, of cigarette-smoke, of sleep. I looked for the light-switch beside the door but failed to find it; so I felt my way, across the thick carpet, round the big double bed to the window; then I took hold of the blind-cord and pulled it. Slowly, as though reluctantly, a quiet, subdued light filtered through the curtains into the room.

I myself did not know why I had come into the room, seeing that there was no sign of Cora. But, as I sat down on the bed and looked around, I understood the reason of this almost automatic curiosity on my part.

In contrast with the other rooms in the flat – which Cora, with a scrupulous care worthy of a museum curator, had kept during those years in their original order, without touching or changing anything, even the smallest orament – upon this room, perhaps because it was the one in which she lived, she had made her own imprint. I recognized, it is true, the cold, simple pieces of furniture in the Empire style which I had acquired and arranged myself: the walnut bed with little pillars with bronze capitals; the commode with its white marble top; the chairs with lyre-shaped backs. But, as happens in churches built at a good period and completely disfigured by the tinsel and papier mâché of a superstitious religion, here neo-classical coldness and orderliness were overwhelmed and submerged by a swarming mass of knick-knacks of a more or less promiscuous and obscenely intimate kind.

All round the head of the bed upon which I was sitting hung a great quantity of toy animals copied from animated cartoons: rats, cats, wolves, rabbits, lions, foxes, giraffes, elephants and so on. They were fixed to the wall by means of hooks and coloured ribbons, but in such a way that they touched the wood of the bed-head; thus, when Cora went to bed after the fatigues of the day, she was able to imagine that all the beasts, with their slyly anthropomorphic faces, bestraddled her during the night, in a wild but motionless dance all round her head. The bed was no longer covered with its original bedspread, which had been, I seemed to remember, sober and lustreless, but with a glossy, shot-silk quilt, a mixture of blue and green and purple. A doll dressed up as an eighteenth-century lady, with a big white cotton-wool wig, a powdered, patch-besprinkled face, with a low-necked bodice and crinoline, was seated, arms and legs outstretched, on the pillow; another doll, this one dressed as a Spanish woman, in black, with a comb in its hair and a black lace shawl over its shoulders, was propped up, also with arms and legs outstretched, against the foot of the bed. I rose and went over to the chest-of-drawers. The white marble top was closely crowded with knick-knacks over which I bent with curiosity. There were little filigree and crystal boxes of the kind that contain wedding sweetmeats; Sorrento musical boxes; small opaline or coloured glass vases; china statuettes of coquettish subjects; little carafes and glasses and cups, and little forks and spoons for dolls' dinner-parties; crystal globes with pansies or the basilica of St. Peter's inside them; ashtrays of various shapes; red or blue velvet pin-cushions; little bottles of scent or liqueurs; small celluloid dolls and so forth. Right in the middle of all this jumble, as though on an altar amongst candles and vases of flowers, like effigies of patron saints, stood a few framed photographs arranged in a circle, of Baba, of myself and of Cora and of a couple of attractive young women whom I did not know.

I turned round, leant back against the chest-of-drawers and looked again at the room. Beside the bed, on the little table, stood a lamp with a red silk shade, and beside the lamp was a red glass ashtray full of cigarette-ends, most of them stained with lipstick at the ends. On the other bedside table, at the other side of the bed, I saw a quantity of pill-boxes and medicine-bottles tidily arranged. I went over to look; there were sleeping tablets, vitamin tablets, tonics, tranquillizers and, surprisingly amongst this varied pharmacopeia, a bowl full of telephone counters. I raised my eyes to the wall: above the toy animals chasing each other round the head of the bed, in the place which is usually occupied by some holy picture, Cora had hung a large oil painting of the kind that is sold in the most commercial type of gallery, representing, in a naturalistic manner, three naked young women bathing in a river against a background of trees and flowering shrubs.

I stood quite still for a long time without thinking of anything, as though I wanted not so much to understand what the room signified as to identify myself with it, through the fascinated contemplation of the bric-à-brac that filled it. Then, suddenly, the telephone started ringing, just there on the bedside table, with a sound that was confidential, ambiguous, intimate, insistent and yet reserved, like a voice that wished to be heard only by the person to whom it was addressed and by no one else. I waited until the ringing stopped, then I went out of the room, closing the door behind me.

I turned back, thinking to go to my own room. Some radio music, coming from behind one of the doors, reminded me that, besides Cora, there was also her daughter Baba in the flat. After a moment's hesitation, I knocked.

The voice of studied, self-satisfied quietness which bade me come in filled me with a vague, indefinable irritation, such as might have been caused by some pointless trick in doubtful taste. I turned the door-handle and went in. Unlike Cora's, this room was lofty, white, well-lit, with a floor of natural wood, well waxed and uncarpeted. One whole wall was taken up by a big built-in cupboard, on the doors of which were painted brightly coloured designs of flowers and leaves; otherwise there was nothing but a divan bed in one corner and a writing-desk in another. The bleak, cold, even light coming in through the curtainless windows gave an appearance of order and cleanliness to this almost empty room, as though the maid had only just left it after throwing open the windows and carefully dusting everything. Seated sideways to me at the desk, Baba looked at me over her shoulder with ostentatious and as it were scientific curiosity, through big tortoise-shell-rimmed glasses. On the desk I saw books and note-books and the portable radio from which I had heard the music as I went along the passage.

I said with some embarrassment, as I stopped in the door-way: 'Excuse my coming in like this, Baba; I'm Francesco, your mother's husband.'

She made no answer but merely sat quite still, turned towards me. I persisted: 'Perhaps you don't recognize me?'

Still silence. I started walking across the room, with small, uncertain steps, as if I were walking over a slippery surface, and so reached the desk. Baba went on looking at me without saying anything; I took advantage of her silence to look back at her. I was struck by the thickness and bear-like compactness of the brown hair that framed her pale, round face at the level of her cheeks. Her forehead was hidden by a fringe, her nose short, robust and straight with rather wide nostrils, her mouth sharply if also capriciously defined, as though carved in an exceptionally hard wood, with two thin, deep furrows at the corners. Then she took off her glasses and I saw her eyes: grey-green and transparent in colour, very large, and with that special fixed, unhappy look that goes with extreme short sight. Finally, with a rather heavy placidity, which sounded to me, however, more deliberate, more studied than derisive, she said: 'Yes, you're Francesco, I recognize you, don't worry. Sit down, Francesco, talk to me, Francesco.'

Something occurred to me at this point which I ought to have said to myself from the very beginning: perhaps I had no right to speak to Baba about the anonymous letter. I sat down feeling rather embarrassed and began prudently: 'Actually I was looking for Cora, because I wanted to ask her something. But Cora isn't there. As I was coming along the passage I heard the radio music, so I came in.'

'You did quite right.'

'But perhaps I've disturbed you.'

'Not in the least.'

'You were studying . . . '

'Don't bother about me. So you came in to tell me what you meant to tell Cora?'

Her tone of voice was highly irritating, on account of its excessive and perhaps impertinent calmness. Suddenly I forgot my prudent intentions and replied almost violently: 'Yes.'

'Well, what is it?'

'It's a matter of – of a piece of information, let us call it.'

'What information?'

'I arrived a short time ago from Iran. Among my correspondence I found this letter.'

'You want me to read it?'

'Yes.'

She took the letter, put her glasses on again, drew the piece of paper out of the envelope, unfolded it, read first one side then the other, and then handed the letter back to me. All this without showing any surprise or other emotion, with a sleepy, sly, yet painstaking air. She took off her glasses again, looked at me for a moment and finally said: 'You want to know if it's true?'

'Certainly.'

'Yes, it's true.'

I sat silent for a little, not knowing what to say, then I asked stupidly: 'It's true? And you say it like that?'

'Like what?'

'Quietly, calmly.'

'How ought I to say it howling and weeping?'

'No . . . But really . . . '

'Really what?'

'After all, Cora is your mother.'

'Yes, she's my mother '

'Well, then . . .'

'Well, then?'

'But is it really true?'

'I've told you it is.'

'But how d'you come to know it, since when have you known it?'

'I've known it for a long time.'

'What does that mean – a long time?'

'Well, let us say six years, at least.'

'Six years?'

'Yes, six years.'

'But how did you get to know it?'

'In the most direct way.'

'What d'you mean by direct?'

'Direct means direct.'

'Have you been able to see anything?'

'I've been able to see a great deal.'

'What for example?'

'Why does it interest you so much to know?'

'Excuse me, but when all's said and done, this does concern me.'

'In what way?'

'Cora is my wife, you are my stepdaughter, this is my home.'

'Are you quite sure of that?'

'Of what?'

'That Cora is your wife, that I am your stepdaughter, that this is your home?'

'As far as one can be sure of anything.'

'All right, in that case I think I can tell you, after all.'

'Well then?'

'Well, here you are, then: six years ago Cora took me to that house.'

'What house?'

'The house mentioned in the letter you showed me.'

'She took you there?'

'Yes.'

'But to do what?'

'To do what is usually done in that kind of house.'

'I'm sorry, I don't quite understand. Cora took you to that house – for what?'

'To put me at the disposal of her clients.'

'And you allowed yourself to be taken?'

'Yes.'

'Without protesting?'

'What could I do? I was only fourteen.'

'Yes, that's true, you were only fourteen; and yet . . . '

'And yet what?'

'Nothing, it doesn't matter. Be quiet for a moment, let me think.'

'Oh yes, think – as far as I'm concerned.'

'Well, now then . . . Tell me, what really happened at that time?'

She looked at me for a moment in silence, then she said: 'I must warn you, in the first place, that I know nothing, or hardly anything, of what happened.'

'Why don't you know anything? It happened to you, and not so many years ago.'

'It didn't happen to me.'

'What d'you mean? Wasn't it you that Cora took to her house?'

'It wasn't me, no.'

'And who was it, then?'

'It was another Baba.'

'Another Baba?'

'Yes, another Baba with whom I've nothing to do.'

'Ah, another Baba? I understand.'

'No, you don't understand.'

'I don't understand?'

'No, you can't understand. It's better for me to explain, then you'll understand.'

'Explain, then.'

She was silent for a little; then, just like a schoolmistress talking to a pupil, in just such a sense and didactic manner, she said: 'The Baba of fourteen years old who was led by the hand by Cora to her house was a different Baba from the one who is now in front of you, and the one now in front of you is a different Baba from the one who, let us suppose, sat for her school-leaving certificate two years ago. D'you understand me now?'

'Perhaps I do, yes.'

'Let's imagine, in fact, that my life is divided into water-tight compartments. In each compartment there's a different Baba, and all these different Babas never communicate with each other, they don't resemble each other, they're not responsible for each other. D'you see now?'

'Very convenient.'

'Why convenient?'

'Just as you said: one Baba is not responsible for another, so anything can happen.'

She remained deep in thought for a moment, then she replied: 'Yes, but above all it's convenient for other people.'

'Why for other people?'

'For Cora, for instance. She did what she did, but I can't reprove her for what she did because she didn't do it to me, but to another Baba.'

'I see. Then tell me what really happened on that occasion.'

'It's *that* Baba who knows about it.'

'So *you* can't tell me?'

'Yes, I can, if you really want me to.'

'Let's suppose I do really want you to.'

'Well, nothing happened at all.'

'How d'you mean – nothing?'

'Just as I say – nothing.'

'It's not possible that *nothing* happened.'

'And yet that's how it was: nothing at all.'

'But Baba must anyhow have seen that first man: who was it?'

'Baba doesn't know who it was.'

'I didn't express myself rightly: what was he like?'

'Baba doesn't know what he was like.'

'But why?'

'Because she didn't see him.'

'She didn't see him?'

'That's right.'

'You mean that Baba and this man met without seeing one one another, in the dark?'

'No, they didn't meet at all.'

'How was that?'

'The man didn't come.'

'He didn't come.'

'Or rather . . . '

'Or rather?'

'Or rather he came, but he didn't show himself.'

'What d'you mean?'

'I mean what I said.'

'And what's that?'

'Well, Cora took Baba into the flat and left her alone in a room, telling her that somebody would come. But that somebody did not come. Or, if he did, he went away without showing himself. And so, that time Cora took Baba home again without anything having happened.'

'I understand. And afterwards?'

'Afterwards – what?'

'Afterwards, no doubt, Cora took Baba back to the house, didn't she?'

'Yes.'

'Cora, then, was determined that Baba should visit the house regularly?'

'So it would seem, yes.'

'Don't you think that, after all, she might have been satisfied with that first time and given up the idea?'

'Why?'

'Well, the man didn't come, or didn't show himself, and surely that was a warning, as one might say, which suggested that she should not insist, which even obliged her not to insist.'

'For Cora it was something different.'

'What?'

'A setback.'

'What d'you mean?'

'She had wished to do a certain thing, according to a certain plan and certain ideas. It had not gone right.'

'And what then?'

'Then she had to try again, as many times as were necessary.'

'Necessary for what?'

'Necessary for the thing finally to succeed.'

'That was why Cora took Baba back to the house the second time?'

'Yes.'

'And what happened that second time?'

'Almost nothing.'

'Why almost nothing?'

'Because, so it seems, Baba was not cut out for that sort of job.'

'Cut out?'

'Cut out, yes; that is, adapted.'

'Who was there that second time?'

'An ordinary sort of man.'

'But what was he like?'

'A middle-aged man, who could have been Baba's father.'

'Unpleasant?'

'No, not in the least unpleasant, very nice.'

'Very nice?'

'Yes, gentle and nice. Fatherly.'

'But who was he?'

'You mean, what was his profession? Baba never found out.'

'I see. And what happened between Baba and this man who was so nice?'

'I've already told you: almost nothing.'

'Why *almost* nothing?'

'Baba had no feeling at all, and no desire to do anything; she was like an inert bundle.'

'And how did the nice man behave in face of the inert bundle?'

'He behaved just as anyone would behave in face of a bundle which he nevertheless believes to be a person.'

'How was that?'

'He tried very hard to make the bundle feel something, to make it take some action; then he got fed up and left it alone.'

'Does it amuse you to talk about these things?'

'Why?'

'I see you're smiling.'

'They're comic things, aren't they? If you look at them from outside.'

'How d'you mean, from outside?'

'Well, imagine telling a friend that you tried to make love with a girl and didn't succeed because the girl failed you in every possible way, imagine telling this in the way such stories are generally told and you'll see that it's a bit comic.'

'Yes, I see. And what happened after that first, or rather that second, time?'

'Cora took Baba back to the house – let us say five or six times more.'

'And what happened all those times?'

'More or less what happened the first time.'

'By which you mean . . . ?'

'By which I mean, almost nothing.'

'Almost nothing?'

'Yes, almost nothing. Baba went on being a bundle. The men tried hard for a bit to make her feel something, to make her take action, turning her over and over in all directions as you might do with a doll in order to find the gadget that makes it speak and move. And then they would get fed up.'

'What d'you mean, they got fed up?'

'They would go to sleep; or else they'd leave the room and go and protest to Cora.'

'And what answer would Cora give them?'

'I don't know. Baba wasn't present when the men were protesting.'

'Anything else?'

'Yes, the last time Baba went to the house one of these men lost patience with her; he slapped her and abused her.'

'What did he say to her?'

'He said: "You turd".'

'And what did Baba do?'

'She did nothing.'

'Did she feel hatred for this man?'

'Nothing much; after all, from his point of view he wasn't wrong. If anything, it was another man that Baba took a dislike to.'

'What man was that?'

'Another man.'

'Why?'

'This man made her tell him her story, and Cora's story too, and he showed pity and even became indignant; afterwards he wanted to make love just the same, like all the others, but it certainly wasn't owing to him that Baba, as usual, behaved like a bundle.'

'You said that Baba didn't go more than seven or eight times to Cora's house. But how did it come about that she stopped going there?'

'Cora changed her mind.'

'How d'you mean, she changed her mind?'

'She changed her mind, that is, she realized her mistake with regard to Baba.'

'She realized her mistake?'

'Yes. After those seven or eight times Cora became convinced that Baba was not cut out for that sort of thing.'

'And what did she do?'

'What does a music-master do when he realizes that his pupil is making no progress?'

'What does he do? I don't know; he would stop the lessons.'

'Exactly. Cora told Baba that from then on she wouldn't take Baba to the house any more. And that Baba must get on with her education.'

'Her·education?'

'Yes, her education; and she said something else as well.'

'What was that?'

'That if Baba ever mentioned what had happened, she would kill her.'

'She said that?'

'Yes, and she picked up a knife and showed it to her while she was speaking.'

'A knife ?'

'A kitchen knife, yes.'

'And what did Baba say to that?'

'It was at that moment that Baba discovered for the first time that what had happened had probably happened to another Baba, different from the one whom Cora at that moment was threatening with the knife. And she said so to Cora.'

'What did she say to her?'

'She said: "For me it's as if it had happened to another person; I don't know anything about it".'

'And what did Cora say?'

'She didn't say anything. Cora never does say anything, you know.'

'And afterwards?'

'After what?'

'After the decision of Cora's, what happened to Baba?'

'Oh, nothing special. She went to school and did well in all the various subjects, she went on to high school and passed her exams with the highest possible marks, then she became a pupil at the University Faculty of Letters.'

'And how about – other things?'

'What other things?'

'Well, let us say – from the sentimental point of view.'

'Ah, sentimental. Nothing extraordinary. Only what might happen to any girl of Baba's age and situation.'

'And what's that?'

'But why d'you want to know?'

'Never mind!'

'I've already told you: Baba is a very ordinary type of person, a person like millions of others.'

'All the same, what happened to her when she was fourteen wasn't very ordinary.'

'But that was another Baba.'

'Ah, of course, I was forgetting. Well then . . . ?'

'Well, let's say that Baba has had a few adventures – not so very many, however – and then a more serious thing. Or rather, two more serious things. One that came to an end after a few months and another that's still going on. As you see, it's perfectly true that Baba is an ordinary sort of person.'

'This last more serious thing – what is it? A fiancé? '

'Yes.'

'Who is he, this fiancé?'

'He's an ordinary kind of person, too. A medical student.'

'And what's he called?'

'This is a regular interrogation, isn't it? But Baba has nothing to hide. He's called Santoro.'

'Does Baba love him?'

'No, but she's fond of him.'

'And does he love her?'

'He does, yes.'

'Will they get married?'

She started to laugh. 'In any case not before Santoro has made, as they say, a position for himself.'

'Why are you laughing?'

'Because you're so curious to know everything. And I can only tell you ordinary things, extremely ordinary things, the sort of answers that any girl of my age would give you.'

'But d'you think it's so very important to be ordinary?'

'I don't think it's important, I just *am* ordinary.'

'Yes, I see. Let's change the subject, shall we? Tell me about Cora.'

'What d'you want to know about Cora?'

'Tell me, are you fond of Cora?'

'Yes.'

'Very fond?'

'Yes, very.'

'Are you being sincere?'

'Yes, I'm sincere.'

'But why?'

'What d'you mean – why?'

'Why are you fond of her?'

'Because she's my mother and I'm her daughter.'

'Is that the whole reason?'

'It seems to me more than enough.'

'All the same, what she did to you . . .'

'I've already told you: she didn't do it to me but to another Baba.'

'Ah, that's true, I was forgetting. Now let's see. Why d'you think that Cora did what she did, six years ago?'

She thought for a moment, then answered with calm, pedantic meticulousness: 'Cora does not believe that there are men who are businessmen or doctors or lawyers. Nor does she believe that there are girls of fourteen or twenty who are her daughters or workers in her dressmaking business. She believes only one thing.'

'What's that?'

'That there are people of opposite sexes who copulate.'

'Does she believe that because it suits her?'

'No, she doesn't believe it because it suits her. She believes it because she's convinced that there's only that one thing in the world, and nothing else.'

'Literally nothing else? How about money?'

'Money is only a means. The end is something different.'

'What is the end?'

'I've already told you.'

'Love?'

'No absolutely no.'

'But I thought you were alluding to love when you said that Cora believed only in that one thing.'

'That thing is not love.'

'What is it, then?'

'It's . . . it's what it is.'

'Why does Cora think like this?'

'I don't know.'

'But you ought to know.'

'Well, let's say it's because it seems right to her, because she likes to believe it and it suits her to believe it, because it seems to her to be the truth.

'If that's so, why then did she change her mind about Baba and, as you yourself said, realize her mistake?'

'I imagine that Cora lives in a world of her own which she considers to be the only possible world and the best of all worlds. Sometimes, however, it may happen that she comes up against a different world, and then – but only for a short time – she recognizes that there are many other worlds besides her own. But for her to recognise it goes terribly against the grain.'

'How d'you mean?'

'She recognizes it only in practice, by which I mean that she doesn't *really* recognize it. In fact – how shall I explain it? – she makes an exception. I was one of these exceptions. But the rule still remains the same.'

We sat silent, at this juncture, for some little time. Baba turned back towards her desk, increased the volume of the radio, put on her spectacles and started reading again, just as if I were not there. I looked at her: she was not tall, apparently, but she seemed to have a good figure, in a concentrated, compact, massive sort of way. This could be surmised from the manner in which she sat crouched on her small chair in front of the desk, her hips projecting beyond the edges of the chair, her robust legs in their tight black trousers barely reaching the floor, her heavy, solid bosom pressed against the edge of the table. As I looked at her, I had a sudden feeling of irritation, the same feeling that had been aroused in me a little earlier by her impudent placidity, and I said, almost in spite of myself: 'Look here, Baba, you can't keep up this game any longer.'

She turned, took off her glasses and looked at me: 'I beg your pardon?'

'This device of splitting yourself up into a number of different Babas, of, in effect, cancelling yourself out, is only a game, and you know it's only a game. Naturally a game of that kind helps you to live. But that's another story, which concerns only yourself. You can make me take part in your game, but only for a little.'

She smiled, then said with a benevolent air: 'I assure you it's not so.'

'How is it, then?'

'It's difficult to explain. I understand perfectly well what you mean, but one thing I can swear to you: it's not a game.'

'It's not a game?'

'No, not in the least.'

'All the same . . .'

'It's a serious thing. I . . . I'm not the person I was six years ago, not in any way at all. And perhaps I'm not even the person I was an hour ago, before you came into the room. I don't know how to explain it to you, but that is the truth.'

'Truth must be proved.'

'The proof, in fact, is that, in order to remember certain things that happened six years ago, I had to make a real effort, not so much to remember them as to imagine them. Just as when you're talking about another person and, on the basis of some piece of information, you make hypotheses about how certain events came to happen. '

'Well, then?'

'Well, I've already told you; Baba who was sitting here reading, all alone, an hour ago, has already become a different Baba, since you came in and talked to her.'

I had, all of a sudden, the rather deceptive and at the same time confusing impression that this was like one of those key phrases, of a conventional kind, which, in a conversation between a man and a woman, are used, after the preamble, to introduce the main subject. I looked her in the eyes, questioningly; but their grey-green irises, to which short sight gave a drugged, fixed appearance, did not enlighten me. Then, with a very sweet smile, of melting intensity, she put out her hand and grasped mine, saying: 'Perhaps another Baba has really come into being with your visit. At least I feel it like that, do you?'

I lowered my eyes. The hand that clasped mine was small but very thick and plump and of a different colour from her face. Baba was pale; but her hand was red, with a dark, smooth redness in which the joints caused very small dimples. Her short fingers were so fleshy that they looked incapable of bending; and so was the palm of her hand, which one felt could never close completely. She clasped my hand with her right hand and held her left hand open in her lap, turned upwards: the inner part of her thumb surprised me with its bulk ; it too was red, but in a less uniform way than the back of the hand, and as it were dappled with white. I also noticed her nails, which were deeply sunk in the flesh, small and oval and painted pink. Then, as I looked at this hand, an idea occurred to me which I was unable to suppress: possibly the whole of Baba's body was like her hand, just as fleshy and of that same crude dark red colour dappled with white. A gross, servile, as it were lifeless body, more like an unspecified quantity of flesh than a body. Then I recalled that once upon a time, when I could no longer endure living with Cora, I had privately called Baba 'The Bastard'; and I felt that there was a link between this nickname and the manner in which I pictured her body. Yes, I thought, there was a link which usually exists between anything that is little valued and its availability and accessibility. And I said to myself that she too, fundamentally, thought of herself as something that had little value; and that this idea had been confirmed, for her, six years before by Cora, when the latter had treated her precisely like an object that can be bought and sold. This explained her otherwise inexplicable claim that she was no longer the person she had been six years earlier, that is, that she resembled an object, which is always new, rather than a person, who cannot help having a past and therefore a story. And the gesture of the outstretched hand clasping mine also became clear: it was an invitation to me to make use of her and to take my pleasure with her, if I wished, without any scruples, since she was nothing but an object at the disposal of anyone who wished to take possession of her and therefore, even if we made love together – although, in a way, we were father and daughter – it would not be incest, as might be thought at first sight, but something quite insignificant which would remain enclosed in the moment in which it had happened, like a dead grub in a desiccated cocoon.

I disentangled all these things later, patiently, as I wrote them down here in my diary with a cool mind; but at that moment they occurred to me, obscurely though forcibly, in the form of an impulse to act in a certain way. I turned my hand round inside hers, took hold of her wrist as it were in a ring between my finger and thumb, and, with a single sharp upward thrust, pushed up the sleeve of her sweater to her elbow, uncovering her round, robust, white forearm, faintly shadowed with a fine, dark down. Suddenly the thought came back to me that often in past years I had concluded that I should never make love again because I could only love nullity; and how can one fall in love with nullity? And all at once I understood that I was face to face with nullity, that Baba was a negative thing and that I was disturbed, not because she was offering herself to me, but because she was negative. She represented the nullity which I would be able to love simply because it was nullity. This love would therefore mean, for me, loving for the second time in my life; the first time had been with her mother, in whom I had loved all the things that I had then believed to constitute reality, and then these things had been revealed as lacking in genuineness and I had given myself over to nullity – that is, to relationships with complaisant girls who came to see me at my flat. Then I had torn myself away from this nullity; but behold, it was now presenting itself afresh with greater force and precision, and it had Baba's body, Baba's face, it was she, Baba; and I felt I could love her because she was an incarnation of the nullity which was around me and within me, in the same way as I had once loved Cora because she had seemed to me to be the incarnation of the many things I believed I had within and around me. But this nullity of Baba's had a name, and it was more by this name than by herself in flesh and blood that I felt myself attracted; and this name was the name that is given to the love relationship between a man and a woman who have the bonds of kinship that existed between Baba and me. And now I became aware that, if it had not been for the idea, or rather the name, of incest, I should probably not have desired her. So it was demonstrated once again that for me there was not, and could not be, any genuine action, even when the impulse to act appeared to come from the depths of my being. My desire, in fact, had been released automatically at the sound of a name, a mere name which was false into the bargain, since, after all, we were not really father and daughter.

I looked up, and this time I detected in her eyes, apart from the usual unhappy short-sighted look, another, more profound, unhappiness, mingled with embarrassment and rejection. I withdrew my hand and said: 'I'm sorry'; and then I let myself fall back in my chair.

I saw that she pulled down her sleeve to her wrist with a gesture of relief, like a woman recovering herself after being assaulted. Then she said, in a quiet, schoolmistressy voice: 'Perhaps there has been some mistake; perhaps we misunderstood each other.'

I agreed frankly: 'I think so too.'

'I took your hand and said what I said, not for the reasons

you appear to have thought, but because I really hope that from now onwards we shall be father and daughter.'

'Father and daughter?'

'Yes. What is there strange about that? We are, in reality, father and daughter, even if so far we've behaved in a different way. Therefore, from now onwards, I should like us to be truly so.'

I reflected that this was a very difficult thing to say, but that she had said it extremely well, even if with a curiously purposive and, so to speak, technical conviction, as though she were speaking of something which we two had to construct together according to a prearranged plan. I said, with an adequate amount of sincerity: 'I ask nothing better.'

'That's splendid; then I'm content.'

She did indeed appear to be content; she smiled at me, put out her hand again and took mine in a brief, affectionate clasp. Then she went on: 'After this you won't go on behaving as you've done in the past.'

'What d'you mean by that?'

'Living like a stranger in your own home and not wanting to have anything to do with your own family.'

'What ought I to do, then?'

'Live with us, with Cora and me, like all the husbands and fathers in the world.'

'Live with you? What does that mean?'

'It means eat with us, go out with us – in fact, really *live* with us.'

'But . . . that's impossible.'

'Why?'

'Because I know what I know and, knowing what I know, the family life you speak of is impossible.'

'But I manage to lead this family life.'

'That's precisely what surprises me.'

'Why?'

'In your place, I should have gone away long ago.'

'I *shall* go away, but not because of Cora.'

'When will that be?'

'Well, I don't know; either I shall get married or I shall take my degree and go and teach in another town.'

Suddenly I got angry; I raised my voice and said: 'But after all, isn't it repugnant to you to live under the same roof as Cora?'

'She's my mother.'

'And to take money from her?'

'That *no*, not in the least.'

'And why, pray? Why not in the least?'

'This city's full of things that are bought and sold. What difference is there between Cora's money and so many other people's?'

All at once I became calm again; and I said: 'All right, we'll be father and daughter, I promise you that. But don't ask me to be a husband to Cora again.'

'At any rate you'll have meals with us – at least that?'

It was strange how, every time she spoke of herself, Cora and me as a family, her voice, usually so calm and expressionless, took on a melting tone. I said drily: 'All right, I'll have meals with you.'

'And you won't be rude to Cora?'

'What d'you mean?'

'I mean that during meals you'll talk to her naturally and kindly, and that, apart from meals, you won't avoid her and you'll show yourself affectionate.'

'Affectionate – that'll be difficult.'

'Yes, affectionate; if you don't want to do it for Cora do it for me.'

'But why are you so eager for me to be affectionate to Cora?'

She answered as before: 'She's my mother', in a tone of someone asserting an unquestionable truth. But I persisted: 'After all, you haven't yet told me why you love her: you must admit, she hasn't behaved like a mother to you.'

She leant forward and squeezed my hand hard. 'Be affectionate to her, won't you? I don't know why I love her, really I don't know, but I feel drawn to love her more and more.'

She squeezed my hand almost to the point of hurting me; I tried to withdraw it but did not succeed. 'Perhaps,' I said, 'perhaps you love her just because she behaved in the way she did.'

'Yes, perhaps, but not in the sense you think.'

'I don't think anything.'

'I don't love her because she doesn't love me. I love her because ... well, I must just go on repeating the same thing ... because she's my mother.'

58

I said sharply: 'All right, I'll try to be, as you say, affectionate.'

She at once let go of my hand and drew back again. I went on: 'I promise you that. Partly because, with luck, my stay in Rome won't last very long.'

'How long?'

'I don't know; a month, two months, time to write the articles about my journey to Iran.'

She turned so that she was sitting sideways to me again, huddled up on the chair that was too small for her, her feet on the bar of the desk. She turned the knob of the radio, increasing its volume, put on her glasses, and made as if to resume the reading which had been interrupted by my visit. I ought now to have gone away; but it seemed to me that there was still something lacking. I said, in a stupid sort of way: 'D'you want . . . d'you want us to go out to dinner together this evening?'

Promptly, as though she were only waiting for this invitation, she turned and answered: 'Not this evening, I've an engagement.'

'Who with?'

'I suppose I must tell you, seeing that you're my father. I'm going out with Santoro, a friend of mine and her boy friend.'

'And where are you going?'

'To dinner, then to the cinema. But tomorrow, yes. Tomorrow I'm free.'

'All right, tomorrow. By the way . . .'

'Yes?'

'Don't tell Cora that we've been talking.'

'You haven't been talking to me but to another Baba.'

'Ah, yes, of course, I was forgetting. Till tomorrow evening, then.'

'Good-bye.'

I left the room with the harsh, drawling and strangely familiar sound of that 'good-bye' in my ears.

Wednesday, October 14th

I am in a room in Cora's *maison de rendez-vous*. I am sure that it is Cora's house, although I am aware that I have never been there before; this certainty comes, perhaps, from the sight of the doll on the pillow of the double bed upon which I am sitting, waiting for the girl whom Cora will shortly produce for me. It is a doll in the semblance of an eighteenth-century lady, just the same as the one in Cora's room in my own flat. But, on looking more closely, I discover, however, that there are differences: this is anyhow a larger doll, and its size appears to increase as I look at it; and then, to my amazement, I discover that the doll's face is the face of Baba: the same grey-green eyes with the drugged, expressionless look in them; the same soft, childish roundness of the cheeks; the same small, broad, robust nose; the same thin, hard mouth with the fine, sharp furrows, like two cuts, at the corners of the lips. It is wearing a white wig, it is true, its face is powdered and patch-besprinkled, it is dressed in a bodice and crinoline; but it is Baba in person, Baba alive and not a doll, Baba dressed up as an eighteenth-century lady, sitting on the pillow of the bed, in Cora's house. And indeed Baba now smiles at me, and then, all of a sudden, she winks at me, in a provoking, equivocal manner. I have a feeling of horror and at the same time of desire, and the horror is born of the desire and the desire of the horror; I exclaim in a loud voice: 'But you're my daughter'; and then, at these words, as at a magic formula that breaks a spell, behold, Baba begins to move away, to diminish, becoming smaller and smaller until, to my relief, she is now merely a doll with a china head and a body made of tow, placed there by Cora to adorn the room. But I still have to wait; soon the door will open and Cora will introduce the girl of the day, quite different from Baba. In fact in a short time the door does open slowly and Cora appears. Cora is not alone, she is leading by the hand a young girl of perhaps fourteen years old, in a red sweater and blue trousers, whose face, however, I am unable to see because she is hiding it bashfully in Cora's bosom. The latter bends down, whispers something in her ear, and meanwhile rolls her eyes at me, as much as to say: 'Of course she's young and she's shy and you must have a little patience.' I notice that Cora's face is flaming and her eyes glittering; she seems to be transfigured by an extraordinary vitality. In the end the young girl allows herself to be persuaded; she turns, and then, once again, I recognize Baba – not the Baba of today, however, but the Baba of six years ago. The girl gives me her hand; she even makes a little well-bred bow; but I look at her critically, with distrust. I am exacting, discontented, capricious, a client and nothing more; and I say without much ceremony that, if the girl's body is not like the fleshy part of her thumb, just as coarsely red and mottled with white, there's nothing doing: it's I who am paying and I wish to have exactly what I want for my money. Cora, quite rightly, at once does her utmost to satisfy me. I watch her as she bends solicitously over the girl and whispers again into her ear. At this point I cry out, for the second time: 'But she's my daughter'; and I awake.

I was damp with sweat, my heart was beating violently; I sat up in the darkness and looked at the luminous dial of the clock on the bed-side table: it was a quarter past four. So I turned on the light and, as I generally do when I awake after a bad dream, I took up the first book that came to hand among the number of books piled up on the table.

It was *Oedipus Rex*, in a popular translation. I opened it at the first pages, and read:

> *Oedipus:* Yes, but where are they? How to track the course
> Of guilt all shrouded in the doubtful past?
> *Creon:* In this our land, so said He; those who seek
> Shall find; unsought, we lose it utterly.

And it seemed to me that these lines had a familiar sound. Then I started reading the whole scene from the beginning. When I came to:

> . . .Well I know that ye
> Are smitten, one and all, with a taint of plague,
> And yet though smitten, none that taint of plague
> Feels, as I feel it. Each his burden bears,
> His own and not another's; but my heart
> Mourns for the state, for you, and for myself. . .

I became aware that I was weeping, with laborious, burning tears which seemed to express the bitterness, not only of what had happened the day before, but also of the whole of my present life. I wept, I put away the book and turned off the light again; and I went on weeping in the darkness and I realized that I was weeping because I found myself in the same situation as Oedipus: the city tainted by plague was my family, which was also tainted; and I, like Oedipus, had questioned the witnesses to find out who was the cause of this corruption and had discovered that the one who bore the guilt of the corruption was myself. But here – and now my thoughts began to be confused by returning sleep – here the resemblance ended. For to Oedipus it had been granted to pluck out his eyes, to transfer his guilt by means of a rite, to free himself from it by changing evil into good. But I? I had to content myself with knowing, beyond any doubt, that I myself was to blame for the corruption, even if in a remote and indirect way; but I could do nothing: I could neither punish myself, nor make any expiation, nor transform what was negative into something positive. Unless . . . upon this 'unless', in which there seemed to be a glimmer of hope, I fell asleep.

Wednesday, October 14th

I awoke when day had already dawned, but it was still early and the house was silent. I got up, dressed, left my room and the flat and went down into the street. I did what I usually did when I got up in the morning, during my visits to Rome between one journey and another – I went to a bar close by and had breakfast: an *espresso* coffee, a roll, and another *espresso*. At the tobacco-counter adjoining the bar I bought a couple of packets of cigarettes, then I went out and bought the morning paper from the newsagent at the corner. Then, with the newspaper under my arm and a cigarette between my lips, I walked back to my own building, looking around me as I went. I recognised all the well-known backgrounds: the rows of apartment houses, biscuit- or putty-coloured, with still closed brown-painted windows, along the still deserted streets; the strips of public garden, with their cypresses and laurels and ilexes, winding in a dark funereal procession along the middle of the road, between the light-coloured blocks of flats; the autumnal sky, of a washed-out blue, over which travelled enormous white, grey-rimmed clouds. I went in at the main door, went up in the lift to the top floor, crossed to the door of my flat, and as I was on the point of opening it, almost collided with Baba who was coming out. She was in sailor trousers and jumper, with books under her arm. 'I got your breakfast ready,' she said to me, 'and put it in your room; good-bye.'

I went into my room and there, in fact, was the breakfast, on the desk beside the typewriter: a neatly laid tray, with a tray-cloth and napkin, a cup and saucer, a teapot, toast, honey and jam. I placed the tray on the unmade bed; but I kept the teapot and the cup on my desk. Then I arranged the position of the desk in front of the window in such a way that I could see two-thirds sky and one-third buildings; and finally I sat down.

It was only now that the memory came back to me of what had happened the day before and during the night: the anonymous letter, the conversation with Baba, the dream, the awakening, the reading of the lines of *Oedipus Rex*. Then I looked at the typewriter and recalled my decision to keep a diary of my stay in Rome; and I wondered if, after what had happened, this was still possible.

I had, in fact, decided to keep a diary of a period of my life which I had imagined would be devoid of events, with the object of extracting from it, later, a novel which would also be devoid of events. But already, from the very first day, this particular diary was shown to be impossible. Ironically, just at the moment when I was getting ready to begin this journal of an uneventful life, that same life was shattered by the violent explosion of something dramatic, exceptional, unbelievable. The novel I had hoped to write, in which the artificiality of drama was to be replaced by the genuineness of everyday life – this novel might be said to have failed from the very start.

I lit a cigarette and started to think, looking up at the sky in front of me through the window-panes. The following idea came into my mind. If I kept the diary just the same and then, as had been my intention, extracted a novel from it, this novel would inevitably be of the kind known as 'romantic' based that is, on a dramatic, or even melodramatic, occurrence, of precisely the type to which the most conventional novelists have recourse, in their congenital incapacity to extract the essence of poetry from everyday reality.

A man goes for ten years without speaking to his wife and daughter, although he lives with them under the same roof. At the end of ten years he comes to find out, through an anonymous letter, that his wife is practising the profession of procuress; that she has tried to prostitute her own daughter.... I was struck by the bad taste – and furthermore the improbability and artificiality – of these facts, in themselves so embarrassing, so distressing and so incredible. I felt that the author of such a novel would be justly accused by critics and readers of having a morbid and over-artful imagination.

But I found myself, alas – or by good luck – in a very different situation: my imagination was by no means led to contrive machinations of this kind – on the contrary; the distressing, embarrassing, incredible thing which I was now obliged to relate in my diary and afterwards to transfer into my novel, these things were not the fruit of a morbid and artful imagination, but real happenings. I had imagined absolutely nothing, incredible as it may seem. I had actually received the anonymous letter; Cora actually carried on that trade; Baba, at the age of fourteen, had actually been taken to Cora's house; and I was now actually sitting at my desk and actually feeling, indeed truly feeling, the painful contradiction that existed between my literary preoccupations and the unavoidable duty incumbent upon me to find, as quickly as possible, a solution – in reality, not in the pages of a novel – to the situation in which I found myself.

And so, while I was able to abandon the idea of writing a novel which I considered to have failed even before it was started, I could not, on the other hand, refuse to recognize that certain things were happening to me; that I ought to take action; and that, in consequence, I would anyhow be taking action even if I in fact did not act, seeing that, in a similar case, to take no action implied, fundamentally, choosing a definite mode of action.

But, just at the moment when I was deciding that I would finally give up the idea of keeping a diary and afterwards extracting a novel from it, my mind was overcome with despair and consternation, as though I were in reality giving up the one and only reason I had for living. I was surprised by the violence of this feeling, and I realized that this was something profound and insurmountable which I could not ignore.

I stubbed out my cigarette in the ashtray and lit another. What was I to do? On the one hand, the novel that I would extract from the diary, supposing I kept the diary, could not fail to turn out just as artificial as the one I had thrown away ten years before; on the other hand, I had pledged myself – and I realized this from the consternation that had seized me at the idea of giving it up – to keep the diary and consequently to extract the novel from it. What, then, was I to do?

Having posed this dilemma to myself, I fell into a profound state of bitter, absent-minded bewilderment. I did not think at all, I merely looked at the tiresome blemishes, in the shape of tears or bubbles, which the minute defects in the window-glass produced in the clouds up above; and all I understood was that I was desperate, with a double despair, so to speak, originating on one side from my family situation and on the other from my literary ambition.

Above all, my mind did not succeed in grasping closely the terms of the problem which nevertheless existed and in which I felt myself struggling. What was it concerned with, in point of fact? Writing a novel? Or putting my family affairs in order? I was dimly aware that, although the two things were different and distinct from one another, they were connected by an unquestionable link and I could not settle one question without settling the other, and *vice versa*.

This link might be defined, in a negative sense, as follows: my family situation – dramatic, to put it mildly – prevented me from writing the drama-less novel I had planned; the plan of the drama-less novel prevented me from dealing with the drama of my family situation by making me feel the artificiality of any decisive intervention.

At this point I was struck by a kind of absurdity in my reflections. I had a painful feeling which, expressed in words, would probably have sounded like this: 'What? You torment yourself so much over miserable literary questions, you're so frightened of giving up the idea of writing one of the usual books with which the counters of bookshops are laden, when you ought instead to be occupying yourself solely with the state into which your family has fallen? Never mind about novels, never mind about diaries. It's a question of your own life. Settle the question, then, not as a novelist but as a man, as anyone in your position would settle it.'

Strange to say, this appeal to good sense had, as often happens, a different effect to what might have been foreseen. I saw, all at once, that I absolutely must not settle my family problem 'as a man', as 'anyone in my position' might settle it. I was not in fact 'a man', nor 'anyone'; but the exact person that I was. I ought therefore to settle my family problem precisely as the novelist I was and could not help being.

It was the word 'corruption' that enlightened me. Yes, my family had fallen into corruption; but this corruption was no extraordinary, sudden, dramatic occurrence, like the plague at Thebes in the drama of Oedipus; it was, on the contrary, one of those facts which, because they have lasted a long time and have become habitual and because they have no definitely ascertainable cause and thus escape both moral judgment and historical investigation, become confused with the normal course of everyday life and are no more important or significant than all the other things that happen daily.

And I was made to understand that this was true by the request of Baba, chief victim of the corruption, that I should show myself affectionate with Cora. Affectionate: fundamentally, therefore, nothing had happened, or at any rate nothing that had importance or significance; everything would continue to run its course in the confused flow of everyday life. And Cora would go on practising her trade; I would start travelling again; Baba would marry Santoro or would go and teach in another town and marry another man, no doubt very similar to Santoro.

Certainly I could refuse to accept this notion of corruption as a sort of crazy normality; I could react with violent moral protestations. But in the name of what morality? Of the confused, hypocritical morality which was discernible in the anonymous letter.

And then, more subtly, the idea which I had formed over the years, of the novel as a means of understanding reality, warned me, as if it had been the voice of conscience, that the notion of corruption as a normality devoid of sense, as a part of everyday life, insignificant in itself, was fundamentally the right one, precisely because of the character of continual organic transformation, so to speak, which the term itself seemed to indicate. Corruption: something natural, biological, perhaps necessary, anyhow inevitable, which therefore could not have any significance, any importance.

I had therefore returned, though by a long circuitous route, to my point of departure. After all I would write my diary, as I had originally decided; and later I would extract a novel from it. And in the meantime, faced with facts such as those I had learned the day before, I would take up the only possible attitude, the attitude, that is, that one adopts in face of the everyday facts of normal life, which take place, indubitably, but have no particular significance in themselves, or at any rate have none until we give it them. An attitude of suspension of judgment, so to speak, and, in short, of contemplation.

I felt relieved as I thought of these things. For, temporarily at least, I had solved my twofold problem of facing the family situation and at the same time writing my novel. I also reflected that all this was not as easy as it might seem. It demanded, indeed, the opposite of the attitude I had maintained in life during the last ten years. This had been, as I have said, an attitude of non-involvement. Now, if I did not wish to have another failure, I must adopt an attitude of involvement. I said to myself at this point that it would be a good thing to emphasize the connection which I seemed at last to have succeeded in discovering between life and the novel. It was not a literary and aesthetic connection, nor was it mechanically imitative. The connection was, as I now knew, one of identification and knowledge.

Wednesday, October 14th

'When did you arrive?'
  'Yesterday afternoon.'
  'Where have you been?'
  'In Iran.'
  'Iran?'
  'Yes, Iran, otherwise Persia.'
  'How long are you staying?'
  'The usual. A month and a half, two months.'
  'Anything I can do for you? Have you put aside your washing?'
  'Yes.'
  'You weren't cold last night? Have you enough blankets?'
  'Yes, thank you, I've enough.'
  'Now look, there are a number of bills to be paid. I've put the whole lot in the drawer of the table in the hall.'
  'Very well. I'll see to it.'
  'Anything else you need?'
  'No, not for the moment. By the way . . .'
  'What is it?'
  'I've been thinking during my journey and I've taken the decision to change the whole set-up here.'

'Change the whole set-up?'

'Yes. From now onwards, if you don't mind, we'll have our meals together. I'm tired of eating in restaurants. And then you and Baba and I will do a lot of other things together: we'll go out together in the evenings to the cinema, we'll go for expeditions together on Sundays, etc., etc. Is that all right?'

'What kind of novelty is this? What's got hold of you?'

'Nothing's got hold of me. I'm tired of living like a bachelor, or a lodger or a widower, when I have a family.'

'I'd have preferred to go on as we were. It's almost ten years now and I've got accustomed to it. Besides, it's difficult to go backwards.'

'It's not a matter of going backwards, it's a matter of going forwards.'

'Going forwards?'

'Yes, going forwards.'

'I don't know what you mean, but we'll do as you wish. After all, you're the master of the house. But I warn you . . .'

'What?'

'I warn you that I have my own life, I want to be free, I don't want any controls. And besides, I can't promise to be with you all the time, except at meals. I have my own friends now, and how could I possibly introduce you as my husband, after having explained so many times that we're separated?'

'All right, don't worry about that; I'll manage with Baba.'

'Then you'll be in for lunch today?'

'Yes, I'll be in for lunch.'

'Today there's grilled liver. Is that all right?'

'Excellent.'

After this we looked at one another in silence. I noticed, as though I were seeing her for the first time for ten years, that Cora was much changed. She had grown thinner, so that the huge, dilated, devouring blue eyes, the German character of the big straight nose, the heavy mouth with its cruel curves, were all more conspicuous in her lean, even rather haggard, face. A strange red light, vivid and fiery – perhaps, I could not help thinking, a reflection of the hot lust of other people which she provoked and promoted day by day – seemed to overspread this face from below upwards, in an unhealthy, feverish way. She put her hand to her mouth and coughed several times, with a dry, seemingly uncontrollable cough; so I asked her: 'Are you all right?'

'Yes; why?'

'I see you're coughing. Besides, you're . . . you've grown much thinner.'

'It's nothing. I had bronchitis this summer and I didn't look after myself and it's left me with a bit of a cough. That's all.'

'What does the doctor say?'

'He said then that it was bronchitis.'

'Then – when was that?'

'Three months ago.'

'No, but what does he say now?'

'He doesn't say anything. I haven't consulted him.'

'Why? If you're ill, you ought to consult him. That's what doctors are for.'

'But there's nothing wrong with me. Why should I see a doctor?'

Once more we were silent. Then I went on: 'One of these days I'm coming to visit you at your dressmaker's shop.'

'What for?'

'To talk to you.'

'To talk to me?'

'Don't be alarmed. Nothing for you to worry about. It's a matter of a novel that I'm writing.'

'And what's that to do with me?'

'D'you remember that I was writing a novel ten years ago?'

'Yes.'

'Well, I've taken it up again. But I'm in need of a few pieces of information.'

'What kind of information?'

'The novel tells the story of our . . . of our love.'

'Nice sort of love.'

'Whether it was nice or nasty, it tells the story of it, or rather it *should* do so. That's why I'm in need of a few pieces of information about our relationship at that time.'

'If that's all you want . . .'

'Then I can count on this? One of these days we'll get together and have a talk.'

'And what's the novel called?'

'It's about involvement.'

'You, who are the most unconcerned man in the world – you're going to write about involvement!' And, with this joking, good-natured remark, in which was expressed all her relief at not having been obliged to speak of the facts of her own life, she went away.

Tuesday, October 20th

I gave notice in the Prologue that I reserved the right, whenever I should consider it necessary, to expand, complete or actually transform events as I reported them in this diary. But I also said that I would give some sort of sign to indicate clearly all those details which I had altered or invented, in such a way as to distinguish them from the true ones, once I had set to work making the novel out of the diary.

And now I suddenly realize that I have been making use of this right, from the very beginning; not consciously and deliberately, as might be expected, but in an almost unconscious way – in precisely the way in which a narrator, carried away by inspiration, mingles the true with the false in spite of himself.

It is not true, in fact, that, when I woke up suddenly during the night after my conversation with Baba, I found *Oedipus Rex* in a popular translation on the bedside table, opened it haphazardly and lit upon some lines that seemed to me to be adapted to my own situation. It is not true. What is true, rather, is that, having woken up in the middle of the night and having thought over what had occurred, I happened to remember *Oedipus Rex* and seemed to remark certain analogies with my own situation in Sophocles' drama; and then, with the usual inclination of the novelist to make good use of the events of his own personal life, even in moments of trouble and distress, I thought that the reference to the tragedy of Oedipus would go well in the novel. Why, then not include it in advance in the diary.

And so, next day, when I was relating the happenings of the night in the diary, I did not hesitate to make use of the discovery of the book which a mysterious hand had placed on my table while I slept – a real *Mene, Mene, Tekel, Upharsin,* all ready for my awakening.

Someone may object: what does it matter? What difference is there, in a case like this, between the thing imagined and the thing that really happened? On the contrary, there *is* a difference; and I think it would be useful for me to explain it. My explanation will serve for all the occasions on which, yielding to the temptation of the narrative, I allow myself to be drawn into such alterations and replacements.

The difference between the thing imagined and the thing that really happened, at least as far as my diary is concerned, is the difference which exists between the inherent reality of falsehood and the inherent reality of truth. The latter stands firmly in place, immediate and direct, it is the fact itself while it is happening; the former, on the other hand, comes through an intermediary, indirectly, and lies, not in the fact itself as it occurs and presents itself, but in the significance of the fact.

And so if, instead of writing as I am doing, I were talking to myself, I think I should address myself in this way: 'You hypocrite, you are indulgent towards the only person to whom you ought not to feel indulgent – yourself. You invented the notion of finding the volume of *Oedipus Rex* on your bedside table in order to heighten the tone, ennoble your experience in some way and, in the last analysis, annul your feeling of guilt in a flattering literary analogy. This, then, is the real nature of your invention, not that of the resemblance between your own story and the tragedy of Oedipus. And only by recognizing and admitting its real nature can you feel yourself justified in leaving the reference to Sophocles' tragedy in your diary.

So that's that. I have admitted the real nature of my invention. Later on, when I start making my novel out of the diary, I shall see whether this hypocrisy on my part can serve any useful purpose, either by denouncing it or, on the other hand, leaving the trouble of discovering it to the reader. After all, my object is not to reform myself but to write a book.

Friday, October 23rd

Baby's birthday; she is twenty today. She informed me of this herself, coming into my study this morning and taking her stand between the desk at which I was sitting and the window in front of which the desk is placed. 'Give me your good wishes.' she said.

'Why good wishes?'

'Because today's my *festa*.'

'Birthday or saint's day?'

'Birthday. I'm twenty today.'

She looked at me with a curiously pathetic yet impudent expression, as though expecting something. With an effort I said, smiling: 'Many happy returns.'

'Thank you.'

She went on looking at me, unsatisfied. I understood and, rising to my feet, went and kissed her, rather awkwardly, on both cheeks, and then, as she offered me her brow, also on the fringe of hair that comes right down to her eyes. But she freed herself quickly from my embrace as though she had not expected it and did not like it, and said hastily: 'Look, you must make a little effort today. I've invited Santoro to lunch; he knows it's my birthday, and you must show that you know it too.'

'How d'you mean?'

'By looking cheerful and contented and affectionate, in fact by celebrating the occasion as much as you can.'

'Yes, I understand.'

'Santoro . . .'

'By the way . . .'

'What?'

'Why d'you call him Santoro and not by his Christian name, Paolo?'

'It's just a habit. Santoro has already given me a present.'

'What has he given you?'

'Some gramophone records.'

'What does this imply? That it would be a good plan if I gave you a present too?'

'Yes.'

'But I don't know what you would like.'

'Oh, anything, provided . . .'

'Provided it's a present.'

'That's right.'

'You might have told me before. I didn't know it was your birthday. Besides, it's late now, and . . .'

'Don't worry. I've thought of everything.'

'What d'you mean?'

'I mean, I foresaw that you wouldn't know today was my birthday and I also foresaw that you would be busy and couldn't go out on purpose to buy me a present. So I've bought the present *for* you. You can give me back the money I spent, and I'll give you the present, and then you can give it to me.'

'What is the present?'

'A most lovely headscarf, just exactly what I wanted.'

'How much do I owe you?'

'Ten thousand lire. Is that too much?'

I took a ten-thousand lire note from my pocket-book, gave it to Baba, and she in turn gave me an oblong box wrapped in red paper and tied with a green ribbon. Feeling a little like an actor in the presence of his producer, I enquired: 'What ought I to do now? D'you want me to give you the present at table, in front of everyone, or d'you want me to give it you here, now?'

'No. It's better here.'

I made as though to hand the box straight back to her, but she looked fixedly at me, with quiet, calculated primness. I understood, rose to my feet and said: 'Well then, Baba, I give you my most sincere and most affectionate good wishes. And this is for you.'

This time it was she who threw her arms round my neck, in the proper style of a daughter to whom her father has given a birthday present. But during this embrace – whether purposely or not, I do not know – the ambiguity that lies at the back of our relationship was once more manifested: Baba's hand lightly but languidly touched my ear and then my hair, in a faint caress which could only have been intentional; her body was pressed against mine in an impetuous, clinging impact; her breast was at first crushed against my chest, then it slid sideways to imprison my left arm, almost, one might have thought, in order to make me appreciate its form and solidity and elasticity; her breath, troubled and eager, wandered slowly over my cheek before being transformed into a filial kiss which was deposited half-way between my mouth and my ear. Finally we separated and, looking at Baba not without curiosity, I saw that she still kept her usual composed, sly expression that seemed to be saying: 'You love me, I know, and perhaps I love you too. But it's understood that we're father and daughter, whatever may happen.'

Baba, however, appeared to guess my thoughts, for, as she undid the knot in the ribbon and took off the paper in which the box was wrapped, she said, in a natural, reasonable tone: 'Perhaps you'll think that I'm putting on a kind of an act with you. But it isn't so. For me at any rate, this isn't play-acting, I swear to you. I've always longed for you to be a father to me, and now I'm so pleased that you accept that position.'

She opened the box, took out the scarf, unfolded it and showed me the design: a whole lot of objects for smokers – cigarette-holders, pipes, match-boxes, cigars, cigarettes, lighters, cigarette-cases, tobacco-pouches and ashtrays; on a cream background with a snuff-coloured border. Then, going, to the looking-glass and throwing the scarf round her head, she said: 'Isn't it lovely? Don't you think it suits me? Tell me how it suits me.'

An hour or two later we were seated at table: Cora, Baba, Santoro and myself. Santoro is a solid-looking young man, stocky and bull-like, with a broad, pale, placid face that makes you think of an under-baked cottage loaf. He has thick brown hair that grows half-way down his forehead, small chestnut-brown eyes, restless but inexpressive, a large chin with a very small dimple in the middle of it. This provincial-looking face wears a serious expression, rather preoccupied but at the same time fairly self-assured, even cold. Absorbed in thought, as if he were alone, he sat between Baba and Cora and, when not eating, was silent, his eyes on the table-cloth, crumbling his bread into pellets with his short, strong fingers. From time to time he raised his head and smiled at Baba, and then two more dimples appeared, one in each cheek. He spoke only when spoken to, and this he did in a slow, precise manner, choosing his words with care and pronouncing them syllable by syllable, reflectively, in a solemn, low voice.

Cora, as usual, sat bolt upright, stiff, completely silent, her huge blue eyes with their dilated pupils fixed upon us, and with a smile, probably unconscious, at the curling corners of her big red mouth.

As for Baba, she was the only one who talked, and one could see why: it was she who had wanted this birthday lunch, she who had planned it, she who was directing it. The design of this resolution was visible beneath the usual ritual of the meal, like a watermark in the transparency of a sheet of paper.

And what did we talk about? We talked, obviously, about all the things that concern Santoro, Baba, Cora and myself. And so, bit by bit, we discussed my journeys and the profession of journalism; Santoro's medical studies and his plans for the future; the fact that Baba is already making a little money by writing literary disquisitions to the order of lazy or incompetent students; and Cora's dressmaking establishment.

Meanwhile Baba superintended the production, as it were, of the conversation without fuss and without showing it too much, quiet and economical in her gestures and her words, putting appropriate and well-timed questions, changing the subject at the right moment, intervening discreetly in such a way as to enliven other people's remarks, yet without interrupting them, behaving, in fact, like an accomplished, self-possessed hostess. To such effect, indeed, that the luncheon-party, which had started in the embarrassment and frostiness of a painful consciousness of all that lay hidden behind our convivial outward appearance, warmed up and rose like well-leavened bread, after the arrival of a big stuffed turkey cooked by Baba (also, it seems, an excellent cook), carried in on a tray, with trembling reverence, by the old servant, who is faithful and affectionate in the traditional manner; and finally it hovered, a balloon realeased from its moorings, in an adequately domestic atmosphere, exactly as the 'producer' had wished. And I myself, for a few moments, had the illusion that I was really what Baba wanted me to be: a calm, affectionate father, a trusting, contented husband, and perhaps even a future father-in-law full of benevolence and sympathy.

But at the end of lunch Baba told the servant to bring in a bottle of sparkling wine and four champagne glasses, and insisted that Cora should be the one to open it. So Cora, with her smooth, white, unchaste hands, took the massive bottle of dark-coloured glass, with its yellow label and neck wrapped in red-tintoil; holding it a little away from herself, with a cigarette in the corner of her mouth and her eyes half-closed, she used her thumb to push up the big cork that had been secured with interlaced wire. Her white thumb, with its oval, convex, scarlet nail, urged the cork gradually from the neck of the bottle. Then came the ritual explosion; Baba uttered a cry, pretending to be frightened and hiding her head under the tablecloth, while Cora, smiling, held out the bottle over the glasses as the wine poured forth, impetuous and foaming. And then, all of a sudden, the family luncheon-party for Baba's birthday collapsed, for me at least, like a piece of cardboard scenery, and I could not help thinking, as I looked at Cora's hand clasping the dark glass of the bottle with long white fingers, and watched the foaming stream surging out into the glasses in a succession of repeated jets – I could not help thinking that in that very same manner, in Cora's house, the male seed surges out, at the moment of orgasm, after long preparation. Suddenly the whole domestic scene was tinged, for me, with an ignoble light, and Baba's efforts appeared to me as vain as those of a producer who persists in putting on a hopelessly bad play.

This thought gave me a slight start; some wine was upset on the table, and Baba, of course, who is always careful to do things as they should be done and as everyone does them, dipped her fingers in the wine and wetted my ear, saying: 'Bless you, bless you!' Then we all rose to our feet round the table, glass in hand.

Luckily there were no toasts; but there was the usual custom of tapping glass against glass and murmuring each other's names: Francesco, Baba, Cora, Paolo; and then the demure drinking as we looked at each other over the surface of the wine which was still fizzing with little gaseous bubbles; these things are in truth more intimate than any toast. Baba jogged my elbow and wanted to drink alone with me, our arms intertwined, she from my glass and I from hers, in the German manner; and as we did this the usual ambiguity in our relations again became apparent, for she cast a meaning look, of obscure complicity, right in my face. Then, in a loud voice, she announced the presents she had received: the records of classical music from Santoro, the dress and the bottle of French perfume from Cora, my headscarf, other presents from girls and boys of her acquaintance. Moreover she took the headscarf out of her bag and showed it all round, and thus the scarf, unfolded, passed from her hands to those of Santoro who examined it carefully and said in a tone of conviction: 'Fine, very fine'; and then from Santoro's hands to Cora's, who looked at it and said nothing and merely passed it back to her daughter.

At that moment I looked between Santoro and Cora at the window and saw a small, distant aeroplane climbing into the sky with lightning-like speed. It went across a bright cloud and I followed it as it flew against the light, a tiny dark speck moving rapidly and finally disappearing as it made its way between two black, towering clouds. And then I could not help thinking, with envy and regret, of the inside compartment of the aeroplane, as it was at that moment, with the passengers sitting in two rows, their heads turned towards the portholes, the hostess on her feet, bending down and smilingly offering sweets on a tray, the luminous panel above the door leading to the pilots' cabin, warning the passengers not to smoke and to fasten their seat-belts; and I said to myself that, if I wished, I myself could very soon be sitting in a similar compartment, in an aeroplane that would carry me far away from Cora, from Baba, from Rome; this depended upon me, and it could even happen tomorrow. But at the same time, indeed just at that moment, I saw Baba looking at me and smiling in a touching way beneath her usual sleepy expression, and then I was ashamed of my thought, and I also realized how strong was the complicated, obscure feeling that I have for her, or rather, that Baba always succeeds in arousing in me, at every moment and in any circumstances, unfailingly, merely by virtue of the simple fact that she exists.

Sunday, October 25th

Today I re-read the whole of *Oedipus Rex*, which I had imagined finding on my bedside table the night after my arrival from Iran. I was especially struck by the obstinate determination with which Oedipus, after so many years of indifference, carelessness and forgetfulness, exerts himself to find out the truth. It is true that this determination is directly provoked by the answer of Apollo, who attributes the plague that is devastating Thebes to the fact that the murder of the King of Thebes, Laius, has gone unpunished. But even this – considering the number of years Oedipus has spent at Thebes, amongst citizens who have known and loved Laius, at the side of a woman who has been Laius' wife, in Laius' own palace, and all this with the consciousness of being himself guilty of a crime, in mysterious circumstances – even this does not prevent one's being forced to think that Oedipus, during those years, has been not so much ignorant as unwilling ever to know that the woman he had married was his mother. Certainly myths do not pay much attention to probability; but it may be reasonably supposed that the improbability of myths has a probable meaning. Now what meaning, what significance is there in the incredible circumstance of a murderer who, having married without knowing it the widow of his victim, never happens to speak to her, during their long and intimate cohabitation, of the crime which deprived her of her mate and, if he does speak of it, fails to recognize the exact details of his own crime in what she tells him? What significance is there except that Oedipus makes himself deaf and blind with respect to everything concerning his parricide; except that he endeavours, unconsciously, not to become aware of the very close resemblance between the crime he knows he has committed and the other crime in which his predecessor has perished?

In truth, during all the years that pass between his arrival at Thebes and the outbreak of the plague, Oedipus wishes to remain aloof from all matters concerning himself, Jocasta, Thebes and, in short, from reality. He wishes, that is, to be ignorant of what lies right under his nose; and, at the cost of a completely unrealistic attitude, he succeeds. For what reality can there be in the life of a man who is the son of his own wife, the brother of his own sons, the father of his own brothers and sisters and the husband of his own mother? The unreality of such a life can be endured only thanks to the anaesthesia of complete non-involvement. But this is the point: why is Oedipus non-involved? One is forced to the conclusion that Oedipus is non-involved because it suits him to be so. This question of convenience can be traced partly to his love for Jocasta, an incestuous love and therefore all the more powerful than normal love, as always happens in the case of anything that is forbidden; partly also to his desire for power, for it must not be forgotten that, thanks to parricide and incest, Oedipus has become king; but above all to the generic fear of knowing the truth.

This question of convenience, however, is unknown to Oedipus himself; if it were not, his tragedy would be merely one of ambition and love. It is unknown, and therefore the tragedy of Oedipus is one of deliberate, presumptuous, frightened, impious ignorance – that is, a tragedy of non-involvement. But Oedipus is a man capable of involvement; and in fact his non-involvement collapses at the first awakening of conscience. Apollo, who by his oracle compels him to pass from non-involvement to involvement, Apollo who splits his own personality and manifests himself in Tiresias, Apollo can be seen, on examination, to be the conscience of Oedipus, never entirely resigned, never entirely obscured. Oedipus abandons himself to the joys of an incestuous marriage, of an unlawful power; but the god is always there, all-present and all-seeing; and, when the moment comes, he strikes the blow unerringly which is to awaken Oedipus from his long sleep. Does Apollo punish Oedipus for having killed his own father and made love to his own mother? Or because he has surrendered himself to non-involvement, the origin of all ills? Apollo punishes Oedipus for surrendering himself to non-involvement. True it is that Oedipus' punishment does not seem to be the punishment reserved for parricides and those who have committed incest, but one which may be imagined as being inflicted upon someone who does not wish to see: Oedipus becomes blind. But, once he has become blind, Oedipus, paradoxically, becomes a seer, like Tiresias who is a seer precisely because he is blind.

And what does Oedipus see after, by blinding himself, he has opened his eyes or, in other words, has passed from non-involvement to involvement? He sees indeed that he is the husband of his own mother and the murderer of his father, but above all he sees himself; that is, he sees how and why non-involvement took the place of involvement in his mind. He sees, in short, that his crime consisted not so much in succumbing to certain passions as in deluding himself into thinking he did not feel them and in making use of this delusion so as to give vent to them with impunity.

I was aware that, in interpreting the tragedy of Oedipus in this way, I was reducing the myth to a psychological and subservient level. There was no doubt that such an interpretation, as far removed from the psycho-analytical as from the traditional explanation, might seem arbitary. But I was searching for the truth not so much about Oedipus as about myself; and it was therefore right that I should make use of the tragedy solely for a better understanding of the situation in which I found myself.

The cross-examination through which, in the tragedy, Oedipus gradually arrives at a knowledge of the truth, finally reminded me that I had hoped to be able to submit Cora to the same sort of cross-examination. The anonymous letter had revealed to me the corruption of my family; the conversation with Baba had aroused in me the suspicion that I alone was really to blame for this corruption; but this was still merely a matter of suspicion. In fact, even admitting that I was directly responsible for the profession practised by Cora, inasmuch as, by ceasing to love her and parting from her, I had destroyed all desire in her for a regular family life and had thus driven her towards her secret vocation; there nevertheless remained the most important point to be cleared up, a point which, for me, was still obscure: why had I stopped loving Cora, or rather, why had I ever begun loving her? Only by questioning Cora should I be able, if not really to find out the truth, at least to check my version of the truth against hers.

Tuesday, October 27th

Towards evening I went out and made my way to the Circonvallazione Clodia, where the dressmaking establishment was situated. I had never been there; during the years when I was still occupied with Cora, it was a different quarter. I parked my car opposite the house; and then, while I was waiting for the green light to cross the street, I took a look at it. It was dark, and all that could be seen of the building was the ground floor and the mezzanine lit from below by the lights from shops and head-lamps; the upper floors remained in half-darkness, against a background of the dark mass of Monte Mario. It was a building of the most ordinary type, with a yellow façade and balconies running all along it at the different floor levels. On the ground floor there was a bar and a few shops; plane-trees thrust their branches up almost as far as the fourth floor. The traffic lights changed from red to green, so I crossed the road and went in. On a black name-plate beside the main door was written, in cursive gilt letters: 'Cora. *Modes.*' Hall, lift, first floor, second floor, third floor, fourth floor. I stepped out on to the landing; and a name-plate, like the one at the main door but smaller, indicated Cora's door. It was open; a second door, of opaque glass and lit by a strong white light, came into view; I pushed it open, setting off a bell; I saw, at the end of a passage, a confused group of women in front of a large table, of the kind that tailors use for cutting out materials; one of these women turned at the sound of the bell, and it was Cora, who cried to me from a distance: 'Go and wait for me in the fitting-room, first door on the right.'

The fitting-room: a sofa and two armchairs; a headless, armless, legless dressmaker's dummy fixed on a pole; a full-length, threefold looking-glass. The carpet was grey, the sofa and the two armchairs red. I sat down, took up a magazine and glanced through it for a short time. Then I threw down the magazine, looked round me once more and, seized by a sudden uneasiness, rose to my feet and went and looked out into the passage.

From the workroom, behind the half-closed door, came the sound of animated conversation. I ventured out into the passage and opened the door: the bathroom; a second door: the kitchen; a third: a bedroom. This time I turned on the light; it was a room just as anonymous as the fitting-room: a very large double bed which left only a narrow space to walk round it; two small bedside tables; a built-in wardrobe; all this in light-coloured wood, with light-coloured curtains and carpet. I said to myself that it was only because I knew about Cora's profession that this dressmaking establishment was, so to speak, visible to me. Otherwise, even though I stood there waiting for Cora, in all probability I should not have seen it, it would have passed unnoticed, as do so many other similar, equally impersonal places. But, after all, what did I see? I saw something which, in the greyness of its familiarity, in a way proclaimed the analogous character – the character of ordinary, meaningless everyday life – of Cora's second profession and of the corruption which allowed that profession to prosper.

I started at Cora's voice, saying: 'Are you looking at the flat? I've had it on lease only for a year. I left it just as it was. There's even a bedroom.'

'What use is the bedroom to you?'

'Sometimes, when there's a lot to do, to take a rest after lunch.'

'Well, have you finished? Can we go?'

'But what are we going to do?'

'Don't you remember – the pieces of information?'

'We can talk here, can't we?'

'No, not here; let's go.'

She said nothing and followed me out. In the lift we did not look at one another, although, on account of the narrowness of the cage, we were very close together. It was not until we were seated in the car that she asked: 'Where are we going?'

An idea came to me: I would go and stop on the Via Cassia, where Cora's *maison de rendez-vous* was situated. I had not yet been there, but I knew the address, which I had made Baba give me: I would stop in front of the gate and in that way I would let Cora see that I knew about her profession, yet without telling her directly in words. 'I don't know,' I replied. 'I think I'll stop some where or other on the Via Cassia.'

She made no comment. We reached the Piazzale di Ponte Milvio, and I started up the Via Cassia. Cora sat motionless, her body upright, her hands clasped on her bag which she held on her knee. We drove on for some time in silence. The houses began to thin out and the country began, as the road ran between grassy slopes surmounted by hedges of elder. I knew that an inhabited area began again after this short stretch of country; but suddenly, all by itself amongst these hedges, I saw a small black iron gate between two red-brick pillars. On one of the pillars I caught sight of the number I was looking for; and by providential chance there was a widening of the road in front of the gate. I turned across the road and came to a stop with the bonnet of the car turned back in the direction of Rome.

I turned off the engine and pulled up the handbrake, looking up at the gate as I did so: there was nothing to be seen because by now it was getting dark, and I had only a glimpse, beyond the bars of the gate, of the vague whiteness of a gravelled path going upwards. The house, a small villa perhaps, evidently stood on high ground; from the road, especially in the dark, there was nothing to be seen of it.

Cora coughed several times, then opened her bag, fumbled in it and drew out a little box of yellow metal, from which she took a pastille which she put in her mouth. As she was doing this, the headlights of cars moving in both directions along the Via Cassia lit up now her face and now her back, with harsh, fleeting intensity. I lit a cigarette and, as I took hold of the car lighter, I displaced the keys which made a little metallic sound as they knocked against the dashboard. 'Well, go on,' said Cora; 'what did you want to say to me?'

'Ah, yes,' I said hastily; 'I wanted to ask you for some information for the novel I'm writing.'

'Oh, of course, the novel.'

'I began this novel exactly ten years ago, then I left it. Now I should like to take it up again. But I need to know a few things from you.'

'Very well. Ask and I'll answer.'

'The novel told the story of you and me, that is, the story of our relationship, from the day on which we met until our marriage. What I should like to know . . .'

I broke off for a moment, embarrassed. What, in reality, did I want to know? I ought to have questioned her about the things that were happening now; but, not wishing to do that, I had to resign myself to questioning her about the things that had happened ten years ago. Nevertheless it seemed to me that even this was a way, though perhaps a tortuous and indirect way, of arriving at the truth. 'I should like to know,' I went on, 'why in your opinion, I fell in love with you and married you.'

She turned her head slightly and looked at me – ironically, it may have been – out of the corner of her eye. 'That's a nice question to ask me! You were fond of me.'

'And why was I fond of you?'

'Why is a man fond of a woman? He's just fond of her; there's no "why" to it.'

'Well then, let's say rather: why, seeing that I was fond of you, has it all come to an end in the way it has?'

'How has it come to an end?'

'I lost all interest in you and Baba, I took to travelling, I became a stranger in my own home.'

'I don't know the reason; it's you who ought to know it.'

'And supposing I don't know it?'

'What, you do things without knowing why you do them?'

'Don't we all act like that? Don't we?'

'Well, I have my own ideas on the subject.'

'And what are they?'

'What does that matter to you?'

'Why, I told you only a moment ago that I was in need of certain pieces of information in order to write my novel . . .'

'Ah, of course, the novel.'

'Don't you believe in my novel?'

'I believe in it and I don't believe in it.'

'Why do you believe in it and also not believe in it?'

'Because you always make use of this novel as a kind of excuse for doing or not doing certain things. Even ten years ago, when you stopped wanting to go to bed with me, you made the excuse that you had to spare yourself in order to write the novel. And none of this was true: you didn't write the novel, and you did go on making love – and how! But not with me, of course.'

'What d'you know about it?'

'I do know.'

'But what has all this got to do with it? Why don't you tell me about these famous ideas of yours?'

She looked at me lingeringly, with an ambiguously benevolent air, with precisely the look of a procuress facing a client and wondering what woman she might suitably offer him. 'You were fond of me,' she said; 'you loved me seriously, about that there's no doubt.'

'Well, then?'

'Wait a moment; you loved me and you showed you loved me. There are some things that can't be faked.'

'I did, in fact, marry you.'

'No, I didn't mean that. Anybody can get married. I'm speaking of the way you made love, until we were married.'

'How did I do it?'

'You did it, to be precise, like a man who loves.'

'Like a man who loves?'

'Yes.'

'And how does a man who loves make love?'

'In the way that you did. Have you even forgotten that?'

'I suppose I did it like anyone who is in love, didn't I?'

'Yes and no.'

'I don't understand you. But, to put it briefly, how was it that this great love came to an end so completely?'

'Because there was a particular thing you wanted, and I, at a certain point, no longer gave it to you.'

'What thing was that?'

'You wanted a woman of a particular kind. When you met me I was exactly the woman you wanted; later on, I ceased to be that.'

'Ah, yes, there may be some truth in that. I was looking . . . I was looking for something which I then called "genuineness" and which it seemed to me I had found in you.'

'Genuineness?'

'Yes.'

'What does "genuine" mean?'

'Genuine, in the sense in which I use it, means "sincere".'

'Sincere?'

'Yes – that is, real authentic, not false, not a parody.'

'A parody?'

'A parody – that is, an ironical imitation.'

'Well, tell me something that's genuine, give me an example.'

'Wine made with grapes is genuine, wine made with powders is not.'

'And how do I come into all this?'

'Well, at that time I had certain ideas, certain feelings. On the basis of these ideas and feelings I had convinced myself that the only repository of everything that is genuine was the working class. You were a working-class girl, and so . . .'

'So you fell in love with me and married me.'

'That's right.'

'But then, if you know what took place between us, why do you want to hear it from me?'

'It may even be that I'm wrong.'

'In fact, you *are* wrong.'

'I'm wrong?'

'Yes.'

'In what way?'

'I've told you already: I have my own ideas and they're different from yours.'

'Then tell me these ideas.'

'In any case the working class is not, as you say, more genuine than other classes. The working class is the sam as the upper classes, only they have the money and the working class hasn't.'

'But it's precisely that difference which makes the working class genuine.'

'Is it? Or may it not be that you call the thing that you like "genuine", and . . . what did you say was the opposite of genuine?'

'A parody.'

'And what you don't like, a "parody".'

'Let us suppose for a moment that that is so. What then?'

'This means that, as far as I'm concerned, what you call genuine was the fact that I was poor and a bit of a whore as well.'

We looked at one another, or rather, I looked at her; and she, on her side, still without turning her head, watched out of the corner of her eye, the effect of her words on my facial expression. An effect there was: I had a disconcerting sense of optical distortion; it was like seeing something familiar from a new visual angle. I objected: 'Yes, indeed you were poor, but . . . but not a whore.'

'You're forgetting where and how we met.'

'We met at the bar in the suburb where you lived, at least I remember that.'

'Yes, but where did we go afterwards?'

'To the house of that friend of yours – what was she called? – Erminia.'

'Yes, a friend.'

'Why, weren't you friends?'

'We were, yes, but not as much as all that.'

'What d'you mean?'

'I mean that Erminia didn't do anything for nothing, and if she lent me the room and introduced men to me, she did it because it suited her.'

'Ah, I understand. Well, I didn't know.'

'You didn't know it the first time. But afterwards I told you about it; have you forgotten that too?'

'No, but you told me you had done it some years before because you were out of work, and that then you had stopped. I didn't attach much importance to the matter, and then I ceased to think about it.'

'Instead of which, I went on doing it even after I got to know you, until the time when we started living together. And it's not true that you attached no importance to it.'

'Why?'

'Because you made me tell you, I don't know how many times, about how I started, and why, and where, and with whom, and when. You pestered me with questions. Oh yes, you thought about it, of course you did. D'you know what you said to me while we were making love?'

'What?'

She turned right round and fixed me for a moment with her pitiless, inhuman blue eyes. Then, muttering between her teeth, she said slowly and with relish: 'You said I was your whore, your strumpet, your pick-up, your slut. And I don't know how many other things of the same kind. And I, to please you, had to answer that it was true, that I *was* your strumpet, your pick-up, your slut, your whore, and that I knew it. I didn't really want to say this, because after all it wasn't accurate; it was a thing I did rarely, and only when I was in real need. But, since you seemed so determined about it, I did what you wanted.' She sat silent for a moment, then added, in an indulgent tone of voice: 'Anyhow there's no harm done, let's agree on that. These are things people say when they're making love. In cold blood they may seem a bit strange. But don't start talking to me about what's "genuine".'

I thought for a moment before replying. Yes, perhaps it was true, perhaps I had said these things; but not more than once or twice; and they were, in fact, as she herself admitted, the sort of things one may happen to say sometimes while making love. But still, it was significant that, amongst so many other things, she should have retained only these. Finally I confessed: 'I had forgotten I said those things.'

'I hadn't, I hadn't forgotten it.'

'Why hadn't you forgotten it?'

'Because the tone in which you said them gave me pleasure.'

'What sort of tone?'

'Passionate.'

'Passionate?'

'Yes. But d'you know . . . ?'

'What?'

'D'you know what you said to me when sometimes I apologized to you for my ugly, mended underclothes?'

'What?'

'You said to me: "Don't change them, don't put on anything else when you come out with me. Your slip with holes in it, your mended blouse, your cotton undergarment, your laddered stockings – all these are more attractive to me than the silk underclothes of the women I have had to do with so far." You were angry with the women of your own class, you had a mortal hatred of them. So much so that one day I asked you if by any chance you were a Communist.'

'What had that to do with it?'

'It did have something to do with it, because you talked like a Communist.'

'And what did I answer?'

'That you were a member of the Party.'

I exclaimed sharply: 'That can't be so.'

'Gospel truth. And why can't it be so, seeing that you really were a member?'

I was confused: I had never been a member of the Communist Party. And, while I was ready to admit that, during love-making, I might have spoken the offensive words she had mentioned, I was ashamed of having lied about a thing so remote from love as membership of a political party. I tried to remedy matters. 'No,' I said, 'I meant that it seems strange to me that I boasted to you about being a Communist. How did that come into it?'

'You didn't boast, you just said that you *were*. And then, d'you know what you did?'

'What?'

'Sometimes you would take my slip, which really was nothing but holes, and not very clean either, and kiss it passionately.'

'Passionately?'

'Yes, really passionately.'

'Now your making out that I'm a fetichist, too.'

'What does "fetichist" mean?'

'It means a man who gets sexual excitement from objects.'

Slowly, rather thoughtfully, she answered: 'No, not that, you were not a fetichist, you truly loved me. But everything that had anything to do with me excited you, not only my slip.'

'For example?'

'Don't you remember when you wanted to go with me to the Gordiani Settlement?'

'Yes, vaguely.'

'Vaguely! Why, we went there at least four times! I had grown up there, but by that time it was some years since I had been living there. However, you insisted on my taking you there, just the same. And when we got there, you didn't want to come away again.'

'Well?'

'Well, you wanted to know everything: where our little house was, what it was like inside, who were our neighbours, what men I used to know there – everything possible, in fact. You wanted me to go with you into the bar and talk to the barman in front of you and introduce you as my fiancé.'

'Well, what harm is there in that?'

'No harm at all. Far from it. And then you wanted me to show you the washing-place where, as a girl, I used to go and wash the clothes, the pump where I fetched the water, the little shop where I bought my father's cigars, and even the public lavatory where everyone went who, like us, had no lavatory in the house. And then – don't you remember?'

'Then what?'

'You even wanted to make love in one of the little houses. And I had the greatest difficulty in persuading a girl called Elda, who led quite a gay life, to lend us her room. I told her we didn't know where to go. D'you know what you said to me that day while we were making love?'

'What a memory you have!'

'It's the good things one remembers, isn't it? You said to me, as you covered me with kisses all over: "It pleases me that you were born and brought up in this place, it pleases me that your mother is a washerwoman and your father a market gardener, it pleases me that you speak the Roman dialect, that you use coarse words, that you're ignorant, that you have a child who is the daughter of an unknown father. If I knew that you were a thief into the bargain, I shoud be even more pleased". And so, to please you, I invented, there and then, a story about my being a thief; don't you remember?'

'No . . . or rather, yes: a story of a theft at a villa, a theft of furs and clothes – wasn't that it?'

'Yes, exactly.'

'And wasn't it true?'

'It was true, yes, but it was nothing to do with me.'

'Who was it, then?'

'Pina, a girl who lived near by.'

'And what effect did it have on me?'

'You couldn't stop hugging me, and you kept repeating like a madman: "My darling thief, my robber, my burglar, my lovely big thief." You really were delighted to think I was a thief. After that day you kept on insisting that I must take you to meet the two young men whom I had accompanied on the job, and you never stopped questioning me, you wanted to know everything – the stuff we'd stolen, how much the receiver had given us, the villa where the theft had taken place. So much so that in the end I had to fall back upon Pina, the real thief, and get her to tell me how it had actually happened.'

'And what excuse did you make to her?'

'I told her you were a writer and wanted to write a novel about all of us who lived at Gordiani. From that day onwards you always carried the newspaper cutting that reported the theft in your pocket-book, together with my photograph. D'you remember? The idea that the words in the newspaper, the usual "unknown persons", referred to me, made you laugh.'

'Yes, it may be that I did something of the kind.'

'And you also told me that you had gone several times to the villa where the theft took place. You said you liked looking at it and thinking that I had been there at night and committed a robbery. Whereas I had never been there at all.'

I should have liked to interrupt her, ironically, with: 'Just as I was never a member of the Communist Party', but I refrained. She went on: 'But the thing that excited you most, in the end, was the fact that for a short time I had been a prostitute. You even wanted us to go to the lodging-house where years before I had taken one or two men, and you wanted to make love in a room hired by the hour, an ugly, cold, dreary room – you who had such a beautiful home of your own. It made me ashamed, doing again like that with you what I had done before from necessity – like acting a play; but then, finally, I thought that after all everyone has his own way of loving, and you, in order to love, needed to believe that I was a guttersnipe and a prostitute and a thief.'

'A fine kind of love!'

She looked at me. Then, as sometimes happens on a still day, when a wind rises suddenly off the ground and strikes a tree, making all its leaves tremble right to the very top, the shock of a memory deeply moved brought sudden life to her usual absorbed immobility. I saw her eyes light up, her nostrils tremble, her bosom swell. In a restrained voice which was yet filled with a deep pride, she said: 'Yes, you can say it out loud, it was a fine love, an intense, violent love, a love that did not stop at the surface but went right down into the depths, a love such as is seldom met with, a kind of love that is never seen nowadays.' She was silent for a moment and then, gazing straight in front of her, she concluded: 'I loved you and you loved me and our love was of the sort that lasts a lifetime.'

'Then explain to me why it lasted only a few years.'

'It was logical. I was attractive to you, and you loved me, because I was poor, because I was a whore, because I'd made you believe I was also a thief. The day I agreed to marry you I became a lady like any other lady; I was no longer attractive to you and you ceased to love me.'

'Logical, as you say. Even a bit too logical, don't you think?'

'Don't you believe me?'

'I believe that you believe you're telling the truth.'

'But it isn't like that; I have proof of it.'

'Proof of what?'

'That what I say is true.'

'And what is this proof?'

'Why, the thing that happened with Gianna.'

'Gianna? Who was Gianna?'

'She was one of my work-girls, a pretty, dark girl, poor, ignorant, from Trastevere, daughter of a bricklayer. That was just at the time when you'd stopped wanting to make love with me. I wanted to see if what I thought was true. I carried out a test. I sent Gianna to you.'

All at once the name of Gianna connected itself, in my memory, with a definite object, and I understood: Gianna was the first of all those hired girls who, during the period immediately after the collapse of my love for Cora, had telephoned me and come to see me at my flat. 'Ah!' I exclaimed, 'so it was you who sent Gianna to me?'

'Yes, it was I.'

'But why did you do it?'

'I've already told you: so as to have a proof.'

'But what proof?'

'A proof that you were attracted by a certain type of

woman and that you had ceased to love me because I had ceased to belong to that type.'

'But wasn't it repugnant to you to make an experiment like that? After all, you did love me.'

'Yes, I loved you, but I knew that you, by that time, no longer loved me, and so it seemed to me that, in sending Gianna to you, I would be making love with you, so to speak, by means of her, that is, through her.'

'Very ingenious. But how did you manage to persuade Gianna to telephone me?'

She looked at me for a moment, boldly and pitilessly. Then she replied: 'I told her that, if she did it, I would give her a dress; and if she didn't, I would give her the sack.'

'But I had other visits too, from other girls. Were they also your work-girls, were they also sent to me by you?'

She became animated, at the same time both impudent and professional. 'Yes, I loved you,' she said, 'and I wanted to go on making love with you, even through a third person. I advised all these girls to talk in Roman dialect, and to appear simple and countrified, the Trastevere type. Some of them were like that in any case, and had no need to pretend.'

'You seem to have had very docile girls in your workroom.'

'Girls, at that age, would make love with anyone; it's according to nature. All you have to do is to put them on the right road and they walk by themselves.'

'And so you put them on the right road, eh?'

'They did it to please me, too. They knew you were my husband.'

'They must have thought I was behind you and that I was making you act as procuress.'

'What does it matter to you what they must have thought?'

'But did none of them, in fact, rebel, did none of them refuse? Is it possible that they were all of that type?'

'What's that got to do with it? They were all virtuous girls. In fact they've almost all got married since then, and some of them have children. It doesn't matter.'

'What is it that doesn't matter?'

'It just doesn't matter: one can do a thing and also its opposite.'

By this time, it seemed to me, Cora was speaking to me in the language of her trade, quietly and openly. I admired the gradual, imperceptible way in which she had reached the point of admitting her own profession to me, yet at the same time without actually admitting it. 'There's one thing I don't understand,' I said. 'You say you participated in my love-making. But how did you manage to do that? Did you afterwards make the girls tell you what it had been like?'

'Yes.'

'And they told you?'

'Yes. But – d'you know . . . ?'

'What?'

'Well, just imagine! Once I even hid myself in the flat and spied on you, you and one of my girls, as you were making love.'

'You did that?'

'Yes. And I saw that you had remained just the same.'

'What d'you mean?'

'The same dirty old pig.'

'Thank you.'

'You're not offended, are you?'

'No, no, I'm not offended.'

'When people make love, as we all know, they're bound to make that sort of impression.'

'All right. But tell me . . '

'What is it?'

'This love-making through a third person, as you call it – did you do it also with other men?'

'What d'you mean?'

'Did you do for other men what you did for me?'

She hesitated an instant, wondering, probably, whether it would be advisable, from her point of view, for us to talk frankly about her profession or not. Then she answered quietly: 'Only for you, of course. I'm not a professional procuress.'

'But you said you did it for love. In ten years it might well be that you've experienced love again in that manner.'

'I've never loved anyone again.'

'Are you sure of that?'

'Why not?'

'You've never loved anyone but me, then.'

'That's right.'

'And you still love me?'

'Yes.'

'Really? You still love me?'

'I've told you I do.'

'And so, if I asked you now to send me one of your work-girls again, you'd do it?'

'Of course.'

'A pity.'

'Why a pity?'

'Because you've kept the same ideas as you had then, whereas I've changed mine.'

'What ideas did you have then?'

'I've told you already: I was searching for something that I called genuineness.'

'Don't you believe in genuineness any longer?'

'No.'

'Why d'you no longer believe in it?'

'Why does one cease to believe in something? Usually because one discovers that the thing does not exist.'

'You've discovered that genuineness doesn't exist, then.'

'Put it like that.'

'I, on the other hand, have not changed.'

'I realize that.'

'I believed in love then, I believe in it now.'

'So I understand.'

'I loved you then, I love you now. And listen, for you I'd be capable of doing something you can't even imagine.'

'What?'

'I've no idea whether you're fond of Baba. Nevertheless, if you fell in love with her and it depended on me, so to speak, whether you and Baba should make love together, I wouldn't hesitate.'

I was not expecting this. I was surprised and troubled and I had to make a serious effort to hide my agitation from her, since she was looking at me, so it seemed, to see whether I would accept her veiled suggestion. And then, during those few seconds of silence, I understood for the first time that I loved Baba; that my love for her was due to the fact that she was my daughter, or at least that I felt her to be so; and that she had a mother like Cora, who had put her up for sale six years before and was now prepared to do so again. I realized too that Cora, with the sure instinct of a procuress, had gone straight to the depths of my heart, and had thus succeeded, even though in an indirect, allusive way, in practising her profession also upon me, revealing what I had not yet had the courage to confess to myself.

No trace of these thoughts was visible in my face – so I hoped, at least, for I was conscious that Cora was watching me. Slowly, cautiously I asked: 'So, even in the case of Baba, you would do this, so as to get the impression of loving me through her?'

'Yes.'

'I am pleased that you love me so much. But surely it's equally true that you're fond of Baba?'

'Why, don't you believe it?'

'Yes, I believe you, but after all, there's a contradiction between the two things.'

'Which two things?'

'That you're fond of Baba and yet at the same time you feel able to encourage a love affair – luckily imaginary – between us.'

'I didn't say I would do it for anyone; I said I would do it for you.'

'There's no great difference, at least as far as Baba is concerned.'

'In any case, a mother may even wish her own daughter to love a particular man.'

'Certainly. But you're forgetting that Baba is my daughter.'

'Stepdaughter.'

'Stepdaughter, if you like. And this particular man, meaning myself, if he had a love affair with Baba, would be committing incest.'

'I don't know anything about incest. I only know that, if you had an affair with Baba, she wouldn't be either your daughter or your stepdaughter or anything else, she'd simply be the woman you loved, that's all.'

'Quite correct. But I wasn't speaking of myself.'

'Whom were you speaking of, then?'

'Actually I was referring to you.'

'And how do I come into it?'

'It might be possible for Baba to be neither daughter nor stepdaughter to me. But it shouldn't be possible for you, even for a single moment, to forget that you're her mother.'

'Of course not.'

'Well, then? How can a mother wish to harm her daughter?'

'Who says I wish to harm my daughter?'

'You said so yourself, a short time ago.'

'But what is this harm?'

'A love affair between Baba and me.'

'But we've just been saying that you're nothing to her. What harm is there in wanting one's daughter to love a man who is nothing to her?'

'So we're back where we started. And supposing the mother wants her daughter to have an affair with a man who is nothing to her, when the daughter is only fourteen? Would there be no harm in that?'

'But Baba isn't fourteen. She's twenty.'

'But let us suppose she's only fourteen.'

'D'you know, you're very curious?'

'Why?'

'Insisting that Baba is only fourteen.'

'She *was* fourteen, once.'

'I almost begin to think that you like little girls.'

'A strange idea.'

'Baba is twenty, she does what she likes, she doesn't depend on me. I didn't really mean what I said.'

'Nor did I.'

'Then why do we go on talking about it?'

'That's what I'm wondering, too.'

We remained silent for some time, during which I reflected that Cora had put up an excellent defence, in the best possible way, that is, by going over to the offensive. I had faced her abruptly with what had taken place six years before; she had at once counter-attacked by accusing me, in turn, of liking little girls. All of a sudden I felt tired, as if after a duel the tension of which had been doubly increased by its indirect, second-hand character. I said slowly : 'Well, thank you, anyhow. You've given me a whole heap of useful information for my novel.'

'Ah yes, the novel. Why, I'd forgotten all about it.'

'Had you? Yet I told you I wanted to speak to you so as to get you to give me certain pieces of information which are indispensable for the novel.'

'You did tell me, yes. But I'd forgotten. I almost had the impression that you were doing it seriously.'

'Seriously – what d'you mean?'

'Well, that you wanted to know certain things for serious reasons.'

'Why, isn't wanting to write a novel a serious thing?'

'Yes, it may be, I don't deny it. But the serious things are the things that are done, not the things that are written in novels.'

'And why, in your opinion, are these serious things done?'

'Oh well, just as things are done in life: because one feels the need to do them.'

'But unfortunately things work differently: to do nothing today may mean doing something, and to do something may mean doing nothing.'

'What's this – a riddle?'

'I'll explain. For me, at any rate, to do seriously the things that you call serious, means doing nothing; and to do nothing, that is, to write a novel, means doing something serious.'

'Why does doing serious things seriously mean doing nothing?'

'There's no "why" about it; it just is like that.'

'Give me an example; otherwise I can't understand you.'

'Well, for instance, I, at that time, seriously did that undoubtedly serious thing which was our marriage. The result has been seen.'

'Yes, but at any rate you did do something. You married me. And one thing leads to another.'

'Yes indeed, one things leads to another. The world was made like that and it has gone on like that ever since: one thing leading to another. Hitler was a monster but the Germans believed in him. And that led to the war and to the death of fifty million people. One thing leads to another.'

'What has Hitler to do with it?'

'He has as much to do with it as anything else. Besides, wasn't Baba's father a German soldier?'

'Well, if that was all that it led to, wasn't I right, perhaps? Isn't Baba a good-looking girl?'

She challenged me with an ironical glance of her flashing eyes. 'We must move on,' I said. 'For one thing, we can't stay here, in front of this gate. We're blocking the way for anyone who wants to get to this villa.'

She said nothing. She turned away, so that her profile was towards me, which was her way of expressing that she was not there. As I switched on the engine, I persisted: 'I wonder who lives in this mysterious, nameless villa.'

'What name would you suggest for it?'

'Oh, I don't know: Villa – anything you like. Villa Cora, for instance.'

'Why Cora?'

'It's just as good a name as any other. Perhaps because I'm sitting with you here at this moment.'

'I only wish it was mine, a villa like that.'

It seemed to me that this hide-and-seek dialogue might go on for ever, so I was silent. I drove the car out of the space at the side of the road and joined the file of all the other cars going in the direction of Rome.

Thursday, October 29th

'Are you sure you made a faithful report in your diary, of your dialogue with Cora?'

'Yes, I'm sure.'

'Really sure?'

'Yes, I'd say so, really sure.'

'Come on, let's read it over together and see if this sureness is well-founded.'

'Very well, I've read it over; the dialogue is the same, there may perhaps be a few words altered or omitted but the substance is the same. And yet, and yet . . . '

'And yet what?'

'And yet I now realize that you are right. As usual, goodness knows why, I have not been faithful.'

'Goodness know why, eh? Come on, don't pretend to be innocent, or forgetful, or the kind of story-teller who composes in an ectasy; because you're nothing like that at all. You know perfectly well that you haven't been faithful, and you know where, and you also know why.'

'It's true that I haven't been faithful at the point where Cora suggested that she would facilitate – in a professional, even if disinterested, way – a love relationship between myself and Baba. Actually Cora did not say anything like that to me and there was no mention at all of Baba. I don't really know why it occurred to me to add this appendix to our dialogue. Perhaps because it seemed to me that Cora was capable of making such a proposal to me and consequently the proposal, even though imaginary, was plausible and, as such, served to define Cora's character and make it more real.'

'Ah, yes, Cora's character. And why not your own?'

'How do I come into it? It wasn't I who made the proposal but Cora; it wasn't I who dragged Baba into it, but Cora. In short, all I did was to listen and, naturally, to feel the full horror which such a suggestion deserves.'

'Yes, it wasn't you who made the proposal, it wasn't you who dragged Baba into it; yes, all you did was to listen, and you felt horror. But, you hypocrite, it was you who imagined that Cora made the proposal, it was you who added this lie to the truth. This you can't deny.'

'I don't deny it; but I've already said that I probably did it because it appeared to me logical and natural that Cora, after all those other girls, should offer me Baba as well.'

'Logical and natural – rubbish! Or rather, logical and natural, indeed; but even more logical and natural that you should have taken pleasure in such a piece of information.'

'Taken pleasure? Why?'

'For the very good reason that you've fallen in love with Baba in a very special manner of your own, which, to be precise, is determined by your kinship with her and by the situation in which you find yourself with regard to Cora.'

'Well then?'

'It pleases you to imagine that it's actually her mother who is offering Baba to you; it pleases you to imagine that you might even, perhaps, possess Baba at Cora's villa; finally it pleases you to imagine, yet further, that Baba is a mere object, a thing, which her mother is selling to you and which you are buying.'

'Are you sure that this is the truth?'

'I am not sure, because one cannot be sure of anything. But you must admit that it is a legitimate suspicion.'

'But then the whole thing may be false, lying, non-genuine. It may even have been a complete invention on my part that Cora runs a *maison de rendezvous* and that she took her daughter there when she was fourteen and that I have been to that house myself, and all the rest of it. In reality I may have invented these things because I have fallen in love with my stepdaughter and because, in order to make love to her, I require to believe that her mother is a procuress and that she tried to sell her own daughter six years ago. In other words, the only thing that is true, objectively true, must be that I love Baba.'

'No, don't try now to shuffle the cards in order to justify yourself. You know perfectly well that Cora really does run a *maison de rendezvous*, that Baba was telling the truth when she said that her mother had taken her there, and that this house exists. You know perfectly well, that is, that your novel, if you ever write it, will be composed partly of objective reality and partly of subjective reality. But you know also that such a division does not, fundamentally, exist. Your novel is yourself. It therefore depends upon you. . . .'

'What depends upon me?'

'To be yourself, completely and without any disguise, through the recognition that some things have really happened to you and others have been imagined by you, rather than through knowledge of the motives of your imaginings.'

Saturday, October 31st

And how about the ordinary everyday life upon which, as on a foundation of granite, I had intended to build my novel? Once again, alas, it had been driven out by drama. I had intended to write a novel without a story, noting down in a diary, day by day, the insignificant, disconnected things that happened to me without my seeking them or wishing for them; instead of which, I have been overwhelmed by a story dramatic in itself and, it might be said, highly significant and well-constructed, a story whose gradual developments I am forced to relate and which urges me continually to take action and to make choices.

Except that – as I think I have already said – this story, apparently so dramatic, fundamentally is not so at all. And in actual fact there are no developments. And what is happening to me is just as ordinary as the things that are generally termed ordinary. I had this feeling today, during the short walk which I usually take in the morning before settling down to work.

I have been taking this walk for years, always in the same way, every morning, during my sojourns in Rome between one journey and another. It is, therefore, the most ordinary thing that I ever do, a thing in which action on my part is reduced, through habit and repetition, to a minimum of automatism and unconsciousness.

I went out today, then, as usual, and walked along the Viale Mazzini from the main door of my own building as far as the newsagent kiosk at the corner of a cross-road. The newsagent is a man of forty, in other words in what is called the prime of life, with a dark, scowling face, small, wide-open eyes, a hooked nose, an up-curving chin and bristling moustaches. A face which has a notable resemblance to that of a stupid, ferocious watch-dog; and indeed, just like a watch-dog in its kennel, he sits crouched in his kiosk, ready, you might think, to sink his fangs into the hand that ventures within to select a newspaper. The newsagent recognized me, of course and said: 'When are you off on another journey, Signor Merighi?' And then, without waiting for me to ask, he handed me, authoritatively, the morning papers, the ones that I've been reading for at least ten years. I put the papers under my arm and continued my walk.

Two streets farther on was the bar: I went in, leant against the counter, ordered a cup of coffee and then looked round, although I know this bar extremely well and it does not contain anything of interest. The upper part of the counter is made of shining grey metal, possibly steel, the lower part of some dark-coloured material that might be wood. There, on the counter, was the coffee-making machine, in the shape of a suitcase; the electric mixer for making milk-shakes; the grill for making toast; the glass case with toast on one shelf and sandwiches on the other; a rounded container of dark red glass with a light plastic lid upon which, in letters fused into the glass, was written: 'Amarena'; a couple of metal sugar-basins with transparent glass lids of the kind that automatically regulate the allowance of sugar in the spoon. The barman, a tall, slim, fair young man with a bumpy forehead and small blue eyes, was standing, an apron round his waist, between the counter and the shelves of bottles, working the levers of the coffee-machine with his big red hands. He too, like the newsagent, recognized me, and cried out, in his loud, harsh voice: 'Here's your usual, small and strong'; and then handed me the cup with a special gesture, a kind of conjuring trick, waving it round in the air in a circle before sliding it on to the counter. I drank the coffee slowly, then paid and went out.

From the bar I went to the tobacconist's in a neighbouring street. I entered the shop, long and narrow like a passage, with the counter running along the length of the shop and the tobacconist sitting behind it – a huge, unhealthy-looking man whose great paunch compels him to sit right back against the shelves, at some distance from the customers who file past in front of him. He recognized me when he saw me, as I realized from the understanding glance he gave me, and, without turning round, stretched out his short arm backwards and, with a neat, pincer-like movement of two fingers, picked up three packets of the cigarettes I usually smoke and threw them down on the counter; then, with his dull, black, feminine eyes, his mouth half-open because of his troubled asthmatic breathing, he brooded over my hand as I selected the softest packet. I took the packet, threw down a silver coin on the counter; and the tobacconist gave me my change without speaking, since speaking was too great an effort for him, thanking me, however, with a look that at once became questioning as it was transferred from my face to the face of another customer who came in at that moment. I took my change and went out of the shop.

I went on to the stationer's shop, next door to the tobacconist's. This shop, actually, is kept by a woman, a pleasing woman of about forty with a pink and white face – the white very white and the pink very pink – and with clear, almost round, black eyes and a pyramid of glossy black hair that may possibly be dyed. Not merely did she recognize me but she spoke to me about my journeys, saying she was glad to see me back, asking me when I should be leaving again and, with a heartbroken air, lamenting the fact that she could not read my articles because they appear in a Milan newspaper. I answered her as best I could and then asked for a ream of paper, a packet of carbon paper, a black typewriter ribbon and a Biro pen. She rose to her feet, displaying a supple, shapely figure dressed, or rather imprisoned, in a tight, shiny black gown; and she collected the things I had asked for from their various shelves. Then she went and sat down again behind the counter and quickly made out the bill on a piece of paper, holding it steady with an extremely white hand with pink nails like those of a little girl. She announced the sum I had to pay, informing me that she was allowing me discount, did up the parcel, took my money, gave me back my change – all this rapidly and expertly. Then she gazed at me fixedly with eyes that looked as if they were painted on two glass balls, as though she were expecting me to talk to her. I seized the parcel and left the shop.

At this moment, as I turned back homewards, I saw my car in the distance standing in front of the main door and recalled that the last time I had driven it had been a few days before, when I had taken Cora along the Via Cassia and had stopped in front of the gate of the *maison de rendezvous*. And then it occurred to me that my morning walk might well have been prolonged to that villa on the Via Cassia, without on that account altering its rhythm and style. So many men preferred to make love early in the morning, when they are refreshed and re-invigorated by their night's rest: a telephone call, then the car drive to the house, the bedroom, the woman undressing and gradually exhibiting all that she can give in exchange for the money, the sexual act, the banknotes in the hand of the procuress. The peregrination which had taken me that day from the newspaper kiosk to the bar, from the bar to the tobacconist's, from the tobacconist's to the stationer's shop, might have continued to the *maison de rendezvous* without any break in quality or interruption of continuity. A series of purchases which included a newspaper, a cup of coffee, a packet of cigarettes, a ream of paper, a packet of carbon paper, a typewriter ribbon, a Biro pen, a woman's body. A chain of events which caused me, in succession, to read a paper, to drink a cup of coffee, to smoke some cigarettes, to type out an article and to make love with a call-girl. And, after the house on the Via Cassia, other peregrinations, other purchases, other events, monotonous and senseless as the waves of the sea on a deserted shore.

But I understood one thing above all: that the newsagent in his kiosk, the barman in his bar, the tobacconist in his shop, the stationer-woman in hers – all these presupposed and justi-fied the girl provided by Cora at the *maison de rendezvous*. I might even speak of corruption. But this corruption had in it nothing dramatic, it lay in the things themselves, in the very material of which they were composed. For that reason it would be more appropriate to call it, as I have already said so many times, everyday normality.

Now under one pretext and now under another, Baba always ends by achieving her object, or rather by imposing her plan, which, so it seems, consists in spending some hours with me every day in an affectionate kind of way suitable to father and daughter. Today her pretext was the choosing of a dog at the municipal kennels. While, in the morning, we were driving towards Porta Portese, where the kennels are situated, I asked her why in the world she wanted a dog. She thought for a moment and then replied: 'Some years ago I had one. Six years ago to be precise. He was run over and killed by a car just at the time when Cora was taking me . . . I mean, was taking Baba to her house. In fact – d'you know what I think?'

'What?'

'That the sadness Baba felt at the death of the dog prevented her in some way from realizing what was happening to her.'

'Was Baba very sad at the death of the dog?'

'Yes. She did nothing but cry for some days and thought to herself that everything was going wrong for her, and that a bad period of her life was beginning.'

'And why didn't Baba get someone to give her another dog?'

'Because she didn't want another one. She wanted *that* one.'

'Yes, I understand.'

We reached Porta Portese. We went through an iron gate into the enclosure containing the kennels. The manager's offices, a building on one floor, long and white with green shutters, lay in front of us; to right and left, scarcely larger than the boxes in which bee-keepers keep their hives, were several rows of the small cages in which the dogs are shut up. We waited for a little, in a deep silence which was at once heavy and full of suspense, and to which the faint wild-beast smell in the air seemed to add a significance of anguished expectation. Then the attendant arrived, a fair-haired, athletic young man with a close-cropped head, dressed in white. We moved, all three of us, in the direction of the cages; and then, suddenly, there burst forth a furious clamour of barking – barking which varied greatly in sound and intensity but which seemed to share in common a single note of heart-rending and perfectly conscious entreaty.

Baba's state of mind, today, somewhat resembled the present state of the weather: a surly, rather bewildered placidity that was, however, pregnant with caprices, very similar to the dark mass of clouds hanging above the city in the mild humming *scirocco* air. She walked along beside the attendant, her hands in the pockets of her coat, which was unbuttoned across her prominent chest, moving her hips, in their tight trousers, with listless, bear-like slowness. As we went past, the dogs rushed to the bars, rising on their hind legs and barking in many different ways and with many different voices, like prisoners from different countries imploring favours in their own language. Baba stopped and stared at them intently for a moment with her dull, grey-green eyes, then moved on again, questioning the attendant with inattentive curiosity: 'How long d'you keep them in here after you've caught them?'

'According to the regulations, three days: usually we keep them up to seven days.'

'And then?'

'And then, of course we send them to the gas chamber.'

'How many d'you kill per week?'

'Ten, fifteen.'

'But there are some pure-bred dogs here – how is that?'

'Their owners abandon them. Or else the dogs run away.'

'But why do their owners abandon them?'

'For several reasons. Because they get tired of them. Or because they find out that the dog doesn't, so to speak, pay its way.'

'How d'you mean?'

'I mean, for example, that a sporting dog hasn't a good nose.'

'But d'you think the dogs know it?'

'Know what?'

'That they've been abandoned and that they're going to end up in the gas chamber?'

'Certainly they know it. The dog is an intelligent animal. He knows everything.'

'But won't a dog like this, once he's been here, be nervous and depressed and bad-tempered afterwards, for the rest of his life?'

'You needn't worry about that. All a dog wants is to have a master. Once he has one, he forgets the past.'

Etcetera, etcetera. This informative chatter, carried on in a calm, casual, leisurely tone while all round us deafening howls arose from every direction, irritated me; and so, since we had to come to the end of the row of cages, I said to Baba: 'Well, now you've seen them all; you must make up your mind.'

She waved her hand at me, as much as to say there was no hurry; then she said to the attendant: 'Let's turn back. I noticed four or five of them that might possibly do.'

So we turned back. Baba stopped every time there was a dog that interested her and, as she mechanically put out her hand towards the animal which, standing on its hindlegs, tried hard to lick it between the bars and implored her with whinings and tail-waggings, she questioned the attendant at great length about the age, the breed, the disposition, the habits and, in fact, every one of the creature's characteristics. All this she did with such minuteness and pedantry that I began to have suspicion that her loving-kindness towards dogs was not devoid of a certain cruelty; all the more so because, during these interminable questionings, the dog was there, straining against the bars, howling and wriggling and supplicating. 'Come on,' I said to her, 'make your choice and let's be done with it. Don't you see you're tormenting these poor beasts?'

'One has to be very careful before taking a dog into one's house.'

'Well then, Signorina, will you take this one?'

'No, that one won't do. He's too ugly, with that face like a calf and those yellow and white spots. A mongrel's all right; but this is a bit too much.'

'The ugliest ones are the most affectionate, you know.'

'Why is that?'

'Because they know that they're ugly, poor things, and they realize that they're alive as it were by a miracle, and they're grateful for it to their masters.'

We went on, from a mongrel which had a remote resemblance to a fox to another which, with a little alteration, might have been a pointer, and then another which, with a little good will, one might have mistaken for a poodle. Baba was talking to the attendant and taking no notice of me. Finally she pointed, in a decided manner, to a cage and said: 'I'll take this one.'

It was a small grey dog, almost a griffon, with a bristling head of ruffled hair amongst which the whiteness of its teeth and its sparkling eyes stood out conspicuously. Seeing Baba's gesture as she pointed it out to the attendant, the dog immediately became quiet and stopped yelping; it had understood that it was safe.

The attendant approved her choice. 'You've chosen well,' he said; 'this is an almost pure-bred dog and you'll see how affectionate he'll become. And certainly you've saved him. We should have had to send him to the gas chamber tomorrow; he's been here six days already and nobody's claimed him.' And so, chattering all the time, he opened the cage, took out the dog and walked in front of us to the offices. Here I signed a register and paid five thousand lire; Baba took the dog in her arms and at last we went out. The other dogs, as though they understood that, from us two at any rate, there was no further hope, raised a deafening chorus of protesting clamour which, the moment the gate closed behind us, ceased altogether.

In the car I said to Baba: 'A real little extermination camp of the Nazi type. There was nothing wanting.'

Baba gave me a hasty glance and then said: 'Yes indeed, but . . . now I come to think of it . . .'

'Now you come to think of what?'

'You remember what I told you about the experience which Cora made me undergo at the age of fourteen?'

'You mean which she made another Baba undergo.'

'Exactly. Well, all that is not to be taken literally.'

'That is to say?'

'That is to say, it was most certainly I whom Cora took to her house six years ago.'

'So it seemed to me, but I didn't dare say so.'

'Gently, now! Yet at the same time it's also true that it wasn't me.'

'But what has all this to do with the kennels?'

She answered me in a pedantic fashion, as though expounding the results of long meditation. 'Those dogs are abandoned by their masters, shut up in cages, condemned to death. If one of them is rescued, what will he do? In my opinion, in order to go on living he will try to imagine that the whole thing happened to another dog, different from himself, and that he is a new dog, with a new master and a new life. Naturally, as I have already said, in an objective sense all this is not true, it is still the same dog that is concerned, the dog that was abandoned by its master and condemned to death. Yet at the same time it *is* true: the dog *is* another dog because, between him and the dog which was abandoned and condemned to death, there stands the precise fact of the abandonment and the death sentence which has split his life in two.'

'They say that dogs have an extremely good memory for injuries and sorrows.'

'It is exactly because of that, in my opinion, that they are able to forget, to pretend to themselves that nothing has happened.'

'Very subtle. It is, therefore, precisely the memory of the past that allows one to abolish it.'

'Exactly.'

'And to look to the future, simply and solely to the future, planning it as one plans a bridge or a building?'

This time she said nothing, but she turned upon me a glance that was sluggish yet hungry, almost cannibalistic and at the same time curiously unhappy, as she slowly stroked the head of the dog on her knee. Then she came to a decision: she took hold of the dog with both hands, half rose in her seat and deposited it on the back seat, with the injunction: 'Now lie down there and be good.' And then she fell upon me, heavily, throwing her arms round my neck and kissing me on the cheek and murmuring: 'Thank you for the dog. And it's not true that I *plan* my feeling for you, as you would like to insinuate. I'm really fond of you, in just the way that a daughter can be fond of her father, please believe me.' As she said this, she pressed her cheek for a moment against mine, and I felt the softness and fineness of her skin, flushed with a fervour I could not define and at the same time fresh with the freshness of youth; and I could not help noticing, as usual, some kind of ambiguity in her embrace, so that almost in spite of myself I put up my hand and pressed her face against mine as though to prolong the contact between our two cheeks. But then she suddenly let go of me, fell back in her seat and said: 'What shall I call this dog? Help me to find a name.'

I started the engine and replied: 'Call him Smoke; his coat is the colour of smoke.'

'No, I shall call him Tuesday, just as Robinson Crusoe called his servant Friday, because today is Tuesday and I myself, like Crusoe, was abandoned on a desert island and have had to start life over again from nothing.'

Thursday, November 5th

'But did you yourself ever take any interest in Cora's profession?'

'In what sense?'

'In the sense of making any enquiry into what she does, when she does it and where she does it.'

'I had no need to.'

'Why?'

'Cora doesn't conceal things from me. No, it's I who have to run away in order to avoid learning certain things.'

'What things?'

'Certain telephone calls, for instance – Cora doesn't hesitate to make them in my presence. And if she does them in code, so to speak, it's not because I'm there, it's because she's cautious.'

'Who does she telephone to?'

'To girls, to men.'

'And you've heard these telephone calls?'

'Sometimes, yes.'

'But what does she say?'

'Oh, nothing very interesting. If I didn't know what it was about, I should think that Cora was in the perfumery business.'

'How d'you mean?'

'For example, she informs someone of the arrival of a certain number of blond or dark tortoiseshell combs, to explain whether the girl is fair or dark. Then she says that these combs have sixteen, eighteen, twenty or twenty-five teeth. That's the age of the girl. Then she may even say that the combs are of a new type, never before seen. That means, probably, that the girl is a virgin. And so on. At the end she gives the address, the day, the hour, and then it's finished;

she puts down the telephone.'

'And how does she justify this perfumery activity of hers to you?'

'She doesn't justify it at all. Cora never justifies herself. She does things and then remains silent.'

'This conversation about combs must be when she tele-phones to men. But to girls, what does she say?'

'She tells the girls that the dress is ready and that they should come and try it on at such a time on such a day.'

'These are the girls who are already in agreement with her. But how about the others?'

'What d'you mean?'

'What I mean is that Cora, on the telephone, must some-times have to do a job of persuasion, of seduction – isn't that so?'

'Well?'

'What does she say in a case like that?'

'Oh, she's wonderful.'

'In what sense?'

'In the sense of doing her job cleverly and well but also with passion.'

'What does this skill consist in?'

'In the way in which she presents the thing.'

'And how is that?'

'As something of little importance, in the first place; in the second place, as something pleasant; and finally as something of momentary interest, which will only happen that one single time.'

'Let's take things in order. How does she set about explain-ing that it's of little importance?'

'She says it's a thing that all women do, that it doesn't have consequences of any kind, that afterwards you go back to your ordinary life and even forget you've done it, that it's just like being with your fiancé – and other things of that sort.'

'And as a pleasant thing?'

'She says it's always a question of men with a great many good qualities of distinction, of kindness, of good manners.'

'And as a thing of momentary interest?'

'The girl is free never to do it again, no one is forcing her to do it, she lays herself under no obligation; furthermore, it is not a question of just any ordinary man, but of someone who has noticed her and would like to meet her, that is, of something which, precisely because it is exceptional, will happen only this one time – and so on.'

'But do all the girls allow themselves to be convinced by these arguments?'

'No, not all. Cora, however, never hangs on to a girl who does not, at the last moment, give her some sort of hope, even a faint one. It's here that she displays her skill.'

'In what way?'

'In transforming a state of mind which is still hostile, but not decisively negative, into a state of mind which is favourable. Besides, when gentleness doesn't do the trick, Cora doesn't hesitate to make good use of forceful methods.'

'For example?'

'I managed, by putting two and two together, to reconstruct what she did on one occasion. A girl, after many hesitations, finally agreed. Cora gave her the address, told her the day and the hour. Immediately afterwards the girl telephoned to say she had thought better of it, she didn't feel like it. So what d'you think Cora did?'

'Did she blackmail her?'

'No, she forced her into it.'

'How did she do that?'

'She rushed off to the girl's home, found her at table with her father and mother and brothers, and told her she had come to fetch her away for I don't know what urgent reason. The girl was frightened and went with her, and so she got away with it once again. Just imagine the courage, the brazenness: in the girl's own home, in front of her family! In the end, it was actually the girl's mother who advised her reluctant daughter to go with Cora, in view of the reason which Cora had invented. The girl didn't want to go, and Cora, in order to make her submit, managed to get the mother to help her.'

'And afterwards?'

'Afterwards – what?'

'What happened to this girl?'

'I believe she got over it and developed quite an affection for Cora; and that since that day she's never made any more difficulties.'

'What does Cora do when she talks on the telephone?'

'How d'you mean?'   .

'I mean, how does she behave? Does she talk a lot or a little, does she raise her voice?'

'She listens, for the most part: she knows how to listen and she knows how to encourage conversations which she then listens to. She speaks in a low voice, like a priest in the confessional, in an even, reserved, subdued tone, hardly opening her mouth. She says little, but very precisely and at the right moment. She never gets excited, she never raises her voice, she never gets angry. Cora's strength lies in the fact that she does not appear interested.'

'Perhaps she isn't?'

'She is and she isn't.'

'But you – when you talk about her, anyone would think you admire her.'

'No, I don't admire her.'

'You say she's clever?'

'It's the truth.'

'But don't you dislike talking about these things, doesn't it disgust you?'

'No.'

'Why?'

'Because these things are, fundamentally, just like any other things.'

'What d'you mean'

'I mean that, if there's one person who has the right not to feel repugnance in this case, it's I – don't you think so?'

'Yes, that's true.'

'Besides, once again: Cora, after all, is my mother.'

'Yes, she's your mother; nevertheless . . .'

'And it seems to me that I'm fond of her precisely because she practices this profession and doesn't hide it from me, and I see it and know about it.'

'But after all, these girls . . .'

'It's the same when she undresses and takes a bath, and then I have to dry her and rub her with a cloth. I see quite well that she's no longer young, that her figure has gone to pieces, I realize that she might even seem repugnant. But since she's my mother and I love her as a daughter loves her own mother, I don't feel any repugnance, in fact I almost seem to love her more, just because she's so flabby and so aged and so unattractive.'

As she said this she looked at me for a moment, her eyelids

half lowered over her motionless grey-green eyes, with a sly, sleepy expression. We were on the Tiber embankment, in the neighbourhood of Piazza Mazzini, and were giving the dog a walk – a new pretext for imposing her usual plan of cultivating our familiar relationship. She looked at me; then, with disconcerting skill, she put her two fingers to her mouth and emitted a long, shrill whistle; and the dog, which had wandered some distance away, at once came running back to us, barking gaily.

Sunday, November 8th

I have been thinking about it at intervals for some days, without coming to a decision; finally today I left the house, got into my car and drove off towards the Via Cassia.

It was five o'clock in the afternoon, on a day which, as usual, threatened thunderstorms. I crossed the Ponte Milvio, joined the column of cars leaving the city, and started driving along slowly and somnolently, in the already dark air, beneath the vault of red and yellow foliage formed by the plane-trees meeting overhead.

As I drove along in this almost somnambulistic manner, I wondered why I should be going to Cora's villa. My first answer to this self-enquiry was as follows: I was going in order that this thing which was to me still incredible – Cora's secret profession – might become familiar to me through seeing it with my own eyes, touching it with my own hands, hearing it with my ears and smelling it with my nostrils; and this with the object of bridging the gap of disgust which made it unreal to me simply because it was so hateful. But, after a more thorough consideration, a second reason became apparent to me: I wanted to see Cora's house because Cora, six years before, had taken Baba to a similar house at the age of fourteen.

Then I thought again of what Cora had said to me about my way of making love, of how I had wanted to go to bed with her in the little suburban house; and I saw that the same impulse, or rather the same project, was now to some extent repeating itself. Only that then, the thing that had attracted me about the suburban bedroom had been the idea of poverty in the guise of genuineness; whereas now, what urged me to visit Cora's villa was, on the contrary, the idea of the nullity which had its abode there and which was practised there every day. And I loved Baba because, with her, nullity found its fullest and most extreme expression in incest; and I knew that through Baba I should be able, if I wished, to plunge to the bottommost depths of this nullity.

Suddenly the car, so to speak, stopped of its own accord, or rather, I braked almost without being aware of it, immersed as I was in my daydreams; and I looked to see what was happening. A traffic policeman, very tall and lanky, with gaiters and belt and leather cap, was directing the traffic by means of a red and green signal; there were a number of cars at a standstill, waiting to proceed; on one side of the road there was a small grey car with a smashed-in bonnet; then there was an expanse of black asphalt, spotted, like a leopard's skin, with dead leaves, red and yellow but covered with a fine sparkling dust of broken glass; and finally there was a big, white, expensive car, long and low, with a crumpled mudguard. I waited for a little while as the cars moved forward in single file past the policeman, then I went forward myself, passing the part of the road where the collision had occurred, and rounded a corner. A man who was walking hurriedly alongside the ditch made a sign to me, and I stopped. 'Will you give me a lift?'

I took a look at him. His face was coarse but not unattractive, the face of a young Roman shopkeeper, fresh, highly-coloured, full-blooded, with bright, impudent, prominent eyes, curly hair over a low forehead and a red mouth with a capricious, fierce expression. He was clasping his shoulder with his hand and seemed rather upset. 'I'm going close by here,' I said.

'So am I,' he replied; 'five kilometres from here.'

'Get in, then.'

He got in, I pressed down the accelerator and the car moved off beneath the trees. 'Was it you who had the collision?' I asked.

'What makes you think so?'

'I saw you were holding your shoulder. Your car was the white one, was it?'

I was prepared for some violent comment; he was the kind of person whom one might expect to have a passion for motorcars. To my surprise he merely said, in a mild way: 'Yes, that was it. But nothing really happened. Just a crumpled wing and a slight bruise on the shoulder.'

'To you; but how about the others?'

'Oh, they went off in a bus. Just a slightly damaged bonnet.'

'But whose fault was it?'

He did not look at me but kept his eyes fixed straight ahead of him, their pupils alight with irritated impatience. Without turning, he answered: 'Mine. I was in a hurry. I overtook another car and we collided. They were on their right side of the road.'

Again I was surprised at his objective and reasonable acknowledgement that he was in the wrong – a truly unusual thing in a man of his type. Unless, I thought, this acknowledgment was perhaps due to something more immediately important to him than his car, something which, in causing him to hurry, had indirectly also caused the collision. 'Are you insured?' I asked im.

'Yes.'

'But the insurance will pay for the other people's damage, not yours.'

'Oh yes, I know.'

Then we were silent again for about a kilometre. Suddenly he put his hand on my arm. 'This is where I get out,' he said. 'Please stop.'

I looked out through the windscreen, upon which the first raindrops were already beginning to flatten themselves in broad, flowery shapes, and recognised, with a sickening sense of inevitability, the gate of Cora's villa. The young man, in the meantime, nimble and impatient, had already opened the door and jumped out. 'Thanks for the lift!'

I pretended to be meddling with the gear lever and stayed where I was, watching him as he turned up the collar of his waterproof round the back of his neck and then walked away towards the gate, pushed it open and disappeared. Then I pressed down the accelerator again and moved off. I drove for about twenty kilometres. The rain, after that first sprinkling of drops like little liquid chrysanthemums, had turned into a heavy downpour, though the air was still clear, and the blades of the screen-wiper succeeded in creating a triangle of visibility only for a moment at a time. Then, as the deluge increased, a livid, swirling mist was intermingled with it; so I stopped, pulled up the window and lit a cigarette.

I thought of the young shopkeeper and of what he was doing at that moment: the nearly dark room, like a well-sheltered cavern; the rain behind the blurred window-panes; the woman's naked, warm body against his; the silent love-making; the explosions of the thunderstorm. And again, identifying myself with him, I understood that it was upon this that the young man's mind was set, with all the impatience of his fevered blood, while I talked to him of the accident, of the damage, of the insurance.

I smoked my cigarette, opened the window and threw out the butt, then closed the window again and lit another cigarette. It was still raining heavily, but not so heavily as to make it impossible to see, as it had been a short time before. I started the car again and drove on for another twenty minutes or so, as far as a cross-roads, where stood the four or five houses of a little country village. I stopped the car and got out, and then, in the rain which was now falling less heavily, I went, jumping over one puddle after another, into a little bar close by. The peasant barman was chattering to two or three customers, also peasants; I sat down in a corner, at a shaky tubular table, my feet in the sawdust that covered the floor, and ordered coffee.

It was a quarter to six. I calculated that the young man had gone into Cora's villa at about a quarter past five, and it seemed to me that his love-making would not have taken more than half an hour, at most three quarters. Therefore I still had about twenty minutes to wait.

The barman brought me the coffee, I drank it and then took up a magazine from a table near by. It was a strip-cartoon magazine, all crumpled and dirty, and in it there was a film romance entitled 'Return of the Past'. I read it, or rather, I looked through it from one picture to another, examining the photographs with attention and carefully spelling out the remarks that came out of the characters' mouths.

The two protagonists, a handsome young man and a sweet-faced girl, both of them dressed with finished elegance, their faces assuming expressions alternately proccupied, sad, passionate, dreamy, affectionate, angry, but always dignified, moved through the rooms of small flats with modern furniture in the Swedish style. As far as I could make out, the girl had

had a lover and had not told her fiancé about it, the lover had reappeared and was blackmailing her, the girl had to decide whether to buy the lover's silence by yielding to his desires or to reveal everything to her fiancé who believed her to be chaste, with the risk that he might abandon her. At a certain point a respectable old lady started to act as mediator between them – an old lady with carefully waved white hair, bespectacled, dressed in black, either his or her mother . . . and then I could not help thinking: 'And suppose my own life were a kind of strip-cartoon like this one? Suppose that, as usual, non-genuineness were lying hidden at the very heart of things? Suppose, in fact, that reality, like these strip-cartoons, were itself constitutionally unreal? And that its significance should be sought, not in events themselves, but actually in their unreality?' I gave no answer to these questions which, in any case, had no need of one; and I went on with my interesting reading. When I reached a cartoon in which one saw the mother urging the girl to speak to her fiancé, with these words: 'Speak to him, tell him the truth. If he can't endure the truth, he's not worthy of you', I called the barman, paid and left the bar. It had stopped raining, and the black puddles on the road quietly reflected the yellow lights of lamps. The air was damp and mild, almost warm, with an occasional feeble puff of cooler wind. I got back into the car, made a half-turn in the road and started back towards Rome. Ten minutes later I was in front of Cora's gate.

I got out and, finding the gate ajar, pushed it open and walked off up the path, between two rows of shrubs dripping and shining with rain. As I followed the path, after a short time I saw the upper part of the villa appear at the top of the hill and then, as I went on upwards, the lower part as well, and finally I came out into an open space in front of the door. As I looked at the façade of the villa, which was dimly lit from below by a couple of luminous globes, I understood why Cora had rented this particular house and no other. No doubt she had done so because of its cheapness, but the lowness of the price, equally surely, was due to the fact that the owner, after he had built it, had realized that he had made a complete mistake and had then wished to get rid of it at all costs. An air of irreparable failure, of fundamental mismanagement, did in fact emanate from this building, which was too large and massive to be suitable for unpretentious living and at the same time too crude to be counted amongst dwellings of the *de luxe* type. The villa was built in the bleak, coarse style in fashion thirty years before, the so-called 'twentieth-century' or 'Fascist' style. Painted in a gloomy grey, its smooth façade, lacking in cornices, mottled with big, dark patches of dampness and streaked from top to bottom with trickles of rust, the villa was flanked by a kind of tower which gave it a sullen, utilitarian look, something between a silo and a mediaeval fort. Two balconies, at the level of the two floors, ran across the façade, and the windows were all closed and dark. I noticed that the door, between the two electric bulbs, was ajar, as the gate had been, no doubt for the same reason. I quickly crossed the open space, pushed open the door and went in. The inside of the villa did not differ from the outside in the crudity, the bleakness and the mistakenness of its construction: there was a long, bare vestibule with a wainscot of dark wood, then an opaque glass door, and finally the staircase, narrow and steep, as though hollowed out in the thickness of the cement. Unexpectedly, at the top of the first flight of stairs, there was a big window of red, green and black glass containing a representation of Saint George on horseback in the act of slaying the dragon. I went up the first flight, stopped a moment in front of the large window, went on up the second flight and found myself in a gallery. Two bare, narrow passages, each with four doors, led off from it, and were lit by opaque glass lamps in the form of cubes. At this same moment a door was opened in the passage on the left, and I only just had time to jump back and take shelter in an archway at the end of the gallery.

I flattened myself against the wall, then cautiously put out my head and saw, standing in the doorway, the young man to whom I had given a lift shortly before and a completely naked woman. The young man's back was turned towards me; the woman was almost facing me. She was tall and well-built, with broad shoulders, robust arms, a long body and strong, firm legs. She had a fine plebeian head: wide-open black eyes, a prominent nose, a wide mouth; all her features, in short, were large and simple. Her hair was dark and grew profusely and thickly on her head, in her armpits and groin; and the half-darkness of the passage brought out the whiteness of her skin in contrast to this darkness. They were standing facing one another; then the young man placed his hands on her shoulders and kissed her – or perhaps bit her – on the neck, and she uttered a cry and twisted her whole body slightly, pressing herself, however, closely against him; then they separated and she said: 'Goodbye, then. But, you know, it frightens me to be left alone in this ugly, dark house.'

He answered in his rough, virile voice: 'If I had my car, I'd take you along. But it looks to me as if it will have to be at the garage for some time.'

'Then wait a little longer. And I can call you a taxi and we'll go together.'

'It doesn't matter, thank you. I'll take the bus. There's a bus stop close by.'

'Why don't you stay? Let's sleep together. It's nice to sleep together.'

'No, I must really go.'

I saw his hand stroking the girl's hip regretfully, almost affectionately, mounting slowly upwards from her leg to her waist. 'I don't know you,' she said, 'I've never seen you before, I don't know who you are, and yet I don't like to let you go. Strange, isn't it?'

'Not so very strange, after all.'

'Why isn't it strange?'

'Oh, well! They do say I know how to do things.'

'Ugh, your vanity! But we'll meet again, promise me we'll meet again.'

'Yes, certainly, I'll telephone the Signora.'

'You say that, but you don't mean it.'

'Yes, I mean it seriously.'

'Why don't you come and meet me at the Alaska Cinema? I work there as an usherette, every day except Sundays and Thursdays. After the show I'm free.'

'Well, I will if I can manage it.'

'I see, you mean you won't come.'

'Yes, I will, if I can manage it.'

'Good-bye, then. And thank you.'

'Thank you for what?'

'Thank you because it's been so good. Good-bye, good-bye.'

He stooped and kissed, or bit, her again on the neck. She wriggled, stifling a laugh, and then, it seemed, put her hand down low and gave him a punch; and he cried out, as if in anger: 'Hey, what are you doing, you hurt me!' and she answered, laughing: 'That's just what I meant to do.' And then, very hurriedly, he said: 'Well, good-bye, see you soon,' and he left her and, with eyes downcast, went to the staircase and disappeared.

I watched her as she went over to the balustrade, leant forward and stood there waving with arm upraised. Then she turned and, leaning her back against the handrail, lifted both arms and stretched and yawned. In her lazy, gluttonous way of stretching herself I sensed her satisfied contentment from the pleasure recently received and given, and I saw that, when she had said: 'It's been so good,' she was not lying. She went slowly back to the door and into the room, and the door closed.

I waited a minute or two, without impatience, reflecting that, if the girl had seen me, apart from a slight surprise nothing would have happened; it would have been just as if two people who did not know one another met in a public place, not like somebody living in a private house discovering that a stranger had slipped in secretly. Finally I came out of my hiding-place and went off down the stairs. Shortly afterwards I was back in my car.

On the way back to Rome I reflected again and realized that my visit to the villa had revealed a reality very different from the fantasies that had suggested my going there. Once inside the villa, I had forgotten Baba and thought of nothing but the two lovers whose leave-taking I had happened to witness. What I had seen had been contradictory to common feeling, which insists that these mercenary encounters have a sordid character. In reality I had penetrated into a kind of temple, open to all, and had spied upon something similar to the last phase of a rite in which, as indeed in all rites, whether religious or non-religious, money, though indispensable, was neither an important nor a determining factor. This, in some way, as a confirmation of what Baba had said about Cora: that her activities were fundamentally disinterested; that she lived in a world which she considered to be the best possible, because the only real, world; and that she was therefore convinced that she was not doing evil, in fact that she was doing good by facilitating other people's sexual relationships – even when it so happened that these were the relationships of her own fourteen-year-old daughter with casual clients.

Thursday, November 12th

One of the unforeseen consequences of my undertaking to keep a diary and planning to extract a novel from it afterwards, is that my behaviour is beginning to come indirectly under the influence of this plan. In other words, when I am on the point of doing something or other, it occurs to me more and more often to ask myself: 'What if this thing which I am about to do, and which, of course, I shall note in my diary, should, in a negative yet irreparable way, alter the novel I am proposing to write later? What if, in fact – to give an example – instead of controlling my indignation and postponing clarification for the moment, I had confronted Cora, as indeed anyone else in my place would have done; should I not perhaps have performed an action which, once it had been reported in the diary, would infallibly have deflected my future novel in the direction of the strip-cartoon or the newspaper serial?'

Here, I think, one can grasp the true advantage of keeping a diary with the object of extracting a novel from it later: the plan does not act as a stimulus, as one might think, to make one perform deliberately determined acts so as then to be able to recount them in the novel – which would be a form of aestheticism, or worse, of cheap journalism; it serves, rather, as a touchstone for everything that is done, and not done, in life. And this confirms what I have already said: for me, the novel has become, with time, a way of understanding my relationship with reality. Incapable of acting in a genuine manner, I re-discover genuineness as if by enchantment as soon as I make the novel a go-between between reality and myself.

This reflection came into my mind today, when I went back in thought to Baba's conduct towards me during these last days. Baba, as I have already said, consciously and consistently and even pedantically wishes that we two should be father and daughter. And, as I have also previously remarked, there is, in the substance of this desire, some profound, yearning quality which partly redeems its deliberately planned character. Yet, perhaps without intending it, she continually places herself and me in ambiguous situations in which we might choose impartially to behave either as father and daughter, or as lovers, or – worse still – as a father and daughter who are lovers.

Furthermore, while all this, with her, is perhaps unconscious and involuntary, with me it is clear and immediate. I know that I am her father or at least ought to be; at the same time I know that I am in love with her and that from time to time I desire, with all my strength, to become her lover.

The ways in which Baba endeavours to be a daughter to me and to make me behave like a father are sometimes truly strange, such as to make one think that she has the opposite aim in view. For instance, it is only rarely that I go out at night because my practice is to write my articles during the evening and until the early hours of the morning. Baba, on the other hand, often goes out with Santoro and with a whole group of students and girls of her acquaintance. Now, since about a week ago, when she comes in late, about midnight or one o'clock, she has developed the habit – as soon as she has undressed and performed her toilet – of coming into my room in her nightdress and throwing her arms round my neck, all of a sudden, coming up behind me on tiptoe and without knocking. What she intends is that this should be her good-night kiss, a family matter and perfectly innocent. But between us two, as usual, it turns out ambiguous.

Her bare arms, cool and rounded, are about my neck; her lips lightly touching my cheek, tickling it gently as they skim across it; her breath, harsh and troubled, travels over my skin; her vigorous, prickly hair titillates my neck and ears. But all this lasts no longer than the time needed to arouse the suspicion of ambiguity. Then, no sooner has the breathless, childish voice said to me: 'Good-night, sleep well,' than Baba has fled away again, as she came, on tiptoe. In reality, as I say to myself each time, she really wanted to wish me good-night; it is not her fault if she did it in such a way as to suggest a different intention.

The temptation is strong, almost irresistible, but each time I manage to control myself in this way: I think of my diary, or rather of the novel I intend to extract from it, and I ask myself what would become of it if I became Baba's lover. I am aware that it may seem strange, incredible and even ridiculous that I should think about a novel I intend writing at the very moment when the woman I love is apparently offering herself to me and when I am violently tempted to take advantage of this; but strangeness, incredibility and absurdity will vanish. I believe, if it is recalled that for me the novel is, as I have said, not a mere literary *genre* but, positively, a way of understanding my relationship with reality. What do I mean by this? I mean that the idea of the novel has become, for me, a kind of conscience, endowed in fact with the proper character of a conscience, that is, the capacity to establish a genuine relationship between myself and external objects. Without the idea of the novel I should not be able to resist the temptation to become Baba's lover and this because, if I did become her lover, it is equally certain that I should not be able, later on, to write the novel.

I say this because I feel with absolute certainty that a love affair with Baba, once it was transferred from the pages of my diary to those of the novel, would lead the latter fatally astray towards the eroticism of a pornographic kind. Thus the project of the novel, being the only sort of conscience that I can make use of, halts me upon a road on which my conscience . . . as a normal man cannot do so. The normal man in me has, in fact, no valid reason to set against this very sweet and tender temptation. The novelist, on the contrary, has such a reason; he is the only one who can say to me: 'Do not do this. If you do it, there reflected as in a mirror, is what you will do.'

But, better perhaps than by these arguments, the truth of what I am saying will be adequately demonstrated by a chapter of my novel which I typed out yesterday evening while I was waiting for Baba to come, as usual, into my room to say good-night to me. Why do I transcribe this chapter? Because I wrote it with the precise intention of having under my eyes, so to speak, all that I should be forced to report in the diary and then in the novel, if I become Baba's lover.

Here, then, is the chapter which I wrote instead of becoming Baba's lover, or rather, in order not to become Baba's lover:

'. . . Again this evening, as every other evening when midnight approaches, I felt that my work was languishing and becoming more and more absent-minded, more and more diaphanous, like a dream in the early morning, when sunlight breaks into the room and its rays penetrate right into the dream and make that which in dreaming seemed reality, appear truly a dream. The sun, in this case, was Baba, or rather my desire for Baba, which, as the moment of her visit approaches, increases and brings a subtle, unconquerable confusion to my mind.

When at last I heard the front door open and there was a sound of someone moving in the darkness of the hall and then, with the usual bear-like awkwardness, bumping against a chair, a sudden idea came to me that I ought to tell her, once and for all, that it would be better for her to stop her midnight visits, which not merely fail to reinforce our father-and-daughter relationship but, on the contrary, serve to weaken and destroy it. No sooner said than done: I rose from my desk, opened the door and, speaking in the dark but in the direction of Baba, whose shadow I could just see in the surrounding shadows, called: 'Baba!'

'Hey, what is it? You frightened me.'

'Baba, come here a moment; there's something I want to say to you.'

Surprised, and immediately pleased, she repeated: 'Something you want to say to me?' Then she stepped forward obediently out of the darkness and walked in front of me into my room. As usual my bed was already turned down: I threw the pyjamas under the pillow, pulled the blankets over it and signed to her to sit down. All this I did in silence because now I suddenly felt agitated to the point of being unable to speak. I watched her as, with slow movements, she took off her sailor jacket, displaying her red sweater and dark blue trousers; then she sat down slightly askew, her elbow on the pillow. She crossed her legs, looked at me in her short-sighted, placid way, and then said: 'Go on, I'm listening.'

I lowered my eyes, and then I saw something which hitherto I had never noticed: between the edge of her trousers and her shoe, round her ankle, a little gold chain caught the light, a rather broad chain which on one side hung down below her ankle-bone. Surprised, I asked her: 'Why, that chain. . . . How long have you been wearing that chain?'

She looked down, gazed at her ankle with a complacent air, and then replied: 'I used to wear it a year ago. Then I stopped wearing it. This morning, I don't know why, I put it on again.'

I went on looking for some time at her rather thick ankle, with the chain dangling crookedly over the ankle-bone – a thing of bad taste, or rather, of a special kind of taste, which inevitably suggested, I thought, both the idea of a slave girl and that of a certain type of rather old-fashioned *femme fatale*. As I looked, I became aware, to my surprise, that my cheeks were burning; and I realized that I no longer had any desire to talk to her about her nocturnal visits, if indeed I had ever had. In the end I said, stupidly: 'Well, what have you been doing this evening?'

'I've been with Santoro and some other friends at a boy's house.'

'What boy?'

'Oh, a University friend.'

'And what did you do?'

'The usual things.'

'And what are they?'

'We listened to records, we danced, we talked.'

'Was it amusing?'

'Yes, of course; why?'

'Oh, nothing. And what did you talk about?'

She looked at me with a hypocritical air and remained silent. I noticed that, owing to the width of the bed and the lack of any support, her body had slipped imperceptibly forwards, so that she was now almost lying flat, her belly offering itself, so to speak, beneath the tightly stretched cloth of her trousers, her legs slightly apart. I was sitting beside her; all of a sudden, with an uncontrollable gesture of impatience, I rose, took a turn round the room and then went and sat down again, not on the bed this time but on the floor, on the carpet, against her legs. Baba finally answered; 'What did we talk about? About all sorts of things. Why, just imagine, we even talked about you.'

'About me?' I uttered these two words in an absent-minded, preoccupied fashion and at the same time put one finger behind the ankle-chain and pulled it a little, as though I wanted to break it. Baba threw me an oblique glance and then replied: 'Yes, about you; there was quite a discussion.'

'What sort of a discussion?'

'Two boy friends of mine attacked you and I was defending you.'

'You defended me?'

'Of course: a daughter has to defend her father.'

I was now sitting with my face against her knees, my arms

raised to clasp her hips and the palms of my hands on the two zip fasteners at the sides of her trousers. Lowering my forehead, I said: 'A daughter has to defend her father, certainly; that's true, perfectly true. And what did these two boys say about me?'

'It's better I shouldn't tell you.'

'Why?'

'It's unpleasant and I oughtn't to repeat it.'

My two hands had grasped the catches of the zip fasteners and were now standing ready, as if awaiting a word of command, to pull them down. I persevered: 'It doesn't matter. I want to know what they said.'

'Well, they were finding fault with you for making a change of front, for going over from the Left to the Right, from a Socialist newspaper to a Conservative one. They said you did it out of self-interest.'

'And what else did they say?'

'But why d'you want to know?'

'Oh well, it interests me.'

'Well, they said that you're a . . . d'you really want to know the exact word?'

'Yes.'

'They said that you're a swindler. Now you know. What advantage d'you get from that?'

Was this possibly the word of command, this 'swindler' insult? I believe so, for, as Baba uttered it, in a rather embarrassed way, as though for her it had a different meaning from the usual one, my hands drew down the catches of the two zip fasteners, sliding them without any hindrance through the double rows of metal teeth; and then the trousers opened on both sides, as if by themselves, like the skin of a fruit, revealing the transparent, creased, pale blue material of the slip. I looked up: Baba was almost flat on her back, supported on her elbows, her chin sunk on her chest, her body thrust forward. Short-sighted, hypocritical perhaps, she might have been thought to be making it a point of honour to ignore what was happening to her own body from the waist downwards. 'A swindler,' I said. 'And you defended me?'

'Yes.'

'Heatedly?'

'Yes.'

'But at the bottom of your heart you agreed with those boys, didn't you?'

'No, I didn't agree.'

'Really and truly?'

'Yes, really and truly.'

I took the two flaps of the trousers at the points of her hips and pulled them down hard. And now, beneath the veil of her slip, appeared, darkly, her navel, like a triangular perforation sunk deep in the plump, youthful flesh of her belly. Another pull, and there was the black triangle, salient and compact, of her groin. My head bowed, I said: 'D'you know what I used to call you, privately, ten years ago, at the time when I couldn't endure to live any longer with Cora?'

'No.'

'I called you "the bastard".'

I raised my eyes and looked at her. She smiled, embarrassed, then said ironically: 'Kind thoughts of a father towards his daughter, eh, Francesco?'

I answered impulsively: 'You're not my daughter.'

'Stepdaughter, anyhow.'

I retorted angrily: 'Neither daughter nor stepdaughter. Nothing but a bastard.'

I looked up again. She was lying down now, her chin glued to her chest, her legs wide apart, naked from waist to knee, and she was smiling at me with a troubled smile, like a suffering animal. Then she pronounced slowly: 'The father undressing his daughter.'

'Do you mind?'

'The stepfather undressing his stepdaughter.'

'Do you mind?'

'The swindler undressing the bastard.'

'Do you mind?'

I saw her shake her head as though she were incapable of speech, and once again I had that painful feeling that she was like a mortally wounded animal. I rose to my feet . . . '

As I have said, I composed this brief chapter yesterday evening in order to become fully aware of what in reality it would mean to me to become Baba's lover. I read it over again and then I wrote a few more pages so as to consign my observations, as I formulated them, to my diary. Here they are:

'The chapter is pornographic, but this pornography consists not so much in the way in which you have described your relationship with Baba as in the relationship itself, which is as it is and which could even be suppressed but not changed. The pornography consists, in particular, in the reasons that make you desire Baba, which are:

1) As soon as Baba arrives home, you rush out and call her, saying you want to speak to her. You pretend to yourself that you want to ask her to stop coming every evening to wish you good-night. But why such a hurry, seeing that Baba will certainly come in later to give you the customary filial kiss? There *is* a reason. Baba is now in sweater and trousers, later she will be in her nightdress. And, since the image of Baba upon which your desire is fixed is that of a girl dressed like a man, you don't want Baba to go and undress. You want Baba to remain in the masculine clothes she has been wearing during the day.

2) The bracelet on her ankle. At first sight, this is an almost insoluble enigma. Baba in fact does not wear, and has never worn, an ankle bracelet. Whence comes, therefore, this mysterious object? It is clear that it comes from something you have seen, something you have noticed, something that has made a sufficient impression upon you for it to remain in the most obscure zone of your memory. It comes, to be precise, from the recollection of similar bracelets observed by you on the ankles of Negro and Indian women during your journeys in Africa and India. The ankles were different from Baba's ankles–dark, thin, bony; the bracelet was a heavy sliver ring; but the underlying idea was the same: the idea of slavery, that is, of woman as an object, as a piece of merchandise, to be bought and sold and possessed, her freedom, her hope of escape, thwarted by means of a chain welded round her ankle.

3) Nevertheless you imagine yourself sitting at Baba's feet, on the floor, so that the sadistic idea of the chained woman is intermingled with the masochistic idea of dependence, of inferiority, of subjection in face of this same woman. Baba is an object, in other words a slave, she wears on her ankle the chain that indicates her character as an object and a slave. But you are the object of this object, you are the slave of this slave.

4) The 'bastard' insult. Here again there is the underlying idea of degrading, of devaluing, and thus of transforming Baba into something of little or no value, into an object, a piece of merchandise. And this through the contempt which,

from time immemorial, has been reserved for illegitimate children. Baba is a bastard, which is equivalent to saying that she is unprotected and available to all, at the mercy of yourself and of anyone who may wish to take his pleasure with her.

5) The 'swindler' insult. You feel a need, at this point, to get yourself insulted in your turn. But here too the real reason is not what it appears to be at first sight. You did not so much wish to punish yourself as, in reality, to get yourself punished by Baba – that is, you once again desired to intermingle the sadism of the insult to Baba with the masochism of the insult to yourself.

6) The father undressing the daughter: the stepfather undressing the stepdaughter; the swindler undressing the bastard. Clearly, there is no need of explanation. Incest judged and condemned the better to practise it. Love conceived as overthrow of restraint and a leap into nothingness.

At this point I stopped writing and thought for a little, then I resumed: 'But even with such feelings and motivations, could you not perhaps avoid pornography? No, you could not. And this is because you have only two roads, both of which lead to pornography, the first to a disguised pornography, the second to an open pornography.

'Surely you could, in fact, do as the traditional novelists did – transform the physical relationship into a psychological relationship; that is, abolish the details of the bracelet, the trousers, the two zip fasteners, the slip, the chemise, the belly, and limit yourself to analysing, in a chaste and subtle manner, merely the feelings, and further, amongst the feelings, merely those that are most indirect and most subordinate. Surely you could. But between you and the traditional novelist there is this difference: they believed in psychology and you do not. If, therefore, you acted like the traditional novelists or, in other words, if you transformed the physical relationship into a pyschological relationship, you would only succeed in creating a mannered psychology or 'psychologism', which is, in essence, a sort of veiled pornography – worse, fundamentally, than open, frank pornography. And so, as I told you, you have only two roads in front of you. At the end of these two roads there still remains pornography.

'But, in conclusion, why pornography? Is not the physical relationship, even if incestuous, a reality like any other reality?'

I stopped for a moment, then I resumed: 'It is pornography because, at the very source of your feelings for Baba and of the physical relationship you might have with her, there is nothing frank or genuine, but something unreal, false, non-genuine in fact, and that is the idea of paternity. This idea is an illusion, but you have need of it in order to love Baba; and you know perfectly well that on the day when you really became her lover you would realize that the illusion had vanished and that Baba was just an ordinary woman, although at the same time she would be something non-genuine, that is, an ordinary woman whom you yet have to regard as your daughter; otherwise you could not love her. Hence the pornography, which is merely a non-genuine representation of the sexual relationship. In conclusion, once again: the falsity lies in the things themselves, before it occurs in the representation of them; and what permits you to recognize it and to avoid it is, in fact, your idea of the novel not as a literary *genre* but as a way of understanding your relationship with reality, or, if you prefer, as conscience. And so, by comparing what you might do with what you would write later on, you are in a position to modify, to direct, to regulate your behaviour. And the novel serves as a touchstone; and the non-genuine remains inside you, in the form of a temptation or a dream; it is not transformed into action and such action, in turn, does not become art – or rather, non-art.

'This amounts to saying: you have a measure for your actions; but this measure, in point of fact, leads you to take no action, the only way, it seems, for you to avoid the non-genuine which is an essential part of any kind of action.'

I wrote all this and then read it through again, and suddenly I felt extremely tired and at the same time almost desperate. I started to undress slowly, straining my ears to every sound. At last, almost automatically, I left my room and went straight to Baba's door. I said to myself: 'Now I shall knock three times. If Baba answers, I shall enter the room, I shall slip into bed beside her and give up the idea of becoming a novelist, once and for all.' I acted accordingly. I knocked three times: the first time gently, the second, louder, the third, louder still. And then I waited, standing at the door, my bare feet on the cold floor. But Baba did not answer; then I went back to my room, got into bed and very soon fell asleep. That night Baba did not come to give me her usual salutation, or perhaps she came and I was unaware of it.

Sunday, November 15th

I had barely finished correcting the typescript of my last article on Iran when Baba came into the room with the dog Tuesday on a lead. For once she was not wearing trousers but was dressed in a black sweater, a narrow flame-red skirt and Cossack boots, black and rather soft, coming up to her knee. She walked straight over to the window and, turning her back on me, stood looking out. I was certain that she had taken up her position there, between the desk and the window, solely in order to get me to admire her boots. Indeed, after a moment, she turned and said: 'Look at my boots; aren't they lovely?'

'They suit you well.'

'D'you know who gave them to me?'

'No, I wouldn't know.'

'*You* did – yes, you.'

'*I* did? What d'you mean?'

'What I mean is, that you *will* give them to me, because I had the bill sent to you. Am I not your daughter, and aren't you my father? It's only right that you should pay my bills.'

She came over to the desk, placed her two hands on the typewriter, contemplated me placidly for a moment, and then went on: 'To inaugurate my boots, I suggest going to lunch at Monte Circeo; what d'you say to that?'

I realized that her proposal pleased me very much, much more than I should have imagined. I could not help thinking: 'Now I shall be able to spend at least eight hours with her.' Trying to disguise my satisfaction, I said: 'All right, let's go.'

'D'you like going out with me?'

For some reason or other her almost hypocritical expression, like that of a little girl laying a trap, aroused a sudden mistrust in me. I answered rather drily: 'Of course. Otherwise I wouldn't come.'

Silence again. Then she said: 'Well then, I'll go and do a little shopping for dinner: I'll come up again and we'll start.' She paused and then added quietly: 'Cora's coming with us, of course.'

I realized I had fallen into the trap. I had been looking forward to a whole day alone with her; and now, instead, there was to be this intrusion by the person whose company I disliked more than any in the world. I could not help exclaiming in irritation: 'But why? Why should Cora come into it?'

'She's not very well. I want her to get some air.'

'But I wanted to be alone with you.'

'You shall be. Cora is very discreet. Once we're on the beach, we'll leave her and go for a walk by ourselves.'

I did not wish to tell her that Cora's discretion disgusted me almost more than her presence: It was the incurably equivocal discretion of the procuress. All I did was angrily to crush out the cigarette I had just lit in the ashtray; then I put my article on Iran into an envelope and sealed it. Baba took possession of the envelope, saying: 'Give it to me, I'll post it for you'; then she went out, dragging Tuesday behind her.

At first I remained sitting at the desk, still in a state of irritation. Then I rose, went to the window and looked down into the street. After a little, Baba came out and I followed her with my eye as, with the dog on the lead, she made her way to the pavement opposite, towards the letter-box. She walked slowly and indolently, hampered by her tight skirt and heavy boots. She posted the letter, walked on to the first turning and disappeared. I went back and sat down in front of the typewriter, lit a cigarette and waited, smoking and looking out through the window at the clouds in the sky. Finally the dog Tuesday came in again, wagging its tail and whining, followed at some distance by Baba. Without turning round, I said to her: 'Listen . . . '

'What is it?'

'I wanted to say: don't think I'm vexed that Cora's coming with us.'

'Why d'you say that to me?'

'Because I protested just now.'

She answered slowly: 'But it's natural you should be vexed that Cora is coming with us. Didn't you say you wanted to be alone with me? Well, I'll go and see if Cora's ready. Wait for me here.'

A little later we were all three of us in the car, on the road that would take us to Monte Circeo, Baba beside me and Cora alone on the back seat. I drove for some time in silence; then at a cross-roads I raised my eyes to the driving-mirror and saw that it was wrongly adjusted, so that, instead of the road, it reflected Cora's face. I was on the point of putting up my hand to straighten it, but a glance at Cora's face stopped me: patchy red beneath the ink-black hair, haggard, the blue eyes painfully prominent and dilated, the big straight nose of a different red from that of the cheeks so that it made you think of a false nose, the mouth contracted into a grimace of unconscious disdain, her face gave the impression of a fixed mask beneath which her real face, wasted and doleful, was concealed. I took a careful look at her, then finally I straightened the mirror and asked: 'How are you today, Cora?'

'How am I? All right.'

'One wouldn't think so.'

'Why?'

'You don't *look* well.'

'Nonsense. I'm perfectly well.'

'Have you a temperature?'

'I haven't taken it.'

'Did you have a temperature yesterday evening?'

'Practically nothing: barely one degree.'

'And the cough?'

'Oh, that! It's much better.'

'What does the doctor say?'

'There's no need of a doctor for a slight temperature and a little cough.'

'Well, I think it would be best for you to send for him.' Baba broke in. 'There, you see: Francesco says so too.'

'You be quiet. I know myself, what's wrong with me: just the results of bronchitis.'

'But after all, why don't you want to send for a doctor?'

'I've a great deal to do. And doctors are all the same: the first thing they advise is a change of air, and I can't leave Rome.'

'But what have you to do?'

'My dressmaking business; the season's just beginning.'

'What season?'

'The winter season.'

I thought that would be the end of the argument, Apart from the dressmaking business, there was the *maison de rendezvous*, of which I was neither able nor willing to speak. However, I said: 'Is the dressmaking business going well?'

'No, it's not going very well; that's another reason why I can't go away from Rome.'

'Why isn't it going well?'

'The customers don't pay.'

'All the more reason, then, for closing it and taking a bit of a rest.'

'You're crazy.'

'Why am I crazy?'

'What does it matter to you about me? Leave me in peace.'

'It does matter to me; you're my wife, after all.'

'Yes, your wife. For ten years you didn't even notice my existence, and now you suddenly discover that I'm your wife.'

'Well, I did wrong. But there's still time to make up for it.'

'No, you're not doing this in order to make up for it, you're doing it to please Baba.'

'How does Baba come into it?'

'It's she who would like me to close the dressmaking business, call in the doctor and even perhaps to leave Rome. And you're in league with her.'

I felt Baba's hand pressing my arm, as much as to say: 'Leave it at that.' But I paid no attention to her. 'Why,' I insisted, 'don't you believe we're concerned for your health?'

'Baba is, yes. But you are, only to please Baba.'

'What d'you mean by that?'

'I mean what I say.'

'And that is . . . ?'

'The better you understand, the less you need to say.'

'In other words, you're implying that I have a feeling for Baba which is not entirely paternal.'

'I don't mean that. I only mean that all this fuss you're making is not on my account, as you'd have me believe, but just to please Baba.'

At this point Baba stopped me from continuing the squabble by intervening hastily, with a sort of affectionate, calculated authority. 'No, no,' she said, 'it's all nonsense, of course; there's not a word of truth in it. I assure you, Mum, Francesco is advising you to consult a doctor for your own good. That's the truth, isn't it, Francesco?'

I felt her pressing my arm. 'Certainly it is,' I said.

'And you, Mum, don't be alarmed; no one's telling you to close down the dressmaking business and leave Rome, nor even to consult a doctor. You can go on living your usual life, and you'll see, your temperature will go down of its own accord.'

There was a brief silence, then Cora said mumblingly: 'I've no need of anybody. I can make up my mind myself.'

'Of course: you must make up your mind about everything yourself. And we three are a family, mother, father and daughter, and now you must show that you don't bear any grudge against Francesco by stroking his cheek. And you, Francesco, shake Cora's hand.'

I wanted to shout: 'No, stop!' But I was too late: she had jumped into a kneeling position on the seat, and twisted round towards Cora, seized her hand and placed it against my cheek. 'Why, what's come into your head?' said Cora. Nevertheless she did not withdraw her hand. With a renewed feeling of repugnance I felt Cora's hand on my cheek, but I went on driving unperturbed; while her hand, impelled by Baba, opened out, clung to my face, stroked it. The palm was damp with sweat, as is natural for anyone with a fever. Baba said: 'Come on, Francesco, shake Cora's hand.' So I lifted my hand, took hold of Cora's, hesitated, and then, with an effort, carried it to my lips. Cora giggled nervously and said: 'No, no, that's enough.' I realized that actually she was pleased, whether because of the kiss or because I had stopped insisting on her consulting a doctor and closing down the dressmaking business, I don't know. Then Cora withdrew her hand and said to her daughter: 'You're a clever one, you are,' – an ambiguous remark that might be equally well attributed to maternal effection or to the profesional appraisal of a procuress.

I felt it necessary to interrupt, somehow or other, this intolerable scene, so I put out my hand and turned on the radio. Then I drove on at a high speed along the straight road with big, crooked pine-trees on either side, meeting the dark, flying banners of the cloud-covered sky. At last we came to the round building at the entrance to Latina, then to the road, flanked with eucalyptus-trees, which leads to Borgo Sabotino, and finally, after a bumpy ride over uneven asphalt, to the houses of Lido di Latina. I turned away along the sea, with the sand-dunes on the right and on the left the marshes. Far away, against a sky full of tangled clouds like the convolutions of an exposed intestine, above a calm, shining sea, rose the misty, shadowy outline of Monte Circeo. I turned in at a lay-by, stopped and turned off the engine.

After a little I put out my hand and shut off the radio. Silence followed and then I realized, from the stillness of the broom-brushes on top of the dunes, that there was not a breath of wind: nothing but the thunderstorm hanging inertly over the sea. 'Let's get out and go for a walk. It's too early for lunch.'

'Come on, then.'

We got out, and the dog rushed forward and disappeared at full speed in the direction of the sea; we followed it, walking over the sand by a path that wound between the dunes. When we came to the top of the dunes, I admired the cold, startling clarity of colour produced by the lack of sunshine and the low ceiling of clouds; the opaque whiteness of the sand, like pumice-stone, the grassy green of the sea; the vivid blackness of the lines of jetsam along the beach. I noticed also that, in contrast with the excitment and the barking of the dog as it ran and jumped about us, the silence and stillness of the day appeared to have become more profound. I stopped a moment to gaze at the sea: a curious ridge of glassy, sparkling water suddenly swelled up, grew larger as it travelled on, broke for a moment into a small crest of foam, then, immediately afterwards, re-absorbed the crest of foam, gradually flatened out and disappeared under the surface without reaching the shore. I said to Baba: 'Let's hurry up and take our walk, it's going to rain.'

Baba answered: 'I'll run on, you catch me up.' She rushed down from the dunes together with the dog, shouting with joy and taking great leaps into the air, her black boots in the white sand. I hesitated, aware of Cora just behind me. But Cora said: 'Go on, take your walk. I shall lie on the sand and wait for you.'

'Won't you be cold?'

'No, it isn't cold. Go along with Baba.'

I watched her as she walked away and then, without choosing any particular spot, lay down on the beach, on her side, leaning on her elbow. She was wearing a dress of her favourite colour, red; and this red, dark in tone and yet bright, suddenly, in that lifeless air, stood out against the sand like a heap of burning embers thinly veiled with ash. With a look of absorption, her head bowed, she took up a little sand in her fist and let it trickle back on to the ground. I went over to her and asked: 'Don't you feel well?'

'I'm all right, but I don't feel like walking.'

'Baba and I will take a little stroll and come back.'

'Yes, go on, go on.'

She coughed two or three times, then took a packet of cigarettes out of her bag and placed one between her lips. I bent down, held out my lighter and struck a flame. She lit her cigarette, inhaled and then blew the smoke out through her nostrils—all this without raising her head. I hesitated and then, in silence, joined Baba who was standing waiting for me some distance away.

We walked for some time without speaking. At last I said:

'D'you know?'

'What?'

'I went a few days ago into Cora's villa on Via Cassia.'

'What for?'

'I don't know. Perhaps because I remembered that six years ago Cora took you to her *maison de rendezvous*.'

'But that wasn't the villa on Via Cassia. It was a flat, in quite a different place.'

'Where?'

'Why d'you want to know?'

'No special reason; I just want to know.'

'The name of the street I don't know, nor yet the number, but I could walk there blindfold.'

'But where is it?'

'If you like, we'll go out together tomorrow and I'll take you and show you the house.'

'Tell me: when was it that Cora took you into the house?'

'Let's see, when was it: it must have been in March 1957.'

'You told me that you didn't go there more than seven or eight times. Isn't that so?'

'Yes.'

'And when was it that Cora finally gave up the idea of taking you there?'

'About May, I think.'

'So the whole thing didn't last more than two or three months.'

'That's right.'

'But those two or three months were important for you, weren't they?'

'You mean for the Baba of that time.'

'Yes, for the Baba of that time.'

'Yes, they were important.'

'It was then that her eyes changed—isn't that so?'

'Her eyes? What ever d'you mean, her eyes?'

'I met Baba one day in the lift—it was certainly in 1957, and it was before March—and her eyes were different.'

'How can you be sure that it was before March?'

'Because it had been snowing, a thing that hardly ever happens in Rome, and I remember that meeting with Baba precisely because there was snow that day. I was already in the lift, and Baba suddenly joined me there before I closed the door. She was wearing ski-ing clothes, with trousers tied round the ankles and a black sweater. She was out of breath and she leant against the wall of the lift, and while we were going down she looked at me intently. She stuck out her chest, and she was hiding something behind her back, holding it with both hands. I was struck by her eyes.'

'What were her eyes like?'

'They were lively and bright, fresh, innocent, childish. Then the lift stopped at the ground floor and Baba ran out in front of me and then I saw what she was hiding behind her back: a little shovel to shovel away the snow.'

'Well, that may be. As for her eyes, it's simple: a year after that Baba began to be short-sighted and since then she's worn glasses.'

'But she had a different look in her eyes.'

'Are you quite sure of that?'

'Yes, I think so. But it doesn't matter. Let's go back to those two or three months which, it seems, were so important for Baba. Tell me, anyhow, why they were important.'

'Oh, for all sorts of reasons.'

'Certainly not because they shook her affection for Cora.'

'No, not that.'

'Nor because, fundamentally, they changed her life.'

'No; nothing, in fact, has changed.'

'Then why were they important?'

'It's difficult to say. They were important, and that's enough.'

'No, it isn't enough. Now listen to me.'

'I *am* listening to you. For some time I've been doing nothing else.'

'No, you shouldn't answer me like that; try and think.'

'About what?'

'About the importance that those months had for Baba. What kind of importance was it?'

'Well, let us say that Baba had an experience.'

'If she had an experience, then it isn't true that there's no connection between that Baba and yourself; to have an experience means to develop and at the same time to be still fundamentally oneself.'

'Why? A man may be run over by a car and after a few hours die in hospital. That man has had an experience, the experience of being run over by a car, but then he has died and therefore it can't be said that he has developed and continued to be himself. He hasn't developed at all and he has never been himself again.'

'I see. You mean that after that experience the Baba of that time died; and since then there has been a new and different Baba; isn't that so?'

'Yes.'

'And what was this experience which was so important?'

'It was the experience—how shall I say?—of being a mere thing.'

'A thing?'

'Yes, a thing, an object.'

'What kind of an object?'

'Just an ordinary object. A chair, let us say, or a vase.'

'But when was it that Baba had the experience of being, as you say, an object? When Cora took her to the house?'

'Not exactly. When Cora took Baba to the house, Baba, actually, still considered herself a person. And it's quite true to say that she was ready to do what Cora had told her.'

'Quite true, was it?'

'Yes, because Baba still thought it was up to her to do or not to do what she had been told by Cora.'

'But what had Cora told her to do?'

'Well, let us suppose she had said something like this: "We're going now to a certain place and I shall introduce you to someone who wants to meet you; try and be nice to him and whatever he does, let him do it".'

'So Baba was ready to do this; and why?'

'Because it was Cora who had told her to, and Cora was her mother.'

'But did Baba not have any feeling of – let us say – surprise?'

'No. It must be said at this point that Baba was then a stupid creature who didn't understand anything—and above all who didn't understand that she didn't understand.'

'You told me, however, that nobody came, the first time. When was it that Baba had the experience of being a mere thing? The second time?'

'Yes.'

'During the love-making?'

'There wasn't any love-making, nothing but embarrassment. No, it was when it was all over and the man had gone away.'

'Why?'

'The man had been with Baba for perhaps an hour, he had talked to her, he had made love, or rather had tried to do so. Then he dressed and went out, saying he was going to telephone, but he didn't come back. Baba, who had gone to the window and was looking out into the street, saw him emerge from the main door, get into his car and drive away. Then she turned back into the room and had the feeling that between herself and the furniture there was no difference. That man hadn't come back to say good-bye to her, just as he hadn't come back to say good-bye to the armchair or the bedside lamp.'

'What does that mean? That Baba expected him to say good-bye to her?'

'Yes.'

'Why?'

'Because, although she had no particular feeling about him and scarcely understood what he wanted of her, Baba had believed that she had some sort of relationship with that man, as between one person and another. You know, if the man had come back to say good-bye, Baba might perhaps have even been able to make love with him?'

'She was very affectionate, then, at that time.'

'No, she wasn't affectionate: it was just that she believed that there ought to be some relationship between people.'

'So it's only necessary *not* to say good-bye to someone in order to inspire the feeling of being an object?'

'Yes, that's enough, at least in certain circumstances. But there was also another thing.'

'What was that?'

'When Baba turned back into the room and had the feeling that there was no difference between herself and the armchair, she also saw, on the marble top of the chest-of-drawers, a banknote folded in four which the man had placed there as he went out, without her noticing it. Then the feeling of being an object and nothing more than an object became – how shall I say? – more real, more concrete. An object can be bought and sold, can't it? And so . . . '

'I understand. And what sort of feeling is it, that of being an object?'

'Much the same as any other feeling.'

'Unpleasant?'

'Not necessarily. For Baba it was, because she did not know she was just an object and stupidly flattered herself that she was something else, and so in a way she had a disappointment. But I suppose it might even be pleasant and that one might actually desire to have this feeling, if only out of curiosity. It depends on the person, of course.'

'Let's go back to Baba discovering the money on the chest-of-drawers and experiencing the feeling of being an object. What did she do then? Did she call Cora?'

'No, Cora wasn't there.'

'What, Cora wasn't in the flat?'

'No.'

'Where was she, then?'

'She went away immediately after she had brought the man into the room; she went out, telling Baba she would come back in an hour's time.'

'I see. What did Baba do, then, when she was left alone?'

'She found plenty to do.'

'What?'

'In the first place she carefully tidied up the room. She re-made the bed, put the bedside rug back in place, picked up the pieces of the little envelope that had contained the contraceptive, also the contraceptive itself which had not been used, and threw them into the waste-paper basket. Then she went on to tidy herself up with the same scrupulousness and the same care. She went into the bathroom, undressed, soaped herself under the shower, combed her hair and finally went and sat in the armchair; then she turned up the volume of the radio and waited for Cora.'

'So there was a radio?'

'Yes, there was a radio; it had been on all the time, with a programme of light music, but very quietly. There was a fireplace too, and the fire was burning. There was everything, in fact.'

'Did she wait long?'

'Yes, about an hour.'

'And what did Baba think, during that hour?'

'She didn't think anything. What does an object think, what *can* an object think? Nothing.'

'Why, did she go on having the feeling of being an object?'

'No, by this time she'd stopped having the feeling of being an object, she *was* an object.'

'What d'you mean?'

'I mean that, from that moment until two or three months later, that is, until Cora finally gave up the idea of putting Baba up for sale, Baba stopped thinking altogether. She was an object and she behaved like an object.'

'How does an object behave?'

'It doesn't behave at all.'

'What d'you mean?'

'Well, it just sits there . . . It sits there, that's all.'

'Yes, I see. And when Cora came back, what did she say?'

'She said: "Has he gone away?"'

'And what did Baba answer?'

'She answered: "Yes, he's gone away".'

'And what did Cora say then?'

'She said: "Isn't it true that he's a very charming, gentlemanly man?"'

'And what did Baba answer?'

'She answered: "He left the money."'

'And what did Cora do?'

'She took the money.'

'In what way?'

'In the simplest sort of way, like something that belonged to her. Without any concealment or haste.'

'And then?'

'Then Cora and Baba went home again.'

'And what did they say?'

'Baba didn't say anything. It was Cora who talked.'

'Really?'

'Yes. She explained her philosophy of life to Baba,'

'And what was it?'

'Baba was only half listening. In short, the substance of what she said was that in life there's only one thing.'

'What thing?'

'The thing that had happened, or rather that hadn't happened, between Baba and the man, just before.'

'How did she say it?'

'She spoke in an earnest, overwrought, excitable, emotional tone; she seemed to be beside herself; it was the first time Baba had ever known her talk so much and with such direct, profound sincerity.'

'But where was Baba and Cora while they were talking?'

'In the car. Cora was driving and talking. She never stopped talking the whole time – a kind of monologue.'

'And Baba – what did she think of the things Cora said?'

'She didn't think anything. I've already told you.'

'Why do you think Cora absented herself while Baba was with the man?'

'I don't know. She only did so that day. On the other occasions, I think she waited in the sitting-room. Perhaps it was in order to give Baba the impression that she was acting in complete freedom, that it was she herself who wished to be an object. That it was she who had chosen to be a mere thing.'

Our conversation was interrupted at this point by the sound of joyful and, in a sort of way, voluptuous barking. We looked up and saw that the dog Tuesday had thrown himself on the ground on his back, paws in air, and was rubbing himself against something that appeared, from a distance, to be a small ridge or a heap of sand. Baba shouted: 'Tuesday!' and rushed towards the dog. As she ran, she said: 'He has a passion for rolling in any kind of filth. Then he stinks and I have to give him a bath.' So, both of us running, we reached the ridge; Baba chased the dog off with blows of the lead, and then, for a moment, we stopped to see what the thing was that the dog had been rubbing against.

It was a carcase, possibly of a sheep, half buried beneath the fine white sand. Part of the carcase projected above the surface, swollen, of a bluish whiteness, glistening with putrefaction under the glassy skin; tufts of wool still remained here and there; the head lay lolling back in an unnatural position, the eye-sockets full of sand and the yellow teeth still clenched. I looked at the carcase, then I looked at the beach stretching white and cold and empty under the low clouds to the furthest horizon, and I saw again the reddish heap formed by Cora as she lay on her side over there below the sand-dunes. And then I could not prevent the inevitable thought taking shape in my mind that there was an analogy between the sheep's carcase and the motionless mass of Cora's body; and I dwelt, not without some satisfaction, upon the physical resemblance which, as often happens, suggested a moral resemblance: both of them inert and corrupt, the sheep in the literal sense, Cora in the metaphorical. After that, for some reason, I thought about the effect which such a comparison would make in my imaginary novel, and I said to myself that it would make an extremely bad effect, as of something stale and in poor taste, such as might occur to a mediocre, old-fashioned writer; and suddenly, as though by enchantment, I ceased to see any resemblance, either physical or moral, between the sheep's carcase and Cora's body; the first seemed to me a sheep's carcase and nothing more, the second a recumbent human figure and nothing more; and I was ashamed of having thought that they resembled one another; and I was grateful to my project of writing a novel, which had served me as a conscience and had awakened this sense of shame in my mind.

Then I looked up and saw that Baba was now playing with Tuesday, running hither and thither along the shore and being chased by the dog which was jumping up and down and barking excitedly. Then Baba picked up a piece of wood and threw it a long way away; and Tuesday rushed after it to fetch it. Black in a cloud of white sand, he went frolicking in the direction in which Baba had thrown the piece of wood, but failed to find it because in the meantime a wave had carried it away. Baba came up to me, breathless and red-cheeked; but with her eyes, as usual, fixed and expressionless and drugged-looking because of her short sight. 'Did you see?' she said; 'the dog's playing. It's the first time he's ever played. Up till now he's always been rather depressed.'

'He's forgotten the kennels at Porta Portese,' I replied.

'He hasn't forgotten them; he's a different dog.'

'Just as you're a different Baba.'

'Yes, but more so than me. I still call myself by the same

name as the stupid little girl who allowed Cora to lead her by the hand to that house. But the dog—goodness knows what his name was. But he now answers already to the name I've given him.'

We went across to Cora. She was still lying on the sand, a reddish mass on a shore that was white and cold under the ceiling of black clouds. She did not move, even when we came close to her: she was reclining on her side, her eyes downcast, two limp locks of hair hanging across her cheeks. Without raising her head, she asked: 'Have you finished your walk?'

'Yes, and what have *you* been doing?'

'I haven't done anything, I was just waiting for you.'

'Let's go and eat. Get up now, it's time.'

For a moment, before she rose, she lay quite still as though she were thinking over what I had said to her; and suddenly I had a feeling of someone who, for some reason or other, has lost all sense of reality. I wondered whether even those simple words: 'Let's go and eat' did not perhaps appear incomprehensible to her and wholly unrelated to what she was and what she was doing at that moment. And now she was thinking it over, in order to establish this connection, in order to throw a bridge across the gulf that separated her from the world to which those words belonged. Then there was a hollow, genial roll of thunder, and the thunder rolled over the flat green surface of the sea like a wooden ball on a resounding floor. Finally Cora stirred and rose to her feet, and walked back with us towards the sand-dunes.

Monday, November 16th

It doesn't interest you to know what goes on in Cora's house and how these things are done and what are the reasons for them and what is their meaning and importance. It is up to you not so much to explain as to *live* these things, that is to identify ourself with them to *be*, one by one, Cora selling her daughter, Baba being sold, the client who buys Baba and even perhaps the bed upon which Baba and the client lay together, and the window from which Baba looked into the street and saw the client going away, and the colour of the top of the client's car seen from above, and the feel of the marble window-sill under Baba's hands, and then the silence in the flat while Baba was tidying up the room, and finally the splashing of the shower on Baba's bare body and her eyes in the looking-glass while she looked at herself combing her hair. You don't require to know anything about the *why* of things; what you require is to identify yourself with the *how*. And your novel, if ever you write it, will be made up of these identifications. And with one identification after another you will perhaps even be able to give the illusion of a sequence of events, of a prolonged happening; but it will be pure illusion because you do not believe in action and in the relationships that provoke and justify action; and all that you can do is, indeed, to identify yourself progressively with what *is*, without taking into account *why* it is.

But at the same time, in contradiction to this, you cannot help attributing significances both to things and to events, transforming persons into symbols, ordering and relating significances and symbols according to ideological systems. And so, inevitably, Baba, Cora, you yourself and what you have done, or rather have not done, and what Cora did to Baba, and what Baba suffered—all these become charged, in your mind, with significance, are transformed into metaphors, are in perpetual danger of losing the weight and density of their reality and of becoming interchangeable parts of a single abstract argument.

Tuesday, November 17th

As she had promised, Baba conducted me today to the house to which she had been taken by Cora six years ago. From Piazza Mazzini, where we live, we went to Viale Giulio Cesare, drove up it past the traffic lights, went on a little farther, and then Baba said: 'Slow down now, it should be a street off here to the left. There, this is it.'

It was a street with featureless blocks of flats on either side; as I turned into it Baba put on her glasses, looked about her and then said: 'You see that butcher's shop with the white marble sign and two bullocks' heads with gold horns at each side of the sign? Well, it's not the door just beside that but the one immediately beyond. That's it.'

I said nothing; there was an empty space a little beyond the door, and I went and parked the car there. I stopped the engine and looked at Baba. She had taken off her glasses, and she looked back at me and said: 'Why have you stopped? What d'you want to do?'

'Let's imagine,' I replied, 'that it's *that* day. Baba has arrived by car with Cora. What happened then?'

'Cora stopped some distance away; you see that baker's shop over there? Well, it was right in front of that.'

'So Baba and Cora had to cross the street?'

'Yes, they crossed the street.'

'How did they do that?'

'What d'you mean?'

'Were they side by side, or some distance from one another, or did Cora walk in front of Baba?'

'Side by side. Cora was holding Baba's hand.'

'Holding her hand?'

'Yes, holding her hand. Baba, in fact, since it was some time since Cora had held her hand, remembered, at that moment, the time when Cora had held her hand often.'

'When was that?'

'When she was small.'

'And what did Baba think of the fact that Cora was holding her hand?'

'Cora had already told her that in that house she was going to meet a gentleman who wanted to know her and to whom she must be kind. Baba thought Cora was holding her hand because she was afraid she might run away.'

'But did Baba know what that remark of Cora's really meant?'

'Which remark?'

'That she must be kind.'

'She knew and she didn't know. In theory she knew what it was, in practice she didn't.'

'Well, go on.'

'Baba and Cora crossed the street, they went to the door and went in, the portress looked out and said "Good day" and Cora answered "Good day". Then they walked up three floors.'

'Wasn't there a lift?'

'No, it was out of order.'

'And then?'

'And then they reached the third floor, and a door without any name-plate. Cora opened the door and they went into the flat.'

'Cora didn't speak?'

'She said there was a stink of smoke inside the flat and she was angry with the portress who, she said, couldn't have done the cleaning that day. She went and opened the windows to let in some air.'

'What did Baba do in the meantime?'

'She sat and waited alone in the sitting-room, while Cora was coming and going about the flat.'

'What was she waiting for?'

'This gentleman. Cora had said to her: "Wait here, he won't be long." '

'And then, did he come?'

'No, he didn't come. I've told you already, the first time nobody came.'

'But how can you be sure that nobody came?'

'Anyhow nobody came into the sitting-room. After a little Cora looked in and said : "I'm going out and I'll be back in about an hour. Leave the door ajar for this gentleman. Don't worry; just wait." Baba said she was all right; Cora went away; but nobody came.'

'It may be that the gentleman came and then, for some reason of his own, went away again without Baba being aware of it. How was Baba sitting in the room?'

'What?'

'I mean: in what position, how was she placed in relation to the door?'

'There was a group of furniture consisting of a sofa and two armchairs, against the wall, right opposite the door. Baba was sitting in one of the armchairs.'

'With her face or her back to the door?'

'Her back.'

'Why?'

'She didn't wish to look the gentleman in the face at the moment when he came in.'

'For what reason?'

'It may seem strange to you: because she felt curiosity and at the same time did not want to show that she was curious. She wanted to give the impression that she was not curious, that it was not the first time, that she was, in fact, self-possessed and open-minded.'

'Well, you see, somebody might have opened the door very gently behind Baba's back, looked into the room and then gone away, and Baba wouldn't have noticed it.'

'Yes, perhaps that's what happened.'

'Why d'you think the man went away again?'

'Goodness knows; perhaps he had a look at Baba and didn't like her.'

'But how could he see her, since Baba had her back turned to him?'

'There was a big looking-glass right in front of Baba, hanging above the sofa.'

'Then Baba also saw the man?'

'No, she didn't see him because she never looked in the looking-glass. She wanted to be seen, yes, but she didn't want to see.'

'But why?'

'For the same reason again: because she wished to show that she wasn't curious. But perhaps, now I come to think of it, there was another reason too.'

'And what was that?'

'Baba felt she was on the point of becoming an object. An object exhibited in order to be looked at, valued, appraised. So Baba kept her eyes lowered and didn't look at the looking-glass, because deep down in her mind was the idea that she shouldn't disturb anyone who was looking at her, that she should show herself, exhibit herself, allow herself to be appraised. Just as an object.'

'But what was Baba doing?'

'Cora had given her a magazine. An illustrated magazine. She slowly turned the pages, one after the other, examining each photograph with care, and all the time with ears strained to hear if anyone was coming. She must have looked through the magazine from beginning to end at least a dozen times.'

'How was she sitting?'

'In a composed sort of way, with her legs crossed and her elbows on the arms of the chair. She thought she ought to maintain a well-bred attitude so as to make a good impression.'

'And how long did she wait like this, holding the magazine?'

'A very long time. Her legs and arms were aching and her

neck was hurting her too. In the end – she must have been waiting for almost an hour – she got up and went on a tour of exploration round the flat. There was no one there. There were four rooms and all four were empty.'

'Was the door of the flat still ajar?'

'Yes.'

'What did Baba do then?'

'She sat down again in the sitting-room and waited for Cora to come back but this time she sat on the sofa opposite the door.'

'Why?'

'Because she wanted to see Cora's face when she arrived and found out that nobody had come.'

'But why?'

'Goodness knows. Perhaps in order to understand why Cora was so anxious for her to meet this gentleman.'

'Did she wait long?'

'No, not long, less than an hour.'

'And when Cora arrived what did she do, what did she say?'

'She didn't show any surprise; she merely asked: "Did he come?"'

'And Baba – what did she answer?'

' "No he didn't come." '

'What did Cora say then?'

' "I expected that." '

'Was that all?'

'No she also said: "He must have been afraid." '

'She said that?'

'Yes.'

'But what was the expression on her face?'

'No expression at all. Cora knows how to hide her feelings.'

'And then what did she do?'

'She said: "Wait a moment; I'll telephone now to someone else and we'll see if he can come".'

'And then?'

'Then she went out of the room to the telephone.'

'Where?'

'In the entrance hall.'

'So Baba heard the telephone conversation?'

'Certainly. The door was left open.'

'What did she say on the telephone?'

'She dialled a number then after a little asked who was speaking, whether it was Riccardo, and then began to press him urgently to come.'

'How exactly?'

'She said: "Quickly, quickly, come here at once quickly; I've something that would just suit you; quickly get into your car and come." '

'How did her voice sound?'

'Pressing, urgent, determined, the voice of someone who wants to settle an affair at all costs.'

'Yes, I understand. Then what happened?'

'Riccardo, on the telephone, presumably answered that he couldn't come at that moment. Cora said: "What a pity, I had it all ready for you here." '

'And then?'

'Then they came to an understanding. Cora said: "All right today at five o'clock".'

'And after that?'

'She came back into the sitting-room and said to Baba: "This one will certainly come. Today at five o'clock." '

'You hadn't told me that the second visit occurred on the same day.'

'You didn't ask me.'

'But what time was it at that moment?'

'Midday.'

'What did Baba think while Cora was telephoning?'

'She didn't think anything.'

'Are you sure?'

'Yes.'

'Why was that?'

'Because she knew that when Cora said: "Something that would just suit you" she was alluding to her. And that remark was all that was needed to turn her as if by magic into a thing, an object, in other words a mere body without thought.'

'In short, she was satisfied?'

'No, she wasn't satisfied.'

'Dissatisfied?'

'Not that either.'

'But the fact that that first client had failed to arrive – what feeling did it arouse in her? Relief?'

'No.'

'Disappointment?'

'Not that either.'

'Well then?'

'Let's say – a feeling of being annoyed with herself.'

'Why?'

'Because she remembered having done all that play-acting in front of the looking-glass and she was annoyed at having done it for nothing.'

'I see. And then what happened between midday and five o'clock?'

'Nothing special happened.'

'What did Cora and Baba do?'

'They left the flat, went downstairs and returned home in the car.'

'And at home, what happened?'

'They had lunch.'

'What did Cora say? Did she talk?'

'She didn't say much. At one moment she said: "Don't pull a long face; for one that didn't turn up, there'll be a hundred others that do. The one you'll meet today, anyhow, is much better; you'll see, he's a really charming person." '

'What did Baba reply?'

'She didn't say anything.'

'Why?'

'She was worried now because, as it was Sunday, a girl friend of hers was to come and do some homework with her that afternoon, and she didn't know what to do.'

'So what?'

'Generally the friend used to stay until supper-time.'

'What did Baba do then?'

'She told Cora.'

'And what was Cora's answer?'

'She said that Baba could perfectly well be with her friend until half past four and then send her away.'

'Didn't she say anything else?'

'No.'

'And afterwards what happened?'

'Baba went to her room and waited there until her friend came. The friend came about two o'clock, and Baba and she went through the lesson together.'

'What was the subject?'

'Italian.'

'Written or oral Italian?'

'Oral. The poetry of Leopardi.'

'Did the lesson go well?'

'Yes, very well indeed.'

'But wasn't Baba absent-minded?'

'No, not at all, she was only worried because she was afraid there wouldn't be time enough before half past four.'

'Time enough for what?'

'For going through the lesson.'

'And then?'

'At twenty-five minutes past four Baba told her friend that she had to go out with Cora, her friend said good-bye and Baba went with her to the door. But the friend stayed there chattering and ten minutes went by, and Baba was on tenterhooks because she knew Cora was waiting. At last the friend went away and Cora at once popped out from the passage and said something disagreeable to Baba.'

'What did she say?'

'Something like: "You chatterbox, I told you to be ready by half past four." Nothing special, but the tone was disagreeable.'

'What kind of tone was it?'

'A tone of impatience. Baba wanted to go back and wash her hands because one hand was stained with ink, but Cora said there wasn't time; she seized her by the arm and pushed her out violently on to the landing and almost made her fall down. Baba was upset.'

'Very much upset?'

'No, only a little, and perhaps more astonished than mortified. Cora seemed nearly beside herself, and this was something new because usually she controlled herself very well. So they went down to the ground floor and drove off in the car to the flat.'

'Did Cora say nothing while they were in the car?'

'No, nothing. She still seemed to be in a rage.'

'And then?'

'Then everything went as in the morning. Cora stopped the car in front of the baker's shop, she held Baba's hand as they crossed the street, they went up together to the third floor, went into the sitting-room, then Cora said she was going into the kitchen to make herself a cup of coffee and went out, leaving the door of the room open.'

'And was there long to wait, this time?'

'No. Baba waited about ten minutes, then she heard the front-door bell ring and Cora went to answer it.'

'Who was it?'

'It was Riccardo. This time Baba was standing by the window. She didn't see him but she heard him talking to Cora.'

'What did they say?'

'Cora said: "You're early. We were expecting you in a quarter of an hour's time; you're lucky to find us." '

'And what was Riccardo's reply to that?'

'He replied that he'd miscalculated the distance between his house and Cora's. He added: "But is this thing here?" '

'What thing?'

'He meant Baba. The "thing" was Baba.'

'What did Cora answer?'

'She answered: "Yes, of course. Come in here in the meantime, and I'll bring her to you at once." '

' "In here" – what was that?'

'In the bedroom.'

'And what did he do?'

'He went in, as Cora had told him.'

'And then?'

'Then Cora looked into the sitting-room and whispered to Baba: "Come on, come along, he's arrived." '

'And what did Baba do?'

'Baba got up and followed Cora.'

'Where?'

'Into the bedroom. The door was open, Riccardo was sitting on the bed and Cora led Baba into the room and said: "This is Gabriella." '

'Gabriella, not Baba.'

'Yes.'

'Why?'

'I don't know.'

'And what happened next?'

'What happened was that Cora told Baba that she was going out as she had things to do, and that in the meantime Baba must keep the gentleman company. With these words Cora went out, shutting the door behind her, and Baba was left alone with Riccardo.'

'D'you mind telling me what happened after that?'

'I don't mind in the least. I've told you so many times: it happened to someone else, not to me.'

'Well then, where were we?'

'We were at the point when Cora had gone away, the door was shut, Baba was standing in front of Riccardo and Riccardo was sitting on the bed.'

'What did Riccardo do next?'

'He was very gentle and very nice to Baba; he took her hand, drew her towards him and asked her a number of questions.'

'What were the questions?'

'I imagine they're the usual ones that are asked in such cases: how old she was, in the first place.'

'And what did Baba answer to that?'

'She added a year to her age; she told him she was fifteen.'

'Why?'

'I don't know. Perhaps because she always did so.'

'And after that what did he ask her?'

'Whether Baba went to school.'

'Whether she went to school?'

'Yes, he took Baba's hand which was stained with ink and asked her if she had got it dirty like that while she was studying. And Baba said yes. And then he asked her whether she went to school.'

'And what did Baba answer?'

'She answered that she did.'

'And did he then ask other questions?'

'Yes, a number of them, but especially about the school.'

'About the school?'

'Yes, he wanted to know everything: Baba's class, the subjects she was studying, the teacher, the other girls, everything. Even the marks that Baba scored in each subject.'

'In what way did Riccardo talk to Baba?'

'How d'you mean "in what way"?'

'What was his voice like while he was speaking?'

'Oh, normal, calm, detached, even rather leisurely.'

'What else?'

'Finally Riccardo asked Baba to recite a poem to him.'

'What poem?'

'Any sort of poem.'

'And what poem did Baba recite?'

'She recited a poem by Leopardi which she had been going through shortly before with her friend: *Saturday in the Village*.'

'Where was Baba while she was reciting?'

'She was standing in front of Riccardo, with her hand in his.'

'What was Baba thinking?'

'She thought Riccardo was kind and agreeable.'

'Agreeable?'

'Yes.'

'But didn't she realize that the object of this conversation was not that of being, as you say, kind and agreeable?'

'Perhaps she did realize it. But it didn't matter.'

'Why not?'

'It's difficult to say. Perhaps because much the most important thing for Baba was to be taken seriously, that is, to be treated as the person she was or anyhow believed she was, and not as the object she still didn't know she had become. If Riccardo had treated her, right up to the end, as a person, who knows? – Baba might even have been able to do what he afterwards wanted.'

'Instead of which, how did he treat her?'

'I told you the other day: as an object.'

'And how was that?'

'Baba was in the middle of explaining something to do with the school, I don't remember what – ah yes, the fact that she was behindhand and would probably have to take the year's course over again – when all of a sudden Riccardo threw himself upon her and caused her to bang her head against the head of the bed.'

'Was Baba upset?'

'Yes, very much upset.'

'Why?'

'Because she wasn't expecting it. She thought that what she was saying interested Riccardo; instead of which he showed clearly, by doing that, that it didn't interest him at all.'

'And then what happened?'

'Baba felt frozen all over and was tempted to struggle and run away. Then she remembered that Cora had told her to let things take their course; so she did. But nothing more. And so the battle began.'

'The battle?'

'Yes, the battle that there can be between someone who is a living person and someone who is merely a puppet.'

'Who was the puppet?'

'Baba.'

'And what did the battle consist of?'

'Riccardo tried to make Baba take an active interest, and Baba didn't put up any resistance, but she didn't react in any way, like a doll whose arms and legs you can put in certain positions but which then stays like that, without moving. Baba tumbled about in all directions, and Riccardo couldn't get her to stay as he wanted her. Finally he tried to undress her, but as Baba didn't help him he made up his mind to undress himself, partly at any rate.'

'Partly?'

'Yes, he took off his jacket and shoes.'

'And then what did he do?'

'He turned his attention to Baba again.'

'In what way?'

'He pulled up her sweater over her head, and the funniest thing was that for a moment Baba remained motionless, her head inside the sweater, sitting on the bed with her arms raised. Then Riccardo tried once again to pull the sweater off, but he didn't succeed, and finally, discouraged, he pulled it down again and Baba's head, with her hair all rumpled, popped out of the sweater again; and then she saw that Riccardo was sitting in front of her, in his shirtsleeves, looking at her.'

'And then what happened?'

'Riccardo looked at Baba for some time, in silence, and then he said a curious thing.'

'What was that?'

' "School, you go to school, to school, to school, to school." '

'He said that?'

'Yes.'

'In what tone of voice?'

'In an unpleasant tone, unpleasant to Baba anyhow. A tone of sarcastic exhortation. But without malice.'

'And what did Baba say to that?'

'She didn't say anything. She looked at her ink-stained hands and remained silent.'

'And then?'

'Then Riccardo hurriedly dressed, said he was going to telephone and went out. But he never came back. The rest you know.'

'Yes, I do. Well, d'you mind having talked about these things?'

'Possibly the Baba of that time might have minded, she was so stupid. I don't mind talking about them.'

'That's good. Well then, wait for me here.'

'What d'you want to do?'

'I want to have a closer look at the house.'

'It's a house like plenty of others.'

'Oh yes, I know that. Wait for me here.'

I got out of the car and walked a short distance among the people who were going up and down along the pavement. It was one o'clock; and there was a festive atmosphere such as is to be found in poor districts when work stops and people go home for their midday meal. Before going in at the door, I looked up to the end of the street and reflected that thus Baba must have seen it on that day: two rows of tall blocks of flats, their surfaces broken by balconies and windows, and at the far end the great slanting wall of the Vatican. I went into the hall, which had a dark red mosaic floor and walls of black-veined yellow marble, looked for a moment at the row of pigeon-hole letter-boxes, then opened a glass door and found myself facing the staircase. The porter's lodge was empty, so I opened the door and called as loudly as I could, breathing in the full blast of the warm, acid smell of cooking that came from the basement. After some little time I saw, emerging slowly from the staircase that led underground and rising with an effort, step by step, the upper part of a head with sparse grey hair coiled in a little bun at the back. Then I saw the face too: big, simple, pallid features; big, ball-like eyes; a big nose, like the clapper of a bell; big mouth, like an octopus' sucker; and then finally the whole person, tall, big, in a striped dress. This was the portress; and when she came out of the little lodge, the following dialogue took place between us.

'Does Signora Cora Merighi live here?'

'No.'

'I mean Signora Cora Mancini.'

'Oh yes, she did live here, but quite a long time ago.'

'How long ago?'

'Well, it must be four years since she left.'

'Could you tell me where she moved to?'

'She left no address.'

'And where did she live, which flat?'

'Third floor, flat eleven.'

'And tell me, what sort of life did she lead?'

'The same as everyone else.'

'But did she sleep here?'

'That I don't know, because at nine o'clock I shut the main door and what goes on in the flats has nothing to do with me.'

I looked at her, and she sustained my gaze with dull apathy. Then I took a thousand-lire note out of my pocket and placed it in the pocket of her apron. She gave an oblique glance at the note but said nothing. The dialogue went on like this: 'Did she live alone in the flat?'

'Yes. She lived alone.'

'But she came there with other people?'

'Oh, yes, she came with other people. Certainly.'

'What sort of people?'

'Oh well, men. And girls too.'

'Girls of what age?'

'Young, for the most part.'

'And the men?'

'Oh, the men, they were of all ages.'

'Some of them not young?'

'Yes, some of them not young.'

'Was there a lot of coming and going in that flat?'

'No, not much. Signora Cora was careful, she didn't like to attract attention.'

'What type of person was Signora Cora?'

'A quiet, serious, ladylike person. I never had any complaint to make about her.'

'She gave you a tip sometimes, did she?'

'Yes, she did: she was generous. As we all know, porters don't earn much and they have to make up for it somehow.'

'Quite right. And tell me: d'you remember the signora coming here sometimes with her daughter?'

'I didn't know she had a daughter.'

'She had, yes.'

'She may have come, but I didn't notice her, because I didn't know she had a daughter. She must have been one of the many girls who came here.'

'I'll describe her and you can tell me if you saw her: a young girl of about fifteen, with a round face, a fringe down to her eyes, her hair cut short.'

'Ah, that one – yes, I remember *her*. Wasn't she always in a sweater and trousers?'

'Yes.'

'Of course I remember her. She came for some time and then she never appeared again. She came with the Signora but also alone.'

'Alone, did she?'

'Yes, all by herself. She used to run up the stairs, two steps at a time. She never took the lift.'

'And how many times d'you think she came?'

'I didn't count the times. I remember her because she was so young and always wore trousers and also because she ran up the stairs.'

'Why didn't she take the lift?'

'Goodness knows. Obviously she liked going on foot.'

'For how many years did she come?'

'Years? Nonsense! It was only months, perhaps for a couple of months and that was all.'

'You saw her with Signora Cora and also alone. And with men?'

'No, not with men. The men came on their own.'

'You didn't see her with *me*?'

'With *you*? Why, did she come here with you?'

'Yes.'

'Well, you know, as I said, I noticed the girl because of her clothes and her age, but I didn't bother to look at the men.'

'Take a good look at me, don't you remember me?'

'No, really I don't remember.'

'Yet I came past right under your nose, holding Signora Cora's daughter by the hand.'

'I suppose I didn't take any notice.'

'I'm looking for Signora Cora's daughter. That's why I'm asking you all these questions.'

'But why don't you go and look for Signora Cora? It can't be so very difficult to find her.'

'Signora Cora is dead.'

'Ah, poor lady, I'm very, very sorry; who would have thought it? Such a nice lady – who would have thought it? And what did she die of?'

'I don't know, I only know that she's dead.'

'Well, I'm sorry, but I can't give you any information about Signora Cora's daughter. In any case she must be a grown-up woman by this time. Goodness knows, perhaps she's even got married.'

'Can I go up to Flat 11?'

'Oh, go up, as far as I'm concerned. But you'll see, they don't know anything about it.'

I went up two flights of stairs and then two more and finally another two. I came to Flat 11: a door of light-coloured wood, with a brass plate on which was inscribed 'Lorenzoni'. I thought for a moment, trying to find a pretext for my visit, then I pressed the bell. It made a prolonged sound, loud and low, rather like the quack of a duck; there was a short silence and then the door opened and there appeared in the doorway a little girl of perhaps twelve years old, in a dirty pistachio-green overall, with long hair hanging loose over her shoulders and on the top of her head a big white bow. Her face was pale, her skin sallow, and there were livid marks under her eyes. She looked at me distrustfully, but without shyness. 'What d'you want, who are you looking for? There's no one at home.'

'I've been sent from the flat above,' I replied; 'there's a leak in the water-main. I'm the plumber.'

She moved aside without making any objection, so I went into the passage – the usual dark passage, with its smell of cooking, always to be found in flats of this type – and hurried to the first door on the left which, according to my calculations, must be that of the room from whose window Baba, six years before, had looked out into the street and seen Riccardo get into his car and drive away. But I was mistaken; I had not calculated the arrangement of the flat accurately; this was a lavatory, a long, narrow little room darkened by the clothes hung up at the window, which, I realized, looked on to the courtyard. I turned back towards the child and said: 'The leakage isn't on this side; where are the rooms that look on to the street?'

She looked me straight in the eye and said in a severe tone of voice: 'If you'd asked me, instead of rushing in like that ...' Then she led me into the room I was looking for. It was a bedroom, as it had been at that time, with a divan bed between two walls hung with a flowered material; there was also a writing-desk; the window had no curtains. I pretended to examine the ceiling as though looking for patches of dampness, then went over to the window and, without opening it, looked down. There was the street, with the people on the pavements appearing, as seen from above, to have their feet stuck on just below their heads; the smooth, oval tops of cars advancing in file, slowly and cautiously, like the backs of cockroaches dazzled by the light; and on the pavement immediately below, the shops at ground level and the people in front of the shop-windows. The child's petulant voice made me start. 'Are you looking for patches of dampness in the street?'

'I was looking,' I replied, 'to see if it was due to an outside pipe.'

'That may be so, but you're not the plumber.'

'Why?'

'In the first place because there's no one in the flat above. It's been empty for two months. Besides, I know the plumber: he's a fair-haired young man and he wears a blue overall.'

'Then who am I, d'you think?'

'That I don't know and it doesn't interest me to know, but you're certainly not the plumber.'

'And what's *your* name?'

'Annamaria.'

'Thank you, Annamaria, and good-bye; sorry to have disturbed you.' I left the flat under the distrustful eyes of the little girl, went down to the ground floor and out into the street. I found Baba reading a magazine. I started the car again and, as I drove off, I said to her: 'There was one thing you concealed from me.'

'What was that?'

'That Baba went there that first day accompanied by Cora, but on the other occasions she went alone.'

'I didn't tell you because you didn't ask me.'

'But why did Baba go there? After all, she could equally well not have gone.'

'Cora told her what time she should be there and gave her the key of the flat. Baba took the key, went on studying until the time of the appointment, then closed her books, left the house and made her way on foot, street by street, to Cora's flat. She went in by the main entrance, ran upstairs two steps at a time, opened the door, and went and waited in the sitting-room with a magazine in her hand. As soon as she heard the bell ring she went and opened the door, the man came in, Baba shut and bolted the front door. Then she led the man into the bedroom. Baba locked the bedroom door, the man threw himself upon Baba and the usual battle took place; then the man went away and Baba tidied herself and the room. Then she went back into the other room and found Cora waiting for her there. Or perhaps Cora was not there and then Baba waited for her to come. Cora and Baba went home, where Baba found her books again and her desk and resumed her studies. Now tell me ...'

'What?'

'Where was there a place for any kind of reflection in this chain of actions? In order to escape, Baba would have had to reflect. But when?'

'Yes, I understand. When you relate all these things in that way, one following on another, I see that there certainly isn't much place for reflection. But, after all, Baba wasn't an automaton.'

'But that's just what she was, nothing but an automaton which Cora had wound up in order that it should do certain things and only those things. But if you prefer, we can say that Baba was dead – I mean the old Baba – and the new Baba was not yet born, and the one that walked through the streets was in reality only a body which had no will of its own and merely obeyed Cora.'

Wednesday, November 18th

Between the decayed and blackened travertine façade of a baroque church and the red-and-yellow plastered front of an old nineteenth-century house, in a quarter of old Rome, my eyes were suddenly dazzled by a neon sign, a horizontal tattoo-mark in purplish-white light emblazoned on the half-darkness of the narrow street: 'Alaska Cinema'. I recalled that that was the name of the cinema where the girl of whom I had caught a glimpse at Cora's villa worked as an usherette; and I went in.

The entrance was flooded with brilliant light; behind the counter of the box office sat a girl with a corpse-like face, with heavily made-up eyes, her head topped by a helmet of fluffy, straw-coloured hair. I went over and asked for a stall ticket, and meanwhile I looked along to the far end of the corridor. There, on either side of the entrance door, like living but un-equal caryatids, stood two women in pearl-grey, red-frogged uniforms so tight and clinging as to go beyond indecency and descend to the ridiculous. One of them was small, blonde and plump with an enormous behind and an enormous bosom and practically nothing in between these two protuberances; the other was tall and dark, robust and well-made. In the latter I at once recognized the girl whom I had seen at Cora's villa. I went up to her and put my ticket straight into her hand; at once, with a brusque about-turn, she preceded me into the hall, projecting the ray of her electric torch on to the floor behind her. As soon as the curtains at the entrance closed behind us, I put out a hand and took hold of her arm, with such force as to bring her to a halt. She uttered a subdued cry of surprise and stood still; then I put my mouth to her ear. 'What's your name?' I asked her.

'Take care! Let me go at once or I shall scream.'

'You silly! Why, we know each other already, we were together at Signora Cora's villa on the Via Cassia.'

She was silent for a moment, then, lowering her voice, she replied: 'My name's Delia. But what d'you want with me? I don't know you.'

'Don't you remember me?'

She half turned in the darkness, waited until a brighter part of the picture appeared on the screen, looked closely at me, then whispered ingenuously: 'No, I don't, really I don't, not at all. I've never seen you.'

I did as I had done with the portress at Cora's former abode: I took a thousand-lire note out of my pocket and placed it in her hand. 'It doesn't matter whether you recognize me or not, let's make an appointment for afterwards, when you go home.'

She looked closely at me once more, half curious and half mistrustful. 'But we don't finish here till one o'clock.'

'Well, then, let's make an appointment at one o'clock.'

'But what d'you want of me?'

'Absolutely nothing. Just to talk to you. Tell me of a café where we can meet, and I'll be there at one.'

'Oh, I'm not afraid for myself. It's only . . . Well, let's meet at the Torino Bar, in the Largo Tritone.'

'That's fine. Till later, then. In the meantime, here's something more for you.'

'Oh, thank you, thank you, you shouldn't trouble . . . But, you know, it's still early, you'll have to see the film twice over.'

'Never mind. Is it a good film?'

'Not bad – a thriller. But tell me, are you really sure you know me? I don't remember you at all, not the least bit.'

At this point some of the spectators began to say 'sh!' Delia stifled a laugh, gave me an understanding pat on the shoulder and walked away.

I sank into a seat and watched the film which was, as she had said, a detective story, with an initial crime of which the perpetrator had to be discovered. And then, as I followed the pictures flowing uninterruptedly across the screen, it occurred to me that there was a certain resemblance between my own situation and that of a detective film; but it was a resemblance in reverse. What I mean is this: the detective film started out from insignificant, every day normality and led to something extraordinary and significant; whereas I myself started out from a situation which at first sight might seem extraordinary and significant but which ended up in the senseless humdrum of everyday life, that is, in the normality of corruption.

I saw the whole of the second part of the film, then the lights were turned up and I looked round me. The long, narrow hall was like an aeroplane hangar; there were few spectators, mostly men, alone or in pairs, sulky, dreary people of the type one usually sees ambling about the streets in the centre of Rome after dinner. Delia was now standing beside the door and, when she caught my eye, she winked at me in a manner so obvious and undisguised that it was almost comic. Then it went dark again and I sat through, first of all the advertisement films, then a documentary about Sardinia, then the news, and finally the detective film, half of which I had already seen. Some time after midnight, not waiting for the film to finish, I left the hall before the lights went on and made my way through dark, narrow streets, over uneven paving-stones made slippery by the dampness of the night, to the café indicated by Delia.

I sat down in the little inside room, on a tubular chair, at a tubular table, in a smell of cold, stale smoke, my feet in the sawdust, the neon light in my eyes; and I ordered a cup of coffee. When I had drunk my coffee, I listened to a conversation between two male voices which came to me in snatches, between the puffs from the *espresso* coffee-machine, from the room adjoining the bar.

'. . . received.'

'. . . on the telephone.'

'. . . on the way. I tried to escape, but I . . .'

'. . . and what has . . .'

'. . . scoundrel. Just imagine that . . .'

'...really? And he?'

'...whereas everybody knows that...'

'...bad. And yet it's also true that...'

Finally I saw Delia standing in front of me; she had come into the little room without my noticing it. She had a grey coat with a rabbit-fur collar, an old bag on her arm, and her large, shapely hands were without gloves. Suddenly she burst out laughing and, looking at me, she said: 'Really I haven't ever seen you, really I haven't. But it doesn't matter. Well, are you going to offer me a snack?'

She sat down, I called the waiter and Delia ordered a cup of chocolate and some sandwiches. The waiter came back in a short time carrying a plate heaped with big, plain rolls with some sort of filling and a large cup of chocolate; and Delia devoured the whole lot without speaking. But, as soon as she had finished, she looked at me and again burst out laughing. 'You know, I really don't remember you,' she said. 'It's true that I've been more than once to Signora Cora's villa, and yet...'

'D'you want a proof that we've been together? You have the scar of an appendicitis operation on your stomach.'

'Anybody might have that scar; a girl friend of mine has one, just the same. Perhaps you're mistaking me for someone else.'

'Wait a moment. There's something else you have, a more special thing.'

'What's that?'

'You have a thin line of dark down that starts from your stomach and goes upwards almost to your chest.'

'You know, you must be a bit of a wizard. It almost frightens me.'

'D'you want to stay here or shall we go away?'

'Let's go away.'

'Where d'you want to go?'

'Take me home, won't you?'

'Where d'you live?'

'At San Giovanni. Have you a car?'

'Yes.'

So I paid, and we went out and walked back to the neighbourhood of the cinema, where I had left the car. We got in, and then, as I drove, we started talking. It was Delia who first broke the silence by asking me: 'And what's your name?'

'Francesco.'

'Some years ago I was engaged to a man who had that same name. Actually, as he was a Tuscan, he liked to be called Cesco. But his real name was Francesco. Now tell me, you know Signora Cora?'

'Yes.'

'Well?'

'No, not well.'

'But what impression d'you have of her?'

'What do you mean?'

'Well, what d'you think of her?'

'I think she's very nice.'

'Nice, yes, but doesn't she seem to you rather – how shall I say? – rather strange?'

'Why strange?'

'Well . . . strange.'

'Explain, why strange?'

She started laughing again, irresistibly, mischievously. 'But if I tell you, you mustn't go and repeat it to her, because Signora Cora has always been good to me and has helped me whenever I needed it.'

'No, I won't go and repeat it.'

'When I say that she's strange, I mean it seems to me that she has, so to speak, a bit of an obsession.'

'An obsession?'

'Yes, an obsession. You know what she does?'

'What?'

'I can't tell you: I'm ashamed.'

'Eh, come on!'

'Yes, I'm ashamed; honestly.'

'Well, what is she obsessed with?'

'She's obsessed with – that thing. D'you understand me?'

'No.'

'Let's say, then, with the physical side of love. Perhaps because she's been ill for some time and can't do it any more.'

'But how does this obsession show itself?'

'Listen, then; it'll make you laugh.

'I'm listening; come on!'

'There's a young man called Marco, who has a shop that sells household electrical goods, who comes to Signora Cora's. He and Cora are friends, and so Cora has contrived that she shall be present every time Marco and I make love. But mind you, Cora doesn't *do* anything, she sits down in the armchair and stays there, quite still, her eyes starting out of her head, watching us two, Marco and me – her eyes starting out of her head, I tell you, so that it really makes me ashamed. And then, just imagine, sometimes she puts out her hand – like this, very, very slowly – and with her finger, with only one finger, she touches Marco just *there*, as though she couldn't believe she was seeing it and wasn't convinced it was really there and wanted to be quite sure by actually touching it, very gently; and then she quickly takes her hand away, as though she were reassured, and stays there quite still, her eyes staring, and I, right in the middle of our love-making, I don't know whether to laugh or to be frightened, because she seems to me to be a madwoman, and with mad people, as we all know, you can expect anything. D'you know what Signora Cora makes me think of at those moments? You may say it's an unpleasant comparison, but it isn't, because I don't mean any harm, and I'm religious and I don't allow any jokes on religious things. She makes me think of the peasant women in my own part of the country, up there in the Friuli, who go into the church and kneel down, and there they remain, perhaps even for an hour or two hours, staring with wide-open eyes at the statue on the altar, and then they kiss their fingers and touch the statue lightly, and all this, so to speak, in a dream, as if they were bewitched. Actually I said to Signora Cora one day: "You look at that thing as if it was something holy. One of these days you'll be kneeling down in front of Marco at the moment when he's making love and you'll clasp your hands and say a prayer to that thing, and I daresay you'll even kiss your fingers before touching it, as the peasant women do in church." And you know what she answered? "It's the only thing that matters in the whole world, and the most beautiful too; you're a silly girl, you can't understand these things." '

'But you – how did you come to know Signora Cora?'

'Oh, that's quite simple. I had to get myself a dress, and I hadn't a penny and so a friend of mine took me to see Cora and I let myself be persuaded to choose a much more expensive dress than the one I had thought of getting. So, when the moment came, I told Signora Cora that, for the time being at least, I couldn't pay for it; and then, although she had always told me not to worry and that she would give me credit, instead of that she threatened to telephone my home and get my father to pay the money; but I didn't want her to telephone because my father, you see, is a doorkeeper and earns very little. Signora Cora, who is intelligent and who takes in a situation at a glance, had understood that I didn't want my father to know about the dress, so she threatened seriously to telephone him, and I had the impression she would really have done so, and therefore I told her I was ready to do anything but I didn't want her to telephone to my father. Then she blackmailed me: either you come and meet me at the villa on Via Cassia and let me introduce you to a gentleman friend of mine, or I'll telephone to your father. It was blackmail, as I said, but she did it so graciously, so tactfully, in such a lady-like way, like a true friend, like a real well-bred lady, saying this and not saying that, hinting at one thing and ignoring another; that I almost got the impression that it was I myself who was asking to meet this gentleman and that she was doing me a favour by introducing him to me and was, in fact, helping me and saving me from a great danger. And so, in the end, we came to an agreement and since then there has never been even the slightest trouble between us and she has always been very good to me and if she wasn't so strange I might even say she was my best friend. But strange she is, yes, very strange indeed, and when she sits there in that armchair, looking at Marco and me making love, with those big, blue, staring eyes, I'm very much tempted to laugh, and I have to make a real effort to stop myself, and then, so as not to laugh, I think about sad things, such as for instance that she's mad and that one of these days they'll take her off to an asylum; otherwise I'd really burst out laughing, and that would be embarrassing not only for her but also for Marco, and it might even do him harm, because it's a bad thing to be interrupted at moments like that....'

And so she went on telling me about Cora with an inexhaustible talkativeness that was at the same time both innocent and mischievous; and at last, with her chattering volubly all the time and myself silently driving, we reached a wide, dreary street outside Porta San Giovanni. Then she told me we had arrived, and I stopped. She gave me a final injunction not to reveal her confidences to Cora, made me promise I would come and meet her at the villa in Via Cassia, declared that she liked me, even if I frightened her and gave her the impression that I was a bit of a wizard, and then added: 'But this time I shall keep my eyes wide open, so that I shall remember you afterwards. But, you know, I really don't recollect having met you? Really and truly.'

I promised that I would get in touch with Cora. She said good-bye, got out of the car, fumbled for a moment with her key in the lock of the huge though humble entrance-door of a block of working-class flats, and then disappeared.

Friday, November 20th

'*Deus ex machina:* theatrical expedient, in use in the classical theatre, consisting in the appearance of a divinity by means of a machine. Such an appearance served to sanction a rite, to establish a local tradition, or even to resolve the intricate knot of the dramatic action. Hence the proverbial use of the term, to indicate a person or thing that intervenes unexpectedly to resolve a specified situation.'

I copied this definition from an encyclopedia, because it seems to me a perfectly fitting description of what Cora's illness might be, if, as I sometimes think, it turns out to be fatal.

There does in fact remain in the depths of my consciousness the suspicion, ineradicable even if arrogant, that, just as Oedipus was to blame for the plague at Thebes, so am I myself to blame for the corruption of my family. To blame for what Cora is and what she does; to blame for what Baba suffered; to blame for the whole situation.

And this idea comes to me at the very moment when I thought I had discovered that there are neither culprits nor victims, but only the indistinct, meaningless flow of everyday life, the senseless, natural normality of corruption.

Logically, my feeling of guilt, like all feelings of guilt, arouses in me a desire for expiation. Certainly I cannot put out my eyes, like Oedipus; but my imagination brings this prospect in a flash before me: have an explanation with Cora, reveal that I know about her second profession, tell her that she is very ill, that she might die, that she ought to go into a sanatorium. And finally make her a proposal which, for me, would be equivalent to the self-blinding of Oedipus: if she agrees to have treatment, I would give up travelling once and for all, would become her husband again and spend my whole life with her. And, to begin with, I would keep her company during the two or three years of her treatment in a sanatorium.

I must point out that I am thinking seriously about all this. To give up travelling, to live with Cora in a sanatorium, to remain all my life at her side – these things, for me, are not just fantasies but, as I am aware, fundamental alternatives in my life. I think of it with such seriousness that my heart aches, as though I were preparing for death; then, from I know not what source, comes a feeling of defiance which helps me to overcome my anguish, and my eyes fill with tears, with real burning tears; and I weep with exaltation and hope.

But at the same time, behind the refuge of this edifying, heroic wish to expiate, rises the shadow of a fear that I shall not be in time, that Cora will start spitting blood and die suddenly. Thus there would be no expiation; everything would fall into place, so to speak, of its own accord. But beware: this fear perhaps merely masks the cynical hope that her illness, like a true and proper *deus ex machina*, may relieve me of my expiation and resolve the whole situation according to the logic of everyday normality.

But what is this 'logic of the everyday' if not the substitution of the things we cause to happen by those which happen to us? In a situation like mine, obstructed by consciousness of the non-genuineness that is an essential part of every mode of action, death by illness, which obviously we do not cause to happen but which happens to us, is the only possible solution. It is, in other words, the *deus ex machina* proper to everyday life, just as providential and just as senseless as the machines of wood and canvas which, in the classical theatre, permitted a divinity to appear and so to resolve the 'intricate knot of the dramatic action'.

The *deus ex machina* of death by illness, moreover, does not only make expiation superfluous but also, as is obvious, the other possible *dénouement* of the drama – punishment. Both of them being non-genuine, punishment and expiation have equal value; in point of fact it seems equally false to imagine Cora either punished or preserved. The only right thing appears to be her death in a hospital bed, from tuberculosis, amongst a lot of other sick people, guilty or guiltless. Something ordinary, in fact, involuntary, insignificant. In other words, the *deus ex machina* once more, serving to resolve the 'intricate knot of the dramatic action'.

Nevertheless, when all is said and done, I cannot succeed in freeing myself from the suspicion that my passivity in face of Cora may finally end in cowardice. Therefore I think that, in spite of everything, I ought to make an effort to expiate and to save Cora. To save her from her illness; to save her from corruption.

So far, so good. But, at the very moment when I am deciding to act, a sudden feeling of uneasiness warns me that perhaps I am going to do something I have already done; and then I wonder whether possibly I am not on the point of relapsing into the unreality of the non-genuine, as I did ten years ago, when I decided to marry Cora.

I feel that, just as, ten years ago, I was wrong in making Cora my wife, so now I should be wrong in dedicating my life to her. Today, as then, action would cause me to plunge into non-genuineness.

But between what happened ten years ago and what is happening now there is, nevertheless, a difference: ten years ago I was writing my novel, accepting the rightness of the things I had done in my most recent past. Today, on the other hand, I shall be extracting the novel from the diary in which I am relating my life bit by bit as I live it; so that my project for the novel, as I have already said, serves me as a conscience for any sort of action I may think of undertaking.

For all these reasons, I decided yesterday evening to test my relationship with Cora by the same method that I used to test my relationship with Baba some days ago, with the novel as touchstone. That is, by writing down in this diary the imaginary scene of my explanation with Cora. The scene is as follows:

'Cora is in bed because she has had a high temperature all day. I knock at the door, enter, tell her that I must talk to her and she, without saying a word, invites me with a movement of her chin to sit down in the armchair at the bottom of the bed.

Before beginning my speech, I look at Cora. She is sitting up in bed with two pillows behind her, the top part of her body wrapped in a dressing-gown of scarlet wool with borders of green silk. Finally I say to her: "I've come here to talk to you. I have to say something to you which hitherto I've never had the courage to say."

"What is that?"

"Can't you guess?"

"No."

"Yet you ought to have understood, from my behaviour towards you."

"What behaviour d'you mean?"

"For ten years I've been like a stranger in this house; then suddenly I decided to make a complete change, to become a father to Baba again, and a husband to you. But in these things no half measures are possible. For ten years I decided to ignore you; now that I've decided to be concerned about you, I must do it thoroughly. Having said so much, it seems to me that it should now be clear what I wish to talk to you about."

"No, it's not clear to me at all."

"Isn't it? Do you still not understand that I am speaking of your second profession?"

"I have no second profession."

"And that I am also speaking of Baba?"

This time she remains silent, betraying neither surprise nor confusion. After a moment I resume: "I think that is sufficient explanation, isn't it?"

Again she says nothing. I continue: "Baba says that for her it's as though the whole affair happened to another Baba, who has nothing to do with her. Let us imagine that everything you have done hitherto has been done by another Cora who has nothing to do with you. And let us come on to the only thing that counts – your health."

"How does my health come into it?"

"Baba has told me that you at last made up your mind to send for a doctor and that he certified a severe form of pulmonary tuberculosis. Is that true, or isn't it?"

"Yes, it's true, but . . ."

"One moment. Furthermore the doctor told you that you can get well only if you leave Rome and go to a sanatorium in the mountains and stay there for a couple of years. Again, is that true, or isn't it?"

"It's true. But I'm not going to a sanatorium. I've too much to do in Rome."

"Too much to do at the villa on Via Cassia, eh, or elsewhere?"

Again no answer. She shuts herself up in a complete and fundamentally contemptuous silence – the silence, I cannot help thinking, of the believer who refuses to admit any discussion about his own faith. I say to her: "So you want to die?"

"Why should I want to die? I'll have treatment in Rome, that's all."

"You can't have treatment in Rome."

"Who says so?"

"The first condition of your treatment is to change your way of life. You must leave Rome and then you can do so."

"I've no intention of changing my way of life. I'm all right as I am and I don't see why I should change."

"Now listen to me, Cora: I'm going to make a suggestion."

"What's your suggestion?"

"If you agree to go away to the sanatorium and, naturally, to give up the villa and all activities connected with it, I make you a solemn promise that I, on my side, will give up travelling and follow you to the mountains and stay there as long as is necessary for you to get well. And afterwards I'll remain with you and won't leave you again."

She looks at me; her eyes are dilated with harsh mistrust. Then she mutters: "I wouldn't dream of it."

"But why?"

"I've already told you: I'm all right here and I don't want to change anything."

I consider her in silence. Then, seeing her there, in the red light of the red silk lampshade, with her wasted, haggard face, all eyes nose and mouth, like a red mask, the redness accentuated also by the reflected colour from her red dressing-gown, I am suddenly assailed by a bitter sense not only of the corruption of which at that moment she seems to be the living personification, but also of the possibility of transforming that corruption into its opposite. I feel that all this is not fatal: there should be a way of tearing off this cruel, impure mask and restoring her human face to Cora. Suddenly, without realizing what I am doing, I find myself pressed tightly against her, my arms round the body bundled up in the dressing-gown, my nostrils filled with the smell of her, a mixture of scent and sweat; and I say to her: "You can get well from your illness, and you can also become a different person, provided you want to. But you must want to, you *must*. And I'll help you to want to."

And I realize that I am crying, my nose buried in the wool of her dressing-gown, my arms round her shoulders, I am weeping bitterly, both for fear that she will refuse, and in the hope that she will agree – both of which eventualities are, for me, equally painful.

But while I stay thus close to her, and talk to her and weep, I feel suddenly that she is beginning to struggle, to make efforts to free herself from me, to pull herself up, to breathe more easily, as if she felt herself suffocating. I drag myself away from her and then, all at once, she sits straight up in bed and starts coughing, and her cough, each time, becomes deeper and harsher, and finally I see her draw herself together and cover her mouth with both hands while her eyes, above the two joined hards, are dilated with terror; and then, in a final burst of coughing, there, in the red light of the red lampshade, with the red face in the folds of the red dressing-gown, there, between the fingers, gushes forth abundantly, the red blood. . . .'

Here ends that part of my diary in which I described an imaginary explanation between Cora and myself. Then I read over what I had written, reflected briefly and finally added this comment below it: 'Sentimental, hypocritical, wishful thinking, unreal, an empty hotch-potch. Therefore non-genuine. As usual, it's a question of something false concealing something true. The false thing is the promise to accompany Cora to a sanatorium, to spend your whole life with her; the true thing is the desire that Cora should die, revealed by the invention of the sudden, fatal gush of blood. But that she should die *after* you have made your promise and *before* you are forced to keep it; in such a way as to let you show to advantage at little expense to yourself and, at the same time, put to rest even the faintest whisper of your conscience.'

Saturday, November 21st

Mild air, presaging rain; a cloudy, thundery autumn day. The travertine stone of the buildings, the flagstones of the pavements, are darkened by dampness. The patches of blue in the sky are continually changing, from great to small, as the huge clouds are driven across them by the wind. Thinly scattered but unceasingly the red and yellow leaves, shaped like hands with open fingers, flutter from the bare branches of the plane-trees in Via Veneto. The asphalt of the street, black and porous like leather, is strewn with leaves that seem glued to it, and here and there are iridescent patches of motor oil and wet cracks in the surface. Baba stopped at a café, pointed to a table and suggested: 'Let's sit here.' We sat down. Someone who was sitting at the next table, hearing Baba speaking to me, moved the newspaper behind which he was hidden just enough to make him visible to Baba and not to me, and said: 'Look who's here! D'you recognize me?'

Baba turned and looked at him, 'Yes,' she said.

'How are you?'

'Very well, and how are you?'

'Very well indeed. And what are you doing now?'

'Studying.'

'Fancy, I recognized you at once, although some years have gone by.'

'Six years.'

'Six years. How the time passes! It seems like yesterday. But d'you know, you haven't changed at all?'

'Really?'

'Yes, really. You're more grown-up, of course; but you've remained the same. Only you're prettier.'

'Thank you.'

'Listen, can we meet?'

'No.'

'Truly no?'

'Yes, truly no.'

'Look, I'll give you my telephone number. Why don't you ring me one of these days?'

'No.'

'I'm sorry, I didn't mean to offend you.'

'You haven't offended me.'

'Well, I must be going. See you some time, I hope.'

'Good-bye.'

I watched him as he walked away with an air which was at the same time embarrassed and self-possessed, whistling, his hands in the pockets of an old but elegant sports jacket, snuff-coloured with green check, a man of about forty-five, with a lean, brown, fine-featured face and a sensitive, slightly melancholy expression, an adolescent whom middle-age had treated kindly – a sympathetic figure, in short, in no way vulgar, and above all gentle, with a gentleness that was revealed when, having risen to his feet, he saluted Baba and his rather sad eyes were lit up with a kindly gleam. I went on looking at him as he walked away, until he turned a corner and vanished. Then I asked Baba who he was. 'It's Riccardo,' she replied, 'the first man Cora introduced to Baba, six years ago.'

Sunday, November 22nd

Cora stayed at home today. I had a glimpse of her through the open door as I passed along the corridor: she was wearing her usual red woollen dressing-gown with green silk borders, and was sitting in the armchair beside the bed, with scarlet slippers on her feet. What does Cora do when a high temperature confines her to the house? She telephones, as I know from the frequent tinklings on the extension in my room: in all probability she telephones to her clients and her girls, arranging appointments at the villa in Via Cassia; she also telephones, no doubt, to the dress shop to find out how the work is going. But I believe that, for the most part, she just sits still, doing nothing, gazing into vacancy, or rather – as I saw her on the beach at Monte Circeo – seeking vainly to re-establish a relationship with reality, across the yawning abysses of her own existence.

But the fever also prevented Cora from going today to see her parents in order to hand over the monthly sum which she provides for their living expenses. So she instructed Baba to take her place; and Baba immediately asked me to go with her, emphasizing, as usual, her position as a daughter, with the right to ask her father to assist her in any kind of circumstances.

We left the flat in the middle of the afternoon, when the early November night was already coming on; and I drove for some time in silence. Cora's parents lived in Via Tuscolana, so we had to go right through the centre of Rome. When we came into Via dell-Impero Baba, who was sitting motionless with her hands clasped in her lap, suddenly said: 'I'm glad you're coming to see the grandparents.'

'Why?'

'Because I know it will give them pleasure. How long is it since you've been there?'

'Almost ten years.'

'They've often asked me about you. Especially Grandma. And I've felt embarrassed because I didn't know what to say. I couldn't say you didn't want to see them any more. I used to say you were travelling.'

'That was the truth, or rather, part of the truth.'

'D'you mind coming? When I asked you, you put on the same face as you did that day when we went to Monte Circeo and I told you Cora would be going with us.'

'What sort of a face?'

'I don't know; something between disappointment and repugnance.'

'No, I don't mind. Or rather, I do mind a little, but not as much as I mind being with Cora.'

'And why d'you mind?'

'That's a long story. There are too many things I should have to explain to you.'

'Well, explain them.'

'Very well then, to put it briefly: what I loved in Cora I loved also in them. Once I'd ceased to love Cora I ceased to feel any liking for them. To see them again is disagreeable to me because it reminds me of my infatuation.'

'What was it you loved in Cora and in them?'

'That's a bit complicated, too; let's say it was their poverty.'

'What is there to be said for being poor?'

'Genuineness. I believed that genuineness and poverty were synonymous.'

'You don't believe that now?'

'No.'

'Actually I knew this already.'

'You knew it?'

'Yes, once when I asked Cora what had happened between you and her, and why you lived like a stranger in the house, she answered "What has happened is that I'm no longer the very poor girl I was when Francesco and I met for the first time. Francesco is like those country landowners who, instead of carrying on with girls of their own class, get crazy about peasant-girls. I'm not saying he's wrong, it's a question of taste; I'm only saying that I couldn't go on being a penniless wretch all my life just in order to please him." '

'Yes, I know that's what she thinks.'

'And you – what do *you* think?'

'About what?'

'About your marriage to Cora.'

'I think I made a mistake, that's all.'

'And, in your opinion, who is right – yourself or Cora?'

'I don't know. Perhaps the truth is somewhere in between, as it usually is.'

'Tell me how you came to meet Cora the first time.'

'What does that matter to you? Why d'you want to know?'

'Oh well, just out of curiosity.'

'Odd sort of curiosity.'

'Well, don't you want to tell me?'

'If you're really anxious to know.'

'Yes, I am.'

'All right then, say what you want me to tell you.'

'I want you to tell me exactly how it came about that you met Cora.'

'I met her at the Gordiani settlement.'

'What is the Gordiani settlement?'

'What *was*. Today it no longer exists, at least so I believe. It was a settlement, in other words a group of houses, or rather, of huts, built and arranged in a special manner.'

'What manner?'

'Like a concentration camp.'

'But what were you doing at the Gordiani settlement?'

'I went there on various occasions.'

'Why?'

'Because I was attracted by places like the Gordiani settlement and by the people who lived in them.'

'You were attracted?'

'Yes, I looked and looked and never had enough of looking.'

'But why did you look?'

'I don't know. Perhaps because I believed in a myth.'

'What kind of a myth?'

'The myth of poverty.'

'What does that mean?'

'A boy may perhaps believe in the myth of nobility. As he doesn't move in aristocratic society, he snoops round palaces, looks at the windows, notices who goes in and out, gets to know all about the life and habits and customs of the people who live in them, and has daydreams of love with a princess. So much so, that one day he may succeed, somehow or other, in forming a part of those coveted, inaccessible circles and finally in marrying the woman, or rather, the noble lady, of his dreams. Only then does he realize that his wife is a woman just like any other woman; but by then it will be too late. It was the same with me. Only for palaces you must substitute settlement huts; for high society, unemployed men and prostitutes and thieves; for the princess, Cora, daughter of a washerwoman and a market gardener.'

'Very well, then: you believed in this myth, but why did you believe in it?'

'People believe in myths because they believe in them. It would take too long to explain *why* they believe in them.'

'Yes, I understand; then tell me how it came about that you met Cora.'

'D'you really want to know the whole story?'

'Yes.'

'But why?'

'Because I've always had a desire to know these things; and Cora would never tell me anything.'

'It was like this. The newspaper I was working for commissioned me to make an enquiry into these settlements. Or rather, I contrived to have the enquiry assigned to me. So I went to the Gordiani settlement one July day, about two o'clock. I must describe the settlement to you, so that you can understand what happened that day. Imagine two rows of huts of only one floor, of an ugly yellowish colour, the windows framed in badly painted white borders, the roofs of grey corrugated iron, on each side of an enormous bare street. Nothing else except the huts and the wide street: not a tree, not a garden, not a shop, not a water-trough, nothing. And in the middle of the street, a hovel with two floors, partly in ruins, with a reddish-yellow windowless wall on which was written in big black letters: Houses! houses! houses! In this hovel there was a bar with the signboard of a public telephone; I got out of my car and went towards this bar.'

'What to do?'

'To telephone to my newspaper and ask them to send the photographer with whom I had made an appointment at the settlement: but he wasn't there.'

'But what sort of people lived in the settlement?'

'All sorts. Prostitutes, thieves, but also workmen, builders for the most part, and other people as well. Your grandfather, for instance, was a market gardener.'

'So you went into the bar?'

'Yes I went in and ordered coffee. Then I turned round and saw a woman in a yellow blouse and a green skirt. She had black hair and blue eyes and her shoulders, chest and arms were bare and very sunburnt, golden almost. It was Cora.'

'What was she doing?'

'She was telephoning. Then she hung up the receiver and I went over to make my own telephone call. The telephone was near the door and Cora was coming towards the counter, so we passed one another in the middle of the room. She looked at me for a moment, in an insistent sort of way, as you look at someone who attracts you. I went to the telephone and then turned round and looked at Cora who was now talking to the barman. She stopped talking and went towards the door, as though to go out. As I said, it was July, and very hot: Cora's arms were bare and I was wearing a sleeveless vest. Then, as she passed close to me, she rubbed her arm against mine, her skin against my skin. Firmly, and looking at me as she did so. Then she went out.'

'And what did you do?'

'I left the telephone and followed her.'

'Why? Did Cora attract you?'

'Yes.'

'And then?'

'She walked in front of me in the strong, burning sunshine and the blinding light, and went to my car, which was the only one in the whole of the street; I opened the door, she got in and we drove off. All this without either of us saying a word.'

'And then?'

'Cora was sitting beside me, looking at the road. All she said was: "To the right, to the left, straight on", giving me directions, and I did as I was told. So we went along various roads – almost country roads – and then under the railway viaduct. At a certain point there was a white, three-storeyed house with green shutters. Cora told me to stop; we got out and went into this house. There was no lift; we walked up two flights of stairs and came to a door with a nameplate on which was written "Torrini".'

'You remember everything.'

'To cut it short, a middle-aged, sullen, disagreeable woman came and opened the door, and Cora introduced her to me by the name of Erminia, and she showed us to the bedroom.'

'What was the room like?'

'A black-painted iron double bed, with four pillows and a red coverlet; a marble-topped chest-of-drawers with family photographs on it; two big bedside cupboards, also with marble tops; a wardrobe with a looking-glass. The window had a lace curtain, yellow with age, with a design of baskets and flowers and birds. I went to the window while Cora was undressing and saw, right in front of me, the viaduct and a train moving slowly, waggon by waggon, across it.'

'And then what happened?'

'What happened was that we went to bed together. D'you want to know the three things that made me fall in love with Cora?'

'Yes, what were they?'

'The first was when, as soon as we were lying side by side on the bed, Cora put her hand down to my belly and, lying on her back with eyes closed and head thrown back on the pillow, seized hold of me and gripped me hard, muttering in a low voice as if in ecstasy: "How lovely that is!" The second thing was when, before making love, she warned me: "I'm a dress-maker. I hardly ever go with men. So you must excuse me if I'm not very good at it." The third was when I put my hand to my pocket-book and she said: "Give me as much as you can, because I have a little girl to support." '

'Why exactly did those three things make you fall in love with Cora?'

'I told you, I was looking for genuineness; it seemed to me that I had found it in those three remarks.'

'And then what happened, after that first time?'

'Oh, then things went on in the usual way of all love-affairs: we met again at Erminia's house, at first rarely and then more and more often; later we went to live together; and finally we were married. A very ordinary story.'

'And when was it you realized you no longer loved Cora?'

'Not long after the wedding, as soon as we came to live in the place where we still live.'

'But do you think Cora was already practising that profession, then?'

'Perhaps so; she was already reserved and mysterious. She said she was working in a dressmaker's shop, but often I failed to find her there. And then she had men and women friends that I didn't know, to whom she would never introduce me.'

'And the grandparents – did you go and see them often?'

'At the time when I loved Cora, I was always looking for an excuse to visit them. They attracted me, just as Cora and everything that concerned Cora attracted me. It was my myth that was working, in short, and they formed part of the myth. Then, when the myth crumbled away, not only did I stop seeing them but it seemed to me almost incredible that I should have gone there so often and above all that I should have taken so much trouble to meet them.'

'So much trouble?'

'Yes, indeed. Cora didn't want to introduce me to her family, I don't know why; I had to go on insisting before I could persuade her to take me one day to her home.'

'And what effect does going there have on you now?'

'It makes me feel rather ashamed.'

'Ashamed?'

'Yes, it makes me feel ashamed, like going back to a place where I got drunk and did stupid things.'

'But perhaps they weren't stupid things.'

'Possibly, but what can I do about it if I now feel them to be so?'

After this, Baba asked me no more questions and I drove on for a little time in silence. Then we came into Via Tuscolana, a deep chasm between two rows of working-class apartment houses. The fronts of the buildings, above the ground floors, were studded with balconies; below were shops, like luminous caverns, and the figures of passers-by were black against the white light of the shop-windows; and there were bars, cinemas, dairies, confectioners' shops and big entrance-doors. Baba asked me: 'Have you never been here before?'

'No. When I used to go and see your grandparents, they lived at the settlement, then Cora managed to earn more money, whatever her job may have been, and so they moved to Via Casilina. I've never been here.'

'Well, stop now. We've arrived.'

I stopped the car, we got out and Baba started off towards a confectioner's shop, saying: 'I must buy something for Grandma. I've always done it and she expects it.'

We went into a large, white, bare hall, where the vibrant neon light glittered on the crockery set out on the counter, on the chromium of tables and chairs and on the big mirrors behind the rows of bottles. The juke-box was turned on full blast, and a group of boys were listening to the noisy music. Baba went to the window, looked for a moment at the trays filled with cream cakes and sandwiches, then selected a box of sweets with a brightly coloured lid and asked me, wishing as usual to make me behave like a father: 'Will you pay?'

I paid and we went out. We walked a few steps along the pavement and then Baba led me through an entrance-door and thence into a courtyard which, as far as I could see in the darkness, appeared to be very large, with extremely high walls, of a prison-like bareness. Baba went over to a door which was lit by a lamp and marked with the letter D. We entered the lift, so narrow that we had to go in sideways. I closed the doors and Baba pressed the button for the eighth floor.

As the lift rose very slowly upwards, we stood face to face, without speaking, so close that we were touching one another. Baba's coat was open so that her breast protruded from it, and a slight oscillating movement, whether voluntary or involuntary I could not tell, thrust her against me from time to time, and then I was aware of the pressure of her bosom against my chest; and I could not help looking at her eyes and was astonished to find in them no confirmation of the ambiguous challenge which there appeared to be in this contact. Her eyes were as always, beautiful, myopic, the pupils motionless and cut in half by the sleepy-looking eyelids. All at once I said to her: 'Does your grandmother know about Cora?'

'You never stop thinking about that.'

'Does she know, or doesn't she?'

'She knows and she doesn't know.'

'What does that mean?'

'Perhaps she knew once, then she wished to forget it, and now, perhaps, goodness knows, she thinks she dreamt it.'

'And your grandfather?'

'He doesn't know. But he feels it.'

'How d'you mean, he feels it?'

'There are people who know things and people who feel things. My grandfather feels them.'

The lift stopped with a jolt which threw Baba against me for the last time, then we got out on to a narrow landing encumbered with a couple of dustbins. Baba pressed the bell and said: 'I do beg you to be affectionate with them, even if you don't feel anything.'

'But why?'

'Do it for my sake, please.'

The door opened, there were affectionate exclamations, then Baba's grandmother embraced and kissed her and was embraced and kissed in turn. Then followed thanks for the box of sweets. Finally Baba moved aside and said: 'Grandma, you see who I've brought to visit you today?'

At the time when I used to see them frequently I had liked Cora's parents, not only on account of my myth of poverty, but also for what I may call an aesthetic reason: with their simple, severe faces, they had looked like one of those peasant couples who sculptured likenesses, hand in hand, are to be seen on the lids of Roman sarcophagi. But a rapid glance now showed me a radical change. In the features of the old woman's face, sunk in fat, glossy new flesh, there was nothing left of the original rustic character. Her light blue eyes, once simple and intense as wild flowers, were now dimmed and half hidden by her bulging, flushed cheekbones; between her swollen, florid cheeks her nose appeared too small; with its twisted, honeyed expression, her mouth made me regret its former haughtiness. I noticed also that her hair was no longer pulled back and gathered in a bun at the back of her neck, but was waved and parted carefully down the middle; and that this hair was not grey but of an ugly artificial colour, between copper and chestnut. An attempt at lipstick disguised her thin mouth; a veil of too-pink powder overspread her rubicund cheeks. She looked at me and exclaimed: 'The professor!'

Ten years before, my mother-in-law had addressed me by the familiar *tu*; and after my marriage she had called me 'my son'. But now, for some reason or other, I had become 'the professor'. Not wishing to delve into the reasons for the change, I replied, with all the warmth possible: 'And how are you, Signora, how are you?'

She led us into the flat, muttering: 'I'm all right, but I'm not what I was'; and indeed I could see that she walked with an effort, dragging her feet in two enormous plush slippers. Once we were in the sitting-room she invited us to sit down on the 'suite' which consisted of a sofa and two armchairs covered in purple satin: 'Sit down here, Professor.' I sat down and cast a glance at the glittering, brand-new furniture of dark rose-wood with sycamore claw-feet. 'What a pretty room!' I said.

'We bought it all on the hire-purchase; we haven't finished paying for it yet.'

'How many rooms have you?'

'Five rooms, as well as the usual offices. There's also the maid's little room with its own bath.'

'So you have a maid?'

'Yes, a young girl that I brought from my own village. She's gone now to fetch the milk.'

I pointed to the big, blind, grey eye of a television set standing in a corner: 'D'you like television?'

'Yes, I like it,' she said, 'especially in the evening, when some of our neighbours come in and we pass the time looking at the programmes. I like the light music best of all.'

She sat bolt upright in the armchair as she spoke, in a slightly unnatural attitude which betrayed her original rusticity. 'But we don't always stay at home in the evenings,' she added. 'Sometimes we go to the cinema. We have a cinema close at hand, right below here. Yesterday evening we saw a film – just fancy, one of the ones that describe the things of the future!'

'Science fiction?'

'Yes, science fiction. But I didn't like it very much, it frightened me. What d'you think, Professor – will monsters arrive from the stars and kill us all, one of these days?'

'Who knows? Probably not.'

Suddenly she exclaimed: 'A cup of coffee, would you like a cup of coffee, Professor?'

'Why d'you call him Professor?' said Baba. 'Call him Francesco.'

'Another time I'll try to, but today I find it difficult, it's so long since I've seen him. Some coffee, then?'

'No, thank you.'

'It's no trouble to make it.'

'Thank you, no.'

She was silent for a moment, looking at me with complacency. Then, with a smile, she said to Baba: 'You know, I don't find him changed at all, the Professor. Just the same.'

To change the subject, I asked her: 'And how about your husband?'

'He's at the shop.'

'What shop?'

'The shop that Cora bought for us, when she took over this flat.'

'What sort of a shop is it? Fruit and vegetables?'

'No, we haven't that one now, they pulled down the building. Now we have a shop for electrical appliances.'

'And how is it going?'

'So so; there's competition, of course.'

'Perhaps your husband preferred the fruit and vegetable shop.'

'Yes, he liked that type of shop better. Naturally, as he'd been a market gardener like his father and grandfather.'

'Is he alone in the shop?'

'No, there's an assistant, a first-class idler. He himself, to tell the truth, is very little in the shop, perhaps an hour or two a day. Ah, he's not what he used to be. His favourite is not his own shop but the wine-shop.'

'He drinks?'

'Does he indeed? Does he *not*? He drinks a very great deal.'

I could not help picturing the ex-greengrocer pulling a new electric lamp out of its cardboard covering and, before selling it, testing it by pressing it into a holder fixed to the counter; and comparing the plump nutritious, varied fruits which he had formerly sold with the bulbs of the present day, all alike, mass-produced, stamped with the number of kilowatts in white characters on the glass. 'Is it a big shop?' I asked.

'Well, yes, it's fairly big.'

'D'you sell nothing but electric bulbs there?'

'No, all sorts of things, but only in the electricity line: stoves, electric irons, lamps.' She turned towards Baba and added, with a smile: 'You know, I recognize the Professor by the questions he asks. It's perfectly true, he hasn't changed at all. Even in those days, he was always asking questions, he wanted to know everything. I remember that once he kept me for a whole hour, asking me what was needed to build an un-authorized hut in a settlement. He wanted to know all about it: how many bricks, how much corrugated iron, how many beams, how much lime. We were living then in the Gordiani settlement, so you can't remember, you were too small. He pestered me with so many questions that in the end I said to him: "Instead of asking me so many questions, you, who are a journalist and know so many people, do something to get me a house, a real house, even if it has only one room." Cora, who was there, was angry, and afterwards she told me I oughtn't to have asked anything from him. That was the last time we saw each other and I thought he must be offended. But Cora said he had gone off on his travels and was never in Rome.

Well, we've got our flat now, you see, Professor? And a fine big flat too, thanks to Cora.'

'Cora is a good daughter,' I said.

She looked at me with half-closed eyes and replied, with an almost teasing smile: 'Yes, it must be admitted, she's certainly a good daughter.'

Baba made a characteristically impulsive, irrelevant gesture: she fell upon her grandmother and embraced her impetuously, saying: 'And your grand-daughter – how about her? Isn't she a good grand-daughter as well?'

'Good and beautiful too ... But keep still, you're untidying my hair.'

'D'you know, Francesco, Grandma goes to the hairdresser once a week and has her hair waved and set and the colour touched up? Just like a girl of twenty?'

'Does Baba come and see you often?' I enquired.

'Yes, at least twice a week.'

'And what does Baba do here?'

'There you are again, with your questions. She behaves like the good grand-daughter she is. She keeps me company, we look at the television or she goes with me to the shops.'

'And Cora?'

'I don't see much of Cora. She's affectionate, she's a good daughter, but she has a lot to do.'

Baba was looking now at me, now at her grandmother, with placid, irritating complacency. Then she said: 'By the way, here's the allowance, Grandma.'

She fumbled in her coat pocket, pulled out an envelope and handed it to the old woman. The latter took it and remarked: 'Cora is so punctual. Never once does she forget the exact day for sending me the monthly allowance.'

Baba added: 'Mother asked me to tell you that next week she'll come and fetch you with the car to go and see that house at Sermoneta.'

'No need to tell you that Cora's a good daughter,' said the old woman. 'I suggested to her that I'd like to have a little house in the country to go to in the summer, when it's too hot in Rome; and she's giving it to me as a present. Yes, she's a good daughter, certainly she's a good daughter.' She repeated her praise of Cora over and over again in a curious sing-song voice, as though she wanted to make fun of it; then she turned to Baba. 'Why don't you take off that coat?' she said: 'it's not cold in here, you'd be better without it.'

'No, I won't take it off because we ought to be going,' replied Baba, rising to her feet.

'You haven't been here long today, you usually stay longer.'

'Yes, but today we have things to do.'

'Anyhow wait until my husband comes in; he should be here at any moment.'

'Where has he gone?'

'Ah, Professor, where d'you suppose he's gone? To the wine-shop, as usual.'

'I'm sorry, Grandma, but Francesco has things to do: he'll see Grandpa another time.'

The old woman did not insist. She rose and led us into the entrance-hall, dragging her feet in her slippers. Without turning round, she said: 'And you, Professor, are you staying in Rome or going away again?'

'I think I shall be going away again.'

'And where will you be going?'

'I don't yet know exactly.'

'Lucky you, to travel so much. D'you know what I'm more sorry about than anything?'

'What's that?'

'Not to be able to take a trip to Russia, to see how they're getting on there, and whether it's true that they're better off than we are. But it's too late now, I'm too old. Have you been in Russia, Professor?'

'Yes, I've been there.'

'And how are the Russians getting on? Is it true they're better off than we are?'

'They're all right, but they're not better off than you, Agnese.'

'Oh yes, we're well off, thank God. But for one family like ours that is well off, you know how many there are that can't manage. Not everyone has the good fortune to have a daughter like Cora who has been able to pull herself up from nothing, so to speak.'

'Yes indeed, not everyone has a daughter like Cora, that's true.'

'But in Russia, Professor, are there any shops?'

'Yes, there are. But they belong to the State.'

'Like our railways, let us say?'

'Yes, let us say, like our railways.'

'But is it true that in these shops a person can take anything he likes and go away without paying?'

'And you, Agnese, do you travel for nothing on our railways?'

'Then you have to pay there, as we do here?'

'Certainly.'

'And so *they* have money too?'

'Of course.'

'You know what *I* say? That if they have money, I have a feeling that they have all the rest as well.'

'How d'you mean?'

'Oh well, all the troubles, just like us here.'

'Grandma, you can talk to Francesco another time. I promise you I'll bring him here next week.'

'Anyhow, Professor, you're a lucky man to be able to travel and see things with your own eyes.'

'Good-bye, Grandma.'

The two women embraced and kissed one another on the landing. Just at that moment the lift stopped at that same floor, the doors opened and out stepped an old man in dark clothes, with the brim of his black hat pulled down over his eyes: it was Baba's grandfather.

I found him changed too, in the same way as his wife. Like Agnese, he had had in the past a head such as are to be seen on Roman sarcophagi, such as are still to be seen today amongst the peasants of the province of Lazio. But, as with Agnese, an increase of fat, by changing the proportions of the features, had also changed the relationship between them, so that now they no longer looked in the least Roman, or at any rate their Roman character was very different from what it had once been. His nose, once aquiline, had grown smaller owing to the plumpness of his cheeks and now resembled a hook of glossy, purple flesh; his mouth, beneath his drooping moustaches, looked twisted as though with discontent; his eyes, which had been blue and simple like those of his wife, now appeared dim between the swollen eyelids. He had been brown and wiry, with a few forceful wrinkles; now he was pink and smooth, with two bulges of fat interlaced with violet veins on his cheekbones.

As soon as he saw us, he made a movement as if to turn his back on us and go back into the lift. His wife, smiling in her own artful way, stopped him. 'Antonio,' she said, 'don't you see who's here?'

'Well, who is it?' The voice was low, hesitating, and at the same time curiously aggressive. I noticed the look in his eyes: it wavered like a candle-flame shaken by the wind. I recalled what Agnese had said about her husband's habits and was convinced that he was drunk. She persevered: 'It's the Professor, Cora's husband. Don't you recognize him?'

'The Professor? It can't be.'

'Why can't it be?'

'He's always travelling and travelling; no one ever sees him.'

Baba burst out laughing. Indulgent, smiling, his wife said to him: 'But it really is him; look at him, it's the Professor, your son-in-law.'

'Don't know who you mean. I haven't any son-in-law.'

'Ah, you haven't any son-in-law. Oh yes, you have, and here he is.'

'Never seen him.'

'A good thing we have Cora's wedding photograph in the sitting-room. I'll show it to you afterwards. He's there, and Cora, and we two.'

'Wedding? What are you talking about?'

'So now you don't even recognize your own relations?'

'I haven't any relations. I'm not a relation of anyone's.'

'Gabriella here, your grand-daughter – at least you'll recognize her?'

'Never seen her.'

'And me – don't you recognize *me*? Don't you remember my face?'

'Nothing, nothing, nothing.'

'But I'm your wife.'

'I haven't a wife, I haven't anybody.'

Here Agnese threw us a glance of connivance and then said: 'You haven't anybody? Really? Yet you have a daughter called Cora, a wife called Agnese, a grand-daughter called Gabriella, a son-in-law called Francesco, and you yourself are called Antonio.'

'Antonio? Who's that?'

'You see?' Agnese, modestly triumphant, as though after the complete success of an experiment, turned towards us. 'You see? When he's been drinking he has a fixed idea, not only that he can't recognize other people, but that he doesn't even recognize himself.' Then she addressed her husband again. 'If you're not Antonio, then tell me who you are.'

'I'm who I am, and what's it got to do with you?' With these words he turned his back upon us and went into the lift again, an old man with a bent back, bow legs, arms dangling in front of him, a true peasant in spite of his clothes, which were not of fustian or corduroy but of dark woollen cloth, and in spite of his shoes, not heavy and hobnailed but thin and sharp-pointed like those of the boys I had seen shortly before round the juke-box in the bar. After he had entered the lift he turned round, stood quite still for a moment, erect inside the cage like a mummy in its sarcophagus; then he closed the door and the lift at once started going down, and through the glass we saw him gradually disappear, first his legs, then his body, then his face, and finally his hat.

Then the old woman said with a smile: 'You see, Professor? He drinks and then he doesn't recognize anybody, not even himself.'

'Wine plays tricks.'

'Oh yes, wine. But that's not to say he doesn't do it on purpose. He has his days. Today, for instance, it might well be that he hasn't had anything to drink at all and that he's just play-acting.'

'But why?'

'Goodness only knows. For no reason, just to amuse himself. You know, Gabriella, some days ago he planted himself in front of the looking-glass in the sitting-room and said to himself: "Who on earth are you? Don't know you, never seen you, you ugly old drunk".'

Baba burst out laughing. Her grandmother was smiling too. Baba went to the lift and pressed the button. Then we stood there, all three of us motionless and silent, the old woman in the doorway, Baba and I on the landing, like three actors who have finished their performance and are now waiting for the curtain to fall; but the fall of the curtain is delayed because something is not working. The lift, after going down to the bottom, took a long time to come up the eight floors again and then finally stopped with a sudden jerk; Baba and I said good-bye once more to the old woman and got in.

The lift started going down again. Baba, as before, was standing in front of me, and again, as we went down, she started swaying slightly backwards and forwards with her whole body; and once more I felt her bosom pressing closely, at regular intervals, against my chest. Finally she said: 'You ought to thank me; I did it well, didn't I?'

'Meaning what?'

'I cut short our visit because I knew it was disagreeable to you.'

'D'you usually stay longer?'

'I usually stay the whole afternoon.'

Sunday, November 22nd

I have read over the pages of my diary in which I described the visit to Cora's parents; and I feel it necessary to state, as I have already done elsewhere, that here too I have modified the truth of the facts. This time, however, the change did not take place as it were in spite of myself, as with my invention of the discovery of Sophocles' *Oedipus Rex* on my bedside table; but it was brought about consciously and deliberately, even if for reasons which, fundamentally, are not clear. What does this mean? It means, I think, that the reasons for which, from time to time, I feel it necessary to alter the facts as I recount them in the diary are manifold and vary according to the nature of the facts themselves and the kind of relationship I have with them. So, in some cases, I amputate or disguise or actually suppress; in others, I develop, I dilate, I reconstruct. . . .

Let us take for example the visit to Cora's parents. Nine-tenths of the visit I recounted faithfully or almost so (I may have changed just a few words or omitted a few sentences); that is, up till the moment when the old grandfather appeared inside the lift; but I invented, or rather I developed in my own way, the whole of the subsequent incident, when the old man asserted that he did not recognize us, took refuge in the lift and went down again to the ground floor.

In reality things went in the following way: the old man came out of the lift, had the appearance of being drunk, swayed and actually stumbled, greeted us confusedly, as though he did not recognize us, and went straight into the flat. Then the old woman apologized for her husband, saying that when he was drunk he did not recognize anybody. Baba and I said good-bye to her and went away.

It is obvious that, by extending and completing the scene when I recounted it in my diary, I altered the true facts. Indeed in the diary the old man not merely fails to recognize us, but he says so, he confirms it, he emphasizes it. His behaviour, in other words, is not confused and ambiguous as it was in reality; it is clear and decided. And whereas in reality the fact that the old man did not recognize us might be an entirely casual and insignificant matter, no more indeed than the effect of drinking, in the diary his failure to recognize us acquires significance and implies a judgment.

From the diary, in short, it might be thought that the old man fails to recognize us, not so much because he is drunk, as because the prosperity due to Cora's money – money of which the old man, according to Baba, 'feels' the origin – has in the end made him a stranger both to himself and to others. In the diary, that is to say, I interpret reality, I adapt it, I reconstruct it, I integrate it, I complete it, according to an idea, or rather an ideology, of my own. Cora's money, according to this idea, being earned as it is earned, cannot fail to produce estrangement and unreality. Thus, by inventing the old man's failure to recognize us, I am not in reality inventing anything; all I am doing is to enlarge a tendency, to develop an embryo. The truth, perceived by intuition and reconstructed, is not fundamentally altered.

Nevertheless, in reality things went differently; and the incident of the failed recognition, of undoubted effectiveness in a novel, still remains an invention. It is true that ill-gotten money generally corrupts and makes people strangers to themselves and to others; this I have often noticed and have had innumerable proofs of it. But that does not at all mean that this is a rule; and that anyhow, even if it is a rule, Baba's grandfather may not constitute an exception to the rule.

In other words, it may very well be that, when all is said and done, it does not matter in the least to Baba's grandfather that Cora's money is made out of the *maison de rendezvous*. He drinks because he likes wine, he knows all about Cora, or rather he 'feels' it, and he doesn't care, he loves Cora just the same, as a father loves a daughter, his conscience doesn't trouble him, and possibly – who knows? – he even approves of his daughter's occupation.

And I myself know nothing of Cora's father, absolutely nothing. I have merely seen him: a speck of colour, a bulky object, something that passed for a moment across my field of vision and then vanished.

Naturally there can be no harm in including the scene of the failed recognition in my novel, in fact it might have some advantages; but I doubt whether I shall include it. Not so much because it is invented, as because what led me to invent it was something false, insincere, non-genuine in short, something from which I want to free myself, precisely by keeping this diary.

Tuesday, November 24th

Yesterday evening Baba did not come to wish me goodnight; and I did not hear her come into the flat. At the time I had a feeling of disappointment, then I forgot about it and went to bed. But I slept little, and this morning, waking up at about seven o'clock, almost without thinking I slipped on a dressing-gown, left my room and went to Baba's door.

I knocked, but there was no answer. After a little I slowly turned the handle and went in. The room was full of light and all in order; the bed untouched. Baba had slept out.

I went back to my study, dressed, had breakfast, and it was after eight o'clock when I sat down at my desk. Then it seemed to me that I heard someone open and close the front door of the flat, walk into the entrance-hall and then along the passage. I went on working until about half past nine, then, suddenly, again without thinking, I got up, left the room and once more went to Baba's door.

The door was ajar; I went in without knocking. This time I saw her at once: she was lying fast asleep on the divan, still dressed in her trousers and sweater, flat on her back with her legs apart, one towards the wall and the other dangling down on the other side of the divan, so that her foot was almost touching the floor. She had one arm over her eyes, as if to shield them from the light. But, in order to sleep more comfortably, she had undone the zip fastener of her trousers on her hip. Through the gap left by the zip fastener there was a glimpse of the crumpled, transparent, pale blue material of her slip, and this last detail reminded me of the imaginary scene of seduction which I had incorporated in my diary some days ago. The dog, as usual, was lying on the carpet at the foot of the bed; he recognized me, but all he did was to raise his head in my direction and wag his tail, without barking.

I walked across on tiptoe. Baba's attitude of sudden, abrupt stupefaction, as though she had fallen senseless on the divan when she came in that morning and had remained exactly where she had fallen, doing nothing except loosen her zip fastening, with no energy to undress and go to bed – all this made me think she had spent the night without sleep and with a man. It was the thought of a suspicious lover rather than of an anxious father. I felt, in fact, unexpectedly, the gnawing of a furious jealousy, and I could not help saying to myself: 'I respected her, I played up to her, and this is the result.'

I stooped down and looked at her wide, capriciously formed mouth: the lips were parted, the upper lip curling slightly upwards and shadowed by a faint line of dark down, the lower lip thicker and curving a little outwards above the chin; both of them of an eager softness that seemed parched by the warmth of her breath, and looking as though swollen and kept open by unconscious desire. I became aware that, almost irresistibly, I was stooping lower and lower towards this mouth, with the idea that I might go so far, if not actually as to kiss it, at any rate to feel the breath which issued from it. At that same moment Baba moved, withdrew her arm from her face and opened her eyes. We looked at one another, our faces close together. Finally she asked me: 'What were you doing?'

I drew myself up and replied: 'I was looking at you.'

She sat up too, and pulled up her zip fastener; then she leant forward, her chin between her hands, and, looking up at me, said in an unpleasantly sententious tone: 'It's dangerous to look at a woman while she's asleep.'

'Why?'

'Because there might be temptations.'

'Why, what temptations?'

She did not answer immediately. She yawned and sat staring for a moment at the carpet at her feet. Then she replied slowly: 'I've been feeling that the time would have to come for an explanation. Well, it's true, I like you, and you, it seems, like me. But we're father and daughter and I want absolutely that we should remain so. D'you see?'

I was again struck by her tone of voice, which was not merely disagreeable but also, as it were, satiated, as though what had happened during the night had made her, for the moment, indifferent and unfeeling towards me. 'I heard you come in at eight o'clock,' I said. 'Where were you last night?'

'I go where I please.'

I realized that I was on the verge of making a retort in doubtful taste. But I could not refrain from replying: 'We are father and daughter. Very well. Then I have the right to know where you spent the night.'

I had the impression that these words did not annoy her at all, in fact, on the contrary, that in some way they pleased her. It was indeed as good a way as any of showing myself to be her father, even if I did so by scolding her. Looking up at me with a hypocritical air, between eyelids heavy with sleep, she admitted: 'Yes, you're right. Well then : I spent the night with Santoro.'

'With Santoro?'

'Yes. D'you want to know what we did?'

I hesitated, then said stubbornly: 'Of course.'

'We were at a party in a villa outside Rome.'

'Where?'

'In the direction of Santa Marinella.'

'And what did you do at this party?'

'We had dinner, we danced.'

'But who was there?'

'Boys and girls.'

'What time did the party finish?'

'About four.'

'It takes barely an hour from Santa Marinella to Rome. What did you do until eight o'clock?'

'Santoro was so insistent that I agreed to go home with him. He's setting up house and there's still nothing in the flat except a few bits of furniture in the sitting-room. We stayed together in the sitting-room until about half-past seven.'

As she said this, she rose to her feet and, looking more than ever like a lazy, sleepy young bear, went slowly and stood in front of the wardrobe looking-glass; then she took a brush and started vigorously scrubbing at her dishevelled hair. After a little, she went on in a negligent sort of way: 'Don't you also want to know what we did during those two and a half hours, between five and half past seven?'

I became suddenly irritated, or rather, I wanted to become

irritated and, to my surprise, I succeeded immediately. 'Come here,' I muttered.

She came over to me, heavy with sleep, her eyes half-hidden by a broad lock of hair. I looked at her for a moment, and she, still not understanding, asked: 'Did you want to say something to me?'

'This!' The slap was aimed at her cheek; but, intentionally perhaps, at the last moment I turned it aside towards her mouth.

She remained standing in front of me, looking at me in a perplexed but not offended manner, as though she had reflected upon the way she ought to behave. Then she put up her hand to her cheek and confirmed: 'You slapped my face.'

'Certainly.'

She gave me another look, then turned her back on me, went over to the mirror and again started scrubbing at her hair with almost frantic energy. Finally, in a quiet voice, she said: 'It's not true that I went to Santoro's flat. Actually we were at Fregene until seven o'clock, in a villa where one of those boys lives. Then we came back to Rome and Santoro brought me here and went off to his own home.'

'Then why did you tell me a lie?'

'To see what effect it would have on you, how you would react.'

'And what effect d'you think it had on me? How did I react?'

She was silent for a moment, then, in an ambiguous, indefinably sarcastic, schoolmistressy tone, she answered: 'It had a bad effect on you and you reacted like a rather old-fashioned father, aggressively and intolerantly. But you're on the right road. Carry on in the same way.'

Thursday, November 26th

'Were you working? Am I disturbing you?'

'No, not at all.'

'I wanted to say . . .'

'What?'

'I wanted to ask you a favour.'

'Well, tell me . . .'

'Is your brother still a stockbroker?'

'I believe so.'

'Well, I have some savings, I should like you to ask your brother if he can . . .'

'If he can what?'

'Everyone says the lira will go down. If he can invest them for me in Switzerland.'

I looked at Cora for a moment in silence. And so, I could not help thinking, this was the use to which my reconciliation with my family, so greatly desired by Baba, was being put: to make me act as an accomplice in Cora's business. To gain time, I enquired: 'How much money is it?'

Without concealing her own diffidence, she replied: 'I'll tell you that afterwards, when I know if the thing is possible.'

'The thing is not possible.'

'Legally, no. But your brother, if he is willing, can do it.'

'My brother will not do it.'

'But why?'

'At the most, my brother will be able to give you some advice about investing your savings in a legal manner.'

'I'm only asking you to find out if he can do it.'

In the meantime I had been thinking. The excuse of the legality of the operation did not hold water: Cora certainly knew that operations of transferring money to Switzerland could be done normally. I said to myself that I could not refuse her the favour she asked of me because I should have to disclose the real reason for my refusal, which was my disgust at the source of her money; and I could not do this without mentioning her profession, which would lead either to a rupture or to a complicity – two possibilities that were equally distasteful to me. Better pretend really to speak about it to my brother, and then tell her that he did not deal with affairs of that kind. After all, it would be a pretext for visiting him; it was seven or eight years since I had seen him.

So I told Cora that I would find out about it, and that same morning I telephoned to Massimiliano. I think nothing can give a better idea of my relations with my brother than our telephone conversation, which I report here faithfully.

'Who's speaking?'

'It's Francesco.'

'Francesco who?'

'Your brother Francesco.'

'Better late than never!'

'How are you?'

'Very well indeed – and you?'

'I'm very well too.'

'All well at home?'

'Yes, thank you. And your family?'

'Matilde and I have parted.'

'I'm sorry.'

'I'm not.'

'And your children?'

'They're very well too.'

'I want to talk to you.'

'To talk to me?'

'Yes.'

'What d'you want to say to me?'

'Oh well, I'll tell you when I see you.'

'Come along whenever you like. Today, even.'

'What time?'

'Come and have some coffee.'

'Can I bring Baba?'

'What on earth is Baba?'

'She's my daughter.'

'I didn't know you had a daughter.'

'She's my wife's daughter, actually.'

'Bring anyone you like.'

So that afternoon Baba and I went to have coffee with my brother. He lived near the Borghese Gardens, in the house which had belonged to our parents, where I myself had lived until the day when I married Cora. As we drove past in front of the Borghese Museum, I said to Baba: 'This is the quarter in which I lived until the day of my marriage. I haven't been back here more than two or three times since.'

'How d'you feel about it now?'

'Nothing at all. It's just as if I'd never been here.'

We came into the gently sloping street: two rows of small buildings, two rows of gardens, two rows of oleanders, two rows of cars parked along the pavement, on either side of the clean asphalt; and at the end the iron gates of the park and, beyond the gates, the trees. We got out of the car, and then I had the feeling that I had lost my way, not because this street was not the one in which I had lived, but rather that the street in which I had lived no longer existed, either here or anywhere else. For there should have been, down at the far end, the white, four-storeyed house, in the *art nouveau* style, in which I had lived for so many years. But this building was not there; in its place rose a modern edifice, ox-blood-coloured, its façade full of tall, narrow windows framed in black marble. I confess that for one instant I hoped that, by some magic, not only the house but also my brother and his family had been wiped off the face of the earth. And I could not help thinking: 'There's nothing left, or perhaps there never was anything. And Baba and I can give up the idea of the visit and go for a drive in the country.' Meanwhile I was approaching the entrance-door, and then I saw the well-known brass nameplate, with my brother's surname which was also my own. And I said: 'You see what happens if one travels and takes no notice of one's own family?'

'What happens?'

'The day one decides to take some notice of them, one comes and finds for example that the family house has been demolished and that an entirely different house has been built in its place.'

'What was your house like?'

'Like that one there, more or less: *art nouveau*, old-fashioned, gloomy, but, as they used to say in those days, "a gentleman's residence".'

'And who lived there?'

'Our whole family. We lived on the two top floors – that is, my parents, my brother, my brother's family and I. On the ground floor was my father's office.'

We went in, past the black and red marble of the entrance-hall, to the yellow-metal lift-cage. We closed the doors and the lift went up to the third floor. We rang the bell and waited; there was a sound of footsteps and the door opened; and then the maid showed us into a room of heterogeneous style, crammed full of objects – or was it perhaps that the big mirrors in burnished metal frames, with their funereal rose-coloured glass, repeated *ad infinitum* the sofas and armchairs upholstered in white satin, the curly, gilt, baroque console-tables, the black-and-purple Louis-Philippe chairs, the blue opaline lamps, the blue-and-cream Chinese rugs, the negro masks, the artificial flowers under glass bells, and the green-and-yellow cage with a live yellow-and-green parrot inside it? We walked over to the glass doors and looked out; the painted whiteness of the iron furniture was out of harmony with the lilac of the terrace floor-tiles in the low light of the dark, frowning autumn sky. 'Tell me what your brother is like,' said Baba.

'He's a monster.'

'A monster?'

'Yes, a monster.'

'And your brother's wife?'

'Another monster. But we shan't see her; they've parted.'

'You don't seem to be very fond of your relations.'

'That's true.'

'But what have they done to you?'

'Nothing.'

A door opened behind us. We turned round, and there followed the rather painful scene that I had expected. My brother shook me by the hand and slapped me on the shoulder with his other hand, saying: 'I'm pleased you've come. Let me look at you, you're not changed at all'; and then, as though yielding to a rush of unpremeditated, irresistible emotion, he kissed me on both cheeks. I drew back immediately after the embrace and replied: 'And you're just the same too.' Then my brother asked: 'And who's this pretty baby?'; and I said: 'It's Baba, my stepdaughter'; and my brother and Baba shook hands, and my brother said: 'Good, good, come and sit down'; and so we all three sat down, opposite the glass doors opening on to the terrace.

I looked at my brother and realized that my old and very special dislike of him had not changed: it was not so much he himself that I hated as his face, and this because it was also my own face, but disfigured by a materialism and a sensuality by which, every morning when I looked at myself in the looking-glass, I feared to discover that I too was afflicted. Both of us, once upon a time, had had faces with very regular, harmonious features; but in my brother's case it seemed that, with the years, the upper part of his face had become pinched and diminished, the lower part broader and heavier. His forehead seemed lower and narrower, his eyes smaller, his nose shorter; in contrast his mouth now protruded in a rather ape-like manner and his jaws looked as if they had developed by dint of chewing. His face had reddened and had a turgid, congested look, a look not of health but of unhealthy swollenness resulting from a plethoric blood-condition. I also noticed with aversion that he was showily dressed – in a shaggy, snuff-coloured jacket, grey flannel trousers and suede bootees. My brother crossed his leg and said to me: 'Well, tell me, you find a good many changes, don't you?'

'Yes, the house itself, to begin with.'

'I had it pulled down, and then I rebuilt in a more rational way. That old house was a waste, in a quarter like this, where the value of building sites has risen enormously. Instead of three flats there are now twelve.'

'I knew nothing about these demolitions.'

'You never put in an appearance. There have been other demolitions too. I've demolished my marriage. I've parted from Matilde.'

'So you told me this morning.'

'It may seem strange to you that we've parted after twenty and more years of marriage. But I couldn't go on any longer with Matilde.'

'Why?'

'Because she's a bitch and a hag and a maniac. Calm and honeyed on the surface, but, under all that sweetness, jealous to the point of madness. To the point of telephoning me every half-hour at the office to make sure I was there. To the point – you'll hardly believe it – of writing anonymous letters to herself about my supposed love-affairs, so as to have a pretext for making scandalous scenes. In the end I told her to get out. She made me buy her a flat, she kept the children, she wanted a packet of money, but at least I don't see her any more. Ugly bitch, pestilential hag, hellcat, scum of the earth, crook.' He heaped insults on his wife persistently, slowly, one might say methodically. 'My life with her,' he went on, 'had become a hell. Especially when she discovered my relations with Popi.'

'Who is Popi?'

'The person I'm living with now. You'll see her in a moment.'

There was a brief silence. With a sudden, guttural sound the parrot screamed from its cage: 'Cretonne!' 'How odd,' said Baba; 'perhaps that parrot once belonged to an upholsterer.'

'Why an upholsterer?'

'Because it said "cretonne".'

'No, it doesn't say "cretonne", it says "cretino"; but as it's a *cretino*, an idiot, itself, it doesn't know how to pronounce it.'

'Who taught it that word?'

'Popi, of course. Now tell me honestly,' added my brother,

all of a sudden, turning towards me, 'you find me a bit fatter?'

'No, I don't find you fatter at all.'

'Oh yes, I know I've got fatter. It's Popi's fault; she makes me eat too much. Much fatter, or just a little?'

'To tell you the truth, I don't know.'

'Let's hear what Baba's got to say; she's a woman. Do I seem fat, to you, or not?'

Baba turned her usual sleepy glance on my brother. 'How do I come into it?' she asked.

'You're my niece, I'm your uncle; or are there some things that can't be said between relations? Well, in your opinion, am I fat or not?'

'I don't know what you were like before. But, compared with Francesco, I should say yes.'

'There you are, you see. The chief thing that's made me grow fat is the joy of not living with Matilde any more. Blasted bitch, idiot, foul, loathsome creature, pious, hypocritical, sanctimonious humbug.' Once again my brother gave vent to his retrospective hatred for his wife. Then, turning suddenly to Baba, he resumed: 'And you – what do you do, Baby?'

'My name is Baba, not Baby.'

'Ah yes, Baba, I'm sorry; I hope you're not offended.'

'No, I'm not offended. I'm a student at the University.'

'And what are you studying?'

'Letters.'

'That's splendid, that's splendid, good old Baba!' My brother leant forward in his armchair, red and congested in the face, and gave Baba a little affectionate slap on the cheek. His big, hairy hand, with its short fingers and spatulate nails and a gold bracelet with a huge watch round the wrist, paused in the air for a moment after this little slap and then finished up with a slight hint of a caress. Baba waited, upright and motionless, for the hand to be withdrawn from her cheek. My brother fell heavily back in his armchair; and at the sound of the door opening, said with a sigh: 'Here's Popi, in other words Isabella.'

We looked. We rose to our feet. Very tall and very thin but with a disproportionately enormous bosom borne horizontally in front of her beneath the close-fitting stuff of her blouse, Popi had a head like a bird, with round eyes and a long, pointed nose, on a long, slender neck. My brother encouraged her to embrace us, both myself and Baba: 'Come on, give them each a kiss, it's my niece and my brother'; Popi obeyed with simpering docility; then we sat down again; but Popi remained standing and offered us coffee from a trolley-table which she had pushed in front of her as she came in.

'How much sugar?'

'You like it without sugar, don't you?'

'One lump of sugar, or two?'

The coffee-cups passed one by one from her thin, tapering hand to ours. She walked on very high heels, with little short steps, impeded by her tight skirt. Her extravagant bosom, on that tall, thin body, made me think of the immense pumpkins and gourds that lie on the ground, attached to long, slender stalks, in vegetable-gardens. Finally she sat down on the arm of my brother's chair and asked me: 'You do journalism, don't you?'

'Yes.'

'Max has told me that you've been in a great many different countries. What a wonderful thing, to travel!'

The tone of her voice was soft, tremulous, melting, full of eager longing, rather silly. Putting her arms round my brother's neck, she went on: 'We're going to New York, aren't we? You promise me?' Then, turning to me: 'I should so love to go to America for our honeymoon.'

'You're getting married?'

'As soon as possible. As soon as Max gets the annulment.'

'But in the meantime,' my brother said to her, 'go and fetch my pipe. I must have left it in the bedroom.'

Obediently the stork rose to its feet and went out with small steps on its long thin legs, the horizontal bosom swaying in the air. My brother sat silent for a little, then observed in a toneless voice, fixing his eyes on me: 'She's twenty-five.'

'Ah, she looks . . . she looks less.'

'She was a model. But her real speciality is cooking. I'll invite you to a meal and you'll see what delicious dishes she makes.'

'I realized she was a model from the way she walks.'

'Shes' a good girl. Of course I'm not even thinking of marrying her, but I let her believe it to keep her quiet. In that way – apart from anything else – she goes straight and stays faithful to me. But certainly I'm not marrying her. I should be crazy. In the first place, one mistaken marriage in life is enough. Besides, what need is there to get married? Women should be changed every two or three years like cars. When they begin to go wrong, they should be replaced by a more up-to-date type.'

Baba said: 'Francesco married Cora – my mother, I mean – and then stayed with her and didn't replace her.'

'But Francesco is an idealist, as we know. We're brothers but we couldn't be more different. Francesco has his head in the clouds, I have my feet planted in the earth. Francesco is a poet, I'm a stockbroker. Different heads and different ideas.'

'But, after all, even you remained with your wife for many years.'

'And I curse the time when I did it. Oh, that evil-eyed slut, that odious crook! When I think that I spent the best years of my life with her, I feel like kicking myself.'

At this point Popi came back, carrying the pipe and tobacco-pouch. My brother put out his hand; but she dodged it, sat down again on the arm of his chair and said: 'I'll fill your pipe for you, you know I like doing it.'

She started to fill the pipe, taking the tobacco from the pouch pinch by pinch, with the tips of her fingers rapidly and expertly. My brother, with a long, slow look that travelled right up Baba's leg from her foot to her hip, said to her: 'D'you always go about in trousers?'

'Yes, almost always.'

Without lifting her nose from the pipe she was filling, Popi cried: 'They're so much more convenient.'

'Trousers suit you well, there's no denying it, because you have narrow hips and straight legs. They don't suit Popi at all well, because she's broad in the beam.'

Popi cried out again: 'You horrid man, it's not true, they suit me very well indeed. Here's your pipe, monster.'

My brother took the pipe between his teeth and continued: 'You're built like a boy, you are, and that's why trousers suit you.'

'She's built like a woman,' cried Popi, 'but the trousers are well cut. That's all there is to it.'

My brother went on: 'It's the first time I've seen them with straps. Let me look.'

Baba gave him her customary sly, sleepy look, then lay back in her armchair, stretched out her leg and placed her foot on my brother's knee. He, his pipe between his teeth, bent forward, red and congested in the face, and touched her ankle under the pretext of pulling the strap to see if it was tightly stretched. Baba said: 'Feel my calf too and see how close-fitting they are.'

My brother stared straight into Baba's face and answered deliberately and without any sense of shame: 'Don't say too much, or I might try.'

'I say!' cried Popi, 'you make me jealous, terribly jealous!'

The parrot in its cage repeated three times over, in a falsetto voice: 'Cretonne, cretonne, cretonne!'

My brother fell back heavily in his armchair and then said to Popi: 'Give me a light, you jealous woman.' Popi took a book of gigantic matches nearly a foot long, struck one and held the flame to the bowl of the pipe. My brother took two or three pulls, puffed smoke out of his mouth, then said to Baba: 'So you're studying at the University?'

'Yes.'

'You can't spend your whole life studying; don't you amuse yourself sometimes?'

'Yes, I do sometimes.'

'And what do you do to amuse yourself?'

'All sorts of things.'

'D'you go dancing?'

'Yes, I go dancing.'

'Where?'

'Oh, anywhere.'

'And whom do you go with?'

'With friends: boys and girls.'

'Are you engaged to be married?'

'No.'

'Would you like to get engaged?'

'Why not?'

'And to get married?'

'Of course, if I get engaged...'

'Would you like to have children?'

'Certainly.'

'How many?'

'Six, eight, perhaps even ten.'

'Splendid! And why so many?'

'Once you start, it's better to have lots, isn't it?'

'I had three and even that seemed to me too many. And what is your ideal of a man?'

'Oh, any kind of man, as long as I like him.'

'Even if he's not young?'

'Even if he's not young.'

'A man like me, or like Francesco, for example?'

At this juncture my brother broke off the dialogue and turned towards me in an abrupt, unexpected fashion, thus showing clearly that his conversation with Baba had had the quality of an animal-like approach, like that of a dog going up to a bitch and taking a good sniff at her; and he said: 'By the way, you know that I have a whole heap of stuff that came from our parents, which really is as much yours as mine, and I don't know what to do with it? I wrote to you at one time to tell you that these things were at your disposal and you answered that they didn't interest you. So I put them into a room opening on to the terrace and thought no more about them. But now I'm wanting that room. I want to make it into a bar, so I think I shall throw the whole lot away. But it would be better for you to have a look at them. Who knows, there might possibly be something there that you'd like to take away, As a souvenir of our parents.'

I looked at him: he was holding his pipe between his strong, regular, white teeth and gazing at me almost with anxiety, red in the face. 'All right,' I replied; 'let's have a look.'

He went on at once: 'Popi, you take Francesco to the terrace room.' Popi did not move. 'I know,' she cried, 'why you want me to go with Francesco. Because you want to be left alone with Baba. That's why.'

'Come on, don't talk nonsense; go with Francesco.'

She rose sulkily to her feet. I looked at him and then I looked at Baba; and it was perfectly true: it seemed that they were both waiting for us to go away. I then followed Popi to the French window, which she opened, crying out again, and not altogether as a joke: 'And don't draw the curtains, we want to keep an eye on you.'

We went out on to the terrace. The mass of low, swollen storm-clouds, broken and frayed, like an enormous net heavy-laden with a catch of dark-coloured fish dripping and slithering through its too-wide meshes, hung suspended over a boundless expanse of pale cement roof-terraces. In the sunless light, colours stood out with chalky, opaque brightness: the lilac of the floor-tiles, the blue and green of cushions, the orange of the big umbrellas, the whiteness of the painted iron furniture. I looked back at the window; and just at that moment, moving silently as if of its own accord, the white curtain started moving rapidly from left to right and finally covered the whole space. Popi, too, cast an angry, sidelong glance at the curtain, and then, as she walked in front of me, said: 'Is it true that you and Max haven't seen one another for ten years?'

'Yes, it's true.'

'Do you find him much changed?'

'Perhaps, as he himself says, slightly fatter.'

'And how about his moral condition?'

'That I don't know.'

'What I really want to know is whether, ten years ago, he was so obsessed by women?'

'Why obsessed?'

'Yes, setting eyes on a woman who's not an absolute monster, and getting his hands on her, is one and the same thing, for him. Did you notice the maid?'

'Yes.'

'She's leaving tomorrow. I gave her the sack because I caught them together. Now I shall get a manservant. Was he like that ten years ago?'

'No, he wasn't like that. He was a man who was devoted to his family. I mean, a good husband and a good father.'

'Evidently he wants to make up for lost time. Perhaps that's why he hates his wife so much. What d'you imagine he's doing at this moment with Baba?'

'I don't know.'

'He's getting busy with her, that's what he's doing.'

She spoke of my brother's sex mania as one speaks of the innocent naughtiness of a child, with resigned, objective, even if angry, deprecation. Meanwhile we had arrived at the door of a small pavilion which occupied a whole corner of the terrace. Popi opened the door and said, as she went in: 'Here you are, this is all stuff that belonged to your parents.'

I entered and looked round. The room was wide and low, with a skylight in the middle of the ceiling. The floor was laid with strips of yellow majolica; the stuff was piled up in a corner. I realized at once, from my first glance, that my brother had got rid of everything which could be sold and had kept only the unsaleable objects – the objects in which, so it seemed to me, intimacy was allied with complete worthlessness.

Enthroned right in the middle of the pile was the white-wood dressing-table, covered with pale blue material and adorned with ribbons of the same colour, at which my mother had sat, every morning for years, as soon as she rose from her bed. The material and the ribbons were tarnished and worn, as probably they had already been when my mother was using it. But now, torn from its customary setting, the dressing-table seemed a positively foul object. Upon it, where once had stood the various pieces of a magnificent silver toilet-set which my brother had evidently had no scruple in keeping for himself, could be seen, one slipped inside the other, two articles of hygiene which my father, who had died after a long illness, had probably used during the last months of his life – a china bed-pan and a glass urine-bottle. Nearby was a wooden stand covered with framed photographs of men and women friends and near and distant relations with which my mother, I recalled, had furnished a whole corner of her bedroom.

Then there was an old radio set enclosed in a piece of Louis Seize furniture, and on top of it, a rubber hot-water-bottle; a trolley-table also in the Louis Seize style, and on its glass top a bathroom cabinet with its paint peeling off, its doors open and its shelves laden with bottles and pots and phials and tubes; an old-fashioned safe, tall and black, which had been in my father's office, its metal-sheeted door now wide open and on its steel shelves rows of light-coloured wooden boot-trees, articulated like feet, such as my father always used; an old-fashioned kitchen stove with four plates, its enamel flaking away, and on it an oval leather hat-box with its lid raised and a few of my mother's small hats crammed into it; a grey marble pedestal in the shape of a pillar, with an old black typewriter poised on its capital; a pile of crumpled French fashion magazines lying on top of a small wooden ice-box; an armchair with a design of flowers and little baskets, worn out and discoloured, which I remembered having seen beside my mother's bed. ...

There were many other objects as well. I noticed that all this stuff had not become amalgamated and confused under dust and spiders' webs, in listless neglect, as happens in ancient lumber-rooms; stacked, without either dust or spider's webs, on that shining yellow majolica floor, it seemed wide awake and full of life, of the ugly, unclean life of everything which is at the same time both intimate and useless. I reflected that these objects were in truth something that it was impossible to introduce afresh into the stream of everyday life; they *were*, in fact, my father and mother at their most private and personal, and therefore, to others, entirely unusable. At the same time, however – and this is not a contradiction in terms – these things that were so private, so personal, so unusable, were also the most ordinary, the most impersonal, the most utilitarian things that could be imagined.

So my brother was right: only a son could take one of these objects and carry it away as a souvenir. But a souvenir of what?

As if to answer my question, Popi walked across to the wall and, one after the other, turned round two pictures that were leaning against it. 'Perhaps you'd like to take these two portraits,' she said. 'Max doesn't want them; he says they're such living, speaking likenesses that they make him sad. Besides, they don't suit our flat. But in yours, perhaps, they'd be all right.'

I looked at the portraits. They had been painted when my father and mother were both over fifty. The middle class had, and probably still has, its poets, its novelists, its sculptors, its musicians and its painters who are entirely different from the artists that are truly representative of the period. To a painter of the middle class, therefore, my parents, like so many other middle-class people, had entrusted the task of portraying them. He was a painter of the 'society' type, that is, a flatterer of the social sort: my father was shown in a light grey suit, with a red tie and a reflected light on his face which was also red, as though he had been drunk at the time; my mother was wearing a yellow silk evening dress, all vaporous and shining, with pearls round her neck, rings on her fingers, bracelets on her wrists and black satin shoes. The painter had been flattering in his style, too: he had painted with broad, swift, impetuous brush-strokes, as if to suggest the idea of an explosive, over-flowing inspiration. The total result could only be expressed by one word: ignoble.

I wondered whether it was the painting which was ignoble, or my parents. And, remembering the impression of non-genuineness made upon me at the time by the novel I had written about my love affair with Cora, I said to myself that probably the quality of non-genuineness was not in the art, whatever that may have been, but in the actual reality. Thus in these two pictures the ignoble quality (which was one aspect of non-genuineness) lay, not so much in the art, as in the subjects of the pictures, or rather, away beyond them, in the very substance of the reality of which they had formed part. I started at the sound of Popi's voice, saying: 'It's true, isn't it, that they're really speaking likenesses? It's just as though they were alive. You'll take them, then?'

'No.'

'Why? Perhaps they make you feel sad, like Max?'

'Very well, let's say they make me feel sad.'

'I understand. If it were just a small photograph to put on your desk ... But these two big portraits are a bit cumbersome. Though they might look nice in a different sort of place from ours. . . . Max told me that you have a traditional type of home. You might be able to put them in the sitting-room.'

'No, I don't think so, there's no room.'

'Is yours a big flat?'

'Yes.'

'Will you invite us there, now that we've met?'

'Certainly.'

'I shall like to come and see you. I'm always alone because Max is either in his office or he goes out with some excuse or other, hunting for women.'

'Don't you think that jealousy makes you see what isn't there?'

'If only that was so! Alas, I know it's quite true, I have proof of it.'

'Haven't you ever taken revenge on him for his unfaithfulness?'

'In what way?'

'By being unfaithful yourself.'

She placed her hand on her breast and said solemnly: 'May I die if I've ever done that!'

'Now look here!'

'May I die, I say.'

I repeated: 'Now look here!', and at the same time, as one does with one's partner at the beginning of a dance, I put my arm very lightly round her waist. As I made this gesture, I saw to my surprise that her face went pale and her lips began to tremble; then, freeing herself from my arm, she went and sat down in the armchair that had belonged to my mother and there burst into tears, bending forward, her face between her hands. I went over to her in embarrassment, thinking that my experiment (for it was indeed a kind of experiment) had had an unforeseen effect, favourable to my brother and unfavourable to myself; and, in some confusion, I said: 'Don't cry, and please forgive me; I'm sincerely sorry. It was a joke, nothing but a joke.'

I saw her shake her head, as if she wanted to reject my apologies. Then she put out one of her hands, blindly, seized hold of my hand and carried it to her lips and started kissing it greedily. I heard her murmur: 'Don't worry; I'm crying because I'm a hysterical person. Tell me you like me, tell me that, tell me you like me.'

She did not wait for my answer. She threw herself back in the armchair, hurriedly unbuttoned her blouse and, with a gesture of a wet-nurse about to suckle a baby, produced, in a kind of explosion, her two enormous breasts, of a transparent, milky whiteness and crowned with large, flat, purplish nipples; then she murmured: 'My breast *is* beautiful, isn't it, don't you think? Tell me, tell me you like it.'

She sat with closed eyes, her tear-stained face against the back of the armchair, frenziedly twisting and writhing, her breasts standing out this way and that, as she sought to entice my hand and press it against them. I looked round and saw close by, on a little table, a triple mirror, of the kind that is used for shaving; and, without breaking away from her, with my free hand I gave the mirror a back-handed blow and knocked it to the ground. There was a sound of breaking glass. Popi sat up hastily, exclaiming: 'What is it, what's happened?'

'Nothing; a mirror's got broken.'

She put back her breasts inside her brassière, buttoned up her blouse and rose to her feet. 'I don't know what came over me,' she said. 'I lost my head.'

'Nothing to worry about.'

'Such a thing has never happened before, believe me.'

'Of course I believe you.'

'I was mad. And now I feel so ashamed.'

'Don't be ashamed. It was just a moment of weakness. It might happen to anybody.'

'Please, don't say anything about it to Max.'

'Don't worry.'

'You're so alike, you and Max. Perhaps it was the resemblance.'

'Yes, I expect it was the resemblance.'

'I swear to you, on all that I hold most sacred, that I have never been unfaithful to Max.'

'I believe you.'

'No, you don't believe me. And yet it's true.'

'I know it's true.'

'Swear to me that we won't do such a thing again.'

'I promise you.'

'No, swear it.'

'I don't believe in oaths.'

'I do. Swear it, to please me.'

'All right: I swear it.'

She was in floods of tears now, standing and looking at me through her tears, with her round, bird-like eyes. Then she stooped down, picked up a fragment of the mirror, looked at herself and re-arranged her hair as best she could. She blew her nose noisily and wiped her eyes. Finally she led me out on to the terrace, saying: 'You know, really I'm quite glad all this happened.'

'Why?'

'It means it can't ever happen again; we can be fond of one another like a brother-in-law and sister-in-law.'

'Yes, that's so.'

'It's such a good thing when people of the same family like each other.'

We walked back across the terrace, and as we passed the French windows Popi said: 'You see, the curtains are drawn back, so they've behaved well too.'

'Why, you were so sure that my brother would get busy.'

'Certainly *he* would, but certainly not Baba. Your daughter's not the type, I saw that at once. In fact, I'm almost glad we left them alone, so that Baba will have given him a lesson.'

We went back into the sitting-room. My brother was leaning forward, thoughtfully smoking his pipe; Baba was sitting in an armchair at some distance from him, and I noticed that she had put on her coat again. She said at once: 'If you want to talk to your brother, Popi and I will go out there and leave you alone.'

'Right. You said you wanted to speak to me.'

'Yes, I wanted to speak to you about an investment.'

'An investment? Always at your service.'

'No, not now. It's late already. I'll come back one of these days.'

My brother warned me, in a professional tone: 'As you like,

but don't let it be very many days. Now is a good moment for certain transactions.'

'All right. In a very few days. And now let us go, Baba.'

'Well, didn't you find anything that interested you in the terrace room? Will you give me the go-ahead? I can't wait to be rid of all that rubbish.'

'You can throw the whole lot away, at least as far as I'm concerned.'

We went, all four of us, into the hall. The two women embraced and kissed one another, my brother shook me by the hand, gave Baba a pat on the cheek, then, with one hand only because the other was grasping his pipe, pushed open the doors of the lift. We went in, Baba closed the doors and pressed the button, and the lift started to go down. Baba said to me: 'As soon as you and Popi had gone out, your brother pulled the curtain and then fell upon me.'

'In what way?'

'Oh, in the usual way.'

'And you?'

'In order to cool him off, I started whistling.'

'Did he cool off?'

'Immediately. He even tried to make excuses. But next moment, seeing that I was not too angry about it, he gave me an appointment for tomorrow, at his office.'

'Shall you go?'

'No.'

The lift stopped and we got out and walked towards the car. 'I'm sorry,' I said. 'I told you he was a monster.'

'No, he's not a monster.'

'What is he, then?'

'Just a man like lots of others.'

'Now you're going to tell me that you really like him.'

'Oh well, yes, I do rather like him.'

'But, good Lord, what ever d'you find likeable in a type like that?'

We got into the car. Baba thought for a moment while I started the engine, then she said: 'I like him because he's what he is.'

'What d'you mean?'

'I mean what I said.'

'And what's that?'

'That is, that I like him because he's what he is.'

'But we're not what we *are*: we're what we *do*. You say my brother laid hands on you.'

'Yes, he undid his buttons, took my hand and squeezed it against his belly.'

'Therefore, my brother is not what he is, he is what he did.'

'That is to say, the man who undid his buttons, took my hand and squeezed it against his belly.'

'What d'you mean?'

'That in reality you're saying the same thing as I am, even if in different words. It's true that we are what we do. But it's also true that what we do is what we do.'

I gave an acid laugh. 'You don't exactly encourage virtue. If my brother is what he is, if what he did is what he did, that is, is not to be judged, then I wonder why it is that I go on behaving towards you in the way I do.'

'What way?'

'In a way, as you know, that goes against my real feelings.'

'But you and I are father and daughter.'

'So what?'

'A father and daughter have to behave in a certain way.'

'Have to?'

'Yes, they can only behave in a certain way.'

'What about an uncle with his niece?'

'Uncles can even marry their nieces.'

'Ah, so that's it. A father plays the part of a father, a daughter that of a daughter, an uncle that of an uncle and a niece that of a niece. And your mother, I suppose, has played, and still plays, the part of a mother.'

'Yes.'

'Are you quite sure of that?'

'I'm sure that Cora is my mother and that I am her daughter.'

'About that there can be no doubt, it's perfectly true: Cora is your mother and you're her daughter. But one has to see what sort of mother and what sort of daughter.'

'Why? One doesn't have to see anything.'

This time I made no answer, then I went on: 'By the way, why didn't you tell my brother that you're engaged to Santoro?'

'Yes, that's true. Perhaps it was because my engagement isn't yet official.'

216

'And what do you mean by that?'

'One's engaged when one becomes *officially* engaged – that is, with invitation cards, written announcements, presents, parties, etc. Otherwise . . .'

'Otherwise?'

'Otherwise people aren't engaged, they're lovers or friends. Your brother didn't ask me whether I had a lover or a friend. He asked me whether I had a fiancé. And I told him the truth, which is that I haven't one.'

Saturday, November 28th

Last night I had the following dream. I seemed to be with Baba in a very beautiful garden, like one of those 'earthly paradises' that there are in Iran, at Isfahan or Shiraz, with a great abundance of fruit trees forming shady groves, streams of clear water flowing amongst beds filled with flowers, weeping willows, cypresses, pomegranate and rose trees. It was truly a most beautiful garden, with the miraculous, magical air which is characteristic of gardens created with great difficulty among the sands of the desert. But I knew that this garden was laid out on the very spot in which there had once been a Nazi concentration camp. And in fact, while I was walking with Baba along these pleasant paths, all of a sudden, in the depths of an orange grove, I caught sight of the blackened opening, the armoured doorway, the iron stretcher of the cremation furnace. Crushed and whitening bones lay all round on the black, greasy earth; above ground, between the trunks of the orange-trees, were strands of barbed wire like long, cruel scars; and at the far end of an avenue of quince-trees, where one would have expected to see a delicious oriental pavilion, rose the guard-tower, squat and crude, with the black shadow of a sentry moving back and forth on the top. I said to Baba: 'But why are they waiting to destroy that monument of barbarity?'; and she answered: 'They don't destroy it because it is still functioning.' I looked again at the furnace; and who should I see lying on the iron stretcher for conveying corpses into the furnace, half in and half out of the opening? Baba: she was lying on her back, her arms folded on her chest, her hair dangling down from the stretcher. And who was superintending the operation? Cora, or rather just Cora's head, hanging and protruding from the foliage of the orange-trees, with the peak of her soldier's cap pulled down over her eyes, and on the cap the swastika sign; the cap, incidentally, emphasizing the Germanic look of her big, straight nose. Then I threw myself on the stretcher, seized Baba under the arms, pulled her out and helped her to get down; and we started fleeing, hand in hand, along an endless, perfectly straight avenue, in the opposite direction to the guard-tower. We ran for some time at a headlong speed, then, all of a sudden, there in front of us was a wide-open gate. Passing through it, we found ourselves in a huge open space round which, in a semi-circle, stood numbers of houses, all exactly alike. They were small white houses, very simple in form, like those which you sometimes see in the vignettes of puzzle-pictures: square, with two storeys and triangular roofs; and on the front of each house, just as in those vignettes, was painted a big black letter. Baba stopped and pointed to the houses, asking me to read the letters. Then, going from left to right, house by house, I spelt out the word: RESTORATION.

An abrupt change of scene. I was with Baba in a palaestra or gymnasium; in front of me stretched a dizzy expanse of shining floor made up of strips of light-coloured wood, like the deck of a ship. In one corner there was a large table of the kind used by architects for spreading out sheets of drawings. Baba was standing in front of this table, completely naked, a ruler in her hand, her spectacles on her nose. With the ruler she pointed, one by one, to the objects on the table, as in a lesson for the children of an elementary school.

'This is a pencil.'
'This is a pencil,' I repeated.
'This is an inkstand.'
'This is an inkstand.'
'This is a pair of compasses.'
'This is a pair of compasses.'
'This is a writing-pad.'
'This is a writing-pad.'
'This is a pen.'
'This is a pen.'

They were all articles of stationery, in fact, and, although this lesson seemed to me a little strange, as I did not feel I had any need of it, nevertheless I could not say that I was sorry to be present at it. Besides, it was true that Baba was naked; but her spectacles, so to speak, sufficed to clothe her, to turn her into a serious, severe, pedantic schoolmistress.

All the more astonished was I when Baba, still pointing with her ruler at the top of the table, announced: 'This is a carcase.'

I looked and saw, indeed, that the whole of one side of the table was encumbered with a reddish carcase, a sheep's carcase, the same carcase, I suddenly remembered, that I had seen half sunk in the sand on the beach at Monte Circeo, a few days before. I was on the point of objecting: 'But what is this carcase doing on that table?'; but I had no time to speak because Baba repeated severely: 'This is a carcase.' And I surprised myself by saying after her: 'This is a carcase.'

The lesson was over. Baba, on tiptoe, led me over that receding wooden floor, in the intense light of very powerful lamps, towards a little door at the far end of the room; she opened it and stood aside, and I leant forward to look out. Then I saw that actually the gymnasium was at the top of an extremely tall, crumbling building, and that beneath us, right to the distant horizon, lay a limitless landscape strewn with ruins and wreckage and scattered fragments and all the débris that comes to light in a town after an earthquake or a fire or some other catastrophe of the kind. But these ruins were, so to speak, in very good condition – not in the least dusty or smoke-blackened or encrusted with damp, but well-furbished, bright, shining, standing in rows along smooth, clean streets, like jewels on a highly-polished metal tray. As I was looking at this view, which seemed to be lit up by the red, oblique light of an invisible setting sun, suddenly I slipped and fell headlong into the abyss. Only for a short distance, however, for a moment later, like a parachutist whose parachute has opened as he falls, I found myself poised in mid-air and hovering round the building at the top of which, on the threshold of the little door, Baba was still standing, hesitating whether to take the plunge or not. I carried out some elegant evolutions, proud to show off my skill to Baba; I turned and banked, I went lower, I rose up again, I hurtled forwards, I stopped, I started again at will. Suddenly I was aware that Baba was there in front of me, that she too was flying, so I began following her. We flew lower and lower, descending in great circles towards the town, towards a great bed that stood in the centre of the square. And now we were lying on the bed, side by side. Shining ruins rose all round the square; and it was understood that Baba and I were there in order to make love. It is true that I felt a certain uneasiness at doing so there in the open, in public; but Baba pointed out that there was no one there, that the town was empty and dead like the casing of a fossil shell. So I threw myself upon her; but then a strange thing happened: I could not manage to possess her, because each time I took her in my arms, behold, we both of us slipped off the bed and had to interrupt our love-making in order to get on to the mattress again. The edges of the bed were too soft and yielding, or perhaps it was our fault for not being able to stay on it; anyhow this persistent ill-fortune had a bewitched quality about it, a quality of fatality, of wilfulness, of malignity. I had an obscure feeling of anger, because I desired Baba and this cursed bed prevented me from giving free play to my desire. And then, suddenly – the final blow to my consuming, ardent longing – I awoke.

And I awoke profoundly irritated, angry, embittered, and at the same time resolved. I said to myself: 'You must bring this to a conclusion once and for all, and all the more so because Baba asks for nothing better. Why go on hesitating?' I got up and, walking on tiptoe in the dark, went out into the passage, turned on the light, went to Baba's door and took hold of the handle. Then, after a moment of hesitation, almost automatically I went back to my own room, huddled down again under the bedclothes and fell asleep almost at once. In the morning I recalled my dream, but I could not manage to make out whether I had really woken up or whether my awakening and my going out into the passage had not also been merely a part of the dream.

Sunday, November 29th

I have re-read the pages of the diary in which I gave an account of the visit to my brother Massimiliano. Again this time I wish to point out, so that I shall remember them when I come to draft my novel, a few additions and developments which, so to speak, escaped my notice while I was writing my report of the visit.

These additions and developments are concerned with the

scene between Popi and myself in the terrace room. In reality things went differently. I had gone to this room with Popi because Massimiliano, with the object of being left alone with Baba, had told me that Popi painted; and why, he said, shouldn't I go with Popi to see her pictures in the studio on the terrace? Popi would be glad to show them to me. So Popi and I left the room and went to the studio which, in point of fact, did not contain things that had belonged to my parents but merely Popi's pictures, curiously formless little canvases which Popi showed my by placing them, one by one, on an easel, while I sat comfortably on a sofa in a corner; the studio was furnished in a dainty sort of way, like a drawing-room. Popi offered to give me two of these paintings, one for myself and one for Baba; I accepted, and she promised to send them to me at my flat in a few days, as she wanted to have them framed. Then we talked about my brother and his sex mania, in a quiet, good-natured manner, without any advances on my side or, on Popi's, any exhibitions or hysterical outbursts. Finally we left the studio, and all the rest happened as I related it in the diary.

I had therefore completely invented, in the first place the detail of my parents' belongings; in the second place, Popi's exhibitionism and her hysterical behaviour. I have reflected upon the motives of these two inventions, or rather additions, and here is the result of these reflections.

Why, in the first place, did I substitute my parents' belongings, in the studio, for Popi's paintings? Those belongings, as I perfectly well knew, could not be in the terrace room; apart from anything else, my brother would certainly not have kept them after the demolition and reconstruction of the house. I thought for a long time and then I remembered: as a boy, I had observed the things in the place where they then were, distributed about the various rooms of our house, and I had indeed imagined that some day they would be piled up higgledy-piggledy, without respect or reverence, in some dusty attic, and would then have that specially repellent look and would be, in effect, all that remained of my father and mother. These imaginings were merely an expansion and an illustration of what I then thought and felt about my parents. In other words, I had imagined something which, as things were or at any rate as I thought they were, was not only possible but also highly probable.

Then, as regards the fact that I had transferred to the pages of my diary these old, cruel fancies of a rebellious youth, I explained it in this way: when confronted with the demolition of my father's house which my brother had perpetrated, I had found myself, so to speak, hanging in the air. I had married Cora, whom I believed to be a genuine person, in order to escape from the non-genuineness of my family. But now, the house whose furnishings could have borne witness to this non-genuineness had disappeared; consequently I could not prove that I had had, after all, a good reason for marrying Cora – to be precise, the non-genuineness of the world in which I had happened to be born. And so, in place of Popi's shapeless paintings, which in fact added nothing to the personality of my brother's mistress, I had put my parents' belongings which, on the contrary, came in useful to me for explaining and completing my own personal history.

And Popi's exhibitionism and hysterical behaviour? Here, in spite of myself, I had lapsed into positive calumny at the expense of that good, faithful girl who never dreamed of offering herself to me nor of weeping and regretting her behaviour. The invention itself was unpleasant; but the reason for the invention was much less so. It was, in fact, jealousy, and anxiety for what my brother was trying to do in the sitting-room, while I was examining the pictures in the studio, which suggested to me the vindictive idea of Popi's infidelity. I decided, naturally, to cut out this seduction scene which, in any case, was not very probable owing to its nauseating parallelism with my brother's simultaneous and comparable attempt. But I was not sorry, after all, to have written it, because it served, if nothing else, as a witness to the strength of my feelings for Baba.

On the other hand, I have not made any decision about transferring the invention of my parents' belongings from the diary to the novel. There was no calumny here; rather, a prolongation and development of the truth. My parents had been what they had been; the things I had imagined as being piled up in the terrace room were not, fundamentally, an invention so much as an emanation, so to speak, of their personalities. Why then not make use of them? I put this question to myself, but I have postponed the answer until the time when I write the novel. Only then shall I see whether it is suitable to cut out the episode, to leave it in, or partially to alter it.

I am no longer working on my articles about Iran. I sent off the last one a few days ago, immediately after my visit to Massimiliano. So at night I sit at my desk and look through my diary, re-writing it here and there, always with an eye to the novel which I intend to extract from it.

Last night, while I was working on the diary in this way, Baba, as usual, slipped into the room without making any noise, placed the palms of her hands over my eyes and demanded: 'Guess who it is!'

Slightly irritated, I replied: 'You're a bad actress acting the part of a good daughter full of affection for her parent.'

She took her hands away from my eyes, walked round the desk and came and stood in front of me. Then she said: 'An idea! Let's play a game.'

I looked at her carefully. Her eyes, as usual, were beautiful – placid, sleepy, sly. 'What game?' I asked.

'Let's play the father-and-daughter game.'

'But what else do we ever do?'

'One moment. Let's play the game of a stepfather who is in love with his stepdaughter, and of a stepdaughter who is in love with her stepfather.'

'And how is it going to end?'

'The end will be that the stepfather declares his feelings to the stepdaughter and tries to make love to her.'

'And the stepdaughter?'

'The stepdaughter, naturally, reacts with the utmost vigour and compels the stepfather to leave her in peace.'

'What does "with the utmost vigour" mean?'

'Kicks and thumps and shoves and scratches.'

As I looked at her, her face wore an amused, placid expression, like that of a little girl describing a game. 'But what's the sense,' I said, 'of playing a game that's so like reality?'

'No, in reality this is a thing that must not and cannot happen. I mean, it must not and cannot happen that you should throw yourself upon me and that I should find myself forced to repulse you. If it did happen, it would be very disagreeable and our relations would be definitely compromised. On the other hand, it can happen in a game, provided we fix the rules of the game beforehand.'

'What would the rules be?'

'That you should try and make love to me and that I should repulse you!'

'In short, you want to make an experiment to find out what my love-making is like; and you want me to make an experiment to find out what it is like to be repulsed by you.'

'No, I just want to play a game.'

'And suppose the game degenerates, suppose – just to give an example – that you *don't* repulse me?'

'That's impossible.'

'Why?'

'Precisely because one of the rules of the game is that I *do* repulse you.'

'I see. Well, I prefer not to play this game.'

'But why?'

'Because I don't play games. To make a comparison, it would be as though you suggested to a thief that he should play at breaking open a safe. There would then be two possibilities, both of them to be deprecated. Either the thief would play the game and thus limit himself to breaking open the safe for fun, in which case he would not steal anything but, being a thief, would find it painful not to do so; or else he would run off with the money – and that would be the end of the game.'

She smiled and said slowly, ambiguously regretful: 'Perhaps you're right. But it's a pity. It would have been amusing to play a game of that sort.'

Wednesday, December 2nd

As soon as we were in the car, Baba asked me: 'Now tell me, who is this Consolo that we're going to see?'

'He's an old friend of mine,' I replied, 'whom I haven't seen for many years. He's a journalist like me. But I'm only a foreign correspondent; whereas he's had a successful career, and a fortnight ago he became editor-in-chief of my paper. In other words, he's my direct superiour.'

'What are we going to see him for?'

'To come to an arrangement about my next journey.'

'So you're going away?'

'Yes, I really think so.'

She was silent for a moment, staring straight in front of her, disconcerted. Then she said: 'What shall I do now about Cora?'

'Why?'

'She was bad all day yesterday. She had quite a high temperature. I told her she hadn't got over her bronchitis and that she ought to call in a doctor and get him to prescribe treatment, and that then she ought perhaps even to leave Rome and spend a few months in the mountains. Because she's been really ill for some time; you're not often with her and you don't realize it, but I'm with her all the time and now I know for certain that she's really ill. And sometines I have a suspicion that it's something worse than bronchitis.'

'What?'

'Oh well, I don't know; some form of tuberculosis. That's what Santoro says, anyhow.'

'Has Santoro examined her?'

'No, but I've described her symptoms to him,'

'And what does he advise?'

'He says, of course, that in the first place Cora ought to have an X-ray examination. And that's precisely why your going away puts me in a difficulty.'

'But why, what has my going away to do with Cora's health?'

'It has a lot to do with it, and it's partly my fault. This morning, when I was still half asleep, I saw Cora standing by the bed, in her dressing-gown, looking terrible: her face was red and haggard and exhausted, with dark marks under her eyes. She looked at me for a long time and then said: "You and Fransesco want me to leave Rome, you want to get rid of me, you want me to go and die in a sanatorium. But I'm not going, I'm staying here, and if I have to die, I prefer to die here.' So I said to her: "Now don't worry; first of all you ought to see a doctor. And anyhow, no one is wanting to get rid of you. Why, if you have to go to the mountains, Francesco and I have already decided that we'll go too and keep you company until you're cured." '

'You said that?'

'Yes, I said that because I know that Cora does in fact set great store by you and what you do for her. And indeed she calmed down at once. She went on arguing for a bit, repeating again that she was not ill and that she would not see a doctor, but fundamentally she was – how shall I say? – already a little shaken. But now you tell me you're going away and I feel embarrassed, because she'll think I told her a lie; in other words, she'll think the truth.'

I remained silent for a moment. Again I detected some sort of ambiguity in Baba's conduct. This compassionate lie that she had told displayed, it is true, her usual policy of filial love; but there was also something else. I realized this from the enticing picture which her lie suggested to me: Cora confined to her room in the sanatorium; we two, Baba and I, not so much close to her as to one another. I said, with a certain irritation: 'You might at least have consulted me before disposing of me in this way.'

As though to confirm my suspicions, she answered quietly: 'To tell you the truth, I gave her that promise partly because I don't dislike the idea of spending some time together with you in the mountains. Did I really do so very wrong?'

'No, you didn't do wrong. Only I absolutely must go away.'

Like someone who had, in fact, foreseen an obstacle, she showed no disappointment. After a little while she said: 'All this, of course, is not at all certain, in the first place because Cora doesn't wish, at any rate for the present, to see a doctor; and also because a doctor wouldn't necessarily order her to go to the mountains. But, supposing for a moment that this did happen, you could make a compromise.'

'How could I do that?'

'Well, you could take Cora and me there, and then, after a week, go off on your travels. The important thing, fundamentally, is that Cora should go to the sanatorium. Once we're there, everything will become easier.' She was silent for a moment, then she concluded: 'As you see, I'm not asking much of you; if you don't want to do it for Cora, at least do it for me.'

This time I said nothing. Subtly, insidiously, the suspicion had occurred to me that beneath this business of going to the mountains there was the idea of a sexual relationship, fleeting, casual, ephemeral, even if complete. A relationship, when all was said and done, introduced into the flow of senseless, gratuitous acts that go to make up everyday life: I would go with them to the mountains, pretending to myself that I was doing it for Cora's sake, and then, at the last moment, perhaps even on the night before my departure, I would linger for a longer time than usual in Baba's room and would become her lover almost without wishing it, as if by chance, and then I would leave next day, just the same, for some distant country. And so, in the end, the whole affair would be re-absorbed, as it were, beneath the uniform, blurred surface of that insignificant normality which I still persisted in calling by the name of corruption. And Cora would die of her disease, as I now knew for certain would happen, and Baba would marry the student Santoro, as I was now equally convinced she would do, and I would come back to Rome and then go away again. In conclusion, I should recognize yet again that it was not necessary to act, because ordinary everyday life takes care of that for us, and all we have to do is to let it take its course, and then there is nothing else for it to do, it summons forth the *deus ex machina* of death and everything falls into place.

In the meantime we had arrived at Via Lombardia, where the Rome office of my newspaper was situated. As I manoeuvred to park the car, I said to Baba: 'D'you really think you'll marry Santoro some day?'

'How does Santoro come into it, now?'

'He does come into it, so answer me: will you end up by marrying him?'

'Yes, perhaps – who knows?'

'But does Santoro know about Cora's secret profession?'

'Yes.'

'Did you tell him?'

'Yes.'

'What does he say about it?'

'He's fond of me; for him it has no importance.'

'That may be. However, it doesn't alter the fact that fundamentally Cora is not entirely wrong.'

'In what way?'

'In thinking that her death would be a convenient thing for somebody.'

'What d'you mean?'

'I mean that for you and Santoro it would be convenient if Cora died.'

I had in fact spoken lightly. She said nothing, but, when I turned off the engine and made as though to get out of the car, she sat still, her eyes fixed on the windscreen. 'Here we are,' I said. 'Come on, let's get out.'

She twisted round towards me, and for the first time I saw a really unhappy expression on her face. 'How can you say such a thing to me?'

'But what?'

'That I desire Cora's death.'

'I didn't say that you desire it. I said it would be convenient for you.' I hesitated and then added: 'It would be what is called a *deus ex machina*.'

'I don't understand you.'

'That is, an external solution, but, to be precise, a very convenient one.'

She sat silent, with an unhappy, absorbed look. So I said: 'Come along, get out, and forget I said it.'

'I'm not coming. You go alone. I'll wait for you here.'

'What's the matter?'

'Nothing's the matter, I just want to be alone for a little.'

'I didn't mean to offend you.'

'I'm not offended. Go on, I'll wait for you here; I'm sorry.'

I didn't try to insist; I got out of the car and went off towards the main door of the newspaper offices, a little further on. The building was an old apartment house with a façade covered with pillars and cornices and brackets and niches, the whole discoloured by the rains and encrusted with the dust of nearly a century; but the editorial offices, where the lift deposited me a little later, could not have been more modern. I passed from an entrance hall with a blue ceiling and yellow walls into a corridor with blue walls and a yellow ceiling, I knocked at a red door framed in golden metal and, when a well-known, sonorous male voice cried: 'Come in!', I entered a room with green walls and a black ceiling. A big, tall man, with a heavily moustached face like a pirate, was sitting behind a teak and iron desk; and as soon as he saw me, he rose to his feet and said: 'Of course you know the story of the meeting of Stanley and Livingstone in the African jungle?'

I knew it; but out of kindness, I replied: 'I don't remember exactly – what is it?'

'Stanley organized an expedition to search for Livingstone, of whom there had been no news for some time. After a terribly difficult march through the African jungle, all of a sudden he caught sight of a group of Negroes carrying a white man on a stretcher. The following dialogue then ensued: 'Dr. Livingstone, I presume?" "Himself, in person." And now I do the same thing with you, Francesco. You sent no news of yourself, I searched for you, and at last I meet you in the jungle of life and I say to you: "Dr. Merighi, I presume?" And you answer ...'

'Himself, in person.'

'Good! I see that ten years haven't changed anything, that we can get on well together as we did ten years ago. But sit down, what are you doing, standing there? Good old Francesco, you know I'm really delighted to see you?'

'So am I.'

'Let me look at you. No, you're just the same.'

I took advantage of the brief silence he allowed himself, and I, in turn, looked at him. Consolo's face seemed to me, unlike mine, to have changed a great deal. Not in the sense of having inevitably grown older, but in a more radical manner. It was still the same face, rather like that of a pirate in a book of adventure stories for boys; but the long face, the drooping moustaches, the hooked nose, the thick eyebrows which ten years ago had gone to make up a living physiognomy, even if of rather a conventional kind, had now the frivolous, empty, artificial look of a mask. I noticed this particularly from the eyes. Consolo's eyes had been like those of a faithful dog – moist, cheerful, ingenuous, a little crazy. Now, beneath the two frowning thickets of his eyebrows, they appeared fixed and glassy, like those of a stuffed animal. I looked at him and suddenly the memory of our old friendship welled up in my heart. 'How are you, Rosario?' I said softly.

Something of my emotion seemed to communicate itself to him, for he looked back at me, tried to speak and then gave up the attempt; finally he passed his hand over his moustache and again looked at me in silence. Then he coughed and said with an effort: 'Forgive me, a moment of sentimentality. I was remembering all the things we did together, all the hopes we had, and I let myself be overcome by feeling. I'm very well. And you know how often I've thought of you during these years?'

'What did you think?'

'Before you joined this paper, I confess that I couldn't help feeling uneasy, each time I thought of you. Goodness me, you were – what shall I say? – my model. Then you and I were separated; I went off to Milan to work on that magazine, and I didn't know if I'd done right. D'you know what I thought?'

'What?'

'I said to myself: Francesco is a reliable man who believes in what he does and never does anything out of self-interest. I, on the other hand, don't believe in anything, I act from self-interest and I'm a buffoon.'

'But after a year, when I started contributing to this paper, you must have thought it was I who was the buffoon.'

'No, on the contrary, I thought there was then some probability that I too might consider myself a reliable man.'

'Why?'

'Because I knew, as I said, that you would never do anything out of self-interest, and therefore, if you did a thing like that, you had your own good reason for it. And in fact . . .'

'In fact what?'

'In fact you had. The events in Hungary proved how right you'd been.'

I didn't dare tell him that Hungary had nothing to do with it and that my moving from the little left-wing paper to the big Conservative paper had had, as its sole reason, my passion for travelling. Consolo continued: 'At the time of the happenings in Hungary I should have liked to write to you, to see you, to talk to you; but you know how it is, I hadn't the courage or the time or the opportunity, so I put the whole thing off and in the end didn't do anything about it. Besides, our ways had parted: you were travelling for the paper, while I was stuck in Milan running the magazine. Never, never could I have foreseen that one day we should find ourselves in the editor's office of the same daily paper.'

'And yourself as editor-in-chief, into the bargain, and I as a mere contributor. And indeed, please allow me to congratulate you. I ought to have done so before.'

He waved his hand, as much to say, 'never mind about that'; but not, so at least it seemed to me, without a certain irresistable, even if remorseful, self-satisfaction. Then, although I had not asked him, he told me: 'As perhaps you may know, I'm married too. My wife will be here shortly. She wants to meet you; I've spoken to her of you.'

'Have you any children?'

'I have one son.'

He was silent for a moment, then, in a gloomily boastful tone, he resumed: 'I want to tell you that, from the point of view of material arrangements, I cannot complain. I have a fairly large flat in town, not at all bad, in a rather expensive block in a good quarter of Milan, I have a seaside villa at

Lerici, I have two cars, a medium-sized one for myself and a small one for my wife. I have a maid, a cook, a housekeeper – everything is as it should be.'

'I'm glad to hear it.'

'You're glad that I am everything I should be?'

'No. I'm glad that what you call your material arrangements are so good.'

'Ah, I thought you were glad that I'm everything I should be.'

Suddenly he started to laugh, shaking all over as if he had the hiccoughs. I looked at him and then, by some sort of contagion, I started laughing myself. We laughed together, sitting opposite one another, for quite a little time. Then, all at once, just as a jet of water stops when you turn off the tap, with the same mechanical suddenness Consolo stopped laughing, so I became serious again too. 'Ah well,' he said, 'that's enough of that. Now the editor-in-chief must take the place of the friend. And first of all, Francesco, there's something I must say to you.'

'What's that?'

'This: that at the present moment you're one of the best journalists on the market.'

'Thank you.'

'Don't thank me, it's not a compliment, it's the truth. I understand about journalism and I repeat: you're one of the best journalists on the market today.'

He was silent for a moment, then, fixing me with his brilliant, glassy, stuffed-animal eyes, he went on: 'But I should very much like to know how you manage to write in that way?'

'In what way?'

'In such a modern way.'

I realized that Consolo was flattering me, as indeed he had done ten years before. Only that then he did it disinterestedly; whereas now it was not impossible that he was having recourse to the kind of flattery characteristic of working relationships, in which the inferior flatters his superior in order to obtain advancement and remuneration, and the superior flatters his inferior to stimulate his output. I asked drily: 'What do you mean by modern?'

Consolo did not answer at once. With his big, hairy hand, the middle finger of which was adorned with a massive gold ring, he took a cigarette from the packet on the desk, inserted it into a very long ivory holder, and, striking a light from a huge cigarette-lighter of the shape and size of a transistor set, lit it. I noticed that his gestures had an air of mimicry, as of an imitation slightly tinged with parody, and all at once I understood: Consolo was not the editor-in-chief of my paper but was pretending to be, in other words he was playing the part. But what *was* he, then? A glance at his staring, glassy eyes suggested to me a bizarre but possibly correct idea: he was merely the fiction, the illusion of being editor-in-chief; outside this fiction Consolo simply was not, he did not exist. And so, fundamentally, he was what he was not; in other words he found his reason for existence in non-existence, although he pretended to exist.

In the meantime Consolo, having inhaled a mouthful of smoke, blew it out partly through his mouth and partly through his pointed, curling, pirate-like nostrils. At last he said: 'You see, Francesco, there are men who, for a brief sometimes extremely brief, moment become identified with their period – that is, in plain language, they become contemporary. Well, as regards journalism, you're one of those men. Tomorrow, even, you may perhaps be old-fashioned and people will no longer be talking about you, but in the meantime, today, you've discovered the formula.'

'What formula?'

'The formula for the modern newspaper article.'

'And what is this formula?'

There was the sound of the door opening behind me. Consolo looked up and said: 'Oh, here's Gioia.' I turned, rose to my feet, and Consolo made the introductions with a solemnity which hinted at something behind it, as though he meant to say: 'Here is Francesco Merighi, of whom we've so often spoken, whom you so much wanted to meet and who so much wanted to meet you; here he is, really and truly in person.'

As we shook hands, I looked at Gioia. A curious lack of proportion between the excessive width of her face and the smallness of her features made one think of certain primitive Madonnas with swollen cheeks, as if they had toothache, and excessively fine, minute lineaments. Everything in that wide countenance was small – the nose, the mouth, the chin, even the eyes which, reduced to a couple of long slits, looked out at me, light-coloured and greenish, with fixed, unwavering curiosity. Her hair was red, a dark, mahogany red; dressed high and puffed out, according to the fashion of the moment, in the shape of a priestly mitre, it seemed to continue and amplify the already disproportionate oval of her pale, freckled, colourless face. I lowered my eyes: narrow shoulders, under-developed bosom, massive hips and legs, knees protruding outside her skirt as she sat cross-legged, in a careless attitude that was perhaps not entirely accidental and that showed a flounce of white undergarment, the opaque hem of her stocking, the clasp of her garter and an inch or two of bare thigh. Her husband took her hand, raised it to his lips and then rested it on the desk, still clasping it in his own. Then he asked her: 'How goes it? Everything all right?'

'Yes, everything's fine.'

The two hands were raised once again slowly upwards to Consolo's lips and then lowered, still clasped together, on to the table. Gioia looked sideways at her husband and smiled at him: she had small, close-set teeth, and as she smiled two shadowy, mischievous dimples appeared in her cheeks, making them look, one might say, even broader than before. Watching them then, Gioia and her husband, as he kissed her hand and she smiled at him, I had the same curious sensation that I had had shortly before when Consolo lit his cigarette, that they were merely a fiction, a fiction which, however, both for Gioia and for Consolo, formed the only reality available to them. Gioia and Consolo were not husband and wife, but were pretending to be. Thus they were what they were not, or rather they were the pretence of what they were not.

Still clasping his wife's hand in his own, Consolo resumed: 'You ask me to tell you what is the formula for the modern newspaper article. I will answer you with an analogy. You know the moving staircases in the big shops, with people going up and down continually and yet standing still on the stairs? Well, you've created what I call the moving-staircase newspaper article.'

I said nothing; just at that moment my theory that the relationship between Consolo and Gioia might be fiction, was receiving an unexpected confirmation. Gioia, as I said, was sitting between Consolo and myself, at the narrow end of the desk. While Consolo was talking, I noticed that Gioia, after gazing at me for some little time with an air of searching, meticulous scrutiny, then turned her eyes to the floor and kept her eyelids lowered as though she were looking at something lying near my feet. I looked down too, and saw that Gioia's foot, encased in a very long, very pointed black shoe, was moving in the direction of my left trouser-leg, my left leg being crossed over my right. It was moving, however, so slowly that it seemed almost not to be moving, and I had to make an effort of concentration to be quite sure that it really *was* moving. For a little time I remained uncertain, then, just when it seemed to me that I could no longer have any doubt that it was moving, I had to raise my eyes so as to give Consolo to understand that I was listening to him. I said rather irritably: 'Moving staircase – whatever d'you mean by that?'

'Moving automatically, like the stairs, that's what I mean. What is the object of moving staircases, as in fact of any sort of machine? To save time and fatigue. And your articles, in fact, save the readers time and fatigue. They jump, so to speak, on to the first line and then, in a moment, without making the slightest effort, almost without noticing it, they find themselves, as if by magic, at the last line. They haven't moved; it is the article that has moved. Actually they haven't even read the article; it is the article that has caused itself to be read, or rather, that has read itself. A moving staircase, in fact.'

Speaking at random, I said: 'Interesting, even if probably inexact.' Then I looked down. Like certain insects which move with extreme slowness over the walls and ceilings of rooms and whose progress can only be measured hour by hour, Gioia's foot appeared now to be motionless, but, when I compared its position with that of a short time before, I was sure that it had moved. 'Our world,' said Consolo, 'is on the way to becoming more and more a world of machines. Machines for living in, machines for doing the domestic work, machines for moving on land, machines for flying, machines for travelling by water. Now your articles, Francesco, are modern precisely because they are small but perfect machines for reading.'

I could not help feeling disconcerted. Consolo's praise confirmed, point by point, the negative idea which I had and had always had about my own journalism. Only that – as is apt to happen – the very thing which I, as a writer or anyhow an aspiring writer, disliked, seemed acceptable to Consolo, the professional journalist. I said, with some bitterness: 'What you tell me is not flattering. An article ought not to be a machine.'

'You're wrong, Francesco. Everything in its own time and place. It is articles like yours which are wanted to day. You have understood perfectly that the reader of today does not so much wish to read as to have the impression of having read. And your articles give him that impression.'

'But reading means, or rather, used to mean, reflecting, understanding.'

'Wrong again. Reading means reading, that is, carrying out the material operation of reading. And the operation of reading hasn't much to do with reflecting and understanding.'

This time I said nothing; I looked at Consolo in silence. I felt that something had become caught in the edge of my trouser leg and was pulling it up, and this thing, I realized, was the long, pointed extremity of Gioia's shoe. Consolo went on talking; and I took advantage of a moment when he was performing his usual editorial pantomime – selecting a cigarette, putting it into his holder and lighting it – to look down. I saw then that, as I had expected, the point of Gioia's shoe was caught in the edge of my trouser-leg and was now pushing and pulling it upwards, uncovering first my ankle-bone, then my ankle, and finally, with a positively violent thrust, the lower part of my calf. I glanced at Gioia: her face now looked wider and flatter owing to the broad eyelids being lowered and smoothed out underneath the eyebrows, which were raised high like circumflex accents; and it had a slightly contemplative look, with an inward-turned contemplativeness that reminded me of the absorbed expression of certain statues of Buddha. Consolo, who had in the meantime finished his cigarette pantomime, said: 'I see that you don't agree.'

'I agree.' I replied, 'but only on condition that the criticism is reversed.'

'How d'you mean?'

'I mean, I agree that my articles are machines for reading, but they are only so because they are bad articles.'

'Wrong, wrong once again. This is the man of letters speaking, for I know you, Francesco, and I know that you are, or rather that you want to be, first of all a man of letters and afterwards a journalist. But literature – forgive my saying so – has had its day. It is a kind of craftsmanship, just like the articles – literary articles – of so many of your colleagues. We live in an industrial age and your articles, thank God, are good, extremely good, industrial products.'

I looked down again: Gioia's foot was now once more motionless, stretched out so as to keep its hold on the edge of my trouser-leg, with the stillness and tension of an insect which, having pounced upon and seized its prey, remains motionless for a moment before devouring it. I looked up at Gioia's face and for a few seconds our eyes met and became, so to speak, fused together, just as the rays of two searchlights are fused together when they encounter each other, and I had the unusual impression that the whole space between us took on, for an instant, the green colour of her eyes and that my own eyes were lost in a confused light like that of an aquarium. Then she turned her eyes away from me and at the same time I felt the tension of my trouser-leg relax round my calf and its edge fall back on to my ankle-bone. Gioia rose to her feet. 'Rosario, I must go,' she said. 'I have things to do. We'll meet at the hotel.'

The husband and wife kissed one another under my eyes and again I noticed the conventional, superficial ostentatiousness of their behaviour; but at the same time I felt that, even had I not been present, the embrace would have taken place just the same, and would have been no less conventional and no less superficial. As soon as his wife had vanished, Consolo turned towards me. 'Let's come to the point,' he said. 'You know why I praised your articles like that? In the first place because I sincerely admire them, but also, and above all, because in agreement with the director, I've decided to ask you to do an important travelling job, a foreign commission that is worthy of you.'

'Where to?'

'To the United States.'

He uttered the name of the country with the generous, paternalistic air of a superior announcing a promotion in rank to an inferior; I felt I ought to show gratitude, so I said: 'It's a flattering commission. But, to tell the truth, I've specialized in under-developed countries.'

'Well, this will be a change for you. You will devote your little machines for reading to the country of machines for living.'

He gave a little laugh, pleased with his play upon words, and then continued: 'You will have to be away longer than usual this time: a year.'

Before I even had time to reflect, something inside me made me burst out: 'No, not a year, that's not possible for me.'

'And why?'

I thought about the reason which had made me burst out in that way. And I realized that, without any doubt, the outburst had been due to an extreme, invincible dislike of being away from Baba for such a long time. I said to myself that I could not bear to spend a year without seeing her; then I thought I would suggest to Consolo that I might go abroad for six months; immediately afterwards I made a mental correction: three months would be enough. I ended up by saying: 'I have serious reasons for not being able to go away for more than ... let us say a month and a half.'

'But what are your reasons?'

I hesitated, thinking: 'What should I tell him? Should I tell him I'm in love with my daughter?' Then I answered: 'You'll perhaps remember that once upon a time I had an ambition to write a novel. Well, I still have that ambition. I have ... I have collected a lot of material. I think that I ought to make a long stay in Rome, as soon as possible, in order to write my novel.'

'A novel? And what sort of novel is it?'

'It's the story of a man who, all of a sudden, decides to become involved.'

'To become involved in what?'

'In what's happening under his nose.'

'What happens to him?'

'Oh, all sorts of things.'

'But what?'

'Well, for example, that his wife is a procuress.'

'But doesn't he know?'

'No.'

'Does he live with her?'

'Yes, he lives with her.'

'He lives with her and doesn't know she's a procuress? Impossible.'

'Why impossible?'

'Because there are some things you can't help seeing, and even more than seeing them, you feel them.'

'Nevertheless ...'

'Nevertheless what?'

'Nevertheless, just to give an example, there are innumerable husbands who don't see and don't feel that their wives are unfaithful.'

'What's that got to do with it? Being a procuress is a much more visible form of activity than being unfaithful to one's husband. Anyhow, in what way does this man come to discover that his wife is practising this profession?'

'He discovers it because, as I said before, he decides to become involved.'

'And what does he do then?'

'He does nothing.'

'How d'you mean?'

'Nothing; he is content to look on.'

'To look on at what?'

'To look on at the things that he sees.'

'But looking on isn't enough.'

'Why isn't it enough?'

'Because a character in a novel has to act.'

'My character doesn't wish to act.'

'And why doesn't he wish to act?'

'Because he has no reason to act, whereas he has many reasons for looking on.'

'What reasons?'

'Good reasons.'

'Well, you know what I say, Francesco?'

'What?'

'That all this would have been interesting fifteen or twenty years ago. Novels like yours were being written then.'

'What novels?'

'Oh well, novels about social, moral, psychological problems. The man who lives with his head in the clouds, the wife who all the time is carrying on the trade of a procuress, his discovery of it – old-fashioned stuff.'

'Why old-fashioned?'

'Because today there are other problems, and above all because there's no longer any necessity to write novels, even from the point of view of criticizing public morality. If a woman carries on that trade, the whole question is settled, without any novels, by a surprise visit from the police, by the closing of the brothel, by compulsory repatriation for the girls, and a few years in prison for the procuress. These are things that happen every day.'

'Yes, they do in fact happen every day.'

'And, as regards information: the public can't be bothered with novels, what they want is a well-managed newspaper enquiry, without any literary frills or inventions, with statistics, places, names, facts, and so on.'

'But I'm not wanting to write a novel about a procuress.'

'About what, then?'

'I want to write a novel about involvement.'

So far Consolo had been amusing himself with my novel like a child with a new toy. Suddenly he became more serious. 'The only objection, then, that I now have to make,' he said, 'is about the theme.'

'What d'you mean?'

'Involvement doesn't seem to me to be at all a topical theme. D'you know what I should discuss, if I were you? Non-involvement.'

I looked at him. He stroked his moustache and went on: 'To me, anyhow, non-involvement seems to be the real theme to be discussed.'

'In what way?'

'In the story of a man who, whatever efforts he may make, cannot succeed in becoming involved.'

He looked at me with a half-smile, under his drooping moustaches. I said, almost involuntarily: 'Your own story?'

'Everyone's story. What d'you think? There's not one single person today who has his mind on what he's doing.'

'I beg your pardon, but do you mean to say that today it's impossible to be seriously involved in things?'

'Yes, I mean just that. And therefore, when you tell me that the character of your novel succeeds in becoming involved, let me point out: this is a novel, well and good, it's a work of imagination. But in life this doesn't happen.'

'What happens in life?'

'Not only in my own life, but in the lives of many people I know, what happens is simply this: that one cannot succeed in becoming involved, even if one wishes to. One way or another, everything passes unnoticed.'

'In your own case, you mean.'

'In everyone's case, Francesco. You know what I feel sometimes?'

'What?'

'It's difficult to explain. I feel as though I were outside time and space, a thousand years ago or a thousand years hence, not in Milan or in Rome but God knows where. Sometimes Gioia, who knows me well, asks me, just to put me to the proof: "What have you been doing this afternoon?" Now in point of fact I've been with her but I cannot manage to remember it, because, while I was with her, I was not, as you call it, involved, I was non-involved. And so, let me repeat again: it would be better that you shouldn't write a novel at all – I mean in the interests of the paper, of course; but if you really must write it, let it be on the theme of non-involvement, not of involvement.'

He was joking; but I realized he was doing so in order to check the emotion which was natural to someone who was speaking of the trouble from which he himself was suffering. He added hastily: 'Of course all this doesn't in any way prevent me from working and doing my duty. I certainly do work, I can tell you. And now, after this literary parenthesis, let's get back to our own affairs. Well, you tell me you can't stay more than a month and a half in the United States. Let's make it three months and say no more about it. Is that all right?'

'When do you want me to leave?'

'As soon as possible.'

I rose to my feet. 'Very well,' I said, 'as soon as possible.'

Consolo also rose. After fluctuating during the whole of my visit between the role of editor-in-chief and that of friend, he chose the latter for our leave-taking and, as he accompanied me to the door, he placed an affectionate arm round my shoulders. 'Let me know the date of your leaving as soon as you can,' he said. 'I go back to Milan tomorrow. Telephone me there. Dear old Francesco, you know I'm really pleased to see you again?'

'So am I.'

We embraced, and Consolo clapped his hand on my shoulder; then I went out and he shut the door. But immediately afterwards he opened it again, looked out and cried: 'And give up the idea of the novel about the procuress. Remember what I told you: literature is dead. Industry has been born. Goodbye, old man.'

I went out into the anteroom, thence to the lift, down to the ground floor, and then hurried out of the building: I was late in meeting Baba. But when I reached the car I saw that Baba was not there. I stood beside the car for a moment, at a loss. Then I reflected that Baba might well have gone off for a little and that it would be right for me to wait; so I got in, sat down and took a newspaper from the locker and unfolded it. At that moment I heard the door open, someone sat down beside me and, without turning, I asked: 'Why, where have you been?'

I was answered by a voice very different from Baba's, a harsh, uneven, impatient voice, whereas Baba's was low-toned, grave and quiet. 'I hid in the entrance,' it said: 'you passed right in front of me without seeing me. Let's be off at once, shall we?'

I turned and, naturally, with a feeling of calm inevitability – as much as to say, how on earth hadn't I foreseen it? – I saw at my side not Baba, but Gioia. Without showing any surprise, I asked: 'Where do you want to go?'

'We'll decide that now, but get started.'

She seemed to be in the grip of an uncompromising, irritable urgency, like one who has a very precise object in mind and is out of patience at having to waste time in searching for the means which will allow of its attainment. I said nothing; I manoeuvred to get the car out of its parking place, then I drove up Via Veneto and went as fast as I could along the Corso d'Italia. 'Have you thought where you want to go?' I asked her.

'Wherever you like. I'd prefer not to go to your own flat. Haven't you the address of some hotel or somewhere where they let rooms? Wherever you like. Even in the country, if you like. Provided we get back in two hours' time, at most.'

'In two hours' time?'

'Yes.'

'And what are we going to do during these two hours?'

'What d'you mean, what are we going to do? Come on, get a move on, turn this way, towards Via Salaria.'

'You know Rome?'

'Of course I do, I'm a Roman.'

'You're a Roman?'

'Yes.'

'Your family lives in Rome?'

'Yes, I'm the daughter of a University professor, Faculty of Law, I have two brothers, one a student and one an engineer, I have a grandmother, I have various aunts, I even have some cousins. Anything else?'

'Why are you so impatient?'

'What need is there of all this information, to do what we

have to do? Let's go as quickly as possible wherever it is we're going, and please don't let us talk on the way.'

'Why shouldn't we talk?'

'What's the need? Words are unnecessary.'

'Unnecessary?'

'Yes, it's all much better if one doesn't talk.'

She spoke with growing agitation, nervously and in fits and starts, sitting with her profile towards me. As we were going along Via Salaria, all of a sudden I felt her hand resting on my leg, and I looked down as far as driving permitted me. Still looking straight in front of her at the windscreen, she moved her hand forwards and then upwards, her long, thin, nervous, light, prehensile hand; then, with a dexterity that was at the same time both hesitant and astute – like that of a blind person making very sure movements in the darkness and being intensely conscious of such movements through the sense of touch – she ran her fingers along the opening of my trousers, pushing the buttons out of their buttonholes one by one, slowly and gently and as though savouring this slowness and gentleness. 'Wait a moment,' I said. 'I don't know of any hotel, and I haven't the address of anywhere where they let rooms.'

'Then let's go out into the country. Drive on along Via Salaria until I tell you to turn off.'

'But where are you staying in Rome?'

'Ugh, you and your questions! In an hotel; where d'you think I'm staying? You'd hardly want to go there.'

'All right, then we'll turn back now and I'll take you to your hotel.'

She said nothing for a moment; but her hand withdrew itself to where it had been before, beside her other hand, in her lap. Then at last she spoke: 'You don't want to?'

'No.'

'You don't want to because you're a friend of Rosario?'

'No.'

'You love some other woman?'

'Not that either.'

'Then you don't like me?'

'That's not the reason.'

'What is the reason?'

'The reason is that I don't feel any need for it.'

She was silent for a moment; then, without any bitterness,

as though establishing a rather surprising fact, she said: 'It's the first time a man has behaved like this with me.'

'Why, does it happen that you do it often?'

'Yes.'

'When?'

'Whenever I want to.'

'And do you often want to?'

She hesitated and then, as though talking to herself, said petulantly: 'I suppose there's nothing left to do now except talk. Let's talk, then. Well yes, I often want to.'

'But on what sort of occasions?'

'Occasions like today.'

'How d'you mean?'

'I mean that at first I feel I should like to talk, to get to know someone, to let him get to know me. But on second thoughts, seeing that it all ends up like that anyhow, I shorten the process.'

'You shorten the process?'

'Yes, I can't help it. I forsee that I'm going to do that thing, and since I'm impatient to do it I try not to wait too long. Logical, isn't it?'

'Yes, it's logical.'

'Why, doesn't it seem to you logical?'

'On the contrary, it seems to me highly logical, even too logical. And then?'

'And then what?'

'After you've ... shortened the process?'

'After that it's finished. I no longer feel any need to talk, to get to know someone, to let him get to know me. It's all over.'

We remained silent for some time. Suddenly, speaking in a jerky way, she resumed: 'It doesn't matter, I'm pleased to have met you all the same. Rosario had spoken to me about you; I was curious to meet you; now I've seen you.'

I nodded my assent. Everything, I thought, was taking place in accordance with a fixed rhythm, in a kind of ritual: first of all desire, then what she called 'shortening the process', then the certainty of imminent sexual relations, then the repulse, and finally, now, the renunciation. Or possibly, I went on to reflect, the decision to postpone the whole thing to a more favourable moment. And indeed she added: 'Soon we shall have a flat in Rome; do at least promise me that you'll come and see me.'

'To do what?'

'To do that thing, even – if, as you said a short time ago, you don't feel the need of it.'

'I don't think I shall ever feel the need of it.'

'You can't know beforehand.'

'But isn't it possible to get to know you in any other way?'

'You can try, but I'm convinced that, anyhow as far as I'm concerned there's nothing else to know.'

'Why?'

'There's no "why" about it, it just is like that.'

'Meaning what?'

'I know that I'm simply *that thing*. That apart from that thing I'm nothing.'

'Nothing?'

'Yes, nothing. Certainly I'm a good wife, an excellent mother, a passable housewife, an affectionate friend, I speak two languages, I even have a nursing diploma; but all this is nothing, not for me at any rate.'

'I understand,' I said; and now she said nothing more. I drove in silence, turning back along Via Salaria towards Piazza Fiume. Here she roused herself from her immobility and said: 'Stop a moment and I'll get out.' As soon as I stopped, she got out quickly, bidding me farewell with a smile which for a moment brought the two shadowy dimples to her broad, pallid cheeks. I looked at my watch. The whole thing had happened in little more than half an hour.

Friday, December 4th

A moving staircase, not that of Consolo's metaphor concerning my articles but a real one, in a big store, today carried Baba and me up and down, from one floor to another, for the acquisition of a number of domestic objects for use in Santoro's still empty home. The student himself hasn't the time, so Baba has undertaken to put his flat in order, making me go with her, needless to say – yet another pretext for furthering the habitual plan of our father-and-daughter relationship.

We got back into the car, our arms laden with parcels, and Baba said: 'Would it bore you now to come with me to Santoro's flat? Apart from anything else, it would be an opportunity for you to see him.'

'I don't really want to at all.'

'Anyhow I have to go there to leave all this stuff. Have you time to take me there?'

'Yes, I'll do that.'

So we left Piazza Fiume and started off towards Piazza Bologna, in the neighbourhood of which Santoro lives. On the way, I did not speak at all. I felt tired and enervated from all the running up and down in that shop. In Via Nomentana Baba suddenly asked: 'What have you against Santoro?'

'Nothing,' I answered drily.

'And yet . . .'

'And yet what?'

'And yet anyone might think you don't like him.'

'That's not true.'

'In any case it's quite right.'

'What's quite right?'

'A father who's fond of his daughter can't really look favourably on the idea of her getting married and leaving home.'

'Ah, so that's it?'

'Yes, that's it.'

'So fathers-in-law have to hate their sons-in-law, just as mothers-in-law hate their daughters-in-law – is that so?'

'More or less.'

Again I was silent. We drove the whole way along the wide, straight Via Nomentana, dotted with moving lights in the smoky twilight as far as the eye could see; we turned off at some traffic lights and came to Piazza Bologna, then went along a side street and stopped in front of an ugly pistachio-green building. We got out and went in, and Baba said: 'It's six floors up. But the lift isn't working.'

'So what?'

'Can you manage to walk up six floors, or would you rather we left the parcels with the porter and then Santoro can see about carrying them up when he comes in?'

'Why, isn't Santoro there now?'

'No, he's not in.'

'Oh well, let's leave the stuff with the porter.'

She said nothing. I watched her as she went to the far end of the entrance-hall, tapped with her fingers on the glass of the porter's lodge, looked inside, and then tapped again. She came back and said: 'The porter isn't there and we can't leave the stuff here. We'll have to carry it up. I have the key, so I can show you the flat.'

'Let's go, then.'

So we started going up, one behind the other, for the stairs were too narrow for us to walk up side by side. First Baba and then myself, flight after flight and floor after floor. Baba advanced slowly, encumbered by the big parcel she was carrying in her arms; and I was also carrying a similar package. I realized that I was examining with excessive intentness, or rather that I was seeing with unaccustomed precision, all the details of the staircase up which we were going – the handrail of the banisters, made out of a mosaic of pieces of majolica of different colours cemented together; the light yellow wall with a mustard-yellow skirting-board; the white marble steps, dirty and dusty. The flights of stairs went up at right angles to each other; on each landing there were two doors and two rubbish-bins; the floors were made of the same majolica mosaic as the balustrade; and although it was now twilight the lamps were not yet lit, so that the staircase was plunged in semi-darkness. Then I reflected that I was looking at each thing with such intentness and seeing each thing with such precision because in reality my intent, precise gaze had been directed towards Baba as she went upstairs in front of me, and I was now switching it from the object at which it had been directed and deliberately turning it elsewhere. After this reflection I went up another two flights with head lowered, then I raised my eyes and looked at Baba and could just see, in the now almost nocturnal darkness, her right side and above that her arm and her hand resting on the balustrade, and above that again her face as she turned slightly to give me a fleeting glance over her arm; and in her eye I detected my own idea, or rather my own presentiment, of what was about to happen. Then the thought occurred to me that I had always feared and at the same time longed to plunge into nothingness, and now this plunge into nothingness was on the point of occurring in the least dramatic way possible, as such things always do occur in every-day life – as a result of an insignificant opportunity involuntarily and readily accepted, through a sudden temptation, without pre-meditation, without preparation, in a casual, passive, idle fashion.

We reached the first flight leading to the sixth floor, then the second, then the landing, in almost complete darkness. Baba, as she stepped on to the landing in front of me, immediately turned round; I stepped up beside her and then, as I had foreseen and desired and feared, we fell into one another's arms.

Baba's mouth crushed itself against mine, lips parted and as it were turned inside out, like the open lips of a wound if pressed against a hard surface; then, with lips still parted in the same position, it started turning round inside my mouth, penetrating further and further as it turned, and then, still continuing its turning, penetrating movement, it opened yet wider, gaping like the gullet of a reptile, forming an empty, dark, warm, dry funnel whose edges, nevertheless, melted with saliva which wetted the chin and cheeks of both of us; and this funnel went on turning and opening, as though Baba were wishing to swallow me, and at the bottom of the funnel, which grew steadily larger, warmer, emptier and darker, was her hard, dry, pointed tongue, which every now and then came forward and then withdrew, with spasmodic swiftness.

The kiss came to an end because suddenly, as though to deny us the protection and connivance of the darkness, the quiet, yellow lamp came on on the landing. We separated at once and Baba bent down towards the door, possibly in order to hide from me her face smeared with lipstick and wet with saliva; meanwhile she was searching for the key in the pockets of her coat. I stood some distance away, looking at her, and saw her fumble in the bag slung over her shoulder, then get rid of the parcel which she was still holding in her arms, placing it against the wall in a corner, and then turn the open bag upside down so that everything it contained fell out on the floor. On to the landing floor rained a variety of tinkling objects, but not the keys of the flat. Baba threw herself down on all fours, looking and searching among the scattered objects; then she raised her face towards me, looked at me, slowly rose to her feet, looked at me once more and finally started to laugh in an ostentatious, insistent sort of way. And then, more or less as had happened two days before with Consolo, I caught the contagion of her laughter and began laughing myself. We stood laughing together for some little time; then Baba stopped laughing and I too became serious again. She threw herself down again on all fours on the floor, put all the things back into her bag, then stood up and said: 'Providential, isn't it, that I've forgotten the key of the flat?'

'Providential indeed.'

'I'm sorry, I wasn't laughing at you, I was laughing at myself.'

'Why?'

'Oh, there you are with your "why's". Because I want us to be father and daughter, I don't want anything else, I swear – may I die if it isn't true! And then, bang! – instead of that I fall into your arms at the first opportunity, and in front of my fiancé's door into the bargain. It's something to laugh at, isn't it?'

'Yes, it's something to laugh at, certainly.'

'There's probably no need for me to tell you that this must be the first and last time we kiss one another.'

'No, there's no need.'

'And now say something to me that a father would say to a daughter.'

'What d'you mean by that?'

'Say something *fatherly* to me.'

We were now going down again, flight by flight, and this time it was I who was in front. I thought for a moment and then said gently: 'Baba mustn't talk any more nonsense, she must keep quiet.'

She started laughing, placed her hands on my shoulders and almost made me tumble right to the bottom of the stairs, pushing me and jumping up and down behind me. This time the porter was there, so we left the parcels in the porter's lodge. Then we got into the car and I turned on the radio full blast, and we drove home without saying anything more.

Once I was in my room, I sat down in front of the typewriter, and all of a sudden, as I looked irresolutely at the blank sheet of paper which I had inserted, I started silently and doggedly to tear my hair and slap myself on the cheeks. Finally I stopped and sat there astonished: I had kissed Baba and wished I had not done so, that was understandable; but I was unable to see why I attached so much importance to the kiss and felt so desperate.

I thought for a long time, then at last roused myself, lit a cigarette and typed into my diary, minutely and faithfully, neither adding nor subtracting anything, all that had happened that afternoon, from the moment when I had left the big shop until I had returned home after the unsuccessful visit to Santoro's flat.

Afterwards I re-read what I had written, and then I understood the reason for my despair. It was directly suggested to me by the manner in which I had described the kiss I had given Baba.

I analysed the long description of fifteen lines, and found I had expressed, in almost every word, a feeling of repulsion, of fear and of horror. Whereas in reality, both on my side and on Baba's, the kiss had been a perfectly normal love kiss, lacking in restraint and full of sweetness almost to the point of insensibility and ecstasy.

But in my diary I had described, not so much the kiss as, through the kiss itself, the feeling which had preceded and followed it. This feeling, to be precise, had been one of disconsolate attraction before the kiss and of horrified regret after it. Attraction and regret: therefore, during the kiss, there had been no sweetness and abandonment but only horror, fear and repulsion.

The clue, in this transformation of the kiss from the innocent thing it had been into something horrible, lay in the choice of words, of metaphors. Baba's mouth became 'the open lips of a wound', 'the gullet of a reptile', 'an empty, dark, warm, dry funnel'. The idea of a snake swallowing its prey reappeared in the description of the 'hard, dry, pointed tongue which every now and then came forward and then withdrew again with spasmodic swiftness'.

In other words, I certainly loved Baba; but at the source of my love for her, instead of a sincere, unutterable, impulse there was the idea of incest as a transgression and as nothingness. This idea, or rather ideology, was just as non-genuine as that which had formerly caused me to love and to marry Cora. Baba, on examination, was not what I liked to think she was, just as, formerly, Cora had not in reality been either a working-class woman or a prostitute or a thief. And in fact, no sooner had I married Cora than I discovered that she was ... Cora; in the same way I knew that I had only to become Baba's lover to discover that she was ... Baba.

Yet in the meantime my feeling for Baba was nourished, inspired and fomented by the ideology of incest as a transgression and as a leap into nothingness. Thus non-genuineness was transferred from this idea to my feeling of love, and from that to my description of the kiss, that is, of love in action. And, instead of the truth of the kiss, I had recounted, in my diary, the falsity of my feeling; which, in time, I could not but transfer into my novel as well.

Therefore, so it seemed, non-genuineness lay in action itself at the moment when one acted. And therefore, once more, non-genuineness revealed itself in the very heart of things, in their composition, that is in the very material of which reality was made. And one could act only in a non-genuine manner, just as probably one could write only non-genuine novels, seeing that a novel without action was not a novel. But between action in a novel and action in reality there was this difference: that action in reality, even if non-genuine, 'worked'; whereas a non-genuine novel, on the other hand, was a bad novel and did not 'work'.

Suddenly I asked myself the following question: 'In the long run all this is nothing but a storm in a teacup. Can't you give a more important and more decisive example of what you are asserting?' I lit a cigarette, smoked and reflected for a little, then said to myself: 'Here was a wholly despicable man, a moral and intellectual cretin, vulgar, presumptuous, untruthful, vindictive, cynical, disordered, cruel, pitiless, blood-thirsty, a monster who was mediocre but endowed with exceptional capacity as a demagogue, as one might say a powerful aeroplane engine attached to the cheap body of a mass-produced car. Here was this monster, grubbing up ideological sweepings, for years, in the taverns, cafés and doss-houses of Vienna and then impregnating this rubbish with hatred and lust for power and extracting from it the essence of a fallacious – in other words, completely non-genuine – political message, and, by the frantic preaching of this message, seizing power, dragging an entire nation behind him, transforming it into a community of cannibals and hurling it against the whole world, causing it to commit the most horrifying crimes with a quiet conscience, and finally plunging it into the greatest catastrophe of its history, with millions and millions of dead, innumerable cities destroyed, infinite suffering and bereavement. Here then was the non-genuine at the level of history, indeed it was in itself history; nevertheless, although it was history, it still remained what it was and could not help being. This is what has changed the face of the world, at least in this century, this convulsion of corruption, this spate of unreality, this whirlpool of non-genuineness.'

I wondered why it had occurred to me to hark back to Hitler at the moment when I was thinking of Baba. And then I recalled that Baba herself had compared the experience forced upon her by Cora at the age of fourteen with that of the Nazi camps, and had said to me that certain things are so outrgeous that they cannot be made up for in any way but must be considered as having been experienced by other people; and I understood the sense of all this: the non-genuine was that which worked, that which was done, that which was acted; but it was not organized and developed in the course of time, rather it passed into everyday life, that is, into a senseless sequence of events in which Hitler's death in Berlin was of the same importance as the rolling of a ball thrown by a child at play at the end of a courtyard.

At this point, however, my thoughts returned to Baba who had been the prime cause of this lengthy reflection, and I said to myself: 'Is he not perhaps rather absurd, even ludicrous, this man who, after doing something he did not wish to do – that is, kissing his own stepdaughter – falls into despair more on account of the harm it will cause to the novel in which he will be forced to recount this kiss than because he has done something which his own conscience forbade him to do?'

But I at once had an answer ready: 'He is neither absurd nor ludicrous because conscience and the novel are one and the same thing, at any rate in your case, and it is impossible for you to separate one from the other.'

Monday, December 7th

In order to please Baba, who insisted on my speaking to Cora and persuading her to call in a doctor, I went out on foot this evening and made my way to the dressmaking establishment. My intention was to wait until Cora had finished work and then to accompany her home and, on the way, to speak to her about her health.

But when I reached the Circonvallazione Clodia I saw Cora come out of the main door of the building that housed her fashion shop. Cora was not alone; she was accompanied by one of those young girls who are employed on all sorts of odd jobs, from delivering dresses to customers to going and buying them cigarettes. By this time I had nearly reached the door, so I hid behind the trunk of a plane-tree and watched the two women who had meanwhile stopped at the edge of the pavement and were waiting for a pause in the flow of vehicles along Via Olimpica in order to cross the road. Cora was wearing a two-piece dress of dark red, her favourite colour, and had her hand on the girl's shoulder, a hand which looked to me both possessive and threatening, like that of a butcher grasping the neck of a sheep he is about to slaughter. The girl looked about fourteen, and could not have been more. She had black hair, of a compact, glossy blackness that shone in the neon lights of a near-by shop; when she turned for a moment to observe the traffic, I saw an olive-hued, southern, boyish face in which, however, there glittered the whites of two large, dark, very feminine eyes, underscored by two deep, purplish marks of painful fatigue. I looked at her attentively and nothing escaped me: the unconscious way in which she suddenly sighed and, with both hands, pulled down her sweater over her meagre chest; the short, narrow skirt that swelled out over the curve of her loins and showed her bare knees; the childish black socks and the grown-up high-heeled shoes; the big hands, red, and with scarlet nails. Cora's hand moved mechanically from the girl's shoulders to the back of her neck; the girl bent forward to look at the traffic lights, pulling back her hip and raising one leg; Cora, erect and motionless, her eyes fixed on the street, spoke; the girl answered, turning towards Cora and showing the whites of her eyes in her dark face. Then there was a pause in the flow of passing cars and they crossed the street, side by side, but now Cora's hand had again moved its hold and was grasping the girl by the arm, below her armpit, as though to hold her up and, so to speak, make her fly across the asphalt.

They went to the parking-place opposite, to a car which I recognized as Cora's; the latter opened the door; the girl went nimbly round the car and got in; Cora also got in and for a moment I saw her in profile, her black hair hanging in loose locks at the side of her severe face; then the car moved away, entered the line of traffic in Via Olimpica and disappeared.

I remained where I was for a little, behind the trunk of the plane-tree; then I went slowly back home. I thought, as I walked, that what I had seen was something perfectly normal: a woman with a young girl, possibly a mother and daughter, or a mistress and her maid, or again a governess and her pupil. But at the same time I knew that it was not so, or rather that it might not be so, and that what I had seen might well be (though I was far from being sure of it) a scene of procuration: Cora removing the fourteen-year-old messenger-girl from the dressmaker's shop to take her to the villa on the Via Cassia, where she was expected by a client of her second profession. Exactly as she had done six years before with Baba.

But then I had a sudden enlightenment. What I had observed had been in truth a normal scene, even as regards the reality that lies behind appearances. This scene was in fact nothing but a minute detail in the continuous, uniform flow of everyday life. On that same pavement there had been, at that moment, innumerable passers-by; and about all of them I might reasonably have imagined the same things as I knew might be imagined about Cora – not so much because the lives of these passers-by resembled Cora's life in detail, but because fundamentally there was nothing to distinguish their lives, even if innocent, from Cora's, nothing, I mean, substantial or original. All these lives, in fact, had in them, one way or another, something of what I could not help calling corruption but which was, on the contrary, merely the imperceptible, unceasing, natural movement of senseless, non-genuine everyday life.

Wednesday, December 9th

Today, irresistibly and almost without thinking, at a time of the afternoon when Baba was not at home, I left my room, went straight to Cora's door and knocked.

I heard her voice bidding me to come in. I pushed open the door and saw her sitting up in bed, supported by pillows and enveloped in her usual red dressing-gown. I noticed that she was doing nothing, neither smoking nor looking at magazines nor reading newspapers; the telephone beside the lamp on the bedside table might suggest that she was continuing, from her bed of sickness, to expedite the affairs of her second profession, but this was merely a supposition. Actually she was sitting motionless, as though she were meditating, or at least contemplating something outside herself that would not allow itself to be either understood or forgotten.

I asked, from the doorway: 'May I come in? I'd like to speak to you.'

She turned her head, took a long look at me and replied: 'To speak to me?'

I went in, closed the door, and went and sat down in the armchair at the foot of the bed; and as a sort of preamble I said: 'I came to the dressmaker's shop yesterday. But just at the moment when I arrived, you were coming out. You weren't alone, you were with a young girl.'

'Ah, yes, Maurilia.'

'Who's Maurilia?'

'A girl I employ for running errands.'

'How old is she?'

'She's sixteen.'

'She looks at least two years younger.'

'Yes, seeing her dressed you'd think she was undeveloped. But that's no more than an outward appearance. If you saw her undressed, you'd think differently. Her breast is already sagging as if she was a woman of forty.'

'Is she an honest girl?'

'What does "honest" mean?'

'Don't you know what "honest" means?'

'Why should you want to know whether she's honest or not?'

'Oh, just curiosity.'

'They all proclaim themselves honest. But then, if you come to look, they're like chestnuts: fine outside and rotten inside.'

She spoke mumblingly, in a disdainful, disparaging tone – the characteristic tone, I could not help thinking, of the procuress, who, to give a light-hearted air to the practice of her trade, is compelled, unlike other traders, to depreciate and belittle the value of her merchandise, decrying it and doggedly denying it any surviving human dignity. I remained silent for a little, then a bizarre idea occurred to me: since Cora concealed her second profession beneath that of a dressmaker, I would try speaking to her about her dressmaking business, alluding, in reality, to her second profession. I wanted to see what effect this would have on me, and above all what effect it would have on her. 'Let's talk a little about your profession,' I said. 'Usually, here in Italy anyhow, women do absolutely nothing. But you're a woman who works. D'you mind if I ask you some questions about your job?'

'But there's nothing to tell. It's a job just like any other job.'

'Perfectly true, it's a job like any other. And yet it's also a job that is different from other jobs.'

'Different, why different?'

'Oh well, in its various technical, commercial, human aspects.'

'That may be so.'

'Then you don't mind if I talk to you about it?'

'No, why should I mind? But I repeat: it's a job just like any other.'

'And I've admitted it. But tell me then, have you a big clientèle?'

'So-so.'

'Why so-so?'

'It's not a good moment, there isn't the money.'

'Yet I should have thought that, in a job like yours, there couldn't be bad moments. You're providing a kind of goods that is always needed, money or no money.'

'Yes, but things are expensive. People who haven't money give up buying them.'

'How d'you manage, in any case, with your customers?'

'What d'you mean?'

'You have all their names written down, with their addresses and telephone numbers – isn't that so?'

'Certainly, of course I do.'

'But where?'

'What a question! In a ledger.'

'Won't you describe this ledger to me?'

'Really, are you crazy?'

'No, I'm not crazy. It's just curiosity.'

'It's a perfectly ordinary ledger.'

'Now make an effort!'

'It's a ledger just like lots of others, of the kind for keeping addresses. I think it has a black back and a marbled cover.'

'What colour of marble?'

'Really I don't know: red and white, I think.'

'And the names inside are in alphabetical order?'

'Of course.'

'But in this ledger there are other names besides those of your customers, aren't there?'

'Certainly.'

'What names?'

'Oh, I don't know – names of work-people, of wholesalers.'

'So it's really the address-book of a business woman, such as you are.'

'If you like to put it like that.'

'And when a dress is ready you telephone to the customer to come and try it on?'

'Yes.'

'What d'you say to them?'

'Why, the usual things: the dress is ready for trying on, come on such-and-such a day, at such-and-such a time.'

'That's what you say?'

'Yes.'

'And do they come punctually?'

'It's in their own interest.'

'How long does it take, trying on a dress?'

'It may take five or ten minutes, just as it may take half an hour.'

'Or an hour?'

'No, not an hour.'

'And why not an hour?'

'Because I'm busy and I can't waste time with a single cus‹ tomer.'

'What are your customers like?'

'How d'you mean, what are they like?'

'Are they easy or difficult, are they capricious or calm?'

'There are all kinds. Some of them drive you mad, others don't.'

'Ah, they drive you mad, do they? What do they want?'

'They want ... They don't know themselves what they want.'

'Wait a moment. They want a dress of a certain type because they feel, even if they can't explain it, that that particular kind of dress suits them, that is, that it will provide them with precisely the enjoyment which is infallibly provided by a dress that pleases them and suits them. Isn't that so?'

'You've said it in a roundabout way, but that is so.'

'And you, on your side, take trouble to provide them with

a dress that will please them and suit them, even if they're incapable of saying clearly what that dress should be like?'

'Naturally.'

'In any case, all they want is to be convinced, isn't it?'

'Fundamentally that's true.'

'And you take back a dress which they haven't examined, or have examined only superficially and then rejected, and you sing its praises, don't you?'

'Yes indeed, that does happen.'

'You praise its colour, its design, its cut, its originality, the fineness of its material, its hard-wearing qualities – isn't that so?'

'Yes, that's so.'

'But tastes vary a great deal, don't they? And you have to be prepared for all these different tastes.'

'Obviously.'

'I imagine there are customers who want dresses that will make them look younger. And that these customers, as a rule, are, precisely, the most elderly. Isn't it so?'

'Yes.'

'And that those who, on the other hand, go for the reliable, the safe, the correct, are the young ones, who don't need so many artifices to look and to feel beautiful.'

'That's true.'

'But there must also be customers who want eccentric, extravagant things, things out of the ordinary. You have to satisfy these customers as well.'

'Yes, of course.'

'When all's said and done, it must be a difficult job, being a dressmaker.'

'It's not an easy job.'

'However, I'm sure of one thing.'

'What's that?'

'That you don't do it for money but out of passion, or rather, not only for the money but also out of passion. Isn't that true?'

'Well, let's say it's true.'

'Do you make much out of each dress?'

'Less than might be thought.'

'But I'm convinced – tell me if I'm wrong – that even if you made nothing out of it, you still wouldn't give up this job. Because, as I said, you do it in the first place out of passion, and then for money.'

'Certainly, without passion you don't get anywhere.'

'That's right, without passion you don't get anywhere. Let's analyse this passion for a moment. Have you time to listen to me?'

'Yes.'

'You have a passion for clothes, for dressing, for procuring clothes, buying clothes, selling clothes, for knowing that these clothes give pleasure, that they are appreciated, desired. This passion, like all passions, arises partly from natural inclination, partly from the void which it has itself finally created in your life, as with everything that is exclusively and passionately loved. You live for clothes and it seems to you that it is not possible to live for anything but clothes. I would say more: clothes and dressing, and the procuring and selling of clothes make all other human activities appear to you colourless, fictitious, false, inconsistent and hypocritical. To press things a little further, one might assert that dress, for you, is the key of reality. You could truly say: tell me how you dress and I'll tell you who you are. As far as you are concerned, everyone thinks first and foremost and solely about dress – rich and poor, old and young, scholars, artists, politicians, professional men and so on. If one could see inside your head, there is no doubt whatever that one would simply see that one thing – dress. And indeed your customers behave just like that: indifferent to everything, they become animated only when it comes to a question of dress. You know all these things and you are conscious that you are not merely the provider of a certain kind of merchandise but also the priestess of a religion as widespread as it is disavowed and dissembled. You know that this religion exists, that there is no one who does not sacrifice at its altars, that it is more powerful than any other power – you know all these things and therefore you think you are performing a function that is not only indispensable but also positive; and so you live on this positiveness, as plants live on sunlight. In other words, dress for you is not a profession but a vocation, and this vocation is connected with the most important thing there is in the life of human beings. Isn't that so?'

At first Cora, accustomed to my extravagances, had answered frankly, even if, as usual, laconically: she thought I was really talking about her dressmaking business. But at a certain moment she became aware that I was speaking of her second profession, and, though she continued to answer me with the same brevity and reserve, the pupils of her eyes, dilated with irritation, betrayed the fact that she was troubled or at any rate considerably disconcerted. Nevertheless, when I had finished my peroration, she merely said, with sincerity: 'I don't know what you're talking about. You say such complicated things. I don't understand you.'

'You're right, it's my own fault. Alas, I can't help making things complicated.'

'Besides, I don't see why you say all this to me.'

'I'm coming to the point. D'you know why I'm talking to you about these things? I'm talking to you because I want you to know that I am aware of the importance your profession has in your life. And that, in spite of it, I've come here to tell you that you must give it up.'

I had spoken in a normal tone of voice; but all of a sudden her eyes were dilated with anger. 'What the devil are you talking about?'

'This, to put it briefly: you're ill, Cora, more seriously ill than you think. You must make up your mind, once and for all, to send for the doctor. Then, as you'll certainly be advised to do, you must leave at once for a sanatorium in the mountains, to have treatment there.'

'You're crazy.'

'No, I'm not crazy; this is the truth. You cough all the time, you have a continuous temperature, you're forced to stay in bed as often as not – in a word, you're ill and you must have treatment.'

'You needn't even think of such a thing; I'm not going to see a doctor and I'm not going to move from here. I have a slight attack of bronchitis, but I don't need any doctors and I don't need to rest; I can look after myself here, on my own account.'

'On the contrary, I tell you most emphatically: you are ill, Cora.' I was silent for a moment and then, for some reason, I further confirmed what I had said: 'You are seriously ill.'

'Who's told you that?'

'It's your appearance that's told me.'

'What's my appearance, then?'

'To be precise, that of a person who is seriously ill.'

For a moment she said nothing, then, staring at me with an

air of defiance, she said: 'Now look here; not even if I knew I was dying would I do what you say.'

Suddenly, before I realized what I was doing, I was on my feet, bending over the bed and shaking her by the arms with a violence that was redoubled by the disgust I felt. 'You've got to have treatment, you've got to go away,' I cried. 'You *shall* have treatment, you *shall* go away.'

She stared at me without reacting, opening her eyes wide; then she started coughing, with a dry, angry, irrepressible cough, raising herself up in her bed, covering her mouth with her hand and gasping for air between one bout of coughing and the next as though she felt herself suffocating. I recalled the imaginary scene in my novel in which I had pictured her death and I immediately let go of her, frightened; but I had not yet given full vent to my rage. Scarcely knowing what I was doing, I took two or three turns round the room and found myself in front of the chest-of-drawers with its marble top swarming with knick-knacks. Then I realized that my words, shortly before, had not been merely a metaphor: Cora was in truth a priestess and this chest-of-drawers was the altar of her religion; and I had an equal loathing for both priestess and religion; and, just as shortly before I had been driven to shake her by a rage that was fundamentally homicidal, so now the knick-knacks on the chest-of-drawers aroused an iconoclastic violence within me. In a subdued voice, so that she should not hear me, I said: 'What did you do to Baba?' And then, immediately afterwards, my arm struck down upon the marble top of the chest-of-drawers and with one single gesture I swept away all the ornaments, as though they were in truth the fetishes of an intolerable, abhorrent idolatry. There was a great crash of things falling on the floor and breaking to pieces; all at once I calmed down, leant back against the chest-of-drawers and said, panting: 'I'm sorry.'

Cora had now recovered herself. With acid serenity, she commented: 'All my poor ornaments – who's going to recompense me for them?'

'I'm sorry.'

'With threats and abuse you'll never get anywhere, I warn you.'

'I'm sorry.'

'In any case I know why you're so anxious for me to go and have treatment in the mountains.'

'Why?'

'Because you want to be left alone with Baba. What d'you think?'

'Whatever are you saying?'

'D'you think I haven't noticed that you're dying for love of Baba? You want to be left alone with her, that's the truth of the matter.'

'You're mad.'

'No, I'm not mad. But if it's true, let me tell you at once that you needn't worry on my account. What Baba does doesn't concern me; she's grown-up, she's at liberty to do what she likes.'

She spoke with professional calm, as though Baba were not her daughter but one of the many girls of the villa on Via Cassia. After a moment she added: 'In short, if you and Baba want to be together, there's no need for you to look for a pretext to send me away. There are some things I quite understand.'

I looked at her and realized then that this was the old Cora yet again, Cora as she had always been, the Cora who had taken the fourteen-year-old Baba by the hand and led her to her house, the Cora whom I had seen the day before crossing the street with her hand on the messenger-girl's neck. The clue to this unchanging quality in her lay in the plausible tone of her voice – that disdainful plausibility which is the unfailing mark of the procuress. So there was now only the thinnest of barriers between us, and it depended entirely upon me to break it down; if I did so, I should find myself suddenly plunged up to the neck in the normality of corruption, since Cora would approve my love for Baba and assist it as far as she could. After reflecting in this way, I answered in a hasty sort of way: 'The question of Baba doesn't exist, and in any case I'm on the point of going away again. They're giving me my visa tomorrow. In a few days I shall be in the United States.'

I saw her face light up. 'Listen,' she said.

'What is it?'

'An idea. Why don't you take Baba with you? After all, she's your stepdaughter, and you can show her a bit of the world, and she could act as your secretary.'

She was not, therefore, renouncing her true self; she was, in fact, proposing herself as intermediary between Baba and me.

I said sharply, looking at my watch: 'I'll think about it. And now I must leave you, I have things to do.'

I went out of the room and she shouted again after me: 'Think about it. It's an idea.'

Thursday, December 10th

Once again today, as I went for a walk in the quarter where I live, I asked myself the question: 'Why, when talking to Cora, did you have recourse to the metaphor of the dressmaker's shop, instead of calling her second profession by its real name? Why, in short, are you not capable of facing the most important question of your life in a frank and straightforward way?'

Of course I made my customary reply: because to talk frankly to Cora meant either condemning her once and for all, or becoming her accomplice – two things that I wished equally to avoid. But I realized that there was another aspect of the problem upon which I had not yet dwelt; and it was this: to talk frankly to Cora meant taking a plunge into bad taste, into the stalest conventionality, into the non-genuine, in short, which lay not in myself but, objectively, in things.

In other words, my situation contained all the elements of what is called a sensational play. The elements, that is, that make people exclaim: 'These are things for a serial story or a melodrama; in real life they don't happen, they've never happened.' Now, on the other hand, these things were actually happening in real life, which was thus revealing itself to be constitutionally non-genuine. That is, the exact contrary was happening of what used to happen, so it seemed, in the past: formerly the serial story was derived from a real life which had the ineffable characteristics of genuineness; but now real life was showing itself to be in every way similar to a serial story, and the writer was faced with the obligaton to extract from it, if he was capable of doing so, something which should be, instead, genuine from the poetical point of view.

I asked myself at this point why this should be happening. The answer came to me in an unforeseen manner, when I raised my eyes as I was in the act of lighting a cigarette.

I was in a side street, not far from my home – two rows of

housefronts and, half way down the street, like the gap of a missing tooth in an otherwise perfect set, a big empty space between two buildings, either because it had not yet been built upon, or because the house which originally stood there had been pulled down.

On the side wall of one of the two houses between which lay the empty space, a tall, smooth, windowless wall, I saw that two gigantic advertisement posters had been stuck up.

The first was an advertisement for a brand of meat extract for soup. It showed a fully laid table, with a tablecloth, crockery, and knives, forks and spoons; and, seated at the table, a family consisting of mother, father and daughter. The man was middle-aged, in a dark grey suit, with well-brushed hair and well-shaven cheeks; the original American model had been touched up so that he should not appear too much of a foreigner to the eyes of the Italian consumer. The wife, slightly younger than her husband, also of an originally American type touched up to make her look Italian, was wearing a coquettish housewifely apron adorned with lace. Finally the daughter, in a sleeveless tartan dress, with a big bow on top of her loose mop of hair, was the only one of the three whose face could not be seen because her back was turned. The wife, as she stood leaning over the table, was raising the lid of a soup-tureen; the husband and daughter, clutching their spoons, were waiting with joyous impatience to be served.

The other poster, on the contrary, was a film advertisement. Oddly enough, it appeared to be the work of the same hand as had painted the meat extract poster. And even more oddly, by a singular coincidence the characters seemed to be the same – a middle-aged husband, a younger wife and a youthful daughter. But the situation in which the little family of the meat extract, then so serene and happy, now found itself, was different: the wife was cowering half-naked on a tumbled bed, her huge thighs veiled by the openwork lace of a black under-garment, her arrogant bosom partly uncovered, one arm stretched forward, her eyes staring in terror; her husband, in a dark grey suit as before but this time with hair unbrushed, was levelling a revolver at her from the doorway; and behind him was a glimpse of the daughter's face, terrified, her hand over her mouth, like a helpless onlooker at the scene of blood-shed.

The two posters, in short, depicted the same family in two

different situations, one of serene happiness, the other in tragic contrast. In both posters, of course, unreality was predominant: the steaming soup-tureen and the levelled revolver were symbols of the same non-genuine quality. But this, fundamentally, was not the question.

The question was a different one, it seemed to me; it was that these two posters were not in fact two falsified, conventional representations of a genuine reality; rather they were faithful and trustworthy representations of a reality itself completely non-genuine at its source. It was not, therefore, that the painter had imagined family peacefulness and tragedy in non-genuine manner; it was that family peacefulness and tragedy had presented themselves to the painter with the characteristics of non-genuineness.

I said to myself, as a conclusion of the matter: 'Advertising, in point of fact, is the folk-lore of industrial civilization. And what can be more genuine than folk-lore?'

Monday, December 14th

More and more frequently, as soon as she comes back from the dressmaker's shop, Cora goes to bed and has her supper there, together with Baba. And so, in order to avoid these embarrassing meals at Cora's bedside, in that room that disgusts me, I have acquired the habit of dining out, making some excuse or other.

This is to explain why it came about that I went back home this evening after dining alone in a restaurant in the neighbourhood. The first unusual thing was that I found the front door of the flat not closed but merely ajar. I went in: the lights were all burning – another unusual thing – both in the hall and in the passage. I hesitated, then went along towards Cora's bedroom.

I did not know what I meant to do; I felt uneasy, as if those two details, the front door ajar, the lights burning, had a significance which it was my duty to interpret. But as I passed along the corridor I noticed, through the half-closed door, that there was a light in the kitchen; so I looked in.

It was possible that Cora had felt better that evening and had preferred not to have her meal in bed: the kitchen was empty but bore all the signs of the supper the two women had eaten there. However, at a second glance, I noticed a curious fact: the meal, for some reason, had been interrupted halfway through.

On the marble table-top I saw two shallow pans containing eggs fried in butter: the yolk of one egg had been broken and had trickled round the inside of the pan but had not been gathered up; the other was untouched, and the piece of bread, ready to be dipped in it, was lying close by on the table. On two plates there was lettuce salad; tumblers and wine-glasses were full; there was a little clear soup and rice at the bottom of two bowls on one corner of the table; the chairs had been pushed well away from the table; on one of the chairs was a crumpled napkin, the other napkin was where a place had been laid. And finally – an incontestable proof that the meal had been recently and suddenly interrupted – a cigarette, still alight, its end stained with lipstick, was burning itself out on the edge of an ashtray.

I went from the kitchen to Baba's room. The light was on, and as usual the room was tidy, except that the wardrobe door had been left open; possibly Baba had taken out her coat and in her hurry had forgotten to shut it. The portable radio on the desk was announcing the stock exchange news in muted tones. I was not ignorant of the fact that Baba had a habit of leaving the radio turned on even when she was out of the room; nevertheless this voice murmuring into vacancy reinforced my feeling of a sudden, unforeseen flight.

I went into Cora's room; here too there were all the signs of haste: lamps burning; the drawers of the chest-of-drawers open; her dressing-gown thrown down on the bed, the wardrobe doors open wide. The telephone receiver had been taken off and placed beside the instrument; from the earpiece came the sound of the engaged signal. I put the receiver back in place and went out.

I went slowly to my own room, lay down on the bed and lit a cigarette. I thought I would wait there until Baba and Cora returned after this inexplicable absence. I said to myself that meanwhile I could pass the time meditating, as I sometimes did on similar occasions, upon the now imminent drafting of my novel. But my thoughts, almost at once, went off in a different direction.

Mysteriously, a memory floated up to the surface of my mind. During my travels in Iran I had stayed in an hotel at Isfahan, and one evening, when I had nothing to do, I had picked up an old number of an American tourist and travel magazine from a table in the lounge. Sitting in a rickety Victorian armchair, I looked through the magazine by the dim light of a central chandelier. Of the large number of articles, I then read one which made a special impression upon me. It was entitled 'The Mystery of the "Marie Céleste".' The *Marie Céleste* was a three-masted schooner which had sailed from Halifax in Canada, in June, one year in the first half of the nineteenth century. On board, apart from the crew and the officers, was the Captain's family, that is to say, his young wife and his two children, one of three years old and the other a baby in arms. The *Marie Céleste* was bound for France, for the port of Le Havre; but she never arrived there. After some months the sailing-ship was discovered in the middle of the Atlantic, in the perfectly smooth sea of a dead calm, with all sails set, drifting with the idle currents of the Ocean. The ship which sighted her had gone alongside, had made signals and even fired cannon-shots; but the *Marie Céleste* had continued to drift. So a longboat had been lowered and the sailing-ship had been boarded. Astonishingly, it had been discovered that she was completely deserted: officers, crew, the captain's family, all had vanished. But everywhere there were signs of a sudden interruption of the quietest and most normal occupations: in the wardroom, the table was still laid, with food on the plates and knives and forks lying on the tablecloth as they had been left. The baby's high chair had been moved slightly back from the table. The other chairs had been pushed back just enough for people to rise from the table without any haste. In short, the meal having been interrupted halfway through, those sitting at the table had left calmly, without confusion or fear. The same kind of abandonment had been noticed also in other parts of the ship; the crew had relinquished their own occupations in a sudden manner but, it appeared, without any sort of compulsion. Moreover these people had left the ship in an inexplicable, not to say mysterious, way, for the lifeboats were all in place; they had gone without touching anything or carrying anything away, and those who were eating had left mouthfuls of food on their forks and those who were mending sails had not pulled their needles out of the cloth; they had gone as birds go from a bough upon which they have perched for a moment or two.

The puzzle of the *Marie Céleste* had never been solved: officers, crew, the captain's family had vanished for ever. Ideally, the Canadian ship should still be rocking on the calm, windless sea, waiting for the solution of the mystery to allow it to sail again. And the solution, as I thought then and as I still think, must be perfectly simple, quite obvious, the kind of solution which lies right under one's nose, so to speak, and which escaped attention precisely for that reason. I recalled that after I had read the article I had spent a couple of hours puzzling over possible explanations of the mystery. Finally I had felt sleepy, had thrown down the magazine and gone to bed.

Now, after finding the flat empty but with the lights on and signs of ordinary life everywhere, the mystery of the *Marie Céleste* came back to my mind as a forgotten enigma that was suddenly re-confirmed by reality. The resemblances were many: the same atmosphere of domestic normality abruptly and mysteriously interrupted; the same impossibility of finding any plausible explanation; the same absolute ignorance of the person or persons who had caused the interruption and the abandonment. And, just as the *Marie Céleste* had drifted, entirely empty, over marine abysses full of darkness and monsters, so the flat, equally empty and uninhabited, hung over the abysses, likewise shadowy and peopled with monstrous creatures, of everyday existence.

I felt sufficiently uneasy not to forget the disappearance of Cora and Baba; not sufficiently to do anything to explain it. In the end I thought the best thing for me to do was to wait until midnight; not till then would I consider the expediency of starting a search for the two women. In the meantime, however, it was only nine o'clock; three hours until midnight, and what was I to do? It occurred to me that my stay in Rome was coming to an end; that in a few days I should be starting on a long journey; that the diary I had decided to keep for the whole duration of my stay would therefore come to an end too, as also, implicitly, the novel which I intended to extract from the diary. Why not, then – even if only in fun – make use of the disappearance of Baba and Cora that evening, or rather, of the explanation I might give of it, as a conclusion both of the diary and of the novel?

But, since it was a question not merely of explaining the absence of the two women but also of imagining the finale of the novel, I might just as well – instead of indulging in vague, disordered fancies – put down in writing whatever imagination might suggest to me as I went along. Apart from anything else, it would be as good a way as any of killing time while I was waiting. So I rose from my bed, sat down at the desk in front of my typewriter, inserted a sheet of paper and, without further ado, began tapping on the keys. This is what I wrote:—

'The site of the ruins of Persepolis is at the far end of an immense plain of a pale, dull green, the yellowed green of innumerable stunted, prickly bushes flattened almost to the ground by wind and dryness. The sky above the plateau, so deep and so blue that it is almost black, hangs above this plain, repeating its emptiness; a vulture circles in the sky, wheeling in slow flight and searching for a prey amongst the bushes; in the plain, equally solitary, a peasant, small and lost-looking in the immensity, drives his plough along the furrows of his field. At the edge of the plain rises a group of rocks, tawny red, scored with deep, purplish grooves; as the car comes closer one can distinguish, on a great rectangular terrace sheltering behind the rocks, a row of indeterminate, uneven columns that look as though made of smoke. These are the ruins of Persepolis, all that remains of the palaces of Darius after Alexander set fire to them during a banquet. As one approaches nearer, the ruins take on a more precise shape, they become more real: the terrace is seen to be constructed of enormous Cyclopean blocks; the columns, so slender when seen from down in the plain, are now shown to be massive, colossal. And here and there, disposed in various strange fashions among the rows of columns, are the cornices, high or low, of windows and doors through which shines the radiant blue of the sky: the fire consumed the wooden ceilings and the walls of mud and straw and spared only these cornices which are made of stone.

'One morning I left the hotel, which stands at a short distance from the ruins, and went up to the terrace; there I sat in the sun on an overturned capital, facing the immense, flat, luminous steppe. My eye was caught by an inscription which had been scratched by means of a nail on the stone of the capital. It bore the signature of a certain J. Logan and the date

1824. It was a Latin quotation: *Vae, vae Babylon civitas illa fortis*. I looked for a little at the writing, then again at the ruins, above which the usual vultures were flying, croaking from time to time in the profound silence; and I reflected that meditation upon the transience of human affairs, upon the reasons for which so many proud civilizations have perished for ever and upon the manifold corruption which had preceded and caused their ruin, was in a way inevitable in a place such as Persepolis. I stayed there for a little longer with eyes half-closed, sitting in the sun, then I took from my pocket an Italian newspaper that I had found in Teheran and re-read with mechanical attentiveness the whole of the page which had been devoted to the bloody and mysterious deaths of Baba and Cora.

'They had been found in the morning by one of Cora's work-girls who had arrived at the dressmaker's shop and found the door ajar. The newspaper, in the usual crime news jargon, with its alternation of the most precise and the most useless information (Silvia Ferrari, aged 22, of 19 Via dei Glicini, Flat 13) with the most stentorian adjectives (a blood-curdling spectacle, a horrifying sight, ferocious cruelty, a monstrous crime, etc., etc.) related, to put it briefly, that the girl had found Baba in the bedroom, lying dead on the bed, and subsequently, in the workroom, Cora, also dead. The way in which the two women had been killed revealed the character of the murderer and at the same time gave a hint of the motives of the crime. Having enticed Baba and Cora to the dressmaker's shop by some pretext or perhaps by blackmail at a time when there was nobody there, the murderer, doubtless the husband of a woman who had frequented Cora's house of ill fame (at least this was the hypothesis put forward by the newspaper), had applied the law of retaliation, possessing Baba in the same way as Cora's clients had once possessed his wife; and had then killed both Baba and Cora. Then we come to the reconstruction of the crime. Baba had been found completely naked but she did not seem to have been assaulted; it appeared that, before she died, she had had sexual relations, unforced though without doubt imposed upon her, with her murderer. Death had been caused by strangulation by means of a nylon stocking and must have been very painful because the murderer, according to the paper, had prolonged the agony, alternately suffocating her and then allowing her to breathe, more or less as happens in the Spanish method of capital punishment by garrotting. As to Cora, she had been struck from behind, with a knife or a dagger, facing the bed on which Baba was lying, probably at the very moment when, having been pushed into the room by the murderer, she had discovered her daughter's corpse. She had fallen to the floor, staining the bedside rug and the lower part of the bed-cover with her blood; then – again according to the newspaper's reconstruction of the crime – she had been dragged by the hair along the passage to the workroom: there were in fact streaks of blood on the floor of the passage along its whole length. In the workroom, the murderer had lifted Cora's body and laid it on the big table which was used for designing and cutting out clothes. On this table, as on a slab in a dissecting room, he had used an axe or a very sharp knife to detach the head from the body, proceeding from the back of the neck to the Adam's apple; then he had dragged the headless corpse to the other end of the room and had placed it in a sitting position in an armchair, upright, with its hands clasped in its lap. Close to the armchair was one of those headless lay figures used by dressmakers for trying on clothes; the newspaper, at this point, ventured the hypothesis that, by depositing the decapitated corpse in this way beside the lay figure, the murderer had given vent to an impulse of mockery and disrespect, as if to signify that Cora was worth no more than a headless tow-filled dummy.

'The paper contained an article about the discovery of the crime, as it had appeared to the work-girl and, immediately afterwards, to the first policeman to reach the scene. But a second article, evidently written a few hours later, contained many further details: for instance that Baba had not been wearing nylon stockings but cotton socks; where then had the stocking come from which the murderer had used to strangle her? The paper explained that one of the work-girls, the previous evening, had washed a pair of stockings and hung them up to dry on a string in front of the window in the bathroom. And now one of the stockings was in fact missing, and this was precisely the one which the murderer had used. The newspaper's reconstruction was convincing: while Baba was undressing in the bedroom, it explained, the murderer had gone into the bathroom to urinate, and thus, as he stood in front of the lavatory bowl, he had noticed the stockings hanging up at the window and had raised his hand, pulled one of them down and put it in his pocket. Then he had returned to the bedroom, where Baba, already lying on the bed, was awaiting him. He had forced Baba to lie face downwards, had thrown himself upon her and possessed her, and then, immediately after the orgasm, Baba being unable to see him because she was lying with her face against the pillow, he had taken the stocking from his pocket, had passed it neatly round her neck and, keeping her still with the whole weight of his body, had alternately tightened and slackened his grip until she was dead.

'About Cora's death, too, the second article in the paper provided some hitherto unpublished details. The corpse had been found in a sitting position, the hands clasped in its lap and without its head. But the head had not been found; what could have happened to it? According to the paper, things had taken place in the following way: the murderer, having put the last touches ot this dramatic tableau of vengeance, had taken up the head by the hair and gone back again into the bathroom, this time in order to clean his hands and his blood-stained clothes. Here, provisionally but not casually, he had placed Cora's head inside the lavatory-bowl, in such a way that only the forehead stood out above the edges of it; and he had washed his hands and had perhaps also tried to clean his clothes. His ablutions had been summary; bloodstains had been found on the wash-basin, on the towel and the soap. Having finished washing, the murderer had turned his attention to the head immersed in the lavatory-bowl; and then, in order to cleanse it of coagulated blood but also, and above all, from the same desire to show disrespect, he had pressed the lever of the tank so that the gush of water should rain down upon the dead woman's head. But the tank was nearly empty, or else it was broken, and so a lot of blood had been found on the edges of the bowl and inside it.

'The head had afterwards been taken away in a very simple manner. The murderer had gone back into the workroom, had opened the cupboard and there, amongst the other junk, had found a tall, oval, white cardboard box of the kind used for carrying hats. It was full of ribbons and remnants of material. He emptied it out on the floor, placed Cora's head in it, tied it up with a piece of tape, and then went peacefully away, the box hanging by a knot from his little finger.

Naturally the murderer had not been discovered. The police formed a number of hypotheses, among which, as I have said, the most probable seemed to be that it was a crime of vengeance on the part of a betrayed husband against the procuress who had corrupted his wife. Of course, every detail of Cora's life was laid bare; and I myself was also mentioned; but it was noted that Cora and I had been separated for many years and that at the moment of the crime I was away on a newspaper job in Iran . . .'

Here I stopped and slowly read over what I had written; and I immediately asked myself the question: why had I attributed the absence of Cora and Baba to a crime, and, to be more exact, to that particular crime?

I lit a cigarette and started to think. Obviously my reconstruction of the reasons for Baba's and Cora's absence had its origin in the fact that my imagination was attracted by tragedy, full of significance as it was, rather than by the senseless normality of everyday life. Probably I was failing to resign myself to the idea that nothing ever happened, or at least, nothing of significance; and almost instinctively I preferred the resounding, consistent quality of drama to the absurdity of the daily round.

Having established this rather important point, I still had to explain why in the world I had imagined myself to be at Persepolis, in Iran (whence I had arrived two months before and where for the moment there was no probabilty of my returning) and why the crime had these definite characteristics. I took up the sheets of paper and read them over a second time, and recalled that I had written them as one might, under the influence of a drug, write a confession of something which has for some time been encumbering the obscurest zone of one's consciousness. In other words, in those sheets of paper I had not only imagined a possible conclusion for my novel, but also – and above all – I had consigned to them something intimate and secret of which I myself had hitherto had no knowledge.

In the first place: Iran. As I said, I had just come from there, and it was strange that I should have imagined myself to have gone back and to have learned there of the deaths of Cora and Baba. It would have been more logical to fancy myself learning of them in the United States, where I knew I should be going in a few days' time. Strange, moreover, that I should have imagined myself to be in Iran at the moment when Cora and Baba were killed – not a day more nor a day less; whereas in reality, if – as was possible even if not probable – their absence was due to a crime, that crime was being committed now, at the very moment when I was writing the description of it in my diary.

Iran, then, must be explained by the fact that it was the last country to which I had been. And the ruins of Persepolis, the fallen capital on which I was sitting, the writing scratched on the stone by Mr. J. Logan (which I had in fact observed during my recent journey) – how were they to be explained? Clearly, by my need to exalt myself, to see myself as a kind of Byronic hero, remote and at the same time superior to the sordid affair of Cora. Yes, I was a rare soul, a man of culture, a poet, a traveller without a goal, sitting among the ruins of a great city and meditating upon the transience of human things, while far away, in another great city – still intact but doubtless also doomed, owing to its corruptness, to a similar destruction – far away in Rome, Cora and Baba were being sordidly, barbarously slaughtered.

However there still remained the fact that I had imagined the crime in a highly detailed fashion and had also formulated the hypothesis, a plausible one, after all, of a kind of law of retaliation applied by a betrayed husband to avenge his own honour. Except that this avenger did not content himself with possessing Baba, as Cora's clients had once possessed his wife; immediately after possesing her he had killed her and had killed Cora. Now one could understand the murder of Cora as a sort of after-effect of hatred; but that of Baba? In reality this crime, cruel and apparently useless, proclaimed me as the true perpetrator of the slaughter, even if only in the pages of a novel. It was I who hated Cora; it was I who loved Baba; I, and no one else. And deep down in the yearnings of my imagination lay incest, in other words, nothingness; to which, after accepting it and practising it, I reacted by killing, in order to punish them, both Cora who had encouraged it and Baba who had endured it. Far from being a husband avenging his honour, it was I who was the real murderer; and this also explained how, having attributed the crime to an obscure, nameless person (obscure and nameless precisely because I myself was hiding behind him), I had come to imagine that at the moment of the crime I was in Iran, sitting among the ruins of Persepolis, admiring them and reflecting upon the transience of human things. Actually Persepolis was an alibi for the crime in which

I was the principal. A literary alibi, of course, since it was all the time a novel, not real life, that was concerned; but it was none the less hypocritical, none the less non-genuine, for that.

Yes; for at the end of all this there was, yet again, the non-genuineness that was characteristic of action and therefore also of the imagination of action. Continually I was doing one thing, believing I was doing another. I believed I was having the two women killed by a husband avenging his honour, instead of which it was I who killed them. I attributed the crime to an excessive and aberrant moral resentment; instead of which the real cause was the attraction, and at the same time the horror of incest – that is, of nothingness. So I found myself again confronted with the non-genuine, which in fact, inevitably, characterizes any sort of action based on, and determined by, nothingness.

At this point I asked myself the question: should I, or should I not, place the imaginary double murder as the conclusion of my novel? I hesitated for a long time and in the end decided not to. Truth, whatever it might be, was always preferable to falsehood. When Cora and Baba returned and I heard why they had vanished, then I would see whether the story of those two months of my stay in Rome really had a conclusion or whether it was left open, without either beginning or end, as often happens in everyday life. In any case the crime could not be made use of.

On the other hand, however, I could not affirm with absolute certainty that the crime I had imagined consisted only of falsehood and unreality. It did not actually happen, it is true, either in life or in the novel; nevertheless it served to indicate a possibility in my mind, it defined my character, above all it threw light on the nature of my relationship with Baba and Cora. Non-genuine both in reality and in art, its genuineness lay in the fact of my having imagined it. For all these reasons, to suppress it would mean, in fact, lying yet again, that is, suppressing a whole part of myself, the part that expressed itself through my imagination and through my wishful longing for the crime itself.

All of a sudden I felt tired. After looking at my watch and seeing that it was past midnight, I rose mechanically from the desk, went over to the bed, lay down on top of the coverlet, fully dressed as I was, and fell asleep almost at once.

I awoke with a start, under the impression that I had slept

for only one minute, so black and profound had been my sleep; but when I looked at the alarm-clock on the bedside table I saw that its hands pointed to a quarter past one. At the same time I realized that what had awakened me was the footsteps of Baba and Cora in the passage.

I listened for a short time, then jumped from the bed, opened the door and looked out.

The passage was deserted, Baba and Cora had already disappeared. I went to the corner and looked again: this part of the passage was also deserted; but the door of Cora's room was ajar and from it came sounds as of sobs mingled with words.

I went nearer, squeezed myself against the wall opposite the chink in the doorway and looked into the room. I was in a good position; I saw the bed diagonally, Cora lying on the bed, and Baba, whose back was turned towards me, bending over Cora.

The sobs, I realized, were Baba's; for I could see Cora's head lying back on the pillow, motionless and with closed eyes. They were sobs that expressed, uncontrollably, bitterness and anguish and sorrow: I should never have thought that Baba, usually so placid and so well-regulated, could sob like that. Between the sobs, broken phrases reached me, such as: 'It's nothing, Mummy, it's nothing, you mustn't worry, Mummy; everything will be all right, Mummy, you'll see ...' Meanwhile, talking and weeping as she did so, Baba was arranging the pillow under Cora's head and pushing back the hair from her forehead. Finally Cora, without opening her eyes, said in a hard voice: 'If it's nothing, why are you crying?'

'Because I'm stupid. Don't take any notice of me; but tell me how you're feeling.'

'Bad.'

'Now you must get into bed and sleep and have a good rest.'

'I can't sleep, you know that.'

'You must take a sleeping-pill.'

'They're no use to me.'

'I'll stay here with you, I'll keep you company.'

'No, there's no need for that. Just help me to get undressed.'

'Really?'

'Yes, really.'

'I'll get you undressed now, of course I will.' Baba began sobbing again in such a noisy way that Cora said once more, in

275

a rude, hard voice: 'Now, once and for all, stop crying, you silly girl. What's the matter with you?'

'I'm sorry, I feel a bit upset; don't worry about me.'

After this, Cora said no more; Baba bent over her and began to undress her as she lay there passively, her head buried in the pillows and her eyes closed. Baba took off her shoes and placed them neatly at the foot of the bed. Then, with both hands, she took hold of the edge of Cora's skirt and pulled it delicately upwards, above her knees. I saw her fingers unhook the top of the stocking from the garter and then, lightly and skilfully, lower it, running her hand round Cora's leg and finally taking her heel in the palm of her hand and slipping the stocking right off. She stooped over Cora again and repeated the operation with the other stocking. Then she pulled her skirt down again as far as her knees, undid the zip fastener at the side, slipped the skirt down along her legs, pulled it over her feet and placed it on the armchair beside the stockings. Cora was now in her green undergarment trimmed with yellow lace. Baba removed this undergarment over Cora's head; Cora, for a moment, was left with only her black slip and brassière; and I was then able to judge how thin she had become since the last time I had seen her. Cora had never been thin, her beauty had been of the solid, muscular kind; but now one could discern the sharp point of her hip, the parallel ridges of her ribs, and higher up the hollows of her shoulders. I remembered her navel as a white, clean, dimple in a surrounding sphere of luminous flesh; now it was nothing but a dark, crushed mark amongst the yellowed folds of her shrunken belly. There was a wide, uneven gap between her legs, from groin to ankle-bone; below her back the buttocks seemed wasted and as though shrivelled; the dull white surface of her thighs was broken by flabby muscles on which the loose skin was puckered and creased. I followed Baba's hands to Cora's chest, saw the two black cups of the brassière lifted and removed, and at the same moment the breasts, no longer held, fell to one side, flat and long like two empty sockets, pulled down, as it were, by the two enormous brown nipples. Baba placed the brassière on the armchair and then enquired, in a sad, exhausted voice: 'Where is your nightdress?'

'In the drawer.'

'Which drawer?'

'The top drawer of the chest-of-drawers.'

Baba turned to go to the chest-of-drawers, so I jumped back and returned on tiptoe to my room. But I did not go so far. Halfway along the passage, I went instead into Baba's room, turned on the light, walked over and sat down in the arm-chair beside the desk. I twisted the chair round towards the door lit a cigarette and prepared myself to wait.

I did not wait long. After about twenty minutes Baba came in and, without saying anything or showing any surprise at my presence there, went across to the wardrobe and started pulling off her sweater over her head, in front of the looking-glass. 'What happened?' I asked. 'Why did you interrupt your meal and rush off in such a hurry?'

She dropped her sweater on the floor, moved close up to the mirror and carefully examined her face, touching her red, swollen eyes with her fingers. Then she replied: 'A depressing, miserable thing happened. Two policemen arrived and took us off to the police-station. There they kept us waiting for more than two hours; then they called Cora into the inspector's room and I don't know what happened – it may have been to do with the Via Cassia villa, or some other thing, Cora wouldn't tell me. I only know that in the end Cora felt ill and fell down on the floor, and then they carried her into another room and called me, and I waited until she recovered and so at last we were able to come home again.'

As I listened to this clipped, laconic account, I had a feeling of disappointment: the most obvious, the simplest, the most reasonable thing – that is, a surprise visit by the police – had not occurred to me, for some reason; instead, I had imagined crimes and cruelty, slaughter and death. I said: 'I saw you while you were undressing Cora.'

'Where were you, then?'

'I was behind the door. You were crying all the time. Why were you crying, seeing that after all everything has turned out for the best?'

After a moment she replied slowly: 'I'm so afraid.'

'But afraid of what?'

'At the police-station, when I saw Cora lying on the sofa, I had a presentiment that she's going to die soon.'

'Why should she die? She felt ill. An indisposition which was, in fact, providential.'

'Don't try to be funny.'

'Anyone might have felt ill in such circumstances.'

'Not Cora.'

'But why should she die?'

'I hope it's nothing. But I'm so afraid she may die.'

I said nothing. I rose from the armchair and went across to her as she stood in front of the looking-glass. Immediately she threw her arms round my neck and we stood there, in a close embrace in front of the looking-glass, which reflected us and confirmed the nature of the embrace, truly innocent this time. Then, pressed closely against her and patting her shoulder gently as one does when somebody is oppressed with sorrow, I could not help thinking that everything was turning out according to the laws of normal everyday life: instead of the black-mail, the ambush and the vengeance of a husband whose honour has been impugned – the surprise visit of the police; instead of murder – death in bed from an illness that might come to anybody. The *deus ex machina*, there could be no doubt, was functioning. Cora would die; I myself should be freed, without any effort, from a stagnant, troublesome relation-ship; Baba, a devoted, compassionate daughter to the end, would be able to marry honourably and would no longer be forced to love her mother for the precise reason that she had no cause to love her.

The end of our embrace marked the end of these reflections. I said good-night to Baba and went back to my own room. It was two o'clock. I went to bed, took up a book on the United States which I had bought that day and read for an hour before falling asleep.

Tuesday, December 15th

I realize today that there is nothing left for me but to go away. The conclusion of my diary, and therefore also of my novel, will be, provisionally, my departure. But if Baba's presenti-ments come true, as it seems probable that they will, the con-clusion can only be the death of Cora – a worthy epilogue to a typical vicissitude of everyday life in which, fundamentally, nothing has occurred and no one has acted in any way.

This morning, naturally, Cora got up and went out, and later telephoned from outside that she would not be coming back for lunch. It is probable that this busy activity on her part was not entirely unrelated to the visit, yesterday evening, of the two policemen; that Cora went out in order to stave off the threat of an arrest; or else to close, provisionally, the villa on Via Cassia; in any case to demonstrate both to herself and to us that she is all right, that she is not ill, that she has no need of treatment or of a sojourn in the mountains. Thus does a boxer in extremities, his face already reduced to a bloody pulp, rise to his feet and seek to deliver one last blow at his adversary.

I asked myself whether the prospect of Cora's arrest, with the consequent scandal and disclosure of my name, frightened me. And I realized, with some satisfaction, that it left me completely indifferent. At most it would be another *deus ex machina*, analogous to that of Cora's death, but of a punitive kind, which would strike not only Cora but also, perhaps not unjustly, myself.

Baba did not come home to lunch; probably she was with Cora, or else she had gone out with Santoro. I ate alone, then went into my room, sat down at the desk and began reading through my diary.

I re-read the page, at the beginning, in which I pointed out that I reserved to myself the right to add to the facts that had really occurred other, invented facts, which would serve as material for the novel I intended to write later; and I fell into a profound meditation.

Why, indeed, had I troubled to point this out? Was it really because I wanted to reserve to myself the right to use the diary as a draft to prepare the way for the novel? Or was it not rather because I wanted to be able to say certain things that in real life did not exist? And to conceal from myself others that did exist?

In truth, if one day I really set to work to write the novel, I should have then not merely to accept everything I had added in the diary with the object of completing reality and, so to speak, making it more real; I should also have to remove all that I had superimposed like a mask on the face of that same reality, every time reality had seemed to me unavowable even in a diary. It was obvious that this work of revision would be far from easy: both the additions which served to deepen and integrate reality, and those which served, on the other hand, to conceal it, had not been made for merely literary reasons to do with the mechanics of a novel, but for extra-literary reasons which I felt it was difficult for me, not to say impossible, to clarify even to myself. The diary, in short, was not only the journal of my life but also the secret mirror of my mind. And I had in fact described in it, apart from a few real, authentic dreams that had seemed to me the most significant, certain events and characters which I knew to be invented but which, like the nocturnal dreams, had served, at the moment when I invented them, to conceal or to give vent to certain passions.

The ordinary man has only dreams, whether they be sleeping or waking dreams; but the novelist, in addition to his dreams, has the inventions he creates in his novels. Like dreams, these inventions are not what they seem; and they signify more than they claim to signify. Now there are two kinds of novelists: those who believe in their own inventions and those who do not. It is permitted to the former to write novels like puzzles, to which however they themselves do not know the solutions; but the latter possess the key to what they write and for that reason are in a position to make manifest that which is concealed. I belonged, clearly, to the second category.

All this may perhaps seem mysterious. But let it be remembered that a diary does not represent the truth because, at the very moment when the keeper of the diary is recounting an event in which he himself was the protagonist, he is no longer the man who experienced the event but the man who is writing about it; and the man who experienced it is a quite separate character to whom the diarist stands in the relation of a judge, or, if you prefer, of a recorder. And while it is true that there is complete identification between the diarist and the protagonist in the events of the diary, it is also true that it is this very identification that lies at the source of any deceit or lie or reticence which modifies, amputates or disguises the events related in the diary itself. In reality the diary is always sincere, always truthful; it is merely a question of seeking out the sincerity and truth behind the events.

This is the reason why diaries, journals, autobiographies, confessions and memoirs are all, more or less, untruthful in a factual sense and truthful in a psychological sense. They are like a mirror in which anyone who looks at himself cannot help assuming an attitude, in some way or other. The truth lies not so much in the image as in the character of the person who, at the very moment in which the mirror reflects his image, creates himself, so to speak, as though by enchantment. But this personage cannot be accepted just as he is; he must be interpreted, submitted to a critical examination. It will then become apparent that he is the result of almost automatic lies and reticences and travesties.

What, in my case, did this critical examination reveal? It revealed that the personage of the diary had been produced through the suppression of an entire part of the reality; and that his true character was determined not only through this suppressed reality but also through the very fact of its suppression.

The personage of the diary was, in fact, a novelist who decided to keep a diary on one period of his life, with the object of extracting a novel from it afterwards. Now the curious thing was this: that, once he had reached the end of the diary, it was actually the project of the novel which destroyed the personage of the novelist. If I really wished to write the novel some day, I should have to admit that it had not been only the project of the novel that had made me keep the diary – had made me, that is, go over from non-involvement to involvement and consequently to knock at Baba's door – but also, simultaneously, something else that was much less elevated and anyhow not literary. This something else had been suppressed by me in order to construct the figure of the novelist; but now the project of the novel compelled me to admit its existence, in fact to base the whole affair upon it.

As I sat reflecting thus, I heard the door of the room open behind me and recognized Baba's footstep. I waited without moving.

She came and stood in front of my desk and asked: 'What are you doing?'

'I was re-reading my diary,' I replied.

I must explain that I had often spoken to Baba about the diary and about my plan to extract a novel from it. So she asked me: 'Are you satisfied?'

'In what sense?'

'In the sense you've always spoken about. D'you think you'll be able to make use of it to write your novel when the time comes?'

'Yes and no.'

'Why yes and no?'

'In some respects yes, in others no.'

'In what respects no?'

'You know that I've made various additions as I was writing the diary, additions that I thought might be useful when I came to write the novel.'

'Yes, you told me.'

'Well, some of these additions make reality more real; but others produce the opposite effect.'

'That's quite simple: cut them out.'

'Yes, they ought to be cut out, but it's not so easy. These additions, for the most part, conceal a truth. If they were cut out the truth would appear.'

'Well, wouldn't that be better?'

'In theory, yes. But . . .'

'But what?'

'It's extremely difficult for me to accept this truth, to admit it to myself.'

'Why?'

'Because it's a truth I'm ashamed of.'

'But what can there be so terrible about it?'

'Oh, nothing really terrible.'

'Well then?'

'Well then, there are things that are easy to say and others, on the contrary, that are difficult.'

'Why difficult?'

'That's just the point. Probably because they were not said at the moment when they ought to have been said.'

'What does that mean?'

'It means that they're just as difficult to say as they were not to say.'

'Why?'

'Because time has buried them under mountains of silence.'

'And so?'

'And so, to be precise, since they're buried, one must go and dig them up – a laborious, disagreeable job.'

'If it's so laborious and disagreeable, give up the idea and continue to keep silent.'

'You'd see what would happen to the novel, in that case!'

'What d'you mean?'

'I mean that, if I keep silent about these things, it will be impossible for me to write the novel.'

'But tell me, then, what is it you're talking about?'

I made no reply; we looked at one another. Baba went on:

'Try talking to *me* about these things instead of to yourself. Sometimes it's easier to confess things to someone else than to oneself.'

'You're the last person I should be able to confess these things to.'

'Why?'

'Oh, for a very simple reason.'

'What's that?'

'Because they concern *you*.'

'They concern me?'

'Yes.'

Again we looked at one another. And then I felt that, although the things I had not the courage to tell concerned Baba, nevertheless Baba was the only person to whom I could confess them. This was because I had loved her and still loved her and I knew that only love made certain confessions permissible. Especially a love such as the love I felt for her, entirely hopeless and now bound up, decisively, with renunciation.

Suddenly, in a troubled voice, I said: 'All right, I'll say to you the things I haven't the courage to say to myself. Let's now do more or less what they do at psychoanalytical sessions; you'll be the doctor and I'll be the patient. But the other way round: I'll stay here, sitting at my desk, and you'll lie down on the bed.'

'But why?'

'I beg you, do as I say.'

She went over to the bed and lay down. I remained where I was, sitting at the desk, with my back turned to her; and I said: 'I'll tell you these things now. I asked you to lie down on the bed because like that I shan't see you while I'm speaking, and at the same time you can listen to me comfortably.'

She said nothing. I went on: 'You remember how our relationship began?'

'What relationship d'you mean?'

'I mean, you remember what happened between us, that evening when I knocked at your door, after I came back from Iran?'

'I remember very well indeed. You showed me an anonymous letter in which Cora's profession was mentioned and asked me if it was true. And I told you it *was* true.'

'Quite right. But did you notice the date of that letter?'

'No, I don't think so; why?'

'D'you know what the date was?'

'What was it?'

'The fifth of October 1952.'

'Ah, then it wasn't true that the letter had arrived that very day?'

'No. Actually it had arrived ten years before. And d'you know what that means?'

'What?'

'Simply that I had already known about Cora's profession for ten years.'

'But you told me you'd never known about it until that day.'

'Yes, that's so. But I lied.'

'Why did you lie?'

'The reason why I lied is exactly the thing which hitherto I haven't had the courage to say, and which now, if you have the patience to listen to me, I'll say to you.'

'I've all the patience you want.'

'When I received the letter – that is, in 1952 – I was no longer having any direct physical relations with Cora. Indirect, yes.'

'What d'you mean?'

'I mean that, ten years ago, I stopped sleeping with Cora because I no longer loved her. Now, just at that same period, in a way which was rather mysterious but in fact fairly normal in dealings of that kind, a number of prostitutes turned up here at the flat, saying they were friends of each other. Anyone else in my place might perhaps have put a stop to these visits from the beginning, but I . . .'

'But you . . . ?'

'It would take too long to explain why I allowed these girls to come to me here at the flat. Let's say then that I was very depressed and that the girls came as just the right moment.'

'Why were you depressed?'

'Oh, for lots of reasons. But what I wish to say now is another mater. It is this: at that same period I received the anonymous letter; I began to have suspicions, I questioned one of the girls and then I discovered the truth.'

'What truth?'

'Not merely that Cora was practising this profession – that indeed was already known to me through the letter; but also something else which was not in the letter.'

'What was that?'

'This: that it was Cora who was sending the girls to me. Cora wished to continue having a love relationship with me through them, and she probably wanted, more than anything, to demonstrate to herself that I – how shall I put it? – that I was not escaping from her, or rather that I was not contradicting the idea that she had formed of the world. Now attend carefully to what I say. The girl whom I forced to tell me the truth was not the last, nor even the last but one, she was one of the first.'

'What d'you mean?'

'I mean that I pretended not to know anything, and I went on playing Cora's game and making use of her, and I didn't put a stop to the girls' visits until a long time afterwards.'

'Why did you put a stop to them?'

'I suppose I had had enough.'

'Was this the thing you hadn't the courage to put in your diary?'

'No, it wasn't that.'

'What was it then?'

'I'm coming to that. Well, in the end I put a stop to the girls' visits, I joined the newspaper I'm still working for, I made my first journey as a foreign correspondent. But, although I had every reason for doing so, I didn't leave Cora; I pretended not to know anything about anything and I went on living with her.'

'Why?'

'Anyone else might say: because I had accepted her services. Seeing that I had accepted them, I couldn't then ... etc., etc.'

'Anyone else might say that. But you?'

'What I say is this: through non-involvement.'

'What exactly is that?'

'I did not wish to have anything more to do with Cora because I could find no valid reason for acting in one sense or another with regard to her. So it seemed to me that the only thing to do was to induce in myself a kind of artificial non-involvement. I succeeded admirably, I assure you.'

'I don't doubt it in the least.'

'I started, therefore, to lead the life that you know of: eight months of the year away and four at home. And during the four months at home no dealings with Cora or yourself, just as though I'd been a lodger and not her husband and your stepfather.'

'Was this the thing you hadn't the courage to say?'

'Not yet. But we're coming to it now. Well, then ...'

'Well then?'

'Well, this life had been going on for four years when a new event took place.'

'What new event?'

'I was in Rome, between one journey and another. The new event was that somebody telephoned me to say that at such-and-such an address, in such-and-such a street and at such-and-such a flat, there was something for me.'

'Who was this somebody?'

'It was Cora. She didn't say she was Cora, naturally. But I recognized the voice.'

'And then?'

'Instead of refusing there and then, or of saying that I realized who she was, I pretended not to have understood and I accepted.'

'And so?'

'And so I went.'

'And then what happened?'

'What happened was that, when I saw the thing that was intended for me, I ran away.'

'What was this thing?'

'Why d'you pretend not to know?'

'I'm not pretending; I don't know.'

'On the contrary, you *do* know, you've always known.'

'But, once and for all, what was this thing?'

'You know better than I do: this thing was Baba.'

'It was Baba?'

'Yes, Baba; and you know it and have always known it.'

'But that's not true. I know and have always known that the first time Baba was taken by Cora to that house, she found no one there and so nothing happened. But I never knew that the man who was supposed to come that day and who didn't come, was you.'

'And yet I have proof that you've known it ever since that day.'

'But what proof?'

'Baba was sitting with her back to the door, which was open, reading a magazine, her head bent; in front of her was a sofa and on the wall above the sofa a big looking-glass – isn't that so?'

'Yes, but it was I myself who said these things to you when I was telling you about that day; don't you remember?'

'Wait a moment. What you didn't say, however – I don't know why – was that, at the moment when I appeared in the doorway and looked into the looking-glass to get a view of Baba's face, Baba, who until then had kept her eyes lowered, raised them and looked into the looking-glass too, so that our eyes met and she, without any doubt, recognized me.'

'Are you quite sure of that?'

'Absolutely sure. Baba recognized me and stayed quite still, looking at me and waiting to see what I would do. What I did, you know: I ran away.'

'By the way, why did you run away?'

'I ran away because I suspected I'd been lured into a trap by Cora and Baba.'

'By Baba?'

'By means of Baba, that is. I didn't know – and how could I have known? – that Baba was in that house for the first time; I thought she had already been there on other occasions; I said to myself that Cora, in agreement with Baba, was making use of Baba to entice me, to implicate me, to compromise me, to bind me to herself. In other words, that she was trying to do once again, by means of Baba, what she had already done years before by means of her girls – to make love through a third person.'

'Was this the thing that you hadn't the courage to say?'

'Yes.'

'Why didn't you have the courage to tell me, since you were convinced that Baba had recognized you?'

'Because, at the moment when I saw Baba sitting in that room, at that precise moment I fell in love with her, and exactly because I fell in love with her I ran away. And so I hadn't the courage to tell you the truth, because I was ashamed of having run away instead of intervening, as it would have been my duty to do.'

'Intervening in what way?'

'Demanding an explanation from Cora, saving Baba from Cora.'

'I'm sorry, but I don't see the connection between the fact that you fell in love with Baba and the other fact that you ran away instead of intervening on her behalf. Logically, seeing that you loved her, you ought surely to have intervened.'

'That was just what I did not feel like doing. I was afraid of myself precisely because I loved Baba. I feared that, if I insisted on an explanation with Cora, I might yield to temptation, I might become implicated, compromised, enticed once again, this time irreparably. Don't forget I was convinced that Baba was inured to this sort of thing. I did not therefore think of Baba, whom I considered to be irretrievably lost, but only of myself. And so I ran away and left Rome next day, a week earlier than I had intended.'

'And then what?'

'And then for six years I went on loving Baba, being at the same time convinced that Baba loved me.'

'That Baba loved you?'

'Yes, I was convinced, as I still am, that, at the moment when our eyes met in the mirror, Baba and I fell in love with one another.'

'But if this was true, tell me why, then, Baba didn't do anything about it, why she didn't come to you and say: "Look here, I saw you, I recognized you, and here I am, I love you." What reasons could Baba have to pretend she hadn't seen you?'

'I suppose she had the same reasons that I did.'

'And what were they?'

'I did not want to be drawn into temptation, nor did she; I for my reasons, she for hers.'

'But what reasons could Baba have?'

'We've talked about it so many times: she wanted me to be a father to her, and she wanted to be a daughter to me.'

There was a long silence. Finally I heard Baba's voice declaring slowly: 'What I ought to say to you now is that Baba cannot forgive you for not having intervened that day, for not having insisted on an explanation with Cora, for not having, as you say, tried to save her from Cora – isn't that so?'

'Yes, it ought to be so.'

'But it isn't so.'

'And how is that?'

'In the first place Baba didn't fall in love with you. I admit it's true that she saw you and recognized you – it's no use denying it now – but she didn't fall in love with you. Baba, at that moment, was as though dead. And how can a dead person fall in love with anybody? No, Baba at that moment felt nothing; later on, however, looking back on it, she certainly had a feeling, but not of love.'

'What sort of feeling?'

'It's difficult to say. The same feeling, fundamentally, that she has for Cora.'

'And what is that?'

'Let us say, a feeling of gratitude.'

'Of gratitude?'

'Yes.'

'But how could Baba feel grateful to Cora who had put her up for sale, and to me who had let myself be tempted to buy her?'

'The gratitude came afterwards. At that moment what happened was the death of the old, stupid, ingenuous Baba. Then, after some time, came gratitude.'

'But gratitude for what?'

'Baba was grateful to you for having caused her to die.'

'What d'you mean?'

'Yes, the old Baba died at the very moment when she saw you in the looking-glass in that room. And that was the reason why, in all these years, Baba never told you she had seen you in the looking-glass and had recognized you. The Baba who had seen you in the looking-glass was dead; and the Baba who now felt gratitude towards you and Cora was the new Baba who, as you quite rightly said, wanted Cora to be her mother, you to be her father and she herself your daughter.'

'But couldn't all this perhaps have happened even without what you call the death of the old Baba?'

'No, it couldn't have happened. And d'you know something?'

'What?'

'Baba considers herself to be a perfectly ordinary person, just like a great many other people of her age, except in one aspect: the people of her age haven't died and then started living again; Baba has.'

'What does that mean?'

'Perhaps it doesn't mean much, only what I've said.'

We were silent for a moment, then finally Baba went on: 'But there's one thing you haven't explained to me. Why, after six years of silence, did you decide to introduce yourself to Baba under the pretext of the anonymous letter?'

'Because I thought I would then do what I hadn't the courage to do six years before.'

'Do what?'

'That first time, at Cora's house, I had run away. Then I had been in love with Baba and had done nothing but think about her, but I had always succeeded in denying myself a relationship which horrified me. That day when I came back from Iran, perhaps because I was tired and nervous after the journey, I suddenly yielded to temptation, that's all.'

'To put it plainly: when you knocked at Baba's door that day, were you thinking of becoming her lover?'

'Yes.'

'Then why didn't you do anything about it?'

'I was convinced that Baba was really just one of Cora's many girls, like all the others. And so, when I knocked at her door, I was trying to deceive myself into thinking I was doing something normal and insignificant. What, in fact, is corruption if not a particular kind of senseless normality? I thought that Baba was a part of this kind of normality which is corruption; but when I came face to face with her I realized, instead, that I really loved her and that this love would allow of only one kind of relationship with her,'

'What was that?'

'Now don't smile, even if what I'm going to tell you seems improbable and actually ridiculous. Not the relationship of a father with a daughter, because I didn't feel like a father with Baba; nor yet the relationship of a man with the woman he loves, because I knew that that relationship between us was not possible. No, it was the relationship – I repeat, don't smile – of a novelist with one of his characters. All this will seem to you, at first sight, highly literary, but it isn't.'

I was silent a moment, and Baba said nothing. Then I resumed: 'In the sphere of relationships in the real world, no relationship is so real as the one that develops between a novelist and his characters. Even the love relationship is less pure, less ineffable, less mysterious, less miraculous, less complete than that. Yes, I love you, and certainly I love you with a love which now, as I talk to you, has freed itself of the last dross, like a metal object that has reached its perfect degree of fusion. And yet even this love is less limpid and less real than the one which will allow me to represent you in my novel, if I ever have the energy to write it. This is because the love that I feel for you in real life is merely a mode of action and there can be no genuineness in action, whereas the love which will allow me to represent you in my novel begins and ends in contemplation and does not become soiled with action, with the dream of action, or with the renunciation of action. I love you with this kind of love, and for that reason I am grateful to you as one ought to be grateful to someone who has aroused in one a rare, difficult, precious feeling.'

I was silent, expecting some comment; but none came. I waited a little longer; then the silence made me suspicious, so I turned round very slowly and saw that the bed was empty. Without my noticing, Baba had risen from the bed, walked to the door and gone away on tiptoe.

Thursday, December 17th

I re-read the last pages of the diary and felt the need to add at any rate a provisional conclusion, all the more so because this time the diary is really coming to an end, since I leave for the United States in five hours' time. However the conclusion, for reasons which will be apparent to anyone who reads further, came to me with, as it were, two faces – two faces which were equally acceptable and equally suitable for bringing the novel to an end, even though profoundly different.

This was the first. 'I wish to point out here, before I go away, that even this last scene of my confession to Baba was wholly invented. It is strange how, as I have proceeded further with the diary, I have allowed myself more and more often to be tempted to invent details, events and sometimes entire scenes; strange, but perhaps not so very strange; in point of fact it is a proof that, as a result of my attention being always concentrated upon the same situation, my imagination begins to warm up, to ferment, to move imperceptibly from the passive observation of reality to straightforward representation.

'Anyhow it is of no great importance that in real life I have never done the things which I have confessed to Baba, nor, consequently, is the confession itself of great importance, nor yet the fact that the anonymous letter did actually arrive that day and that before that I had known nothing of Cora's second profession. It is of no great importance because, in the first place, whatever the reason may have been, I had for ten years taken no interest in Baba and her destiny, whereas I ought to have looked after her, since she was my daughter and I had agreed to be her father, and, in the second place, because I really loved Baba, and it mattered little whether this love had lasted for six months or six years.

'The only remaining problem, if anything, is to know whether I shall conclude the novel with the confession. Or whether I shall leave it open after the surprise visit of the police and the return home of Baba and Cora, in expectation of the fatal, forseeable *deus ex machina* of Cora's death from illness, which will allow of my finishing the narrative as I began it, under the heading of everyday normality.'

The other possible conclusion is as follows. 'I am forced to admit it, because, if I don't, I am sure I shall never be able to write my novel: the scene of my confession to Baba did really happen, with those very words and precisely the revelations I mentioned. What was invented and untruthful, on the other hand, was the note I appended to the scene a short time ago, in which I declared the scene itself to be untruthful and invented. Furthermore I should now like to know why I was unwilling to admit certain things even to myself; why, as soon as I had admitted them, I regretted it and denied having admitted them. Possibly because, in admitting them, I also admitted that, fundamentally, the shame aroused in me by the past was not, as I wished to have it believed, the shame which is aroused by an illusion to which one has succumbed; but rather the shame which can be caused by a fault of which one is guilty.

'But it was also true that, by accepting Cora's offer and going to that house, I had equally succumbed to an illusion. The illusion of which Cora was the dispenser and the promoter. The illusion, to put it in a nutshell, in which the more general illusion of life was manifested in a more essential, more complete way. And so the project of the novel had served, more than anything, to do this: to free me from the shame of having lived.'

So much for the two faces of the conclusion, both of which, as I said, were suitable for bringing the novel to an end; but each of them in an entirely different sense and different manner.

To begin with the second, the one that confirms the reality of the confession, it endows the whole novel with the character of a well-made machine. It is true that this machine is, so to speak, entirely 'interior', dealing, fundamentally, with psychological developments rather than with real events; but it is also true that the anonymous letter shown by me to Baba ten years after I received it; my visit to the *maison de rendez-vous* and my flight from it without being recognized; and then the silence maintained for six years about this visit and this flight – it is also true, I say, that all this savours strongly of contrivance, of mechanism, of romantic, even if mainly psychological, intrigue. Nevertheless it must be recognized that all this, and more, happens in life. And that, if romantic novels are written side by side with others in which nothing happens, this means, in fact, that even in reality as it is lived, side by side with the lack of events there is a super-abundance of actual events. Finally it must be observed that the confession to Baba introduces a de-mystifying note into the novel. As much as to say, non-involvements that last for ten years do not exist without there being a reason for them. And now the reason is explained. As in *Oedipus Rex*, there can be no mysteries either for the author or for the reader, only for the character concerned.

The first face, on the other hand, the one that denies the reality of the confession, transfers the novel from real happenings to the consciousness of the novelist. It ceases to be the story of a feeling of guilt originating in a fault actually committed; rather it is the story of how a novelist faces the problem of the representation of guilt and of the feeling of guilt. With the first face of the conclusion I should have a dramatic novel, with the second, the drama of a novel.

Someone may now wish to know which of the two conclusions corresponds to the truth. That is, to what actually happened. But this I shall not say, because in fact it is not necessary for me to do so. Indeed, when all is said and done, my problem, after all, is not so much to accuse myself, to justify myself, to reveal myself, as – much more simply – to write a novel. And it is true that one cannot write a novel except by telling the truth. But who could deny that both the conclusions are truthful, even if in different ways?

The *deus ex machina* of death by disease worked punctually, as I had foreseen. After I had been for about three weeks in New York, a letter arrived from Baba telling me that Cora had at last made up her mind to see a doctor and that the doctor had diagnosed a fatal disease. It was not a question of tuberculosis, however, as we had all thought, but of lung cancer. Baba also told me that the doctor had given Cora from six months to a year to live. And that it was therefore not necessary for me to return to Rome immediately.

I received a further couple of letters, quite optimistic: Cora was better, she was steadily improving, the doctor couldn't understand it, there was actually talk of a miracle. Then, suddenly, an abrupt change: a telegram which announced that Cora was dying.

While I was flying across the Atlantic, I asked myself what it was that I now most strongly desired. And I realized that I desired, above all, to arrive in Rome *after* Cora's death. The idea of Cora at death's door, with Baba and myself sitting at her bedside, which to Baba, with her obstinate plan for the restoration of family affections, would certainly be pleasing – this idea was infinitely repugnant to me. I did not wish to restore anything. For me, Cora was what she was, Baba was what she was and I was what I was. And it was impossible to talk about 'family'; and, to me at least, it was preferable to be what one was than to try and be what one ought to be.

The *deus ex machina* benevolently granted my prayer. When I arrived in Rome, I found nobody at home; the maid told me that Cora had died on the morning of the day before and that Baba was at the nursing home for the funeral. After a moment's hesitation during which I wondered whether it would not be better to pretend I had not arrived and to stay at home, I plucked up courage and went to the nursing home. I reached it just in time to hurry to the chapel and see four undertaker's men lift the coffin and carry it off down a staircase to the hearse which was waiting outside. The coffin was of light-coloured, almost raw, wood, of the most ordinary kind; and as I followed it down the stairs, together with Cora's parents, Baba and Santoro, I was struck by the speed – one might say, in fact, the frantic, precipitate haste – with which the four bearers carried it, almost at a run, down the stairs, lifted it as if it had been a mere piece of straw to the opening in the hearse, thrust it inside, closed the doors and then jumped into the vehicle, one on either side, while the other two got into a little black car. The noise of the doors being violently slammed echoed in the silence of the garden, and immediately there was a roar from the engine and the hearse moved off. I got into my own car, Baba sat down beside me, and off we went, a little procession of four cars – the bearers' car, Cora's parents', Santoro's and mine – off we went at full speed behind the hearse which was already rushing headlong down the drive through the nursing-home garden. We reached the main gate and came out into Via Cassia; there was a lot of traffic, but the hearse, as though it had gone mad, rushed along without slackening speed, recklessly overtaking, continuously hooting, insinuating itself between one car and another, taking advantage of brief empty stretches to achieve the greatest speed possible, braking suddenly and then leaping forward again. I said to Baba, who kept her face resolutely turned to the side window: 'Whatever's the matter with them? Why are they rushing like this?'

'Perhaps they're in a hurry. They may have another funeral.'

I said nothing, but if I had spoken I should have had to say what I was thinking, or rather, what I was feeling: it may indeed have been true that the undertakers were in a hurry because they had to press on with another funeral as soon as possible; but this haste seemed nevertheless to be inspired by another desire – to get rid of Cora, to put her underground as rapidly as possible and never to think of her again. Cora was something foreign, hostile, negative, destructive, anyhow in the world to which the undertakers belonged. A disturbing, fearsome presence, Cora must be eliminated as soon as possible, just as a body eliminates a thing that is not only foreign to it but also harmful: a poison, a splinter of wood. Cora had believed in nothingness, had represented nothingness had fostered nothingness. Now they were hurrying to get rid of her; and if her body was not to be thrown on the rubbish-heap but buried with all the rites of religion, this was certainly not due to piety, but to the inflexible integrity of the world she had rejected and insidiously attacked.

Thus, while I was still reflecting on these matters, we

arrived at a great speed at the cemetery, which had evidently been inaugurated only a short time before, as I noticed when we had driven through the gates and were proceeding along a bare, bleak avenue, between small, stunted cypresses supported by stakes and plots of ground with a few scattered brand-new graves of glossy coloured marble and glittering gilt lettering. It was a very cold, dull day, such as there are in Rome in the winter between one spell of rain and another, with a uniformly grey sky and no contrasting tone or outline of cloud, as though, instead of blue, grey were its habitual colour. The hearse, still travelling at the same frantic rate, twisted and turned between one plot of ground and another and finally came to an abrupt stop in an open space. We were on the side of a hill; there was a line of burial-vaults in four rows, one above the other, against the slope. From the open space where we stopped there was an immense but melancholy view of the Roman *campagna* – pale green, with no trees, no houses, and at either side, like the wings of a theatre, the low, undulating lines of inconspicuous hills, one behind the other, stretching away to the far horizon. The doors of the cars were opened and we all got out – Baba, Cora's parents, Santoro, a young girl who was presumably Santoro's sister, and myself; but we barely had time to walk over to the hearse before the bearers opened the doors at the back, pulled out the coffin and carried it away, at a run, to one of the many vaults that were still empty. A couple of men followed with two small wreaths of flowers, and we all went after them, hurrying along as fast as we could. The vault was in the top row, and in front of it was a small scaffolding with a ladder leaning against it; the bearers quickly went up the ladder carrying the coffin on their shoulders, quickly thrust the coffin into the vault and quickly came down the ladder again; two bricklayers climbed up in their turn, one with a basket full of bricks, the other with a bucket of lime and a trowel. Then, still with the same rapidity, the opening of the vault was walled up by the two bricklayers, smartly and briskly, as they squatted on the scaffolding: first a row of bricks, then a layer of mortar, then another row of bricks and another layer of mortar, and so on until the opening was completely closed. We all stood there, round the scaffolding, looking up; and suddenly the thought came to me that Cora had been walled up inside the vault not dead but still living; this was perhaps because it seemed to me that all this haste was more suitable to an enemy still capable of doing harm than to an innocuous life‑less body.

Once the vault was walled up, the bricklayers, pressing it against the bricks, fitted in the stone that bore Cora's name and the dates of her birth and death, placed the two little wreaths on either side of the stone and then climbed down again. All this may perhaps have lasted quite a long time – after all, time is needed for walling up a vault and fixing a stone against it; but to me it seemed that it had taken only a few minutes. Finally, in an embarrassed, hypocritical silence, there were the usual handshakes, the usual remorseful head‑nod‑dings. Baba said to Santoro: 'Paolo, I'm going with *him*. We'll see each other later.'

We got into the car and I drove down the avenues much more slowly than when we had come in following the hearse. We left the cemetery and joined a line of cars moving along Via Cassia in the direction of Rome. I glanced hastily at Baba. She was dressed in black and was very pale, her eyes swollen and red from weeping. I could not help thinking, without any irony, 'truly the inconsolable daughter weeping for the death of her mother: everything as it should be'. Finally, without looking at me, she said: 'I'm sorry, but I shan't be able to be with you much while you're in Rome. I've been living with Santoro for nearly a month.'

I said nothing. After a moment she added: 'We're getting married in two weeks' time.'

'Are you pleased?' I asked her.

'Yes,' she answered, 'It was what I wanted, after all.'

Everything that there had been between us, or rather that there might have been, was condensed into that 'after all'. 'After all' – as much as to say, I have loved you, I still love you, I might have gone so far as to commit incest with you; but it's better for me to marry Santoro, whom I don't love, and have children and a family life with him, and for us two to remain, or rather to become, once and for all, father and daughter.

I communicated nothing of these thoughts to Baba, feeling that I could now no longer be completely sincere with her. After a silence, she enquired: 'And you, what will you do?'

'I shall leave again for the United States, tomorrow.'

'And then what?'

'Then I shall go on doing what I've always done – journalism.'

'And the novel you were thinking of extracting from your diary – will you write it, later?'

'I don't think so. Anyhow I shall devote the day I'm spending in Rome to this problem. I shall examine the diary and see what I can make of it.'

And those were the last words I exchanged with Baba. For shortly afterwards we arrived at Piazzale Flaminio and she told me to stop. We got out and embraced, she with filial impetuosity and I with fatherly passivity; then I got back into the car and drove home.

I wanted to examine the diary, but I felt tired after the long flight from the United States and the funeral. And so, after turning over a few pages, more or less mechanically, I rose from my desk and threw myself down on the bed. I fell asleep at once and had the following dream. Baba and Cora were coming towards me, walking hand in hand down a very long, bare avenue which I recognized as that of the cemetery: indeed it was flanked on either side, as far as the eye could reach, by rows of brand-new tombs made of glossy marble which glistened in the sunshine. These tombs were in the form of chapels, of little temples, of pavilions and miniature houses; I found myself beside one of them, the bronze door of which was wide open so that one could see perfectly well that the inside of it was empty; above the door there was something written in gold letters, but the sun was beating down upon it and the gleam of the gold prevented my reading it. Meanwhile Cora and Baba had come up to me, Cora dressed, as usual, in a red coat and skirt, Baba, on the other hand, incongruously, in a wedding-dress, with big, vaporous white veils falling from her head down on to her shoulders, a wreath of orange-blossom, a white silk dress and a long train. I looked at them and then noticed to my alarm that Cora's face, enclosed between two tresses of loose black hair, was not her face as it had been when she was alive, so florid always and with eyes so blue, but the face of Cora dead – yellow, with the black-shadowed yellowness that goes with death, the eyes sightless, dim, almost white. But Baba did not appear to notice this. Suddenly she raised Cora's hand to her lips – the hand, too, a yellow and dead as the face – and kissed it devotedly and uttered in a loud voice a sentence which sounded like this:

'This is my mother Cora and I owe everything to her, and Cora did for me what no mother has ever done for her daughter, and I love her and my gratitude will never cease, for ever and ever.' At these words Cora nodded her head in agreement; but in a feeble, spectral sort of way, like a dead woman. Then together they made their way to the tomb beside which I was standing, Baba still holding Cora by the hand and appearing to guide her. Cora entered the high, narrow tomb that seemed too small for her, and the bronze door closed. Baba now had her back turned to me, and at her side was Santoro, dressed as a bridegroom, in black clothes, with a bunch of flowers in his right hand. Baba was holding his arm and they both walked away down that long, long avenue, between the two rows of tombs, they walked away into the distance until finally they were nothing but two little black spots; and at this point I woke up.

I was still feeling frightened by the dream, and I seemed to be preoccupied by something sinister and menacing. But then I started to reflect, and I realized that what I had dreamed, in the images of a dream, was in fact what Baba had once said to me in words: that she was grateful to Cora because Cora had made her die, and then she had risen again from the dead, and without Cora all this would not have happened and she would have been like so many of her contemporaries who did not know what life was, precisely because they had not experienced death. This reflection finally calmed me down; I got up and washed my face in cold water, then sat down at my desk. I no longer felt in the least tired; I opened the diary at the first page and started to re-read it, and I read it right through during that afternoon. And in the end I saw with absolute clearness that I must give up the idea of extracting a novel from it, as had been my intention in the beginning.

The diary consisted of two unequal, quite distinct parts: the first, which was the longer of the two, contained a large number of short pieces in the nature of essays, as well as the many inventions which I had not been able to refrain from adding as I recounted events; the second, which was shorter, comprised what had really occurred. Now I had written the part consisting of essays and inventions with the underlying idea that it should not be transferred to the novel: it dealt, basically, with all those things that may occur to the mind of a novelist while he is reflecting upon the novel he is going to write – things that may even perhaps help him to write the novel but which, obviously, could not figure in it. And yet, if I discarded this part, there would be very little left for the actual novel. During those two months, in fact, almost nothing had happened, or at any rate nothing that could be used to form the structure of a narrative. Besides, nothing having happened, I had not recorded the details of daily life in the diary, as at first had been my intention: the exceptional character of the situation in which I found myself had prevented me. But at this point I made a discovery of something obvious and manifest, which I ought to have thought of from the beginning: it was not necessary for me to extract a novel from the diary; I had already written the novel without realizing it.

This novel was simply the diary itself, just as I happened to add to it day by day, not only with the few events that had actually occurred but also, and above all, with those that had not occurred at all, those that I had either dreamed or invented or even merely stated as a hypothesis.

I had always thought that the novel I planned to extract from the diary must be a normal novel with a protagonist, which would be myself, and a number of other characters. But my diary, which in reality was a ready-made novel, had, as its protagonist, not a living character but a literary entity – in other words, precisely the novel which I had intended to extract from it later.

The novel, in short, was the true protagonist of the diary, not I myself who was keeping the diary. And the diary was a ready-made novel because I had recorded in it, not my own story, but the story of a novel I was planning to write.

Furthermore, I became aware that the novel, the protagonist of the diary, was not just an ordinary novel but, as I have already said many times, a way of understanding my relationship with reality. In my diary I had, in fact, recorded how this way of understanding the relationship with reality had gradually begun to take shape, becoming articulate and organized, and how in the end it had prevailed.

At this juncture I imagined, nevertheless, that some reader might object: 'If so many things in this diary are, by your own admission, the result of invention – that is, in point of fact, dreams – who is to guarantee us that the things you give as being real are not also dreams, and that the whole diary, in short, is not an invention pure and simple – in other words, a dream?'

A legitimate objection; but I told myself that the only answer I could give was that not only was my diary a dream but also, as the title of a celebrated Spanish play suggests, the whole of life. The difference between the things called real and the things dreamed was in fact very slight. It was a question of first-rank, second-rank, third-rank dreams, and so on. But it was also true that, by reversing the design, one could say that some of these dreams were reality of the first rank, others reality of the second rank, others again reality of the third rank, and so on. In fact, while it was, in a way, true that the things that were dreamt were not real, who could doubt having dreamed, and having dreamed precisely those dreams and no other? Who could say to someone who was telling him about a dream he had had: 'No, you're lying, it's not true, you weren't dreaming'? And so, while perhaps the things dreamed were not real (or at least not real in the manner of the things that are called real) the fact of dreaming, without any doubt, *was* real.

In other words, if it was true – as I was convinced it was – that a novel cannot but be realistic, my diary demonstrated that there were no limits to realism, that nothing could be excluded from reality, not even dreams; not even lies, not even the vital illusion which had once made me ashamed of having lived.

The only lesson, if any, that I had derived from the reading of the diary was that one should contrive, if one could, to dream only certain dreams. How that could be possible, I was unable to say; all I could do was to indicate the probable solution of the problem. Anyhow, even if partly made up of dreams, it seemed to me that the diary was better fitted than the novel I might have extracted from it, to give an idea of what the novel itself would have been: something I would have written in order to find out why I was writing it; just as it had always seemed to me that I was living in order to find out why I was living.

I had kept my diary so as to find out why I should write the novel. It would be better to preserve this character of investigation and not to give a definitive form to something which probably could not have such a thing.

For this reason I decided to publish the diary as it was, just as I had written it, limiting myself to changing the names of the persons concerned and of a few places. And this is what I have done. What now appears in the form of a novel is in fact nothing but my diary, with the addition of a prologue and an epilogue.

SOME PANTHER AUTHORS

Norman Mailer
Jean-Paul Sartre
Len Deighton
Henry Miller
Georgette Heyer
Mordecai Richler
Gerard de Nerval
James Hadley Chase
Juvenal
Violette Leduc
Agnar Mykle
Isaac Asimov
Doris Lessing
Ivan Turgenev
Maureen Duffy
Nicholas Monsarrat
Fernando Henriques
B. S. Johnson
Edmund Wilson
Olivia Manning
Julian Mitchell
Christopher Hill

Robert Musil
Ivy Compton-Burnett
Chester Himes
Chaucer
Alan Williams
Oscar Lewis
Jean Genet
H. P. Lovecraft
Anthony Trollope
Robert van Gulik
Louis Auchincloss
Vladimir Nabokov
Colin Spencer
Alex Comfort
John Barth
Rachel Carson
Simon Raven
Roger Peyrefitte
J. G. Ballard
Mary McCarthy
Kurt Vonnegut
Alexis Lykiard